WHEN THE GERMANS COME

DAVID HEWSON

BLOODHOUND
BOOKS

PART ONE

CHAPTER 1

While battling Spitfires fill the air, the bastion of England awaits the enemy
Jessica Marshall, Special Correspondent to
the Toronto Inquirer

Another year, the coast would be crowded with holidaymakers. Charabancs of visitors making the day trip from London. Picnickers on the famous White Cliffs admiring the view across the Channel to the coast of France. Bathers on the golden sands waiting for fish-and-chip time and a pint of warm beer.

No longer. Dover, England's nearest neighbour to mainland Europe, the town invaders from Julius Caesar on have identified as the entry point for any coming invasion, is readying itself for combat, close and bloody. Forces are gathering, professional and amateur. Shelters are being dug, gas masks distributed. On the winding country roads of Kent, signs are being removed to confuse the coming invaders. War is on the way, and all of Dover knows it.

The harbour town received a premonition of its fate in May when the Dunkirk evacuations brought more than 300,000 weary and wounded British and Commonwealth soldiers across the Channel in a flotilla of rescue boats, large and small. Most have now moved on to camps elsewhere, training for the expected Nazi invasion. The sick and the wounded remain in Dover's hospitals and field facilities, helpless spectators as the town built around the forbidding hilltop Castle, home to Roman conquerors and English kings, finds itself under constant attack from air and land, readying its fortifications, visible and hidden, for the expected assault upon its coast.

An understandable secrecy surrounds the preparations Dover is making for the future. The Castle fortress is now home to a busy military complex barred to all but the privileged. Scattered around the town, barracks and gunnery emplacements going back to Napoleonic days are similarly out of bounds.

How fare the ordinary townsfolk who stay behind, knowing they might be in the midst of war in weeks, perhaps days? Nervous, brave, determined and with no small sense of urgent wildness rising in their blood. Most schoolchildren have been evacuated to safer homes, some as far away as Wales. Those that remain run the streets, through bombsites and artillery emplacements, untutored, untrammelled, parents too occupied to care.

The civilian population has dwindled to those divided between the business of war and the cares of everyday life. Specialist advisers and strategists mingle with fishermen and grocers while naval crews man the harbour guns and its busy fleet, moored beneath a forest of barrage balloons that offer hopeful protection from daily aerial sorties launched across the Channel. Few bobbies patrol the lanes and alleys. Most are engaged in war preparations wreathed in secrecy and subterfuge, unconcerned with the everyday and untroubled, it seems, by petty theft and the occasional outbreak of disorder. The Germans are coming. Nothing matters more than that.

The stalwart English bulldog spirit the prime minister seeks to summon remains, though more muted than in the capital. Shells fall randomly throughout the town daily, aimed at the military installations one assumes, but frequently missing their mark. The list of civilian casualties grows, marked by fresh graves in the cemeteries. More than a hundred ordinary men and women have died from stray missiles that have destroyed homes and even entire terraces in parts.

Bombardments come swiftly, sometimes with little chance for civilians to flee to the shelters. These men and women of Kent are a hardy race, not made for cowering underground without good reason. Instead, proud of their insouciance, they stroll through the charred, wrecked streets as if life were normal, and danger a mere inconvenience.

The day before your correspondent arrived, a butcher was killed mid-afternoon while taking a delivery basket to a nearby home. The man was caught by a shell from an artillery installation twenty miles away, across the slender stretch of water the French call La Manche. Death may arrive from thin air without warning, save for the tell-tale whine that says nothing except you are too late.

As Hitler rolled his *blitzkrieg* across Europe, your correspondent has followed the cities it has engulfed. Each approached the possibility of occupation in its own way, through varying combinations of fear and defiance, organisation and panic. Dover is unlike any other she has encountered: aloof, alone, stranded, almost an island in itself, cut off from the norms of England, the rules and strictures that maintain that legendary sense of British decorum and calm.

Nights here can be feral, reckless, with burlesque shows for the drink-filled soldiery, talk of houses of ill repute, little sign of sobriety after hours for those on leave. Few locals feel happy to speak to outsiders freely, aware that the town may be vulnerable to traitors, spies and careless talk, conscious too that they are insular folk, not given to gossip or trusting strangers. I was able to talk to one of the burlesque show dancers. Dawn Peacock she called herself, a woman from the East End of London, eager to speak, unlike most. Thirty-two, with long ringlet blonde hair, a cigarette set between her carmine lips, the flowery smell of gin about her, she spoke admiringly of a town so in dread of the future that it had resolved to take, in her words, 'each day as it comes'. Here, after dark, the law barely exists, and where it has some presence turns a blind eye, focussed on the greater issue, the enemy across the water, not any felon within. Assignations, discreet for the most part, are made and paid for, prophylactics handed out to the soldiers for free to stave off disease. Such is life on this strange frontline. Only the moment matters, not what follows.

Why, I asked Dawn, did she risk being in such a perilous location? The trains are running back to London and relative safety. No civilian need be this close to the frontline unless they crave it.

'Oh, sweetheart,' she said, with a cheery Cockney cackle. 'Have you never heard that saying? The devil's favourite piece of furniture is the long bench. We're not good at putting things to one side. If there's a job to be done, folk get on with it. Anyway, the closer you get to the grave, the more you seem alive. I've never felt happier in all my little life. Besides. Them men out there... Brave lads. They shouldn't have to face all this without a spot of entertainment and female company, should they?'

Company that is brief, perhaps sweet, and invariably paid for one way or another. Dover sits at the very edge of Britain, like a sacrificial victim waiting for the onslaught, anxious, prepared and in some wild, strange way, free. A nation's past is embodied in its ancient stones, its future in the people who walk its cobbles strewn with debris, dust and blood.

Shakespeare might have had Dover in mind when he wrote...

This fortress built by Nature for herself
Against infection and the hand of war,
This happy breed of men, this little world,
This precious stone set in the silver sea...
This blessed plot, this earth, this realm, this England.

The fortress remains, a fragile bulwark against a much-feared enemy, more bruised than blessed now. Dover is the realm of King Lear too, the White Cliffs where the blinded Gloucester – a reminder of the English propensity for cruelty – bade his son lead him to the 'very brim of it' so that the crippled lord might leap to his death.

At the 'very brim of it' is where Dover, her men and women, and even a few children, now stand. Waiting on tomorrow and tomorrow and tomorrow.

CHAPTER 2

'Louis,' Aunt Veronica barked down the telephone. 'I need you to go round to Crooks and buy me seven tins of chicken liver pâté and a bottle of decent Sauternes. Danvers was supposed to find some, but the wretched man says there's none anywhere.'

'I...'

'Saturday night drinkies. The lord lieutenant's coming, the king's personal representative in Kent. I can't serve him a jar of chopped pork with margarine.'

'Why not? It's what most people eat.'

'These are most decidedly not most people.'

'One bottle won't go very far.'

'At what point did I say it was for them?'

It was a bright summer morning, almost noon. Louis Renard had been at work since seven and was due to knock off early to attend his aunt's afternoon drinks party in Temple Ewell. The town had seen little activity except two shells landing on the vast military complex up the hill at the Castle. A quiet day for Dover. Almost peaceful three miles inland at the smart village where he was now living with his aunt.

'Perhaps Danvers is right. The war and everything...'

'Don't be so defeatist. The lord lieutenant will be in attendance, along with our new vicar and his wife. Since it's impossible to buy any *foie gras* these days, chicken will have to do. Find some.'

Renard shuffled through the pages in front of him again.

'I'm straight from duty. I doubt I'm fit for fine company.'

'I note you said, "on duty". Not working.'

A fair point. He'd been at his desk in Dover nick a week and was still trying to adjust to the place. Before he was wounded in the Dunkirk evacuations, Renard had spent his entire career in Scotland Yard, rising to the post of inspector in the serious crimes division which, more often than not, meant murder. Then came the horrors of the French beaches and his return on a boat, wounded, something he barely remembered.

After that, the hospital. Blackouts. Wild dreams. Despair.

A small coastal police station was meant to offer a route back into the routine of work. But it was a very different kettle of fish to the Yard, a provincial outpost starved of resources and manpower at the best of times. In war, the place barely seemed to function. Two nights before, he'd wandered the town during what was supposedly curfew and come across open drunkenness and prostitution that would have warranted immediate arrest even in Soho. Dover police had neither the men nor the energy to do more than issue the odd warning and walk on.

'These are important high society people,' his aunt continued. 'Even if they weren't, it's time you made new acquaintances. I want you smart and polite. Life's like a train. It always moves on.'

'Clearly you haven't caught a train recently.'

'Have you bought a new suit yet?'

Renard had thought little about clothes since they'd let him out of hospital.

'Dover's hardly the place for bespoke tailors.'

'You truly are the most infuriatingly crumpled nephew I know.'

'The only nephew.'

'Crumpled and pedantic, too. Great shame. You would be passing handsome if you had a decent haircut and smiled more. Not as much as your dear father...'

Constable Kelly cleared his throat from the other side of the desk. Renard had turned up for work in an old sports coat and slacks, all taken from the wardrobe of Veronica's late husband, Maurice. The uniform superintendent Chalmers, the man usually in charge, gave him a filthy look most mornings anyway, but that was more to do with him being an unwanted outsider than any sartorial failing. Not that CID counted highly in Chalmers' view. Two officers, one senior, one junior, comprised the entire office much of the time.

Kelly pulled up a chair, leaned back, spread out his legs, grinned his cheeky chappie grin and listened.

'Chicken liver pâté and Sauternes,' his aunt declared in that loud, theatrical voice that had once graced stages around the Empire, from India to Hong Kong, Australia to Jamaica. 'Do not return home without them.'

Then the line went dead.

Chapter 3

The telephone was a black candlestick type, the sort that might have been in service since before the Great War. Renard placed the receiver back on the stand and wondered if there was any point in trying to find something more modern.

Dover CID meant a small, grubby room furnished with an ancient desk, two rickety chairs and a typewriter the officers had to use themselves since the secretary had been sent to work in the Castle. Somewhat different to the facilities he'd enjoyed in the Yard. With some conspicuous prompting from his aunt, a woman of no small fame and influence in East Kent, he'd agreed to serve there for a while. The previous inspector had been badly wounded in a German artillery attack from the long-range guns newly installed across the Channel. The work, Veronica assured him, would be light and rarely taxing, a good way of getting him back into the job. She seemed to be right insofar as it seemed the posting was remarkably free of anything that might be labelled "crime".

'Dame Veronica, by any chance?' Constable Kelly asked.

Renard was thirty-seven, single, a man of middling height and a benign appearance most people seemed to find unmemorable. He cared little for tailors or barbers and it showed. His face was gently ascetic for a policeman, more that of university professor or a member of the clergy, a fact that meant he had to pull out his warrant card more often than most to prove his position. Even now, with a horizontal scar across his forehead from the mortar that felled him on the crowded beach that May. His hair was brown, wavy, often barely combed and, as Veronica frequently pointed out, in need of the attention of a barber. In his bachelor flat in Bloomsbury there'd been three identical suits, three almost identical pairs of shoes, four shirts, all white, and seven removable collars that ran to the nearby laundry on a schedule roughly twice that of all other laundry. London was grubby and most of the muck, it seemed to him, gathered at the neckline. Not that he'd set foot in the capital since the medics took him to hospital after they fetched him back, along with a dozen wounded soldiers, in a small coastal fishing boat that managed to cross the Channel and dock in Ramsgate. By the time he was discharged, the Bloomsbury flat had been destroyed by a Nazi bomb, everything in it lost. So he was now reduced to the clothes Veronica had recovered from her late husband's wardrobe, all of them several years old and a marginal fit at best.

Finding new and better ones, and a haircut, had hardly seemed a priority. Nevertheless, Renard hated the word "crumpled". He'd heard it far too often.

'Was it that obvious?'

'Can't mistake that voice of hers. Don't know why she needs to use the telephone at all. She could just shout, and we'd hear her all the way from Temple Ewell.'

Veronica Sallis had been a stalwart on the West End stage for almost half a century, and the screen for a good two decades, latterly making her name in a series of films produced at the studio owned by the late Maurice in Barnet. Comedies, dubious historical dramas and crime capers mostly, in which she seemed fated to play seductresses of ill repute, in pearls and silk and daring period dress. After Maurice's death she'd retired to his family home, a small

Georgian mansion known as The Pantheon. Fronted by a Palladian portico, copied from its namesake in Rome, the house stood in extensive gardens by the river outside tatty, bombed-out Dover. Slim, statuesque, with the face of a Botticelli beauty as she approached seventy, she could still turn heads anywhere she walked into the room.

'I had occasion to pull the lady up once driving her Bentley down the wrong side of the road on her way back from Sandwich Golf Club,' Kelly said. 'Gin had been liberally taken, I believe. She was as polite as she was slurred and called the chief constable after I drove her home.'

'What happened?'

'I got a boot up the arse and she took to getting her handyman to chauffeur her to and from the golf.'

Veronica used Danvers, a genial local, as her retainer for everything from shopping to repairs on the crumbling mansion. His sister helped out in the kitchen and with the laundry and cleaning. The pair seemed to adore her and worked for a pittance, which was just as well since Veronica was always pleading poverty.

'And how,' Renard asked, brandishing the newspaper copy by one Jessica Marshall, 'did you come across this?'

The pages had the stamp of the Ministry of Information office at the top and were probably retyped from the original.

'Found them in the bin outside Superintendent Chalmers' office,' Kelly said, straight off. 'What do you reckon?'

'I reckon you shouldn't be going through the superintendent's wastepaper basket.'

'Everything chucked away's fair game, isn't it? He does have a bit of a habit of throwing stuff without reading it proper. If they're going to make me a detective, I'm bound to be a bit nosy. That's what being a detective means.'

Kelly was twenty-two, a sporty type, muscular and keen on gesturing with his fists from time to time. He'd been a constable in the Dover police for just over twelve months. Some year too, as he'd told Renard in great detail. He'd joined three weeks before Britain declared war on Hitler, worked through the idle vacuum of the first few months, then, like the rest of them, had thrown himself into helping with Operation Dynamo, the Dunkirk evacuation. The conflict was suddenly real. Kelly was a master of station gossip and rapidly discovered Renard was one of the wounded retrieved from the beaches across the Channel. He soon found out, too, that his new boss had no intention of talking about what happened or why he was there.

The young man was voluble, impetuous and blessed with an occasionally infuriating charm, which was probably why Chalmers had taken him out of uniform and thrown him into CID with the unwanted newcomer from London.

'Don't do it again. Chalmers doesn't have a sense of humour.'

Kelly frowned like a teenager just told off.

'This showgirl the woman's writing about. Dawn Peacock.'

'"She called herself". Didn't you notice that part?'

'Yes, but–'

'So that may not be her name at all. She might not even exist. Reporters make things up.'

'Not actual people, surely.'

'I just said. She might not be a real woman.'

Kelly remained unconvinced.

'So, this Dawn woman, imaginary or not, is supposed to come from London, like you?'

'And?'

'"The devil's favourite piece of furniture is the long bench". Never heard a saying like that. What does it mean?'

Kelly had a point.

'Read the story. It means you shouldn't reward procrastination.'

'Is it a Cockney thing?'

'I'm not a Cockney myself, but it's new to me.'

'And that woman reporter who wrote it. The gorgeous-looking one who was here last week, the Yank...'

It was Renard's first day. He'd seen the press party only briefly and made sure not to talk to them. He wasn't a fan of reporters. Though the woman did stand out, elegant, confident, knowing. Or so it appeared.

'She was Canadian, I believe.'

'Same thing really. She shouldn't be going on about all the bad stuff here. The girls from the shows. They're not all tarts.'

'The woman's a reporter. As I keep saying.' He passed over another note from the Ministry of Information office down by the harbour. 'Seems she's back here.'

Kelly glanced at the message and shook his head.

'Hungry for the big story, eh? Adolf on British soil. She's either brave or stupid. God knows what happens when they turn up.' He sighed, looked serious for a moment. 'Have they given you a gun yet, sir?'

'Not me. They're short of them. Has anyone got one?'

'Don't think so.' Kelly hesitated, uncertain for a moment, then said, 'What exactly are we supposed to do when Hitler puts his head round that door?'

'Ask me that when he knocks.'

'The thing that struck me,' Kelly went on, 'is they'll still need coppers. Us. Speaking English. They can't manage on their own, can they? I was talking to Joe Dobson. The sergeant. Now he's a Londoner, so local blokes here don't like him much. But Joe made a very good point. The bastards might invade, but they can't run everything. If we've lost and they're here, no choice about it really. Anyone still alive is going to have to knuckle down and carry on with the job. Does that make you a traitor? If you go back to work for them instead of leaving it all to the Krauts?'

Renard didn't want this conversation.

'Let's hope we never find out.'

Kelly wouldn't shut up.

'If you ask people out there who they'd rather have on the streets I think you'd find it's us, not Herman the German. Suspect the villains would say that too.'

Renard picked up the story the Marshall woman had written.

'I want you to promise you won't go looking for material like this again.'

'All right,' Kelly said, so quickly the pledge was clearly meaningless. 'Do you mind if I ask a question?'

'Depends on the question.'

'Ben Muirden's not coming back. So they say. Nasty injuries. Are you temporary, sir? Visiting, as it were? I'm confused. We don't normally get chaps down from Scotland Yard. Well, never, as far as anyone knows.'

Renard thought about it.

'Talking about me, are they?'

'Well, yes. You hopping over to Dunkirk like that. Coming back on a stretcher. What's a Yard bloke doing *there?*'

He tapped his nose and left it at that.

'Sorry if I'm prying. Just wondered, that's all.'

'Think of me as a man of mystery, Kelly. Now. We should keep an eye out for Jessica Marshall. Reporters roving around the place. They need watching.'

The young constable grinned.

'That won't be hard. She is quite the looker.'

'Pleased to hear it.' Renard pulled some money out of his wallet and passed over a tenner. 'Go round to Crooks, whatever that is, and get me seven tins of chicken liver pâté and a bottle of Sauternes.'

Kelly blinked, looked round the office then said, 'But I'm on duty.'

'This is duty. Do you want to tell my aunt otherwise?'

A quick cough, then Kelly got up and headed for the door.

Renard followed him out. Dover nick smelled of bad drains and stale tobacco as always. The reception area was stuffy, a good couple of degrees hotter than CID. Joe Dobson, the sergeant who'd been making some unwelcome remarks to his fellow officers it seemed, was heading for the front door.

'You back off up to see your secret squirrels up in the Castle, Sarge?' Kelly called out.

Dobson just gave him a cold look then walked out.

'Funny chap. Never quite know where you stand with him. No one does.'

'We've yet to meet,' Renard said.

'Quiet fellow. Got a few problems at home. Teenage daughter. Joe didn't want her evacuated with all the other kids. Don't think his wife's best pleased. Women, eh? A mystery to me. How about you?'

'These... secret squirrels?'

'Something the army's up to. All very hush-hush.' He held up the tenner. 'If you don't mind me asking... what's sorter... er...?'

Renard scribbled it out on a pad.

'Sauternes. A sweet wine from Bordeaux.'

'Fremlin's man myself.'

The inspector blinked.

'Beer. It's beer.' He waved the tenner. 'We could always go for one later if you like.'

'I have a social appointment. But thank you for the offer.'

Louis Renard went back to his rickety desk and wondered if the cleaners had given up on Dover police station. The place was covered in dust. The rubble and wreckage of recent bombings meant the town lived in a constant cloud. All the same... the Yard was never this messy.

He read the newspaper piece the Ministry of Information had sent Superintendent Arnold Chalmers once more. It was a curious thing to throw in the bin. A curious item to send to the nick at all.

CHAPTER 4

Jessica Marshall caught a morning service from Victoria. The train was mostly empty as it wound its way south. Most civilians wanted to flee the coast, not get nearer. She had her accreditation papers as a correspondent for the *Inquirer* in Toronto and clearance to travel, all checked before she boarded and again by a police officer on the journey. Bacon, eggs and devilled kidneys were available in the buffet car, smoked salmon if she wanted it. Rationing hadn't quite reached the malachite-green first-class carriages of the Southern Railway company. Third class was crammed with soldiers in khaki and sailors in navy blue, all looking pensive while munching on their sandwiches. As she boarded and searched for a seat, they'd ogled her and made the occasional tasteless comment. Marshall gave a little wave and smiled.

This would be her second visit to Dover in a week. The first had generated just a single story, one she'd struggled with for days, finally typing something she thought deeply unsatisfactory the previous morning then sending it off to the agency to be wired to Toronto. She'd kept a carbon copy and reread it late the night before, wishing she could rewrite the whole damned thing. It was a skimpy colour piece, lacking in detail. Perhaps a little too literate for the paper back home, but she'd had to pad out the scant information she had. All she had to work with was the highly controlled visit organised and run by a couple of humourless hacks from the Ministry of Information. They were desperate for heart-warming stories to neutralise the continuing misery and bad publicity of the Dunkirk debacle three months before.

She wasn't going to write that crap and told them so on the train home. All the same, Dover did get under her skin. It wasn't just that this was the closest to the real war she could find. The place had an air about it, frantic, nervy, exciting, almost sinister. It was living on the edge and that was a place that drew Jessica Marshall like a magnet.

Just turned thirty-one, she'd spent the previous four years travelling Europe for the paper, from Rome to Berlin then Paris. When that city was about to fall, she'd found her way onto one of the last ferries out of Boulogne to Folkestone. The paper wouldn't let her stay in France to report on its capture by the Nazis. They'd have no choice when the invasion of England began. This was going to be the biggest story she'd ever covered. The fall of Canada's mother nation. As she'd told Mark Calhoun, the nervy foreign editor, an Englishman, no one was going to deprive her of the opportunity to cover that. Or the chance to be close to the fighting when it began. Calhoun had never allowed her near the frontline. Mostly, she'd reported on politics and local colour. He'd always said the military side of the conflict was to be left to others – men, naturally – often stringers risking their necks to be close to bloodshed. Calhoun doubtless knew what she really wanted, a break onto a bigger paper. One of the New York titles or London. From time to time, he'd tell her to forget it. She wasn't good enough. Sometimes, struggling to find the right words for the perfect, elusive story in her head, she thought he might be right.

———

As the train pulled into Priory station, she waited for the thick smoke of the engine to clear then found a porter to take her to the Lord Raglan Hotel. It was half a mile away in Flying Horse Lane. She wasn't wrong that first time. Dover possessed the intriguing scent of war, an atmosphere that was tense and expectant, soldiers and sailors everywhere, gun emplacements, the dust and burnt-out rubble of bombed terraces and shops, cordoned off, abandoned. The contrast with the money, grandeur and confidence of London was marked. There had to be a smarter side to the town, but the streets she saw were mostly terraces – two floors, narrow, modest to the point of mean – and small shops, all with blacked-out windows, some with obvious damage. Above everything stood the fortress on the hill, the Castle, a towering citadel out of an adult fairy tale now surrounded by more modern buildings, all buzzing with distant activity like a beehive in summer, one barred to ordinary civilians by armed guard posts.

The Castle was the focal point of the frontline waiting for Hitler, a massive complex cut through with tunnels that housed facilities so secret the Ministry drones clammed up when asked the simplest of questions. They'd never let her write a piece that so much as hinted at what went on there, even that the evacuation of Dunkirk was masterminded from within its subterranean control rooms. Under the latest regulations any stories that mentioned troop movements or the frontline had to be submitted to the censor's desk first for approval and would usually be returned amended or spiked altogether. Chafing against the rules was pointless. Better to find a way round them. The piece she'd filed the day before skirted the danger areas carefully. That was why it took so long to write. Evading the truth with conviction was so much harder than simply telling it.

The porter with his trolley said nothing when she asked him what happened behind the secure enclave of the Castle. The fellow simply moaned about the weight of her luggage. He had good reason. Dover was somewhere she planned to stay for as long as necessary. Everything she owned was in the battered leather suitcase that had followed her around a disintegrating Europe. Most importantly, a Remington Noiseless portable typewriter and a Zeiss Contax II 35mm rangefinder camera along with several rolls of film.

Not that she'd risk taking the camera out without permission. Journalists, especially foreign ones, were always under suspicion from the authorities. In Berlin, she'd been arrested for taking a few shots of building work near the Brandenburg Gate, supposedly a new command bunker for Hitler. It was only an intervention by a brief lover, an attaché at the Irish embassy, that saved her from a beating or perhaps worse. After she got out of jail, the man had driven her straight to the Adlon hotel to pick up her things, then put her on a train to Paris. He'd made it clear he thought she'd been a fool and never wanted to see her face again. No great loss, she thought, and at least she still had her Remington and the Contax.

The trip with the Ministry of Information had been a single night only, and that spent in a spare and windowless annexe of the officers' quarters in the barracks at the Citadel. Now she needed a place of her own, privacy, as much freedom as she could get to move around. The Raglan turned out to be a small Georgian hotel by an equally modest river, well-named the Dour. The travel agent in London had said he'd found her one of the finest places in town. That she found hard to believe.

The porter stopped outside and held out his hand.

'I thought it might be swisher,' she said, handing over a shilling. Enough for twenty cigarettes. It seemed generous, not that he was going to allow that to show.

'You're in Dover. What do you expect? The Ritz?'

An equally poker-faced man who introduced himself as Eric came out and took her bags. Reception was a bar. The place, it seemed, was more a pub than a hotel.

She placed her passport on the counter, along with the fee they'd demanded for a two-week stay.

'I may need to be here longer. I trust that's not a problem.'

He snorted at that.

'I don't know what'll be happening tomorrow, let alone in a fortnight, love.' Eric was a spindly man of about fifty with a tweedy suit and the permanent stink of pipe tobacco about him. 'Canadian, I see. Shame your chaps didn't make it over here sooner. Maybe things might have turned out different.'

How many times had she heard that? Britain and France declared war on 3 September the previous year. On that same day, a Nazi U-boat torpedoed a passenger ship, the *Athenia*, en route from Belfast to Montreal, killing 117 passengers and crew, a ten-year-old Canadian girl among them. Seven days later Canada joined the conflict, but distance and a lack of preparation meant troops only reached France the following June. By then, Paris had fallen and the British forces and their allies were trapped in Dunkirk. No sooner had the Canadians arrived than they were racing to Brest to be evacuated. The landlord of the Lord Raglan had a point.

'At least we came. Unlike the Americans. May I ask again? If I need to stay longer—'

'You're the only guest we have, Mrs Marshall. Stay as long as you like. Unless Jerry comes along with different plans.'

The suite was large, plain, a desk, a double bed and a separate bathroom with a tub that looked as if it dated back to Victorian times. The so-called river view was little more than a lookout onto a stretch of stream overgrown with elder and willow. The Castle up the hill dominated the town. As she watched, a formation of aircraft flew past, heading north. The recognition posters for friend and foe planes were in her case. But these were close enough to see. They were Messerschmitt Bf 109 fighters escorting a group of Dornier Do 17 light bombers, out to wreak havoc somewhere inland.

Eric grumbled as he lugged in her case and deposited it by the bed, then glared at the window and the noise there.

'That'll be London they're going for then.'

'I doubt it. First, they'll be taking out the southern airfields. London will be next.'

'I stand corrected. You obviously know a lot more about this than me.'

'Just what a man on the train told me, actually.'

'But you are a reporter?'

'More a writer, really.' She opened the case and retrieved the Contax. It felt like an old friend in her hands.

He stared at the camera and said, 'Zeiss. That's Kraut, isn't it?'

'Made in Dresden. A beautiful place. Have you ever been to Germany?'

'Why would I do that? Go somewhere they don't even speak my language? When I've got England?'

'I don't know. Maybe to... see what somewhere else is like.' It wasn't worth the effort. 'Contax. Best camera in the world for my kind of work. Find me an English one as good and I'll buy it.'

Eric didn't look happy.

'Don't worry,' she added. 'I'm a journalist, not a spy. You hang them, don't you?'

'Only if they're one of ours, I believe. If they're foreigners, they get shot.'

———

He handed over a front-door key then left her to unpack her things. The typewriter and the Contax went on the desk by the window, along with the paper and the last few carbons she had. She'd need to find out where she could wire copy back to Toronto. Some means by which she could send her undeveloped films to the AP office in London where they could dispatch the best across the Atlantic with their wirephoto machine. Writing stories and taking pictures were sometimes the easy part. Getting them delivered was time-consuming, occasionally impossible. Fleeing the Nazis through Europe, she'd lost count of the films that had got lost in transit, worthwhile pictures vanished for good.

Ten minutes in, there was a knock on the door. Eric with two envelopes, one a familiar telegram. Had to be from the paper. She ripped that open first.

STILL AWAITING COPY. BUDGET EXCEEDED. UNABLE TO ADVANCE FURTHER SUMS. MAKE ARRANGEMENTS FOR YR RETURN ASAP. CALHOUN.

She whispered a bitter curse. The story was filed in good time the day before, to meet the morning's edition in Canada. The paltry budget was agreed when she was in Paris never expecting to have to pay for a rapid exit across the Channel. She'd been as parsimonious as she could and was down to her last few pounds. He could pay up or she'd find someone else to write for. As for going back to Canada... the last thing she was going to do was join a passenger ship that might get torpedoed by a German U-boat. Even if she did feel like being scared away from the frontline. Calhoun was a pen-pushing executive sitting safely behind a desk in Yonge Street. If the man had a clue how hard it was to file and stay in touch on the road, he didn't show it.

The second envelope was plain with just her name on it written in neat capital letters.

Inside was a single sheet headed "Ministry of Information" with the address of the unit's headquarters, the requisitioned Senate House of the University of London, a grim, grey tower block in Bloomsbury she'd had to visit to get permission to work in Dover. An ugly, modernist pyramid that wouldn't have been out of place in Nazi Germany or Mussolini's rebuilt Rome, it was filled with men, always men, who couldn't wait to stop her getting on with the job.

The typed message read...

Welcome to Dover, Mrs Marshall. Your immediate presence is required in my office, 21 Waterloo Crescent. You will find us by the harbour, with a guard outside the door.

Capt. David Shearer.

CHAPTER 5

May Dobson was in a flimsy blue checked cotton dress, the kind of thing she'd worn at school. For Harry Lee it was the usual – torn brown corduroy trousers mucky from farm work and a cheap and ragged cotton shirt.

She picked at the daisies on the grass and said, 'If my dad knew I was here, he'd kill you.'

'Best not tell him then, eh?'

'He finds things out. He's a copper.'

'I'm a Lee. You think I don't know that?'

She'd been a couple of classes below him. Long fair hair, bright blue eyes, the face of an angel. May didn't laugh at his crooked teeth, the port wine stain on his cheek, the haircut his dad did with a pair of kitchen scissors. Didn't treat him like a thick yokel unworthy of the odd smile or the time of day. That made a change.

Her old man had come up to him in his sergeant's uniform earlier that summer when Dover was full of sick, tired, flea-ridden squaddies newly evacuated from Dunkirk. Warned him he didn't like the way Harry hung about to linger round his daughter when she came out of school. He'd thought of saying, 'Ain't you got better things to worry about, mate?' Everyone knew Joe Dobson was the softest copper in town. Smart chap, May told him. Always down the Workers' Educational Association doing courses, reading things. Hardly seemed a copper at all.

That said, the Lees and the law had previous, what with his father being a bit of a thief and getting a spell in Canterbury jail. But time was served and now he was back home. Harry still missed his mum, who'd died just before war started, cancer in the Institution Hospital. But you had to get on with things, his dad said. It was only those with money who had the chance to look back. The Lees were poor, always had been, and for the poor the only thing that mattered was the present. A war was on, the Jerries again, who else? Farmers needed working men because a nation fought on food and couldn't get it from anywhere but its native fields. Sergeant Joe Dobson and the like wouldn't be picking on folk like the Lees for a while, not if they knew what was good for them.

'Your dad wouldn't hurt a fly, I heard. He's too nice to be a copper. Likes books, don't he?'

'Doesn't yours?'

Harry found that hilarious.

'He can't hardly read, May. I have to do it for him.'

'Maybe he's just bone idle. You thought of that?'

He hadn't and he realised she was probably right. Not that reading mattered much anymore. Since Frank Lee got out of prison, the war had taken a big turn for the worse. There was no school, for one thing. No one had a clue when there might be. Or whether, when the classes finally came back, the first thing they'd be learning would be German.

Most of the younger kids had been evacuated, sent packing on special trains, bags by their side, gas masks over their shoulders. Lots had gone to Wales, which might have been another country, and from some of the letters they sent back not a friendly one either. It was pot luck. Some kids landed up with kind folk. Others seemed to be working as little more than agricultural slaves. May stuck around because her dad had this thing about the family staying together. Joe Dobson didn't like the idea of his pretty young daughter getting pushed off to live with strangers on the other side of the country. She was the sort of girl who turned men's heads, made them stare at her and whistle as she passed. Straying hands kept wandering her way – and invitations. There was a glint in her eye that made it look like she just might take them, too. May said her mother wanted her somewhere else, but that cut no ice in the Dobson household. Her dad, quiet as he was, still ruled the roost.

They were on the footpath at the edge of town, beneath the military area of the Western Heights and the Citadel. All around, hundreds, maybe thousands of soldiers lived in their barracks, drilling during the day, drinking and the rest at night. Quite how many, no one knew. That was a secret. Just asking might get you into trouble.

Harry could hear the distant rumble of Merlin engines. The daily ritual of aerial warfare was so familiar he barely thought about it. All the same he strained his neck, shielded his eyes and pointed.

'Right, girlie. Plane-spotting time. What are they?'

'Ours. And I'm not a girlie.'

'I know they're ours. What kind of plane? If you're wrong...' He took a deep breath and decided to say it. 'If you're wrong, I'm owed a kiss.'

She laughed at that.

'You a good kisser, Harry Lee? Lots of experience?'

He didn't answer.

'No. Thought not.'

May dropped her smile and gazed across at the broad and busy harbour. Ugly grey barrage balloons floated high above the jetties. More were tethered to ships outside the port. They looked like the cast-off toys of giants, desperate to fly away from all the daily commotion but tethered down by steel hawsers.

Harry snorted at them.

'My dad reckons they're useless. Don't bother the Jerry planes one bit. Some bright spark who ain't too bright in London thought them up. Typical.'

'Your dad hates everyone who doesn't come from Dover.'

'Quite a few who do, as well. Like they hate every Lee that's ever lived.'

She couldn't take her eyes off the view.

'We used to have picnics here.'

There were more planes now. A good dozen of them hugging the coastline, probably from Hawkinge. The sights, the cliffs, the Castle, France on a clear day across the Channel, were something he'd grown up with, taken for granted. Nothing special but for the younger May they were still the coast, a magical place you went on holiday. She was just turned eleven when they'd moved from Bermondsey, astonished, she said, to discover they had schools at the seaside at all. Everyone was meant to be on holiday, having fun, down on the beach, in the arcades and on the rides, not getting bored stiff stuck at a desk.

'They're going to be fighting again, aren't they, Harry?'

'Our lads aren't up there for joyrides. Do you want to watch?'

Her delicate fingers gave him the lightest of slaps.

'It's not like Saturday morning cinema. This is real. People die.'

'They die whether we're looking or not.'

'I ought to go home.'

He put out a hopeful hand to stop her.

'You know your dad's going to be busy till God knows when. Your mum won't be back from the hospital for ages. All them sick soldiers from Dunkirk...'

'Why aren't you working? I thought you'd got a job at Miller's farm.'

He shrugged.

'Got fired. Had an argument with the foreman.'

'Not nicking stuff?'

'No... not nicking stuff. I saw him whacking one of the horses and told him if he did that again I'd be whacking him.'

She kept staring at the balloons and the harbour. Harry had a reputation for whacking people when they got annoying, a habit inherited from his dad, the one man he'd never dare whack in return.

'If they start bombing,' she said, 'we'll have to go down one of the shelters.'

'The shelters are in town. We're not. It's safer here.'

'What if they make a mistake? Even Germans do that.'

The Hawkinge planes had turned over the sea and started to climb. They'd probably been scrambled to meet a group of Messerschmitts or bombers heading out over the Channel. He'd watched enough of those deadly tussles over the previous weeks to get a feeling for the rhythm, what prompted them.

Rumour was Churchill had some kind of control room built into the cliffs beneath the Castle. People there were directing all those planes, like football managers telling their players where to be. The Battle of France was over, Churchill said. Now it was the Battle of Britain. Lose this and Hitler would be in London before Christmas, lining Winnie up against a wall, flying swastikas over Buckingham Palace, putting the king's brother back on the throne in a Nazi uniform. Jerry would invade Dover long before that. A couple of days away, maybe. Not that you read it in the papers. Just in the faces of some of the men who fell out of those secret offices and tunnels in the Castle, wandered into town to a pub, to a flophouse or the shows and couldn't keep their traps shut from time to time.

He pointed at the sky and said, 'What plane?'

'Spitfire,' she said immediately.

The dry grass smelled like old hay. He rolled onto it, put his hands behind his head and closed his eyes, laughing. He so wanted to touch her, hold her, but didn't quite dare.

'I give up. I really do. If they come that way, they're from Hawkinge so they're Hurricanes and then there's the shape and–'

Something light and gentle brushed his forehead. She kissed him, primly, quickly, but on the lips. He felt the heat run through him, the hope, the ache. When he opened his eyes May pulled back and giggled, blushing. Of course, she knew they were Hurricanes.

'You are the most beautiful thing I've ever seen,' he whispered.

'A thing, am I?'

'You know what I mean.'

She touched the red mark on his cheek and said, 'You'll have that forever, won't you? There's nothing they can do.'

'No. Do you hate it?'

'Just a bit of skin, Harry. That's all. Young skin. I like young.'

He didn't understand what she meant.

'It's a stain. I walk round with a stain on me. All day long. People look and stare. They say things.'

'And when they get your goat, you thump them.'

'Yeah.' He laughed and shook his fist. 'You bet I do.'

CHAPTER 6

Waterloo Crescent was a terrace of four-storey Georgian houses that looked out onto the busy grey waters of the outer harbour. Before the war the docks were the departure point for England's wealthy, taking ferries to Calais, Boulogne and Dunkirk, headed for the ski resorts of Switzerland or the promenades and casinos of Monte Carlo and Nice. Dover was a transport stop along the way, never a pretty seaside resort, even with the White Cliffs and the spectacle of the fortress on the hill. Still, Jessica Marshall could imagine the town might once have possessed a sense of gaiety, the affluent toasting the ferries as they left the Eastern Docks, flutes of champagne in their hands as they wound their way to the continent.

All that was gone. Naval craft, heavy functional cargo vessels, swift slim launches and troop carriers crammed the broad bay, a forest of guns pointing skyward from deck after deck. The air was filled with the sound of machinery, the stink of raw diesel and the cries of men sweating and scuttling around ship after ship. Little from the sky above the barrage balloons at that moment. The storm of aerial warfare always shifted like angry summer clouds and the planes were elsewhere. Inland, perhaps over Canterbury or closer to London, Maidstone and the genteel suburbia of Sevenoaks. War was spreading steadily, relentlessly towards the capital.

Number twenty-one was in the middle of the terraces, two soldiers in khaki outside looking weary, windows boarded up, a sign that said, "Mountbatten Hotel" sitting crookedly by the double front doors. A quarter of a mile along the way the skeletons of scaffolding were wrapped around a building with bomb damage, ragged walls like broken teeth held up by girders. It didn't look fresh. This was a part of the town that the organised visit of the week before had omitted. They'd never even seen much of the harbour, only the Castle and a meeting in a function room with a few locals primed to tell the story they'd been fed, about patriotism and courage and how everyone felt the way Churchill did, determined to the end.

Now she saw one more reason why the harbour had been off-limits. At the western end, close to what she'd heard was a submarine unit, lay the obvious wreck of a larger ship, a destroyer possibly. It sat there, half out of the water, torn like an abandoned child's toy, while salvagers clambered over the hulk.

An elderly man in baggy black trousers and a pale-blue shirt was ambling along the harbour pavement, taking a Yorkshire terrier for a walk, whistling what sounded like an old music hall song. He seemed an archetypal English pensioner, tubby, cheerful, a little scruffy in his old clothes and in need of a good shave. Taking his little dog for a stroll as if there was no war, no Hitler, no threat of bombardment across the Channel at all. He stopped next to her, smiled, and seemed to be enjoying the view.

'Excuse me,' she said.

'Madame.' He doffed his cap. 'A beautiful summer day, all things considered.'

'It is. I wondered...' She gestured at the wreck. 'What is that boat?'

'Ship, love. That's a ship.'

He had an accent she half-recognised as northern.

'Not anymore. What happened?'

He hesitated, pulled the dog to him and said, 'You're not local, then?'

'Down from London.' She pulled out her press card and showed him. 'Just curious. It's my job.'

He laughed, looking at her photo, four years younger, on the ID from the paper.

'Now there's a coincidence. A fellow warrior of the press. *Toronto Inquirer*, eh? Sounds fancy.' He held out his hand. 'Fred Lumsden. Chief reporter on the *East Kent Mercury* till I retired. Not my choice you understand, but times are hard as we all know, and the paper was kind enough to give me a little pension.'

'That's nice.'

'It is. I think you're having a more varied career than me, mind. I just covered flower shows and the odd pub punch-up, mostly. Dover's a quiet place when there isn't a war.' He glanced at the sea. 'The last one was nasty enough. Never thought I'd see that nightmare come back twice as bad. When will we learn?'

'The wreck...'

'Well...' He looked at her press card. 'Jessica... you won't be writing about that piece of junk over there. Not for a good while. They won't let you. Not even been a word in the local paper, and we all walk past it every day.'

'I guess. I just wondered.'

'You know your Samuel Johnson, I hope, young lady? No writer nor essayist should be without him by their side.'

He squeezed his eyes shut, thinking.

'Let me try and remember. "Among the calamities of war may be numbered the lessening of the love of truth, by the falsehoods which interest demands and credulity encourages".' He looked right at her and added, 'Or to put it more succinctly, as I believe our so-called American friends once did... The first casualty of war is truth. I may envy you your youth and dedication, but I don't envy you your job. Ask away, then. Won't make a blind bit of difference.'

'I did.' She glanced at the half-sunk remains of the ship.

'HMS *Codrington*. Took a few thousand of our lads out of Dunkirk. Saw that myself. Did a lot else besides, or so I hear. Which I didn't witness, so I won't talk about it. Nor would you want to know, you being a reporter who deals in facts not hearsay.'

The dog kept staring at her as if expecting a treat.

'A couple of weeks ago, she was in the harbour for a boiler clean or something. Jerry bombers came in. Broke her back. No one killed, from what I heard. Can't see them moving a wreck that big quickly, can you?'

No, she couldn't.

'Are you just drifting through, like most of the press people we get down here?'

'No. I'm here to stay. Until, well...'

There seemed no need to say more.

'If Jerry comes, he won't take kindly to a foreigner with a press card, love.'

'They won't take kindly to lots of things. If they come.'

He pulled a fountain pen out of his jacket pocket then a small ring-bound notebook. Once a reporter, always a reporter.

'Here.' An address. 'Twenty-seven Blenheim Avenue. Dover's not as big a place as people expect. I've been on my own since my wife died. Just me and Benny here.' The dog looked up and wagged his tail. 'Stop by if you want a cup of tea and a chat. I moved here from Yorkshire forty years ago so while I may not quite count as a Dovorian – you need a bloodline back to the days of Nelson for that – I could offer some local colour.' He nodded at the guards on the door of the Ministry of Information base. 'A few truths as well, and you might not get them from the chaps in there. They won't give you the time of day, not unless it suits them.'

'Thanks,' she said, and he ripped off the sheet of paper, handed it over, then doffed his cap again.

'Come on, boy. One quick turn of the harbour and let's hope Jerry don't catch us on the way.'

CHAPTER 7

Veronica's party was in full flow on the lawns of The Pantheon when Louis Renard returned. He parked his sit-up-and-beg Hillman Minx at the end of the line of luxurious saloons by the dry-stone ha-ha that led down the gentle curve of the Dour. Ever eagle-eyed, his aunt was soon marching over from beneath the Palladian portico, pearls around her neck, silk dress flapping in the warm breeze.

Brown trout were so common in the little river that idled through the estate you could almost tickle them out of the clear chalk stream. Hoping to introduce him to a pastime, Veronica had ordered some fishing gear from Hardy's in Pall Mall: a fly rod, Cascapedia reel, five different wet and dry lines and a selection of trout flies. The way the war was going, she said, they might end up fishing for their food before long.

Every time he struggled with casting a line, the sleepy brown shapes mocked him from the infuriatingly limpid water. He was thinking about how to improve his dubious casting technique when his aunt marched up and seized the bag from Crooks.

'Aha!' she cried, holding aloft the cans of Fortnum's pâté. After that came a flurry of theatrical curses when she picked out the bottle. 'Madeira? Your poor mother must be turning in her grave.'

'She was cremated, if you recall.'

'Pedantic *and* crumpled. God, you look a tramp, Louis. And here I am introducing you to the cream of Kent gentry.'

'I sent someone out to see what he could get. That...' he pointed at the bottle, '...was the best they had.'

'Ugh,' she said and threw the Madeira into a garish bed of petunias. 'Time to mingle. I know you don't do mingling, but you're thirty-six–'

'Thirty-seven.'

'Even pedantic about your age. Follow me and learn. I've been mingling all my life and I'm damned good at it.'

'Perhaps I should go and change...'

She jabbed a painted pink fingernail in his direction.

'No. You'll only skulk in your room with a book and the blasted wireless. Meet people, boy. You've been solitary enough.' His eyes were still on the river. 'You can always pretend to instil some terror in the trout later. It's not as if they're about to come to any harm. Come along...'

CHAPTER 8

'What do you think's going to happen?' May kept trying to make a daisy chain out of the tiny white flowers wilting in the dry summer grass. 'I know everyone says we'll win in the end. They've got to, haven't they? But the way my Dad's been talking. People don't believe it, do they? They're just trying to keep us quiet.' She scowled. 'Like we're children. Best seen, never heard.'

He sat up, put his hands round his knees, and looked out to sea. The day was so clear the French coast stood out in detail on the horizon, the distant cliffs there almost a mirror image of Dover's own. A swarm of planes had gathered mid-Channel like warring flies, RAF roundels meeting Luftwaffe Balkenkreuz, ready for the deadly dance they performed most days.

'Are you going to say anything, Harry Lee? Cat got your tongue?'

'Don't your dad talk about it? What we're going to do when they show up?'

'Not if I'm around. Told you. He thinks I'm a child. Does yours?'

He plucked a yellow flower from the sharp grass, smiled, held it beneath her chin and said, 'You like butter.'

'I know I like butter, thanks very much. Are you going to answer me?'

The idea had been buzzing round his head all day. If he was found out, God knows what hell there'd be to pay. If May really was impressed, then...

'I could show you something. You'd have to promise not to tell anyone. I mean... anyone.'

She was sweating a bit in the heat. The thin dress made the shape of her more obvious. He had to fight to stop staring at her bare legs. The shoes she wore were odd, though. Tan, shiny, recent, they looked too grown-up. Something a smart woman, a secretary or a teacher, might have worn. Not a girl just out of school.

'It's not something you've nicked, is it?'

'Just because I'm a Lee doesn't mean I spend every day nicking stuff.'

'What then?'

'A bit of a surprise,' he said, and started walking along the cliff path.

It was like laying a trail for the foxes when the hunt was out. Something he and his dad did every time there was a meet. Dug the cubs out of the ground too with the terriers given half a chance, did a bit of poaching – hares, pheasant, partridge and deer – on the side. The Lees had always lived off the land one way or another.

His old man kept a close eye on what was happening with the coppers. Made good sense. May's father was working with the military in the Castle now. The police force of old – one that kept all the drunks in check, knocked on the door of the Lees every time something went missing, gave you a kicking if they couldn't get you into magistrates' court – was gone. What few coppers weren't up at the Castle spent their time checking people's papers and looking out for dodgy foreigners, not whacking the heads of anyone they didn't like or kids who'd been out nicking apples. His dad reckoned you could kill someone right then. In broad daylight, too. Not much chance of them investigating that.

'When Jerry gets here it won't be over. It's just the beginning.'

He put a finger to his lips and kept on walking.

'Where are we going?'

'Shakespeare Cliff.'

'That's miles.'

'Worth it. Promise.'

'Why?'

He winked.

'Wait and see, May Dobson. You won't believe your eyes.'

CHAPTER 9

Veronica, while a fervent atheist, had been persuaded to arrange the drinks to mark the arrival of the new vicar of Temple Ewell. It was the kind of responsibility that came with owning The Pantheon, once the manor house of the village. Jolyon Partridge and his wife Linda had arrived from Canterbury, where they'd both worked in the archbishop's office. St. Peter and St. Paul's was a good three-quarters of a mile from the house, up a steep hill which Veronica, not one for exercise any more than she was for religion, refused to climb. Partridge turned out to be a nervy, unsmiling man of fifty or so, bald and chubby with a clean-shaven face nicked by clumsy razor work. His lean and sharp-featured wife was a good two inches taller, an expert in church architecture, or so she claimed, very gushing. The pair had been working in Europe for a while, with English congregations in Berlin and Brussels, before returning to England two weeks before war broke out.

'A very pretty church,' Renard said, though he'd only seen it from afar.

'Indeed,' Partridge agreed. 'I'm sure Linda can tell you all about it, can't you, dear?'

'Founded by the Knights Templar,' the woman declared.

'Fifteenth-century tower restored by the Victorians. Triple lancet windows, which are very Kent. There's a marvellous mortuary with rather finer examples in Selling.'

'Probably be needing that soon,' Partridge grumbled.

'The most interesting feature,' his wife continued, 'lies in the chapel glass. Undoubtedly German, early seventeenth century. *The Annunciation*. Very fine work given the local heathens once allowed the place to be used as a cowshed.'

'Any weddings planned?' asked Veronica.

'None,' said Partridge. 'Though the funeral trade looks busy and about to get busier. Seems I'm expected to help out in Dover as required, too. That was never part of the arrangement.'

Veronica smiled and introduced the pair to a man in tweed and plus fours who was, she announced, 'the master of the local hunt, and a jolly devout fellow.'

'Heavens,' she whispered, dragging Renard over to a gaggle of people by the tables on the patio. 'If that's what the grace of God looks like, kindly spare me. The man's a misery and the woman can't shut up.'

There must have been a good twenty-five locals scattered round The Pantheon's lawns and manicured flowerbeds, mostly of a certain age and countenance. Renard found himself being introduced to landowners who wanted him to come hunting, businessmen who couldn't wait to get him on the golf course and a chap who said he was a film producer friend of Veronica's late husband and wondered if he'd like to act as technical consultant for a crime film he was about to shoot back in Barnet.

The buzz of aerial traffic apart, it almost seemed the war was happening somewhere else. As if there was a border that set off grim Dover as the place for death and bombardment while genteel Temple Ewell sipped dry sherry and ate canapés.

'Funny name you have there,' said a ruddy-faced chap called Terence – he was unsure if that was the man's first or last name – who was a regional manager for a banking chain. 'Foreign.'

'We're all foreigners if you go back far enough,' Veronica said with a forced smile.

'It's Huguenot,' Renard added quickly, before her fuse was truly lit. 'Our family were silk weavers in Lyon. They came over in 1685 and settled in Spitalfields after Louis XIV revoked the Edict of Nantes and said every French child had to be raised Catholic. We were refugees.'

'Just like the Jews, then.' It was clear the man had been hitting the drink. Veronica looked ready to explode. 'And what do you weave now?'

'Nooses to wind around the necks of any murderers I can find. I'm taking time off from Scotland Yard. Inspector. Murder mostly, though I'll stoop to robbery with violence if there's nothing more interesting around.'

The man went white and stuttered, 'What in God's name are you doing here?'

'Looking for trade. What else? If you happen to know where I might find some...'

'You won't find criminals in Temple Ewell.'

Renard nudged the chap's elbow and spilled his drink, quite deliberately.

'Oh, if you look hard enough, you'd be amazed what turns up in the most unlikely of places...'

The bank manager stuttered something, then wandered off to the trellis table and the wine bottles.

'Dreadful little shit,' Veronica grumbled as he vanished. 'If I didn't need to keep him sweet about money, I'd never allow the fellow through the door. And...' she prodded Renard in the chest, 'you are the most infuriating man I know. Meek as a mouse one moment then you bare those fangs and take them down with one bite.' She kissed his cheek. 'Maddening and adorable, nephew. You should have followed me onto the stage. At least I could get you a decent wardrobe then. Brown shoes with a blue suit. Bloody hell.'

'I sometimes feel I have,' he said, looking around. 'Followed you onto the stage, that is.'

This was the relationship they'd always had, even when he was a precocious child. Playfully antagonistic, with a touch of light comedy on the side.

She pointed out a young woman with bright-red hair, tight jodhpurs, a riding crop in one hand and a voice that carried all the way across the lawn.

'The Bellamy girl's single. Comes with money. Father owns a small brewery. Spends all day with her damned horses, as you can judge from her arse. But no one's perfect. I think she plays the cello, too. If you like I could introduce–'

'Thanks, but no.'

'Louis.' Her voice had softened, her hand crept over and squeezed his. 'You can't be a hermit forever. Please. Indulge me. You need more than an ancient aunt for company.'

He was saved by an angry buzzing overhead. Two aircraft performing an aerial duet, so distant it was impossible to identify the types let alone which was British, which German.

Watching them, he found the garden party on the lawn of The Pantheon vanished altogether. There was little he could think of except two men fighting to kill one another high in the clear blue sky of Kent. Another time, too, a few months before. The beach of Dunkirk, the scramble to get on the ragtag flotilla of boats come to rescue them. Blood and shrieks and fear everywhere, beneath the scream of German dive bombers, crows pouncing on carrion. Then an explosion and a darkness punctuated by a multitude of variations upon the theme of pain.

'Stop that now,' Veronica said and slapped him on the wrist. 'I know what you're doing.'

The aircraft above them twisted around like two cats fighting over an invisible ball of wool. Then came a long rattle of gunfire and a line of grey smoke appeared near the tail of the plane that had rolled beneath the other, as if in submission.

'It's Jerry, thank God,' someone said.

There were flames and the Messerschmitt began to plummet towards the green fields. They could see the black cross on the side. The cockpit was thrown back, a figure flew out. Then a parachute opened.

'Shoot the bugger to pieces, Tommy,' someone yelled. 'They'd do it to us.'

'That,' said an elderly aristocratic-looking man, 'is not war, sir. It's murder.'

The British plane came lower. A Hurricane. The fighter performed a slow victory roll past the German pilot floating gently towards the ground, little more than a mile away. The tall gentleman who'd spoken so severely had a pair of opera glasses out as he followed the descent.

'Veronica. I'll deal with this,' Renard said as he took the keys to the Hillman out of his pocket, wondering if there was somewhere he could borrow a gun, just in case.

'No, you won't,' the fellow with the glasses said. He held out his hand. 'James Mortimer. Your aunt was about to introduce us, I'm sure.'

The Lord Lieutenant of Kent. The king's representative in the county. The man who should have had *foie gras* but looked content enough with liver pâté out of a tin.

'Sir. If an enemy combatant lands on English soil...'

'He's coming down on Freddy Lancaster's estate. Freddy's men will deal with him soon enough. Besides...'

He handed over the glasses. Renard took a moment to catch the distant figure. The German was floating to earth, head slumped on his chest, his pilot's vest burned the colour of cinder. His face too, by the looks of it.

'I imagine you know what a dead man looks like, Inspector,' Mortimer said. 'Care to comment?'

'I believe things that I can touch and see close up, sir. Someone needs to follow up on this. Not a bunch of farmhands, either.'

The man laughed.

'A village constable is on his bicycle as we speak. Be assured of that.' He raised his glass. 'We have more weighty matters to consider. Come...' He took Renard's arm. 'Are you... are you well enough now? Excuse my asking.'

'I believe so.'

'Good. Then we must speak.'

His aunt walked with them.

'Two glasses of something or other, please, Dame Veronica. Then kindly leave us. Your nephew and I need to talk. Alone.'

CHAPTER 10

The soldier on the door of the house in Waterloo Crescent checked her passport, looked at a list in his pocket and waved Jessica Marshall through. It was obvious the place had been a hotel before. There was a reception desk next to an empty lounge bar that bore a sign, "Visitors Waiting Area – Do Not leave unaccompanied".

Fifteen minutes later an unsmiling young woman in a plain grey skirt and cardigan walked in and said in a bored, upper-class voice, 'Captain Shearer is ready for you now. Do you have a camera?'

'I always have a camera. It's my job.'

'Leave it here with your bag and pick it up on the way out. If we see you take any photographs inside or in the vicinity they will be confiscated, along with your equipment. Only make notes if you are asked.'

'Welcome to Dover,' Jessica Marshall muttered as they headed for the winding staircase.

Shearer had an office on the first floor surrounded by rooms full of busy people, the clatter of typewriters, a telegraph terminal, what looked like a small telephone exchange run by two women in uniform. He had a minion with him, who introduced himself as

Ian Henderson. 'Local,' Henderson said, as if to point out that was rare in Dover's Ministry of Information outpost. The captain was a tall man in a dark suit, custom-made, probably. Neat black hair, lean saturnine face, thirty-five, perhaps forty. He had the pallor of someone who didn't sleep much. Henderson looked quite provincial next to him: a portly, pale-faced chap in his early twenties, round glasses, brown-rimmed, the cheapest you could find, barrel chest filling out an old tweed jacket with leather elbows.

'Why didn't I meet you last week?' she asked before the captain could say a word.

'Because it was needless and inconvenient,' Shearer replied. 'Do you find the Lord Raglan comfortable?'

Unasked, she fell into a seat in front of his desk. Henderson pulled up a chair and took out a notebook and pen. Marshall watched him write: Pitman shorthand, the same system she'd learned at college when she was desperate to get into newspapers. She caught his eye and said, 'Comfortable enough. You're either a former court stenographer or a reporter like me, Mr Henderson.'

He grinned at that.

'Ian, please. Sports reporter for the *Dover Express*. Football, rugby and cricket. Stringer for the *Sketch* for a while too. Ordinarily I'd be covering a match on Saturdays but... well. I hope to make it to Fleet Street one day, when all this nonsense is over.' He shrugged his sturdy shoulders. 'Can hardly call myself a journalist really, not next to someone with a career like yours. All them places. Rome. Berlin. Paris. I did a ferry crossing to Boulogne a while back, summer beano organised by the paper. Chucked my guts up on the way back. Bit rough, bit pissed too, if I'm honest.'

'You do know a lot about me. Did your research tell you I'd be lost at football, rugby and cricket?'

'Oh. I'm sure you're a fast learner, Mrs Marshall...'

Shearer gave him a sharp glance and Henderson shut up.

'Introductions over,' the captain said. 'This...'

He threw a sheaf of papers on the desk. She recognised them straight away and the heat started rising in her cheeks. It was the wire version of the piece she'd filed in London the day before. The colour story, few facts, much padding, something she'd hoped would keep the distant Calhoun on the foreign desk in Toronto as happy as a miserable creature like him could be.

'What the hell are you doing with my work?'

'Saving you the embarrassment of seeing it in print,' Shearer said and tore the pages in half in front of her.

'I sent that to be wired yesterday...'

He ran his fingers through the shredded pages.

She was ready to explode.

'Some bastard in London killed it?'

'Never got further than the operator. Since we knew you were on your way here, they asked me to deal with it.'

'That's my job. I've been late with my copy anyway. You could get me fired...'

Shearer picked up another sheet of paper and pushed it over. It was a copy of the message she'd received from Calhoun when she arrived at the Lord Raglan. His warning about being over budget. How he refused to send any more money and demanded she make arrangements to return home.

'You've no right–'

'I've every right. We're in the throes of a conflict that could see Hitler on our doorstep any day. The only privileges you have are the ones I accord you.'

She knew the limits. The piece she'd filed, so carefully phrased, crossed none of the boundaries the Ministry drones had laid down in such fine detail, the mention of troop deployments, weaponry, casualties, anything close to being a statistic.

'I didn't break your rules, Shearer.'

He rolled his seat back, closed his eyes, put his fingers together in a tent, the kind of gesture a teacher used when dealing with a slow pupil.

'No. You were cautious in that respect. But let's not be picky. We both know there's the question of morale–'

'I'm not here to raise your morale. I'm here to report the facts. As accurately as I can, within the restrictions you've set out.' She picked up some shreds of torn typescript. 'That's what I did. It's a damned impertinence you're intercepting my private communications with my newspaper. When they find out–'

He laughed. So did Ian Henderson, probably because it was expected.

'You know,' Shearer said, 'for a war correspondent you seem remarkably ignorant of the way matters work.'

'Really?'

'There isn't a wire goes in or out of this country involving people like you, people under our supervision, without us seeing it first.'

'Your supervision?'

Henderson jumped in.

'The tone's the problem. We found it... unhelpful.'

'For God's sake!' Too loud, she thought. Too shrill. 'This is Dover. You're staring down the barrel of Hitler's guns. You want me to make out it's some kind of holiday camp?'

'The mood,' said Shearer, 'was defeatist. We don't like defeatist. We don't believe our allies like it any more than we do.'

'My boss–'

'Mark Calhoun.' Shearer was checking some notes in front of him. 'Englishman. Worked in Canada for seven years. Formerly of the *Yorkshire Post*. Do you get on?'

'We get on fine.'

'Even though he sacked your husband?' Henderson asked.

'Jesus...'

'How is Michael?' It was Shearer this time. 'Have you heard from him and his girlfriend in Seattle?'

'What do you know–?'

'I know he's an American citizen who got fired from the

foreign desk for having an affair with a woman on the city beat. I know the two of them are trying to scrape by on the West Coast working for some pathetic little rag there. If there's anything you'd like to add...'

'You tell me. You read my mail.'

'Calhoun won't give you any more money,' Henderson said. 'He told you. Told us, too. He says you've spent a small fortune. Times are hard. They don't think you've been great value and–'

'It's a goddamned war! I spent what I had to...' *Quieter,* she thought. *Calmer.* 'And anyway, it's none of your business. What goes on between the *Inquirer* and me. None at all.'

Shearer was running through some of the torn pages.

'You write with some style. Very readable. Literate without being fussy. I like it.'

'I am so grateful.'

'It's just a shame you choose to use it to focus on the negative. When there are so many positives to be found here.'

'Fine.' She got to her feet. 'You made your point. I'm going back to London.'

'Sit down.'

'Screw you...'

He got up from the desk.

'Sit down, please. We're not done here.'

'Did you not hear me?'

'Do you have the train fare?' Henderson wondered.

'Yes. I do.'

'And then what?' Shearer, now. They were a polished double act. Must have rousted no end of people like this. 'Do you have money for a hotel? Food? Film and wires?'

'Calhoun will send it...'

He smiled, took out a silver cigarette case, lit one for himself, no one else.

'Calhoun won't send you another penny. The next telegram you get from him is the one that fires you.'

'Bullshit,' she snapped.

He opened his desk drawer, pulled out the familiar envelope and threw it across the table.

'The only wire terminal in Dover is in the next room. Along with the only wirephoto machine. A darkroom and the best man for developing and processing film in Kent.'

'Andy Bell,' Henderson said. 'Lovely chap. Used to run D and P for the paper. Can work magic, even with terrible photos. Can't say the ones we've seen of yours have been, well, *Picture Post* quality, Jessica. Hope you don't mind me being honest.'

She sat down and ripped open the envelope. The message was timed just after midnight in Toronto. Calhoun never liked working late. He wouldn't have sent a message like this unless someone ordered it.

```
SERIOUS DISCREPANCIES FOUND BY ACCTS RE
EXPENSE CLAIMS. POSITION TERMINATED WITH
IMMEDIATE   EFFECT   DUE   TO   FINANCIAL
MISCONDUCT.  SUGGEST  CONTACT  CANADIAN
EMBASSY ABT REPATRIATION. CALHOUN.
```

Shearer pushed his silver cigarette case across the table.

'Have a smoke. They're Du Mauriers. You won't find them easily anywhere else. Not even on the black market right now.'

She didn't move.

'Who the hell do you think you are? You and your cut-price spy sidekick?'

Captain Shearer stared right at her and opened his arms wide in a generous and welcoming manner.

'Who am I? Why, Mrs Marshall... I'm the fellow who's going to make your career.'

CHAPTER 11

Harry Lee led her to the highest stretch of Shakespeare Cliff, chalk meadow running seven mostly unspoilt and verdant miles to Folkestone, home to spider and bee orchids, rock samphire foraged by the locals, all the many coastal flowers of southern England. Rampant wild grasses ran to the ragged edge, fading to gold and rapidly going to seed. Gulls and terns hovered in the hazy summer air, barely moving their wings in the stiff sea breeze.

A dizzying distance below, on the slender shore of a shallow rocky bay, was a short railway stop where the London line through Folkestone emerged briefly from twin tunnels. Nearby were some abandoned workings the school used for history visits. They were the start of a Victorian pipe dream, another subterranean shaft, this time to France beneath the Channel, hardly begun before it was abandoned for fear the foreigners might use it to invade.

When the teacher said that, Harry'd laughed out loud. The idea was stupid. How could they smuggle an army down a passage barely wide enough to take two tractors? With the onset of modern war, it seemed even more ridiculous. Jerry could shell England from his gigantic artillery placements on the other side. Fly his fighters and bombers across the bright blue sky. Land his troop ships somewhere along the Kent coast in his thousands. A tiny burrow that ran from coast to coast was surely beneath Adolf and his generals. All the same, the army had created a camp next to the little train platform that carried the sign, "Shakespeare Cliff Halt". Maybe they knew something the ordinary folk of Dover didn't.

Close to the cliff edge a local birdwatching group had built a hide, a large wooden hut with benches and slit windows. There they would spend days watching the rich and changing wildlife, swifts and redstarts, the occasional osprey, wheatears, stonechats and spotted flycatchers, all recorded in a logbook kept on a table inside the door.

The place was always locked now but, half hoping, he'd stolen his father's key. All the same, the padlock was undone when he got there. Some idiot on the team not doing his job, Harry guessed. He pushed it open and waved her inside. She'd been on the same school visit as him to the halt below, and the hide. Straight away she went to the logbook to check. The last entry was the previous December. Just one paragraph. Black redstarts and ravens, a short-eared owl and a flock of kittiwakes.

'Those birdwatchers can't use this place anymore, can they?' she said, flicking through the pages. 'Soldiers down below. We shouldn't be here, either.'

He sat on the bench by the window slits. She didn't join him. May had a mind of her own. No one was going to order her around. In some odd way, now he'd got closer to her than ever, she almost seemed older than him. Angry, hurt about something too. That came across in her prickly, awkward nature.

'You're with me, May. No one's going to bother us.'

She did sit down then, but at the end of the bench, away from him.

'What makes you so special?'

He wasn't supposed to tell anyone. Not a soul. His father had made him swear on his dead mum's grave. Whatever that meant.

His old man never took much notice of her when she was alive. He couldn't work out why either of them should bother now she was gone.

'You asked what was going to happen. When they came.'

There was the low, guttural rumble of a Merlin engine overhead. So low, so loud they had to stay quiet until it passed.

'If they come. Might not happen,' she said when the plane drifted away, out over the sea.

'When they come. They will. Maybe even tomorrow. If they do, there are plans.'

'Well, yes.' She laughed. 'I imagine there would be. All those soldiers up at the Castle. Churchill on the wireless and in the papers day and night. Of course there's plans.' She shrugged. 'They'll still be here, Harry. So will we. My dad thinks...'

She stopped abruptly, as if she'd said something she shouldn't.

'Your dad thinks what?'

'He says if they turn up and we lose we'll have to get on with it.'

This was interesting. He shuffled along the bench to get closer to her.

'What does that mean?'

'It means... we get on with it! The Jerries aren't here to kill us all, are they? They just want to run things. Boss us about. Make us do what they want. Like Churchill and his lot do anyway. We're just common folk. If we've lost, we've lost. We're going to have to learn to live with it.'

'Is that really what your dad reckons?'

She looked sulky, suddenly. As if she'd said too much.

'Winnie reckons–'

'Oh yeah, Winston Churchill,' May grumbled. 'Him! That man sent in his soldiers to break the General Strike, my dad says. Same lads he's got fighting for him now are the ones he was fighting then. Listen to all his guff. "We'll fight them on the beaches, in the streets, the fields".'

'What's a general strike?'

'God, Harry. Don't you read anything?'

'We don't ever surrender,' he said, trying to remember what else he'd heard listening to the wireless at home that June when the Dunkirk evacuations were filling the town with miserable, flea-infested soldiers stumbling out of the ships, some no more than fishing boats. It was stirring stuff, made him want to be brave, to volunteer and fight himself. He'd have enlisted on the spot if they'd taken him, but you had to be eighteen. A few months to wait. One day... a pilot, he reckoned. Spitfire or Hurricane, it didn't matter so long as it was just him up there in the sky, alone with his fearsome machine spitting death and bullets.

'We won't give in, May. We're not like that.'

'You mean we're different? Really?'

'Yeah. We're British.'

'Better than everyone else?'

'Yeah. We are.'

She waved a hand at him.

'You believe all that nonsense? Politicians have to spout that stuff. Doesn't mean it's true.' She tapped her chest. He stared. 'Makes no difference if I surrender or not, Harry Lee. I'm not going to walk out into the street and fight them, am I? I wouldn't know how. Or my mum. Or Gran up in Bermondsey. She's turned seventy and half daft. You think she's going to grab a rifle or something soon?'

'That's not the point.'

'It is. It's the only point. If we never surrender, we all end up dead. That won't happen. We'll... I don't know. Get on with it. Like I said. Stay... safe.'

'Like your dad said. Be German, you mean?'

'No!' She looked furious, scared a bit, too. He couldn't imagine the kind of conversations they must have had in the Dobson house. All he ever talked about with his own father was work and money and the odd bit of mischief. Then, lately, the fight to come. 'We'll always be us.' May reached out and took his hand. 'We're just kids, Harry. You...' Her eyes were sharp and wouldn't leave him. 'You're more a kid than me. It's not our war. We didn't start it. Lots of things can change. They won't unless we're still here to make them.'

He got up, walked away from her, bent down, and gazed out through the slit windows. The camp beneath the cliffs was tents mainly, khaki, with a line of field guns set to one side. Men were busy all round, dragging tarpaulins over the artillery to hide them. So many hours went into putting massive installations like that into position, so many hours after that trying to disguise the fact they were there.

It was hard to picture what an invasion might look like. He'd asked his old man, not that he had a clue. Did they come ashore in some kind of special boat? If they tried that at the foot of Shakespeare Cliff they'd run straight into that battery of guns, a bunch of hard soldiers and no easy way to get into town by foot except along the train line where they'd be like ducks in a shooting gallery at the fair. Maybe they'd parachute down. Though they'd need thousands of soldiers to take a place as tightly protected as Dover. Even the Germans, he thought, might be hard put to manage that from planes, especially with the RAF harrying them all the time the way they did now.

Boats. It had to be by sea, head-on. Dover was a harbour town. If it fell it would be from the Channel, fast, brutal, massive. A *blitzkrieg* like they'd called it in France.

May had a point, though. All civilians heard was what the government told them. Which was sometimes as good as lies. There'd been things happen, bombs, arrests, damage to the Castle and the harbour, that never appeared in the papers or on the wireless. Stirring speeches like Churchill's sometimes made no sense at all when you picked them to pieces. She was right about what her old man said about no surrender. If it was true then every last man, woman and kid in Britain would die fighting. That wasn't going to happen.

'Better a live coward than a dead hero, then?'

May winced. It was a stupid comment. This wasn't going how he planned it at all.

'No.' She came over, touched his chest, the cheap cotton work shirt, red-and-blue plaid. 'It's not that simple. Being dead's just dead, isn't it? If it's not, the Jerries who cop it are heroes too. At least to the people who love them back home. I just think there's a point where, if it comes to it, we'll say fine... put a picture of Hitler on the wall. Boss us around for as long as you can get away with it. Do what you like. Just let us live, let us be ourselves. And maybe we can change things one day. Except... we're not supposed to say that now. I shouldn't be saying it. You don't like it.'

All the young who'd stayed behind in Dover were growing up fast. But that wasn't a fifteen-year-old girl talking. Even a quick and bright one like May Dobson. It was her dad, the awkward copper, the one who liked his books.

'I shouldn't have brought you here. We ought to go.'

She didn't move. He could tease as well.

'Why did you?'

'To show you a secret. Except it's one you won't want to know about. So best...'

'Oh.' She ran a finger down his chest again, slowly this time, pressing against his shirt. 'I thought you brought me here for something else.'

And there she'd got him again. All the heat, the want was back.

'Don't know what you mean,' he mumbled, tearing himself away from her, hard as it was.

The way in was hidden under a length of old carpet at the far end of the hide. Beneath was a circular iron handle screwed to a trapdoor, on the underside a tin box supposed to contain a battery torch and two oil lamps with a cigarette lighter to bring them to life.

The torch was missing and there was only one lamp with the lighter. Must have been the same fool who'd left the door unlocked.

He lit one of the lamps and held its waxy yellow light over the gap. She came and looked. A line of steep wooden steps descended into darkness.

'There's this as well.'

Chapter 12

The wine was Muscadet, a little fusty, warm. Aunt Veronica used to go to Le Touquet for breaks and bring it back by the crate. Now she was down to her last few bottles and since it was somewhat inferior, intent on serving it to her guests.

'Oxford, was it?' Mortimer asked.

The lord lieutenant had taken him to one side, a spot close to the river by a bank of unruly rhododendrons.

'Cambridge.'

'Law?'

'History.'

Mortimer sighed.

'Culture's fine for those who can afford it. The real money's in law. Always has been. Always will be. Unless you're lucky enough to be born to wealth like me. A strange trajectory. From Cambridge to Scotland Yard.'

There was a handful of Oxbridge graduates in the Metropolitan Police when Renard arrived. All treated like misfits by the regulars.

'It wasn't strange for me. The work sounded... interesting. Different. I like different.'

Sir James Mortimer sipped at his wine, pulled a face and said, 'What do you know of finding spies?'

'Nothing.'

'Do you think you could learn?'

Renard glanced around the garden party. He felt he might always be a stranger to this part of England. There were no such social events in Bloomsbury.

'I could try. But I think you might be better served by someone local.'

Mortimer must have been pushing seventy, a fit and handsome man, craggy-faced, hair silver and sleekly greased. He had the air and demeanour of an old soldier or the master of a hunt and was probably both.

'It pays to think like your enemy, Inspector. If you were Hitler, where would you want your friends right now? London? Or here in Kent, where you hope to be landing, perhaps next week? Perhaps tomorrow?'

'Both.'

He laughed.

'Very good. But it's the friends here that concern me. They've been around for years. Being so very... English. Or so they'd like to think.' He eyed the bank manager across the throng. The man was on his own and looked dead drunk, sullen, lost. 'You met the clown from the Midland, I see. What did you make of him?'

'Unpleasant. Fond of the booze.'

Mortimer seemed to approve.

'He was once a member of the British Union of Fascists. Though he got out when he realised events might threaten his middle-class, mediocre career. He believed we didn't know.' A smile. 'He's wrong. I told him when he arrived, which may explain his condition. I do wish Veronica had cleared the guest list with me. They're picking him up this evening and sending him to the Isle of Man. There to remain for the duration, however long that might be.' He pulled out a short cigar and lit it. The smell was acrid, overwhelming. Renard stood back a little, not that Mortimer noticed. 'I see his poor wife's not here. I rather imagine she'll be grateful.'

'If you've further intelligence you wish to pass on...'

'Oh, Christ.' Mortimer gave him a filthy look. 'If I possessed that, do you think we'd be having this conversation?' He sucked on the cigar then looked Renard up and down. 'All we know is they're here. They're trying to penetrate our preparations against any coming land attack. The obvious ones, military and visible. The covert ones which, in the end, may make all the difference. Have you met Captain Shearer?'

Renard had heard the name mentioned, rarely with affection, around Dover nick. But that was all.

'I've never had the need to deal with the Ministry of Information.'

Mortimer guffawed.

'You will soon enough. David Shearer's much more than a petty censor. His licence runs far and wide. Nor is he a lowly captain. The Ministry of *Mis*information's more like it. What did you make of the new vicar?'

Renard struggled for an answer.

'I barely met the man...'

'He and his wife worked in Berlin for three years then a spell in Brussels. If you can call what he does working.'

So did many Britons, Renard believed. The continent was far from distant.

'That doesn't mean much, does it? Hardly makes him suspect.'

'Probably not.' He shrugged. 'The point I'm trying to make is that the important people we're looking for are far more likely to be here, drinking Dame Veronica's awful wine, than hanging around the docks in Dover trying to pick up morsels of information. They have men and women doing that no doubt. But the brain...' he tapped his head, 'will always be elsewhere. Hidden where you least expect it. That is how intelligence works. The fellow you should suspect is the one you rarely do.'

'You seem familiar with the process.'

'Do I really? What do you know of Cordelia?'

'As in *Lear*?'

The man groaned.

'There's an answer. Cordelia is the means by which we hope to delay Hitler on his way to London, should all else fail. If it's compromised, Jerry will be flying his swastika over Buckingham Palace in weeks. We must keep its methods, its men and its lairs to ourselves.'

'I understand.'

'I hope so. Why did you flee London to go to Dunkirk? It seems an extraordinary thing to do.'

Renard hesitated, wondering how much to say.

'I wanted to help.'

'And damn near died, from what I heard.'

Renard raised his glass and stayed silent.

'Of course,' said Mortimer. 'One rarely wants to talk about such things. Head wounds can affect a man. For quite a while, or so I hear.'

'I'm well enough, as I said.'

'And Scotland Yard?'

'Perhaps one day. My aunt has this place all to herself. I didn't like leaving her in the circumstances.'

'Dame Veronica,' Mortimer said with a chuckle, 'would cope with the Germans rather better than most of us.' He glanced at her admiringly across the lawn. 'There's an entire generation of my age still in love with your aunt. A fine-looking woman who stands no nonsense. Nor should she. I fear for any Kraut who tries to order her about.'

'That, sir, is one more reason why I'm here.'

Mortimer seemed satisfied. He patted Renard on the arm and said, 'Good. Have they issued you with a firearm yet? They're meant to, but I gather they're hard to come by. Others, our feral chaps in Cordelia for example, take precedence.'

'No.'

'If I gave you a Webley .38 would you know how to use it?'

'That is the handgun of the Metropolitan Police. Yes. I believe I could manage.'

'Then follow me.'

They went to a shiny black Bentley by the conservatory. There were more people there behind the glass, half-hidden among the orange and lemon trees and aspidistras. Mortimer retrieved a large leather case from the boot of the limousine. It was made for weapons, six places set for them, only one occupied with a holster alongside.

He picked out the weapon and handed it over.

'I wouldn't carry it as a matter of habit, Inspector. People will ask questions. But if you feel you're near a suspect...'

Renard held the gun, turned it in his hands. It seemed identical to the ones they used on the rare occasion the Yard felt the need to be armed.

The brown leather holster, very new, and two packs of shells followed.

'Good luck, Inspector.' Mortimer held out his hand and the two men shook. 'If you need anything more, do call.'

'I will.'

'Oh. And should you encounter the young lieutenant in charge of Cordelia, do pass on my regards.'

'You know him?'

Mortimer smiled.

'I do indeed. He's my son.'

CHAPTER 13

The military meant paperwork, even for an insurrection against the Nazis. Joe Dobson had learned that early on when Superintendent Chalmers said he was to be attached to the secret unit based in two Nissen huts in the lee of the hill behind the Castle. There was no arguing, though perhaps Chalmers simply wanted him out of the nick. War deprived you of that privilege. Nor could he discuss a word of his work outside the tiny team in shacks A and B.

He reported to Lieutenant Tobias Mortimer, all of twenty-four, fresh from the Royal Military College at Sandhurst. He was ever-optimistic, fond of morale-raising speeches for anyone who would listen, utterly ignorant of police work, the law and war. A man, it seemed to Dobson, who anticipated meeting "the Boche" in battle the same way he looked forward to the start of the game season.

The government had been working on creating a civilian resistance force for some time, with mixed success. Initially called the Local Defence Volunteers, the effort had been dogged by patchy recruitment, poor training and low morale, not helped when Anthony Eden, the Secretary of State for War, announced the effort with the proclamation, 'You will not be paid, but you will receive a uniform and will be armed.'

That was in May, the month Churchill was made prime minister in the hope of turning the tide of what was rapidly becoming a fight for national survival. The new man soon pounced on the failings in the LDV and demanded the effort be restructured and renamed the Home Guard, effectively a civilian militia charged with fighting alongside the conventional army.

The brief Mortimer had been given was to set up the Dover section of something entirely different. His would be one of a series of covert armed units code-named, in the case of Kent, Cordelia. Each would embark upon a guerrilla campaign in the event of a Nazi invasion. Their initial brief, once the Germans had launched from France, would be to work alongside the police to capture any suspect locals who, for lack of damning evidence, had yet to be interned. These had already been named in a Home Office and MI5 dossier listing suspected British Nazi sympathisers, whose 'recent conduct or words indicated that they were likely to assist the enemy.'

After that, the members of Cordelia would go underground to harass and delay the enemy as the Nazi forces tried to fight their way to London. Terror was the answer: street assassinations, the delivery of bloody mayhem to the new invaders. Bright-eyed Mortimer thought Cordelia "terrific fun" and had taken to dressing in civilian clothes and trying to adopt the local rural accent and vernacular to ready himself for the task.

To Joe Dobson, the son of a trade unionist railway worker from south London, the man's efforts to be anonymous only made him stand out a mile. Not that he ever said so. Mortimer seemed a nervy soul beneath the surface, still living in the time of the phoney war, believing the only blood to be spilt was that of the enemy and the heroic few. Yet he was no fool. He had to know he was sending poorly trained civilians to their deaths, as must some of the volunteers the team had recruited over the previous weeks.

Perhaps, Dobson thought, one of the secrets of war was to conceal reality from oneself. To pretend the worst might not happen at all. Tobias Mortimer wished to adopt a Panglossian bravado, hoping that all would indeed be for the best in the best of all possible worlds.

The lieutenant's underground warriors amounted to thirty-four local men between the ages of forty and sixty, all of whom had received the minimum of training in signals and intelligence, and directions to a series of hidden safe bunkers they could use when they wanted to disappear. The last part of the process was the most important: they needed to learn how to kill, quickly and efficiently, with the minimum of weapons. The previous Friday they'd been issued with military daggers – sharp, well-balanced knives designed to pierce a man fatally in seconds. Now it was time to issue each with a Webley .38 service revolver, along with thirty-six shells each, enough to refill the cylinder six times. That, for the moment, was as much as the army could afford. Once the necessary bureaucracy was complete, they were to visit the armoury firing range where a brigade instructor would teach them how to clean and maintain the guns while they were in hiding, vital if the weapons were to remain serviceable for the guerrilla war ahead.

The revolvers the volunteers were being given were old and rejected by some in the military who preferred the standard issue Enfield No. 2. But the men who'd volunteered for Cordelia were only too happy to receive free firearms and had turned up on a rota during the day for their approval by Mortimer, followed by a spell on the firing range. Joe Dobson knew a good few: tradesmen, fishing-boat skippers, farmers, a couple of layabouts. Some of those picked for Mortimer's underground army were clearly infirm, chosen for the boasts they made about killing Germans in the Great War. A few, he felt, were entirely unsuitable to be trusted with weaponry at all. Not that the lieutenant was interested in his qualms. He waved a dismissive hand at every quibble the sergeant raised, then sent the trainee in question to be armed and taken to the range.

The racket of aircraft buzzed over the office constantly. But the whistle and explosion of shells in the town was absent. From the distant sound of explosions, Jerry's land-based guns, the batteries on Cap Gris-Nez, were probably targeting shipping in the Channel. Dover's turn would, inevitably, come later.

Dobson was getting heartily sick of the whole exercise. There were better things to be done. The handful of music halls still working were now given over to lurid shows that skirted the edge of legality, though the police were under strict instructions to ignore them. So popular were they with the military that performances would be halted from time to time and the names of men required back at their station read out in front of the audience. There were whores working the back streets, black market touts, pimps and thieves, everywhere. Plenty of genuine police work to be done in the real world while he stamped pieces of paper that were meaningless in the extreme. Except the real world no longer existed, and he'd no idea when it might return.

Beth, his wife, was a nurse who worked in the Institution Hospital, mostly caring for injured soldiers. May, the daughter he kept close while all her peers were evacuated, was growing ever more surly and rebellious. He'd no idea how the girl, so pretty, so naive, so vulnerable as she hovered on the cusp of adulthood, could possibly be better off with strangers than she was with them. Though the essential work, his own and his wife's, meant May had to be left alone for long hours on end, something that worried Dobson greatly.

When the Germans landed, Dover might fall within days, perhaps even be abandoned after a fight, to allow the home forces to concentrate on the larger battle to prevent the Nazis reaching the capital. Yet a nagging inner voice kept whispering that the town under occupation might be safer for his family than if it was subjected to daily bombardments. Though this was a treasonous thought, one he was not minded to share, even with his wife.

'Sergeant Dobson. Are we awake?' Mortimer asked in a dry, laconic tone.

The accent was Eton once more. The man couldn't keep up his fake rural Kent act for more than a minute.

'What is it, sir?'

'Your mind seems to be somewhere else. We haven't finished, have we?'

'No...'

He looked up and saw the next man in line for a free firearm and ammunition to go with it.

Frank Lee, a local criminal Dobson had taken to court the previous Christmas, last seen waving a fist at him as a Black Maria carried the thug off to jail.

'Lieutenant,' Dobson said as a grinning Lee came and stood before him, taking off his flat cap and giving a quick and disorderly salute. 'I need to talk to this man in private. Would you like to go for a cup of tea?'

'No time for tea, Sergeant. We've a bunch of deadly rascals to assemble, remember?'

Mortimer vanished for breaks, lunch, and dinner, whenever he wanted.

There was the deep boom of artillery beyond the windows and the Nissen hut shook with the force of the noise and recoil of the nearby guns.

'I hope to God we got that bastard,' Frank Lee said with a gap-toothed grin. 'If not, sir, I'll happily do my best to pay Jerry back twice over should you allow me the opportunity.'

'That's the spirit!' Mortimer cried and banged his fist on the desk.

'If I could have a word...'

Dobson might as well have been talking to himself.

'You look young enough to fight,' the lieutenant declared. 'Why aren't you in uniform already?'

Lee, a stocky man, ruddy-faced, wiry ginger hair, still in his blue farmworker's overalls, coughed into his fist.

'May not look it, but I'm forty-two, boss. Too old for call-up. Frankly, if you saw my medical record you wouldn't want me volunteering for the army anyway.' Another throaty cough. 'Bad lungs, the doctor reckons. Got it something rotten. It's the fags, you see. Nasty habit but one I'm on top of now. All the same, I'll be the first to put a bullet in Jerry if he's got the cheek to turn up here, that I promise.'

'This man's record,' Dobson said, 'is six months for burglary and that's just what we know about. He only got out of jail a few months back and–'

'Is this true?' the lieutenant asked.

Lee put on a hang-dog look.

'Every word, I regret to say. Sergeant Dobson would never lie. I overdid the beer one night and broke into someone's home to have a kip. All the strain of thinking about the war, me out of it, doing nothing and nobody any good. It gets to a man.'

'I don't recall that excuse at the time.' Dobson remembered every detail. Lee had tried to terrify the woman he'd robbed into withdrawing her statement. The burglary rate in town had tumbled the moment the man was safely in jail. 'There's more–'

'Beggars can't be choosers,' Mortimer said, waving at him to be silent. 'The fellow wants to fight for his country. He's had his dagger training already.' That must have happened when Dobson was back at the nick returning the files. 'I see no problem...'

The lieutenant stamped the permit, shook the man's hand, and wished him well.

'How about you and *me* have that cuppa, Sergeant?' Lee said with a crooked grin. 'Clear things up. I'm on the side of the angels for once. Just like you.'

Dobson nodded at the door.

'We can't be choosy, Sergeant,' Mortimer said.

'So I gather...'

Frank Lee marched out grinning, with a final quick salute.

The telephone rang. Mortimer grabbed the handset, grunted and said, 'It's for you.'

Beth, from the hospital.

'You know you're not supposed to call me at work, love.' The lieutenant was glaring at him already. 'Got a lot on and–'

'One of the nurses just saw May walking up towards Shakespeare Cliff.'

'Are you sure?'

'Yes. I'm very sure!'

He sighed.

'She knows she's not supposed to go out. I'll have a word when I get home...' Another word. So many. 'She knows...'

'May shouldn't be here in the first place, Joe. She should have gone with all the other kids when they left.'

Mortimer had waved the next man in line to come forward and was rubber-stamping his papers already.

'We went through all this. She's safer here.'

Just a crackle on the line. It was never good lately. Maybe people were listening in. Then Beth said, 'She was with the Lee boy. That creepy little horror who's been following her around like a dog on heat...'

He swore.

'Joe. Don't lose your rag with her. That won't do any good.'

'What *will?*'

'Not that–'

'I'll deal with it,' he said and slammed down the handset.

There were five or six men still queuing for their passports into Cordelia, a covert killing machine in their heads, an amateur army of unsuitables in Dobson's.

'No private calls, Sergeant,' Mortimer said with a hard stare. 'I shouldn't need to tell you that.'

'Sorry, sir. May I be excused? Urgent personal business.'

The man glared at him.

'The only urgent business here is beating Hitler. Nothing personal comes before that. Not for you or me. Or anyone.'

Dobson bit his tongue. On a night off he'd taken a turn round the streets, off-duty in plain clothes, ticking off all the things happening just then that would normally have seen him wading in to stop them. No more. There were plenty of sordid goings-on in the alleys nearby, drunks puking in the gutter, the making of fights, squaddies and their women entwined in the hot, dark night. Towards the end, when he was cursing himself for letting all this pass, he'd spotted Mortimer wandering round town looking very satisfied with himself. Civvy clothes, off-duty. Unmistakably a man out for pleasure, or returning from it.

'I wouldn't ask if it wasn't important.'

'We'll finish the line, Sergeant. Then you can go.' He waved to the man waiting by the door of the hut. 'Next!'

Chapter 14

They were inside the bunker at the foot of the steep wooden stepladder. Harry had found the spare lamp lying on its side, leaking oil. The battery torch seemed gone. Some fool had been messing around and left the place disorganised. From what his dad said about the men who ran the unit, they'd be less than impressed when they found out about that.

'Who made all this, Harry?'

'Bunch of army engineers. Did it all in secret last year when they thought Hitler was on the way.'

'Can't be that much of a secret. Those birdwatchers must have known.'

'Well, I guess they're English. In on it.'

'Right...'

There were three separate chambers, timber walls and floor set against bare earth that was working through a few of the cracks. One was the armoury: combat knives all ready, other weapons and ammunition soon to turn up, or so his father said. Cans of food too, bully beef, beans, pork, plum cake and oat biscuits, tins of soup and a small stove with a bottle of meths to light the burner. The second room had maps, codebooks, a set of car batteries for power and a small petrol generator attached to a pipe system that took the fumes outside. There was a radio with a microphone headset and a telegraph key, all connected to a mast hidden in the roof of the hide.

May put the headset on and said in a loud, theatrical voice, 'Hello. This is the BBC in London calling. The news today is Harry Lee's wriggling around like a daft teenager with something in his pants he's trying to hide...'

'Stop it.' He took the set off her long, soft hair, giggling, both of them. 'What are you doing, talking like that?'

'True, isn't it? Wandering hands and prying fingers. That's you. Or who you'd like to be if you had the spunk.' She grinned. 'You're blushing, Harry. Don't you know that word? Spunk?'

He stuttered something, he wasn't sure what, and stumbled into the third room. This one had two single beds, crude, uncomfortable-looking military things, high metal frames, rough sheets and blankets. He flashed his oil lamp that way briefly, too nervous to go any further.

'Aren't you going to ask what all this is for?'

May was in the shadows so he couldn't read her face.

'Obvious, isn't it? A place for men to play soldiers.'

'Not going to be playing. Not for much longer. Dad reckons Jerry will be here any minute.'

'*If* they come.'

'What do you mean? Did your old man say something?'

'Dad's not the only man I talk to.' She winked. 'Lots else besides. Wouldn't you like to know? If Adolf's on his way he has to do it now. You know what the sea's like after that. Foggy and horrible. Jerry won't want to set sail in that.'

She seemed so sure of herself. He couldn't work out why a girl would know that kind of thing.

'I suppose you're right.'

'Oh, I am. If Hitler doesn't come dead soon, he's looking at next year. Who knows where we'll be by then? Maybe the Yanks will join in. Won't just be us against Jerry. Maybe the whole world'll be at war.'

All his hope and faint confidence were ebbing away in front of her certainties, the way she seemed to know so much.

'Do you think I should be getting you home, May?'

She laughed in his face. Wrinkled her nose when she did that. He felt both elated and deeply miserable. It was stupid to think he could ever hope to trap a beautiful butterfly like her.

'I thought you were the big brave type. Is that an act, then?'

She snatched the lamp off him and went and sat on the nearest mattress, very primly, knees together. Then she glanced at the grey military blanket next to her. It was supposed to be neatly folded the way soldiers made their beds. Instead, it was ruffled, a mess. Whoever was in here last hadn't tidied up at all.

'Tell me all about this hole of yours then,' she said, when he sat next to her. 'Everything.'

'Shouldn't really.'

She took his hand and put it on her knee.

'Oh, but I know how to make men talk, Harry Lee. You go fire up that little stove out there and get me a cup of tea. Some biscuits. Some plum cake.'

'Can't do that. They'd know.'

'In that case I will go home.'

She stood up, stopped, and waited.

He muttered something then went and got the little stove going with some meths. Found the kettle and a bottle of water and opened a packet of plum cake.

'No biscuits,' he said, coming back with the tea in two tin mugs and the cake in a couple of pieces on a plate. 'I'm in trouble enough as it is.'

'Don't be silly.' May was on the bed again, knees tucked underneath her. 'We'll tidy up afterwards and they'll never know. You're a little criminal, aren't you, Harry Lee? Don't you know how to tell a few fibs? How to keep things hidden? I do. We could both be villains together.'

Except he was always getting caught. Carrying the blame for stuff he'd never done sometimes, too.

'What is this place, Harry?'

'It's called Cordelia. They could shoot me just for saying that.'

CHAPTER 15

Jessica Marshall didn't go back to the Lord Raglan after she left Shearer's office, the stink of his Du Maurier cigarettes still on her clothes. She got her bag and the camera and walked up towards the Citadel, furious, lost, unsure what to do.

The man seemed to know more about her plight than she did. If Calhoun cut off her money from Toronto she was screwed. She still owed the hotel in London, had barely enough to pay for another week in Dover. Shearer's offer – work for him, write the kind of stories he wanted – was insulting. As was the promise he'd pay for the hotel, food, and lodging, as well as give her ten pounds a week on top, cash in an envelope. The real bait – and they both knew it – was his claim that he could get her not just back on the front page of the *Inquirer* but published around the world, in London too, through high-level contacts he had on Fleet Street.

She wanted her work out there, her name on it. Without that all those years of struggle, first in Toronto, later in Europe, trying to claw her way up the ladder, would be in vain.

The day had been mostly quiet except for the drone of aircraft overhead. Plenty of action in the Channel and some around the Castle. But little in town. Walking round was dangerous, she felt sure. The sky could become alive with aircraft or artillery at any moment. But she was picking up a little of the attitude of the locals. A blunt determination not to be bowed by the threat of those giant guns across the sea. If the sirens sounded, she'd probably stride off to the nearest shelter, in the caves or one of the tunnels near the town centre. Till that happened she'd walk where the hell she liked.

The conversation in the Ministry office in Waterloo Crescent was still rattling round her head. There were so many things she might have said, so many objections she could have raised. All of them only coming to mind now, too late.

As she climbed the shallow hill a stiff old man appeared, a jaunty little dog by his side.

'Well,' Fred Lumsden said, doffing his cap as he came to a halt. 'If it isn't our new Canadian visitor, Mrs Marshall. Benny here needs his little walks. Three daily. Not much else for us to do. We try and go out when Jerry's not dropping shells on us, naturally. Not that you can always get that right. That cup of tea, love. You look like you could use it.'

'What I could really use is a story. Somewhere to place it. The paper just fired me.'

He didn't look surprised.

'A wise man from Fleet Street once told me you were no real reporter until you got the sack. Didn't happen to me, which is maybe why I never made it beyond Dover. I think you have to be a touch stroppy, a bit of a rebel, to make a real name for yourself. Not that I ever wanted it really.'

'Captain Shearer said he could get me back into work.'

'Ah.' He frowned. 'At a price, I imagine. Not the sort of chap to hand out favours lightly.'

So he knew who the man was.

'I just have to do what he wants. Something... patriotic. Perhaps manufactured.'

The dog was sitting on the pavement, listening too.

'Did you meet young Henderson? His sidekick?'

'I did.'

'Ambitious lad, despite appearances. Always trying to muscle in on other people's patches when he was a reporter.'

She eyed the barrage balloons and the busy maritime traffic in the harbour.

'I'm going back to London.'

'But you've got no work. Or so you said.'

'True.'

'Expensive place, up there. Dover... you can live here for a fraction of the price.'

'Money's not everything.'

'The story is and that's here, isn't it? I got the impression that's why you came. You want to see what war looks like. Real war. All the blood and thunder.'

'I've spent the last year being told a woman's not supposed to go anywhere near the front. As soon as I get here, they try and take it away from me.'

'I can imagine that must be very galling. Having to choose between your conscience and your career.'

Lumsden seemed to measure every word he said. She envied him that.

'Do you think you could write what you want and keep Captain Shearer happy?'

'I write what my editors want. Not some Ministry drone.'

'I think you'll find Captain Shearer's a bit more than that. If you got fired your editors don't seem much interested, do they?'

'Thanks for the reminder.'

'Surely you could try and square the circle, Jessica? Give it a go?'

She hesitated. He was offering something.

'If I had a story. The trouble is... everything here I should be writing about...' She pointed to the wreck of the *Codrington*. 'That boat–'

'Ship.'

'Sorry.' She laughed, just briefly, and so did he. 'That ship. The defences. The state this place is in. Ready, waiting on something they're all trying to pretend won't happen. Still knowing it's just round the corner.'

'Perhaps. Nothing in war's certain in my limited experience.'

'Doesn't matter. Shearer won't let me near it. The only wire machine in town is his. The only wirephoto. What am I supposed to write about? How people still go to church? Run... flower shows or something?'

'Is that such a bad idea?'

'Yes. For me it is.'

'Human interest stories,' he said. 'That's what most readers want. Not politics. Not military strategy. They want pieces that bring them here. Put them in our front rooms. Out on our streets. You should tell your tale through Dover folk. Ordinary people. With ordinary stories about the cards war's dealt them. Shearer won't object to that. It's to do with morale. You've heard Winnie on the wireless. All that lovely rhetoric. It's bollocks really, excuse my French. Beautiful, uplifting bollocks. The kind of thing we need.'

She was certain of it now and thought it was time to say so.

'You know that do you? That Shearer would be happy...'

'Not exactly–'

'I'm sorry, Fred. But I'm no great believer in coincidences. Or beating about the bush. I don't think it was chance you bumped into me this morning. Or now. He sent you.'

Lumsden whistled, long and loud.

'No flies on you, Jessica Marshall, is there?'

'I hope he's paying you.'

For the first time she thought she'd offended him.

'You think I need paying to do my patriotic duty? Good God, no. It was Ian Henderson who asked me to keep you company, by the way. Captain Shearer's mostly above dealing with little folk like me.'

'Why? Why do you do it?'

'Lord above. If I can help a bit at my age...'

She turned to leave.

'I'll go back to London. I can't deal with this shit.'

A curse from a woman seemed to surprise him. Offend the man, even.

'If that's what you want, love. But first let me introduce someone you might want to talk to. You've got your notebook. Good shorthand, I hope.'

'A hundred words a minute.'

'Well, you won't need that for this sad lady. She'll speak soft and slow. Come on, Benny. Now you behave, lad, too.'

She didn't move.

'Who?'

'Her name's Edith Winter. Fisherman's wife. She's fifty-seven so you won't have to ask her age. Last Friday her husband went out to pick up some crab pots in Langdon Bay. Just him, a little fishing boat.' He wagged a finger. 'And that *was* a boat. A Messerschmitt spotted him. Seemed the pilot just saw a Spitfire down one of his mates or something. Any road... he took it out on Alf Winter. Shot the man up – and his dinghy. The coastguard found his body washed up by the Western Docks after the high tide. Boat was in pieces. More left of that than there was of him.'

He blinked at the harsh August sun.

'Are you up to interviewing a war widow, Jessica Marshall? Or is that beneath you now?'

CHAPTER 16

'Cordelia?' May said. 'Like that Shakespeare thing we did in school?'

It rang a bell, not that he'd listened. Something about an ancient English king, his murderous family, war, and the French invading.

'Miss Harkins took us up here, Harry. She said this was where some of it happened. An old man barking at the wind like a lunatic. Then someone gouges a bloke's eyes out.' She shuddered. 'Didn't like that.'

'Never bothered to listen,' Harry said.

He tidied away the tin mugs and the plates and returned with one of the combat daggers. It was unlike any knife he'd ever seen. Just under six inches long, slender too, but the metal didn't give. The edges were as sharp as a razor and the ringed hilt fitted the palm so perfectly it was hard to imagine dropping the thing unless you wanted to.

'You can gut a man with that. Push the blade right through his ribcage. Slash him with it. Kill him outright in one go. My dad showed me.'

'I bet he did,' May whispered.

He held out his arm, bent it as if he was gripping someone round the neck.

'You can come up behind and slit their throat. Stab him in the back. Or just straight up front. No noise. No squeals. He's gone. That's how we fight.'

'In Cordelia?'

'It's just a name.'

There were groups like that being formed all along the coast and inland on the way to London, he said. When Jerry came, they'd go underground, live in places like the Shakespeare bunker, come out at night and create mayhem, killing, bombing, making the Germans pay.

'That's what terrorists do, isn't it?'

She always had a question, one he couldn't answer.

'Someone's got to fight them. Won't be your dad, will it?'

'No. I don't think it will be. You could die.'

'If I have to.'

'Why? What for?'

'For England.' It seemed the strangest question. 'For us. For who we are.'

She moved the pillow up so she could lean against the timber wall behind.

'Put that stupid knife back where you got it then come back here,' she ordered.

He did. When he returned, she was lying on the bed, legs up so he could just make out her knickers.

'Sit.'

She patted the sheets.

He did that too.

So close he could feel her breath on him she said, 'You think they'll thank you for it, Harry? The people who live.'

'Don't matter. It's duty.'

'Duty?' she repeated with that dry, cruel laugh she sometimes had. 'You're seventeen. A child. Never done anything all your life.'

She stared hard at him. 'Never even been with a girl, have you? I bet you sit in bed fiddling with yourself night after night, dreaming.'

Tongue-tied, all he could do was look at her, hungry, and doubtless showed it.

'Say something then, won't you? Do you want to die a virgin, Harry? Are you too scared to find out what it's like?'

This wasn't how it was supposed to go. He was the one meant to be saying it all.

'Do you want to die that way too, May?'

That laugh again, a look that went right through him.

'Too bloody late for *me,* sunshine. That ship sailed a while back.'

He blushed at the thought of it. May Dobson, so perfect, so untouched.

'You're fifteen. That can't be right. Your dad could lock a bloke up–'

'I'm me. I get the shivers and the shakes once a month. The pain and the blood. Isn't that enough?'

It was cold in the bunker and the place smelled of damp. All the same, he was sweating.

'Don't want to get up the duff though,' she said. 'That would be... awkward.'

She reached out and gripped his thigh.

'Did you bring a little present for me?'

'Like what?'

'Like something that stops babies. They call them rubber johnnies. In case you didn't know.'

'I didn't think you'd ever. Not really...'

She shuffled up close, whispered in his ear, hot breath and the smell of something sweet on her. Then she reached inside the breast pocket of her dress and pulled out a tiny tinfoil package.

'Always come prepared,' she whispered. 'Don't want you shooting off without one on you.'

'Where'd you find–'

'Does it matter?'

He kept quiet.

'Oh.' She creased up giggling. 'I get it now. You think I'm some sweet, angelic virgin who's been saving herself just for you. Christ, Harry. You been following what's been going on here all these months? People getting blown to bits walking down the street. Squaddies everywhere with drink and money and...' Her teeth fastened on his ear, just for a moment. 'And rubber johnnies. Millions of them going for the asking.'

He ripped at his shirt, struggling to take it off, one hand going to his belt too. She stopped him.

'Don't rush. First time. I want you to remember this.' There was, for a moment, something like doubt in her face, caught as it was by the yellow waxy light of the lamp above them. 'I want you to promise you won't come down here again. You'll never be a part of this stupid Cordelia thing. Leave it to the old men. Your father. All those fools. We're young. We've got things to look forward to.'

She touched him through his trousers, and it was like an electric shock ran right down his spine.

'You have now, haven't you? Something to look forward to?'

May Dobson stretched out on the single bed, head on the pillow, and opened her legs. He stood up to look at the wonder of her.

'Promise, Harry?'

'Promise. What do you want me to do?'

'Take my knickers off, stupid. What do you think?'

CHAPTER 17

There was a pile more paperwork in the hot, dank Nissen hut. Lieutenant Mortimer saw to that. Beth called from the hospital again, which only made the army man madder, more determined to keep him there as long as he could.

To Dobson's annoyance his wife had changed her tune. Now she was begging him to do nothing. May was out there somewhere with Harry Lee, an ugly, damaged lout from a tribe of thieves and thugs. Leave it till later, she said.

'The nurse who saw them... maybe it was a mistake.'

'Didn't sound like a mistake when you called before.'

Tobias Mortimer was glaring at him. There were now a couple of new men in the line to process.

'Just drop it, Joe. Will you? Please?'

'Sergeant Dobson!' the lieutenant cried in a voice so loud it filled the tin shack. 'We have work to do.'

'You heard the man. I have to go.'

'I can't get out of here right now. Don't do anything rash...'

Women, he thought, as he put down the telephone.

It seemed to take forever to clear the last volunteers. Mortimer was picking through every last detail in a way he hadn't until

Dobson asked to be excused. The army was like that, the officers anyway. He was still, on paper, an employee of Kent Police. Officially, the man couldn't order him around. But he'd do his damned best to make life awkward if he wanted. There was no choice but to wait.

When the last man, a former ticket inspector from the buses, fifty-five, chain-smoking, grey-faced, ill by the looks of it, was sent to the armoury for weapon training, Dobson got up from the desk, ready to leave.

'Care to join us for a bite to eat?' Mortimer wondered. 'Free food and drink in the officers' mess. Waiter service, too.'

'Thank you. I've family matters to attend to. As I said.'

Mortimer reached out and took his arm to stop him.

'If we don't stop Jerry you might not have a family, Sergeant Dobson. Have you considered that?'

'I think of little else,' he said and walked straight out.

CHAPTER 18

Edith Winter lived in a run-down cottage on Cowgate Hill, a dead-end lane leading to the military bastion of the Western Heights. This was one more fortified area from which Jessica Marshall, like all unauthorised civilians, was banned. She'd had a heated argument about access the week before. Marshall was good at research, a busy reader. An old tour guide from the 1920s had told her the Heights had all the colour for a good piece, the Citadel built to repel Napoleon, barracks, gun emplacements and a parade ground from Victorian times. There was a series of small defensive forts linked by dry moats and an extensive deep staircase through the cliff, the Grand Shaft, that could take soldiers from the Heights to the harbour without fear of bombardment.

The answer was a flat no. Now, she could appreciate why. The whole area was hectic with activity. A forest of artillery batteries ran up the hill, military vehicles and snaking lines of squaddies moving all around them. A few thousand men or more could be living behind its tall, well-guarded walls, loosed onto the streets of Dover, to the pubs and the wild nightlife, off-duty. All waiting on the inevitable, an assault from the sea, from the harbour and perhaps by air onto the cliffs to the east and west. From the tactics

89

the Germans had used in France – rapid, all-out attacks based on might and aerial mastery – there seemed little reason to believe Hitler would launch anything but a massive frontal *blitzkrieg* on England.

The Winters were a fishing family. They'd lived on Cowgate Hill all their lives, inheriting the tiny cottage from her husband's father. There were a few pictures on the tiled mantlepiece: a heftily built man in a fishing bib and brace, a jaunty sailor's cap to one side. He was pictured aboard a small boat, little more than a dinghy, crab pots at his feet. In his hand was the biggest lobster Jessica Marshall had ever seen. A line of silver cups and trophies ran along next to them. Alf Winter looked a handful, burly, with a wicked smile and a full fisherman's beard. A man to be noticed. Painted on the bows of the boat in old capital letters was what she assumed to be its name, *TO THE LADIES*.

She jotted this down in Pitman as Edith Winter watched.

'He won all those for rowing.' The woman pointed to the cups and shields, dusty on their wooden plinths. 'He loved the sea, did Alf. Felt more at home there than on land, he always said. No women to nag him on the waves.'

Fred Lumsden had gone into the kitchen to make a pot of tea. The terrier was curled up in front of the sooty grate looking bored.

'What happened?' she asked, as Lumsden returned with a tray, chipped china cups on chipped china saucers, a plate of digestive biscuits.

A stupid question but it seemed the only place to start. Better than, 'How does it feel?'

It was as simple, as trite almost, as Fred Lumsden had said. Winter had gone fishing off the eastern shoreline as he did most days. A German fighter spotted him and raked the boat with gunfire. The coastguard station on the cliffs had watched, helpless. By the time a rescue craft was launched from the Eastern Docks, Winter's boat was in pieces and the man lost to the surging tide.

She'd never taken an assignment as personal as this before. It was always a question of talking to people primed to respond, politicians and military officials ready to face the press. The questions didn't come easily, or without a sense of embarrassment.

'What was he like?'

The woman glared at her and said, 'How am I supposed to answer that?'

'What Jessica means,' Lumsden cut in, pouring out the tea then sitting down as the dog came up to him to be stroked, 'I believe is... can you paint us a picture of him? Something Jessica can share with her readers? Bring home to them how war feels out here on the frontline? Most of them haven't got a clue. Especially those in Canada. If you could–'

'He was a brute, Fred, and you know it. Beat me black and blue when he felt like it. Especially when he came back from the pub half-cut after a night with the rest of them. Or some lady friend.'

The tea was weak, the biscuits damp and old.

'I'm sorry, Mrs Winter.' Jessica Marshall glanced at Lumsden. Time to leave.

'Your boy, Edith,' Lumsden went on, not moving an inch.

'What about him?'

'Tell us about Brian. He joined up the moment he could, didn't he?'

She went to the mantlepiece and took down another photo. A young man, burly too, in an ill-fitting army uniform. It looked like the Citadel behind him. He was smiling, but something in his face said that didn't happen a lot.

CHAPTER 19

Her knickers were white, soft cotton, the elastic that held them so loose they came away easily as he slipped them down her legs and she wriggled to help.

'Fold them up and put them on that chair. I don't want them getting dirty.'

He did and when he'd turned back, she'd pulled up her dress, right up to her shoulders. Women wore bras, or so he thought, but not May. He could only stare at the dark nipples and the subtle shape of her breasts, the tiny rose of her belly button, the nest of brown hair beneath, a secret within he could only guess at.

'You really never seen a girl bare before, Harry?'

'Not... not exactly.'

'Jesus. There you were thinking you were plucking my cherry. Instead, it's me plucking yours.'

May edged further down the bed, closed her eyes, put her hands behind her head, stiffened her palms against the wooden walls.

'Well then... get started.'

Something didn't feel right.

'How do you know all this?'

'All what?' she asked, all wide-eyed innocent.

'About, you know...'

'Say what you mean.'

'About... it?'

She screwed up her eyes.

'It? Shagging?' May winked then grinned. 'Fucking? There. I said it. Did you really think I never knew that word?'

'How...?'

'Christ, you thickhead. Do you even listen? We're here like stupid sitting ducks. Any day now Jerry might be killing you and raping the likes of me. Got to...' She stumbled over the words and for a moment he thought she might break and cry. 'Got to live the way we want first, haven't we?'

'How many... boys?'

She shook her head, mouth open, a sarcastic expression that said: amazed.

'Oh, millions. What business is it of yours? And anyway, most of them were men. Do you want to do this, or don't you?'

He'd imagined it differently. Warm and rosy and full of love like they hinted at in the films he saw down at the Regal. Still, he struggled out of his trousers and sat there, waiting for something to happen. She took the rubber johnny out of the packet and rolled it in her fingers. There was a smell, something chemical, industrial.

'You are the most beautiful thing I will ever see,' he whispered.

'I am,' she said, and touched him there. 'I always will be.'

CHAPTER 20

Joe Dobson kept his police bike in the racks by Canon's Gate. From there a short tunnel and a winding road took him back into town. The Castle complex had already been given over to the military by the time he moved his family to Dover. A shame, he thought. There was much to see and appreciate on this hill above the White Cliffs and he so wanted to share his thirst for knowledge, for improvement, with May, even if she rarely seemed much interested. Perhaps the remains of a Roman lighthouse, ancient gun batteries with strange names like Shoulder of Mutton and Shot Yard might make a difference. Or the church called St Mary in Castro and the imposing fortress itself with its baileys, barbican, and great tower. There was no way of knowing now. She was growing up, too quickly, and the war might stand in the way for years.

Parts of the Castle complex were off-limits to all but the chosen few. The admiralty quarters where, rumour had it, some of the top brass in the navy had overseen the escape from Dunkirk, working to marshal a civilian fleet alongside their naval vessels and ferry the vast, dejected armies across the Channel to safety beneath the onslaught of German air attacks. The radar station to the east was home to a technology that seemed to come out of science fiction, one that could pick up enemy aircraft unseen, even at night and in thick fog. The most secret parts lay in the tunnels, a warren of them, some ancient, some new, burrowing ever further through the clifftop above the eastern harbour, level after level of them, worked by gun crews and intelligence officers, intelligence units preparing for the pitched battles to come.

Dobson hated the fact Beth and their daughter had to live with all this threatening military activity on their doorstep. Hated the idea he might soon have to accede to his wife's pleas and let them leave before the Nazis arrived and Dover turned into a bloody last stand on the road north. There was no safety in the world at that moment. Only the faint sense of security he could cling to if he could see them, touch them, try to hold them together each night when he came home.

He raced the police bike beneath the tunnel and into Canon's Gate Road. The hill was so steep coming down from the summit he wouldn't need to touch the pedals until he emerged at the foot of the lane in Castle Hill Road. Then a ride through the chaos and confusion of the town, past rubble and the shells of buildings, military posts, anti-aircraft batteries, and ordinary Dover folk wandering through it all to do their shopping, chat in the street, get to work if they still had it.

When he took the job, he thought leaving London for the coast might cheer May's moods, provide some kind of holiday for her away from the Bermondsey kids, the wrong sort always, but the ones she liked to be with whenever he wasn't watching. Dover was never a jolly place, even when they turned up. They should have stayed where they were, safe in a poky terrace in south London. Now all Beth could do was nag about the fact he'd turned down May's place in the evacuation and wouldn't even let them go to stay with her mother in Peckham instead. Keeping them together was driving them apart. It was his fault, his alone.

Shakespeare Cliff was a good twenty or thirty minutes from

the foot of the hill. The second the momentum of the incline failed to carry him he began to pedal, sweating in the heavy uniform and the stifling summer heat.

May and Harry Lee.

He'd told the creepy little bastard to stay away from her. If the kid had half a brain he would have listened.

Joe Dobson was the only copper in Dover nick disinclined to give local toerags a shoeing from time to time.

That, he thought, was a habit he could lose.

CHAPTER 21

'So, Louis? Do tell.'

Danvers and his sister were clearing up after the last guests had departed. The garden was littered with spent glasses and plates, cigarette ends and the odd cigar butt. The Pantheon seemed made for such celebrations. He could imagine Jane Austen there, writing about the elaborate and bickering private life of the local aristocracy. Nor, strangely, did he find it in the least odd that the sole occupant of its airy halls, a banqueting room, a garden with a gazebo and the Dour trickling away at the foot of the lawn, was his widowed aunt. Both building and owner shared an elegant English grandeur on the fade.

'Tell what?'

They sat at a table close to the ha-ha, taking a break from clearing up. Veronica always insisted the Danvers were helpers, not servants. There to aid in domestic duties, not manage every last task around.

'Whatever Sir James Mortimer had to impart that took so long, there were at least three fascinating young women I wanted you to meet. Well, as fascinating as rural Kent gets. Instead, all you did was spend your time with the lord lieutenant then vanish into the drive so he could give you a gun.'

She had eyes in the back of her head.

'He asked me if I had any experience in tracking down spies.'

'Oh.' She seemed surprised by his frankness. 'Do you?'

'No. Just thieves and thugs and murderers.'

'Spies could be any of those three. Or all.'

'He said there's a list of people they're going to intern as Jerry sympathisers. Your half-cut bank manager is on it, for one.'

Veronica laughed.

'Tell me something I don't know. They've been quietly picking up people for weeks. I'm amazed it's taken them so long to get to that fool. He used to boast about how close he was to Oswald Mosley. The idiot thought he'd be running the Bank of England once the jackboots took control. I can only imagine the people in charge think him no real threat at all.'

It had been nagging him for a while and now had to be said.

'Would I be wasting my breath if I said you ought to go and stay in London? There's that actor friend of yours. Gerald, Gerald...'

'Gerald Harker? Called only the other day. He has another young boyfriend in tow. Last thing he needs is me spoiling the fun. Also, his flat, which he insists on calling an "apartment", is some bohemian dive in Islington. I am never going to live in Islington. West London or die. Not that I'm a snob. It's more a case of genetics. And age. If one couldn't walk to Harrods, what's the point?'

He knew this was going to be hard.

'The Germans will have a field day. They'll requisition places like this.'

'Let the bastards try!'

'They'll be picking up anyone they think are the awkward squad. I don't think it'll be for a trip to the Isle of Man, either.'

She laughed.

'Do you think I'm on their list?'

'I do recall you going to Germany. Just after Hitler came to power, wasn't it?'

'Back when Berlin was fun. I played the murderous lady in the Scottish play on tour. Does that mean I'm damned?'

'I don't know. How were the reviews?'

She threw back her head and snorted.

'Terrible! It was a modernist thing. They made Banquo a robot or something. Berlin was gorgeous. Such a wonderful city. Then that fraudulent monster came along and cheated his way to power. As Mosley would have cheated himself into Downing Street if we'd let him.'

'The monster's on the way. He could be here any moment. It's going to turn bloody.'

'Louis...' She took his hand and peered at him, eyes twinkling, a thespian always. It was never easy to separate the player from the part. 'I realise you're still here because you want to offer your doddery old aunt some protection. You're also intelligent enough to know I see matters in much the same fashion, just the other way round. Let's strike a compromise. We both agree to look after one another. This will be over one day. In the meantime, I will flit around my acquaintances here as always. While you, it seems, will hunt for villains and spies.'

He wondered whether to say it. But Veronica was no fool. She probably knew already.

'Mortimer dropped a pretty big hint the man I'm looking for may be among them.'

'Or woman. Don't be naive.'

'Or woman,' he agreed.

'Love, if Jimmy Mortimer knew who he was really looking for, do you think he'd be asking favours of you? Now...'

She got up, clapped her hands and started looking round for something.

'Let's tidy up a little more. If there's time you could fetch that very expensive fishing rod I bought you. Danvers gave me a couple of flies the poachers use on the Dour. The most effective is called the "Brown Bugger", or so he'd have me believe. I've cadged you a few.'

'If there's time,' he agreed.

Renard really wasn't sure he was made for angling.

The gardens were silent save for the buzzing of bees and the distant chatter of Danvers and his sister clearing up in the kitchen. The Pantheon was a special place, a haven of peace and solitude. He could understand why she'd refuse to abandon it.

'Oh,' she added as he rose to his feet. 'You know that German pilot we saw bale out?'

'What about him?'

'Freddy Lancaster's farmhands caught up with him when he landed. The poor sod was dead, sadly. Wounded, burned as well.' She patted him on the back. 'Did you know you lost a distant uncle in Gallipoli?'

'Really?' That was a surprise. 'No one told me.'

'The Renards are no strangers to war, Louis.'

'Indeed. I...'

Veronica wasn't listening. She was brushing her feet through a bed of bright red and yellow petunias, wilted from the long hot summer.

'What are you looking for?'

'That blasted bottle of Madeira. What do you think?'

CHAPTER 22

Harry Lee didn't know what happened next. Didn't know anything really and the fact the lamplight only cast him in darkness didn't help. Sex was something that was supposed to come naturally, an automatic act, the knowledge of it locked inside you like all the other bodily functions. But as May fumbled with the johnny and his cock kept struggling to get harder, bigger, it was all so different. Not like those times he'd been trying himself, getting hot and grunty alone in his room, at all.

'What am I supposed to do?' he asked, sliding over on the sheets.

'Me, stupid. What do you think? Will you stay still?'

Still, she hadn't got the rubber on him.

'Will you stop wriggling around, Harry? This is like putting a scarf on a little snake.'

'Not so little now,' he said and laughed.

'Seen bigger.'

She didn't sound amused.

He bent sideways, leaned against the wall, opened his legs a little, tried to edge towards the dusky lamplight. Maybe the oil was running out. It seemed to be fading and the second lamp was on the other side of the room.

'Dammit, Harry,' she muttered. 'Can't you get it harder?'

'Thought that was your job and...'

Something happened with her fingers. They gripped him more firmly, moved more quickly. Then, so fast he couldn't hope to stop it, the rush was on him and it was like the times back home, a hot spurt running out while he gasped and choked and cried out, couldn't stop it.

'Bloody hell,' May yelled. 'Don't want your spunk all on me, do I?'

She pushed him away and let it squirt out onto the floor. He watched it, felt it, said, 'Now what?'

'Now...' She ruffled down her dress so he couldn't see much anymore. 'Now I go home. This was all a stupid idea.'

'Why'd you bother then?'

'Maybe because I felt sorry for you!'

That was the worst answer she could have given.

'You're meant to be the first.'

'Not my fault.'

'The only one I ever wanted.'

'What?'

'The only one...'

'Oh, for God's sake. Don't start that.'

May tried to get up. He pushed her back onto the pillow.

'You wait and I can get it up again.'

'Romance isn't exactly your thing, is it? I mean...' She glanced round the little room, dug into the earth above the cliffs. It didn't smell good. Damp and now it had the stink of him shooting off as well. Something else too. Something worse. 'I'm done with this.'

'No!'

His fingers were round her throat and for the life of him he didn't know how they got there. Just that they did, and it felt right too, as if that was a good place. A place that stirred something.

Until she pushed him off.

'Just wait, will you? I'll get it up. You find that johnny and I'll put it on myself this time and–'

'Shut up. I'm not another pillow for you to shag.'

That didn't sound right.

'Aren't you? How many fellers you had then, May? Me thinking I was going to be the one and–'

She flapped him away with her hands.

'You got no right to expect that. I'm going. If I tell my dad...'

'Tell him what? You came down here with me and took your knickers off? Like you done for all them other blokes?'

That shut her up.

He remembered how his father used to talk to Mum.

'You'll do as you're bloody told, girl. You'll wait for me to get it up again and...'

Her nails came out and scratched his cheek. The red fire rose then, and his hand was on her again, harder this time, relentless, choking her pale-white throat and there, for the first time, was fear in her eyes, glinting in the dying light.

That worked. That made him stiffen, harder than he'd ever known before.

'I'll do you proper,' he said, then pushed her back onto the mattress, lifted her dress, grabbed at her skinny chest. 'No johnny either.'

Something hard and bony caught him in the eye. He screamed. Her elbow struck him on the chin, her nails and fingers clawed at his cheek, then a knee lunged fast and angry right at his balls. She was a fury. He was a fool.

May spat in his face, swore, rolled off the bed, onto the soft earth floor.

'Fine,' he muttered. 'Next time.'

Won't be one, he thought and that hurt most of all.

'May...'

Apologise. Be kind, be humble. He'd played the scene in his

head so many times in the days before, listening to the planes and the bombs, craving to know the secret of what it was like to be inside a girl. Not any girl. Just her. Then the two of them had hidden away in Cordelia's bunker, locked together. It should have been perfect.

'May. I'm sorry. I never meant to hurt you.'

Except, a little voice inside said, you did. His hand around her throat, that glint of terror in her eyes, they were what brought him upright when all else failed.

'I said...'

But she was quiet and that wasn't like her.

He pulled up his trousers, looked at her crouched on the floor. Staring at something underneath the crude iron bed, more full of fear than she'd ever been with him pawing at her skin.

'What is it?' he asked, scared himself now.

May didn't speak. Just turned to face him glassy-eyed. She held up a hand, covered in dark, thick blood. The smell of something earthy and foul was all around them.

She ran for the steps, panting, half screaming.

After one quick look he wasn't long after.

CHAPTER 23

'Here.' Edith Winter handed her son's photo over, along with the picture of her dead husband on his boat. 'That's our Brian. Can't see much of a resemblance to his dad, thank God. Twenty-two years old. He was supposed to be a fisherman too, not that Alf gave him much choice. Brian didn't want it. No money. Hard life, all weathers. The Channel's a nasty stretch of water. He was desperate to get out of here. Talk about frying pan into the fire. Didn't know he'd be up to his neck in mud and shite and blood in France.'

'Is he all right?'

A scowl then she said, 'Bullet in the leg. That'll heal, they reckon.' She tapped her head. 'What's wrong with him up here... who knows? He's in some army sanatorium outside Faversham. I'd go and see him if they'd let me, but they say no. He's not up to it yet. And anyway...'

She sipped at her tea.

'When he's ready, they'll send him back to fight, won't they? By then Jerry's going to be here. Lot of that to be done. All to save Winnie's skin.'

'You're proud though, Edith,' Lumsden said. 'Proud he signed up.'

'Why?'

'Because Brian's a patriot. Like Alf was. Good Englishmen.'

She screwed up her eyes and peered at him.

'Are you serious? One of them used to whip me when he felt like it and now he's dead. The other's daft in the head and fool enough to do what anyone tells him. What's there to be proud of there? You tell me. This bloody war...'

'Edith...'

'This bloody war...' Her voice was rising. 'Don't know why we're having it in the first place. Alf voted for that man Oswald Mosley. Hitler's mate. Does that make him a good Englishman? Told me to vote for him or he'd beat me black and blue. I didn't like the chap. Nasty toff with a nasty moustache. Never believed a word he said. Mind you, if we'd followed him none of this would have happened, would it? I mean nobody likes the Jews, anyway.'

It was Fred Lumsden's turn to wear a sour face.

'How many Jews do you think we've got in Dover?'

'Haven't a clue, but it's too many. Does this woman know what happened with Derek Farrell?'

'Who...?' Marshall said. 'Who's he?'

'Had a big pleasure boat in the harbour. Wealthy fellow. Lawyer up in London. Took it over to Dunkirk, twice. Got Jerry firing on him there and back. Didn't blink once. That man brought home a good number of ours, my Brian among them.'

Fred Lumsden finished his tea, waited for her to take a breath, then said, 'Derek Farrell was a member of the British Union of Fascists. Big cheese with them. Met Mosley himself. Almost stood for Parliament. In it for years.'

'So was Alf.' She laughed, quickly, with no humour at all. 'There. You didn't know that, did you? My husband hated Jews. Folk from London. The coppers. Women, except when he wanted one. True patriot, he always said.' She tapped Marshall on the knee. 'That Farrell fellow got back from Dunkirk, was having breakfast with his wife and kids in their posh house up in

Womenswold. Coppers came around and arrested him. Interned God knows where now, lots of others with him. Free country, my arse. Say the wrong thing to the wrong man and you're banged up. Shot, for all I know.'

'Regulation 18B,' Lumsden said. 'That's what happens to Blackshirts.'

'He rescued our blokes!'

'And if Hitler had landed he'd doubtless have put out a welcome mat.' Lumsden shrugged. 'This is war. Not going to be fair. I wondered about Alf, to be honest. He did say things from time to time. But so did lots of them.'

'Now you'd be locking him up too, wouldn't you?'

He smirked and she didn't like it.

'Oh, Edith. Don't be so naive. Alf was a fisherman. Not very bright. I doubt anyone would have thought him important enough. Now, Brian's a soldier–'

'My son had nothing to do with Mosley and his nonsense. He hated his dad as much as I did. Got punched enough, too.'

'Are you proud of him?' Jessica Marshall asked, unable to think of anything except to repeat Fred Lumsden's earlier question.

'I'm proud he had the guts to get out of this dump. If they let him back now, I'd tell him to pack away his guns and stupid ideas. Go and let some other fools bleed and die for what Churchill and all those other toffs want. Why's it always us? I got no money now Alf's dead. Can't go to the doctors about my feet. Have to scrape around for food. How's it going to be worse if Jerry comes? Tell me that. I'm no Jew. No Jew lover either. Alf had it right there for once. This isn't our war. We shouldn't be dying for it.'

'Thank you,' Lumsden said, getting to his feet. 'Jessica? Unless you have more questions?'

She picked up the photos, father and son, and asked if she could borrow them. There was no point in asking if she could take out the Contax and snatch a portrait of Edith Winter too. The woman was so forlorn and dishevelled. Marshall didn't want the responsibility of broadcasting that to the world.

'Why do you want the pictures? You're not going to write about them now, are you?' Edith Winter said. 'One a Blackshirt, the other sick in the head.'

'If I could just borrow them for a day... I may be able to get you a pound or two. You'll have them back. I guarantee.'

The woman scowled at the cups and photos over the fireplace.

'Keep the one of Alf for all I care. I'll have Brian's back and some cash, thank you very much.'

CHAPTER 24

Dobson raced his bike towards the long, steep hill that led to the stretch of cliff west of the town. War had always marked this coast. There were Martello towers across Romney Marsh from Napoleonic times, a narrow canal designed to halt the march of Boney's soldiers. On the heights before Folkestone stood a sound mirror, a vast cement dish that served as a listening post for approaching aircraft, some poor technician once stationed in a hut beside it for hours on end. Now it lay abandoned, replaced by the radar system run from inside the tunnels below the Castle, one more secret buried under white chalk and brown Kent earth.

East, around Deal and Sandwich, places he'd taken May and Beth for the beaches, walks and fish and chips, lay the remains of more ancient fortifications, castles built by kings from history books, earthworks going back to Roman times. Dover and the land around it was England's soft and vulnerable underbelly. Exposed and now more vulnerable than ever.

As usual, the town was preparing for a night bombardment. Squaddies sheltered in their barracks while the grey men from London laboured away in their lairs beneath the Castle, monitoring radios, checking the radar, contemplating the disposition of their diminishing resources of planes and ships. Joe Dobson was a man who liked order, calm and harmony, saw it as his job as a police sergeant to deliver those things to the public at large. But Dover didn't want any of that. It was an island now, almost cut off from the rest of England, bait dangled in the face of Hitler, anticipating when the Nazis might strike. It occurred to him that a good few of the men around him relished what was coming too. As if this was what the town was made for, this was how it proved its English worth.

He was out of breath by the time he got to the top of the hill. The light was fading, evening coming on.

There was nothing there but a single battery manned by soldiers smoking idly at their station, waiting on the nightly bombardment to begin.

Dobson pushed his police bike over and asked them if they'd seen anyone. A young girl. A teenage boy.

'Aye, that we did,' said the corporal with them, a Scot by the sound of it.

'Where?'

They made him ask.

'Along the way,' the man said. 'Back towards that hut place ye cannae see beyond the rise.'

Dobson climbed back onto his bike.

'The young have got to have their fun, Sergeant,' the Scot said, watching him. 'Times like these... It's a cruel man denies them that.'

'You think...?' Dobson yelled back as he set off along the dry, late-summer grass.

Over the rise, hidden from view of the battery and the road, there was the hut. A hundred yards beyond that, two figures. May, on the ground, looking as if she was weeping. Looking like there was blood on her, too.

Harry Lee walking round, talking, pleading maybe.

Joe Dobson bellowed something, he wasn't sure what, and pedalled on.

CHAPTER 25

The sun was fading as Jessica Marshall and Fred Lumsden made their way down from Cowgate Hill. The harbour looked busier than ever and there were distant shapes in the sky well out to sea.

'Jerry will be making his presence felt soon enough,' Lumsden said, tugging the dog away from something on the pavement. 'Planes or bombs from across the water.'

'Or both.'

'Or both,' he agreed.

'How did you know Alf Winter was a Blackshirt?'

The dog gave up and they carried on. Lumsden was insistent he'd see her back to the Lord Raglan. There was something very old-fashioned and gentlemanly about him.

'Shearer's got a membership list of all of them. More and more are getting added all the time. They're just the ones they know of. Or think they do. The real villains... well. Still, it's best for everyone all round. At least they're not getting hanged or shot like they would in Germany.'

She stopped. A lone fighter had appeared on the horizon, smoke streaming from its tail.

'One of ours,' he said. 'Hope he makes it.'

The plane was edging lower and lower as it approached the cliffs. The engine, that Merlin rumble she recognised, was stuttering. A Hurricane, or so she thought. Couldn't have been more than four hundred feet above the ground when it passed overhead. They waited for the sound, a crash, metal biting into hard Kent earth, an explosion. But nothing came.

Fred Lumsden crossed and uncrossed his fingers.

'You'd be amazed the scrapes they get out of. Nothing's quite as it seems, as good or bad. Everyone wants war to be black and white. Truth is it's always a muddy shade of grey.'

She made a mental note to remember that. Good for some story to come, so long as it passed Shearer's red pencil.

'You could find some copy there, Jessica. Alf Winter and his poor son. They're still victims.'

'Were there many like him? Blackshirts?'

He smiled then sighed.

'Oh, please. They'll tell you the British could never have gone down the road that Hitler did. The hate. The Jews. The terror.' He shook the dog's lead, egging him on. 'Don't get me wrong. I'm a patriot but patriotism's not about being blind. People are the same everywhere. We're not special, we just think we are. We've got an empire. We rule half the world, don't we? And we'll do that forever because God, our God, gave it us. There's plenty who didn't like the Jews round here, that's for sure. Plenty still. You're not...?'

He looked worried for a second.

'Jewish?' she said. 'Not that I'm aware.'

'The Nazis would have found out when you were in Berlin. They have a talent for that, it seems. No, I meant... you're not one of them who blames the poor blighters for everything?'

'No. I'm not.'

'Good. You've got your story, then? One that'll make the captain happy?'

She shook her head.

'What? That the fisherman who died in the Channel was a

Nazi sympathiser who beat up his wife and his son? A son who signed up to get away from him and now he's wounded and half-crazy in hospital?'

'Harsh, Jessica. Harsh.'

'Hardly.'

They were down the hill, in the town proper. All the signs of war – the damage, the barricades, the soldiers – lay around them. It was a gorgeous summer evening in all other respects, balmy with a radiant, setting sun. At any other time, she guessed, the Kent beaches would be full of holidaymakers, not soldiers building barricades and manning machine-gun stations.

'A wise chap I worked with – he went on to join the *News of the World* – told me no one wanted to be reported verbatim,' Lumsden went on. 'They wanted you to write the words they wished they'd said. All the awkward bits, the stutters, the malapropisms and clumsy phrases taken out. Makes them look better, you see. Cleverer.'

That wasn't a great journalistic secret. Every direct quote was rarely word for word. People didn't speak the way they felt they ought to look in print. What mattered was the sense, not a precise record of speech.

'He's still a Blackshirt wife-beater.'

'Peacetime reporting's maybe about getting down what the people you talk to want to say. War's different. It's about what the people in charge want the rest of us to hear. Comfort. Hope. Something stirring to strike a little light in all the darkness. And besides...' He winked. 'Alf Winter's dead. A Blackshirt like you said. I don't think anyone's going to complain about you mucking around with his memory. Least of all that poor widow of his.'

She had no answer to that. Ten years she'd been working as a reporter, clawing her way first from the City desk in Toronto on to Foreign, always looking for the best story, the exclusive, the meaningful. Talents that meant nothing now because the copy they produced would never get through Shearer's wire machine on Waterloo Crescent, the only one she could use.

'I do have a few ideas,' he added. 'If you'd like them, that is.'

She said nothing. Fred Lumsden chuckled again.

'What's funny?'

'You. Every reporter I ever worked with who went somewhere was the same. Never wanted help. Never wanted to be told what to do. Peacetime scribes, Jessica. Doesn't work anymore. We need all the help we can get. Every last one of us.'

She nodded.

'What ideas?'

CHAPTER 26

May Dobson knew that voice so well. She just didn't recognise the fury inside it. Her dad never got mad, not really. Just quiet, firm, determined.

Not now.

He was pedalling furiously across the grass towards them while she sat on the ground, picking at the daisies like a child.

'Bugger,' Harry muttered.

She'd stopped crying. Stopped listening to him pleading for her not to tell anyone. They could walk away, pretend it never happened. Forget there was a dead body down there and her hand had slipped onto cold flesh and tacky blood as she fought him off, scared all of a sudden by the way his hands had wound around her throat.

Fat chance now.

Her dad was there and off his bike so quickly, Harry never had the chance to leg it.

One hard fist to the head, another to the gut. He was a big enough kid, hard too, from what everyone said, except when it came to girls. Just not when a man in a sergeant's uniform was on him, hands flailing, mouth spitting swear words she'd never heard from her father before.

May let him kick Harry around a bit. He'd asked for that. Then she sniffed, got off the ground, aware she had no knickers still, just a thin blue-and-white-striped dress now stained with blood.

'Dad...'

Harry was on the brittle grass, snot and gore coming out of his nose. Joe Dobson stood over him, fist raised, looking as if he couldn't work out where to hurt him next.

'Dad!'

A kick. Harry screamed something about how it wasn't his fault. Nothing, she guessed, ever was.

She put out a hand when her father went to land another blow, got between them, tried to ignore the anger, hate even in his eyes, because just then it seemed aimed right at her.

'It wasn't...' she said, as quiet, as calm as she could manage. 'It wasn't his fault. Not really.'

'You're bleeding,' Joe Dobson said. 'I'll see this little bastard in jail for this.'

'No, you won't. It's not my blood. And Harry's just...' She wondered how to put it. 'A little idiot. I was sorry for him. I egged him on. Blame me.'

'What...?'

It occurred to her then. He'd really no idea. Her mother must have kept her word.

Harry crawled off the ground, bleeding, wheezing, cursing, then broke into a run as he headed for the road that ran behind the cliff.

Her father went for his bike and picked it up.

'Stop it, Dad.'

'I don't know what's gone on here, but I'm going to find out. That little toerag won't get away from me.'

'No. I'm sure he won't. There's...' It was hard to say the words because they just brought back the memory. 'The point is... there's a body down there.'

That stopped him.

'A woman. She's dead. Cut about, I think.' May held up her hands. 'It's her blood. Not mine.'

'Down where?'

'In that bunker they built inside the birdwatchers' place...'

The bike fell to the grass.

'How do you even know about that?'

She ignored his question and began to walk towards the hide. Some things needed to be faced. All she'd seen, all she'd felt in the semi-darkness of the bunker was the cold and clammy skin of something crammed beneath the iron bed, the way a child hid broken toys, something that was a source of shame. Then blood on her fingers and the stench as she'd rolled, terrified on the floor, hearing Harry grunt above her.

The door was still open, and the latch to the bunker. May stood at the top of the steps, aware that her father was following, not thinking about him at that moment.

She had led Harry Lee on. She didn't know why really. Saying she felt sorry for him was just an excuse. She wasn't sure why she'd done any of those things that summer. Maybe it was boredom. Or some kind of rebellion against the idiocy of the world. Dover, a town she hated anyway, was fragmenting into pieces more every day and she felt herself breaking with it. Or it was the fact it was men who were supposed to enjoy what went on beneath the sheets and women who were there to provide it. That seemed wrong. She liked what happened there too, loved the way the wild heat took her out of all the dreariness and briefly stole her away to somewhere else.

May walked down the steps and went into the chamber. One of the lamps was on its side. She set it upright, wondering what might have happened if the oil had spilled and set fire to the wooden floor.

Her father followed. Smelling something now, rank and foul. She bent down, blinked once then looked away, determined that brief and blurry picture would never become any clearer in her head.

'That,' she said, 'is where the blood came from.'

Then she went and stood at the foot of the steps, gulping the hot foul air until she retched hard, choking bile, and puked into the corner.

When that stopped, she clambered up the steps, walked out of the hide into the fading evening sun. There was artillery fire from somewhere and over the harbour a searchlight had started sweeping the dusk sky. War had taken a holiday for a few strange hours. Now it was back, maybe for most of the night.

After a while – she didn't know how long – he came and joined her.

'What is it?' She had to ask. 'I couldn't look, not really.'

'A woman. I think she's been stabbed.'

May sobbed and wasn't sure who for, herself or the corpse beneath the bed.

'What did Harry Lee do?'

'He didn't do anything. We were just messing.'

'Didn't look like nothing.'

She turned and faced him.

'You don't know who I am, do you? You're not even bothered.'

They didn't have real arguments much. Only silences.

'Someone murdered that woman, May.'

'It wasn't Harry. I saw his face. He was as scared as me. Maybe more so. We always blame the Lees for everything, don't we?'

He threw something on the ground. Her knickers.

'Make yourself decent. I'm taking you home.'

They rode the bike back into Dover, May on the saddle, Dobson upright on the pedals though the hill did most of the work. The artillery positions were starting to sweep the barrels of their guns around the darkening sky where a forest of searchlight beams ranged the clouds, desperate, hunting prey.

CHAPTER 27

There was something waiting for Jessica Marshall behind the counter of the Lord Raglan. A bottle of Scotch, common Johnnie Walker wrapped in plain brown paper, with it a note in neat, very legible handwriting.

> *Mrs Marshall. I apologise for any abruptness this morning. Time's short and getting shorter and on occasion, my temper with it. You're free to choose the path you wish. Return to London if you want. Stay here beneath our wing, should you, as I hope, see fit to join we few, we occasionally happy few, this band of brothers who would welcome a Commonwealth sister in their midst.*
>
> *Bring me a story tomorrow and I will find you an audience across the free world. Readers everywhere will know your name.*
> *David Shearer (Capt.)*

'A man came round from the funny brigade down the harbour,' Eric told her. 'Had a piece of paper that said they were paying your bill from now on. Room, food, drink, everything. That right?'

Yes, she said. It was. He grunted something she couldn't hear.

'We don't normally allow outside drinks on the premises,' he added as she unwrapped the bottle.

'Would you like to take that up with Captain Shearer?'

No answer. She ordered a cheese and tomato sandwich and a carafe of water and ice to be brought to her room.

'Tomatoes are like gold dust round here,' the landlord said. 'Ice? This isn't The Savoy.'

She scowled at him.

'At what stage of your life did you decide you were destined for the hospitality trade, Eric?' No answer. 'Do what you can. I need to work.'

Ten minutes later there was a knock on the door. A cheese and tomato sandwich, a carafe of water, an old and battered ice bucket with a few cubes.

She had her notes and the additional information Fred Lumsden provided as they walked. Local colour, the kind of material she could spend days searching for usually. What was true and what was invented, she'd no idea. Right then it scarcely mattered.

Jessica Marshall took the Remington Noiseless out of its battered leather case, rolled in two sheets of blank paper, a carbon between them. Then she poured herself a Scotch and did what she'd done so many times. Stared at the empty page, hunting for the intro, the words that would kick the story into life.

It was different this time. There was another voice in her head. Not just Shearer's. Fred Lumsden's, too.

All the same, it was her name that was going on this piece.

She retrieved the carbon copy of her old story, the one Shearer spiked, wondered what she could recycle from there, and began.

CHAPTER 28

The job of sergeant came with a police house, a featureless 1930s semi in Priory Hill, twice the size of their terrace in Bermondsey, one reason he took the position. Dobson dropped his daughter off there without a word, then set off for the nick, five minutes away in Park Street, next to a stretch of the Dour that still looked like river, not the meagre trickle of water it became by Flying Horse Lane and the Lord Raglan closer to the harbour.

By the time he got there it was blackout, no obvious illumination anywhere except for the searchlight beams still sweeping the night sky. The station was barely manned in a conventional way anymore. Law and order were set to one side for the moment, in their place the preparations for the Nazi onslaught to come.

Had Frank Lee been caught breaking into a terrified woman's home of late he'd have walked away with a caution, not a spell in Canterbury jail. As it was, the man now counted himself a secret soldier in the private undercover squadron of Lieutenant Tobias Mortimer, was gifted his own deadly weapons – a gun, an army dagger – plus the knowledge of how to use them. Privy to hidden refuges like the bunker beneath the bird hide on Shakespeare Cliff. The knowledge of which he must have passed on to his son.

Superintendent Arnold Chalmers was still on duty, a local who'd worked his way up from lowly constable until he as good as ran the place. Pushing sixty, built like a rugby player with the face of a judgemental Old Testament God, he was an officer with a long list of those he didn't like. Anyone from London. The Scots. All foreigners and those with a suspect skin. The man was a widower and seemed to spend every hour he could in his office, mostly tidying his papers. The less work there was to do, the more time he wanted to put in.

'Sergeant?' he said as Dobson came in and took a seat without asking. 'I thought you'd be home by now. Or...' He stopped. The air raid sirens had come to life. One was on the nick roof. No one could talk over that racket. A good minute later Chalmers said, 'Or playing soldiers up at the Castle.'

'We've got a murder, sir.'

The man winced as if someone had jabbed him with a knife.

'Don't tell me that.'

'There's a dead woman in the bunker used by Mortimer's people on Shakespeare Cliff.'

'You're sure of this?'

'I am. I saw her for myself. Looks as if she's been stabbed and hidden away there. I don't know.'

'What the hell were you doing on Shakespeare Cliff? I thought you were supposed to be with Jimmy Mortimer's boy in the Castle.'

He wasn't answering that.

'I'm pretty sure I know who she is as well.'

Chalmers raised his eyebrows and waited.

'A woman called Dawn Peacock. A dancer at the Hippodrome. A tart I think, as well. I picked her up for what looked like soliciting a couple of nights back.'

'Oh, that's useful. Thanks so much,' Chalmers said with a

pained look on his face. 'Hitler on our doorstep and you're arresting women who are keeping the troops happy.'

Dobson couldn't believe it.

'I warned her, like we do. Let her off.'

'Good.'

'I filed a report. Haven't you seen it?'

Chalmers tapped the neat pile of papers on the side of his desk.

'These are from the army, the navy, faceless creatures in London. Our friend Captain Shearer down the harbour. I regret to say reports of my men picking up local whores for no good reason may well have slipped through my fingers.'

'She spoke German. That's why I filed something.'

'What?'

Dobson remembered it clearly. The woman had been drinking when he found her walking out of an alley behind the Albion pub, a place squaddies used to pick up women nightly.

'She was dead mad with me because I'd stopped her. Said I had no right. I'd get into trouble if I didn't watch out. When she walked off, I heard her mutter something. It sounded like she was cursing me. In German.'

'What did she say?'

'I don't speak the lingo. I wouldn't know.'

'But you know what it sounds like?'

'I know it wasn't English. I'd like to take someone up there with me to record the scene. You can send a team from the hospital to deal with the body.'

Chalmers rolled back in his chair and glared at him.

'You really think a German spy would mutter something in her own language in front of a Dover copper? Are they that stupid?'

It was a good question, and he didn't have an answer. Maybe it was just the drink, but the woman hadn't seemed untroubled by his interest in her.

The sirens went again. The glare of searchlights was just visible beyond the blacked-out windows. The rattle of artillery, from the harbour by the sound of it, ripped through the night, along with the distant drone of aircraft. Before the siren ended there was the roar of an explosion. Not so near. The Castle probably.

'A woman's been murdered,' Dobson said when there was a brief lull. 'She was soliciting men in the military. I'm pretty sure she spoke German. We should have investigated already.'

'Are you living in the real world, Sergeant Dobson? Do you have any idea what we're trying to deal with right now?'

'Murder's murder. War or no war.'

There was another explosion. Nearer this time.

'If I were you,' Chalmers said, 'I'd go home and get your family into a shelter if they're not in one already. I'll be there soon. So will anyone with any sense.'

'Sir...'

'You're a street copper at heart, Dobson, and always will be. God knows how you got three stripes. I'll deal with it. Now goodnight.'

CHAPTER 29

The death of a fisherman spurs the spirit of a frontier town
by Jessica Marshall, Special Correspondent

Another year, the coast would be crowded with holidaymakers. Charabancs of visitors making the daytrip from London. Picnickers on the famous White Cliffs admiring the view across the Channel to the coast of France. Bathers on the golden sands waiting for fish-and-chip time and a pint of warm beer.

No longer. Dover, England's nearest neighbour to mainland Europe, the place invaders from Julius Caesar onwards have identified as the entry point for any coming invasion, is readying itself for combat, close and bloody. The war here is real and deadly, meeting it head-on a price the stalwart locals pay, whatever the cost.

Alf Winter had worked the grey and unforgiving waters of the English Channel since he was a child. There wasn't much money to be made from the crabs and lobsters he caught in his pots beneath the famous White Cliffs. But Alf, a popular figure in the town's pubs and social institutions, didn't mind. This was the trade he was born to, the one his father and grandfather had followed. Dover was where he earned a meagre living to support his loving wife and son in their modest fisherman's cottage beneath the great green hill of the Citadel, twin fortress to the better-known bastion of the Castle to the east.

Dover was where, on a warm summer morning, he set out to lay his pots from his little inshore boat named "*To The Ladies*", a craft first learned when he was twelve years old, tutored by his fisherman father.

Dover was where he died in a firestorm of machine-gun shells, torn to pieces by the vengeful pilot of a German warplane. One more defenceless civilian caught in the sights of a Nazi killer desperate to destroy anything of England he could find.

Rarely do the relatives of the town's civilian victims talk to outsiders. This is a community intent on keeping its grief to itself. Only through local kindness did your reporter manage to speak to Alf's widow Edith, now alone in her tiny home beneath the Citadel hill. She sat by a mantelpiece covered in pictures of her late husband and her son, Brian, both victims of the Germans, both stirring her pride and determination that Dover, the very frontier of England, within sight of the French coast, will never bow down to foreign might.

'This,' she told me proudly, 'was when he won a cup for rowing, back in the old days. He loved the sea, did Alf. Felt more at home there than on land, he always said. My hubby was Dover through and through. Hard, like fishermen need to be. You didn't mess with him. You should have seen him when Brian came back from Dunkirk…'

Edith breaks off, sips her tea, takes a bite of a biscuit. Alone now with her memories. Brian, their twenty-two-year-old son, volunteered for the British Expeditionary Force the moment he could. Much as he loved his hometown and the sea, fighting the Germans was a mission he would not shirk. One his father would have shared if he wasn't too old to enlist.

'We're patriots in Dover,' Edith says. 'We know the pain, we understand that someone's got to pay. Brian was lucky getting out of Dunkirk. Got Stukas firing on him there and back. Didn't blink once even though he got wounded. Bad leg. Might not walk for a while, but he don't mind.' Edith raises a finger. 'Duty, you see. It's in our blood.'

How fare these ordinary townsfolk who stay behind, knowing they might be in the midst of war in weeks, perhaps days? Brave, determined, and resolute. Most schoolchildren have been evacuated to safer homes, some as far away as Wales. The older ones who remain run errands through the streets, past bombsites and artillery emplacements, as dedicated to the town as any of their older fellow citizens.

That stalwart English bulldog spirit the prime minister seeks to summon runs through these men and women of Kent, a hardy race, not made for cowering underground. Instead, proud and defiant, they walk the streets as if life were normal, and danger a mere inconvenience that will one day fade away. *Invicta* is the motto of Kent – "undefeated". One that dates back two millennia to when the county was the only area of southern England that refused to bow to Roman rule. A motto men and women hereabouts are certain to remember in the weeks to come.

Dover sits at the very edge of Britain, a fierce English lion prepared for any onslaught Hitler's storm troopers may plot. Shakespeare might have had the place in mind when he wrote…

This fortress built by Nature for herself
Against infection and the hand of war,
This happy breed of men, this little world,
This precious stone set in the silver sea…
This blessed plot, this earth, this realm, this England.

This England waits, proud, determined, grieving for the fallen like the lone fisherman Alf Winter, poised for vengeance against the foe across the water, ready and willing to meet the bloody challenge ahead.

CHAPTER 30

Night in Temple Ewell. Louis Renard listened to the wireless for a while, wondering if Dover would ever produce a case of interest. Then, bored, unable to sleep, he took out the Webley Sir James Mortimer had given him that afternoon. It was identical to those he'd trained with at the Yard, a heavy weapon, crude but deadly. Renard was always careful around firearms. There'd been accidents in the Met among those who were slapdash.

He broke the gun and checked there were no shells in the cylinder. Then he held up the barrel to the light and peered down the machined metal tunnel where the shell would travel.

He was still doing that when Veronica knocked on his door. The gun was back in the holster in his wardrobe before he answered.

From the long window of the landing, he could see the sky was lit up over the coast. A red haze hung above the town, tracer fire running up from the ground like fiery rain in reverse. Frantic searchlights pierced a sky devoid of stars and moon.

'I made cocoa,' Veronica said and passed him a mug.

He thanked her and walked out to see more closely.

'You are not leaving this house, Louis.'

'They're bombing the town.'

'They do that from time to time. I thought you'd noticed.'

'I should be there.'

'To do what?'

She took his arm then guided him gently downstairs to the study. There was a grand piano there, walls full of books, photos of her on the stage in London and New York, on the sets of films with some well-known stars, British and American. It was the place she came to feel safe, he thought. Even Dame Veronica Sallis had her fears, not that she was apt to show them easily.

'I'm doing nothing here, am I?'

'On the contrary,' she said. 'You're saving yourself for the time when you can do something useful. Dover's well used to these nights by now. The firemen, the soldiers, what few police we have. They know how to handle these things. You don't.'

He raised the mug in a toast. The cocoa tasted foul, but he didn't want to show it.

'This is disgusting,' Veronica said, grimacing at the mug. 'Not the real thing at all. Nothing is anymore.' She took the drink off him and suggested a couple of glasses of the Madeira. Renard declined. There was less than half a bottle left, and he hadn't touched a drop.

'You could always try fishing at night,' she said, pouring herself a small one. 'The trout do bite sometimes. I've had poachers at two or three in the morning.'

'What do you do?'

'I tell them they can take a couple at the most, not to make a noise and to keep the place to themselves. People are hungry. We are privileged. Many are not.'

She'd always had a liberal streak about her. Something that annoyed his late father, a surgeon with a wealthy practice in Mayfair.

'If I was going to fish now, I'd need a torch. There's a blackout. I wouldn't want to get you in trouble.'

She chuckled at that.

'You're a police inspector, dear. I imagine you'd be in more trouble than me.'

Not now, he thought. Now, anything seemed to go. There was no time to be pedantic about the law.

The telephone rang. He was first to it.

It was Chalmers, still in the nick, sounding worried.

'On my way, sir,' he said without waiting to hear what he wanted.

'No, you're not, man. Don't be so stupid. There's an air raid going on. The last thing I want is you driving a car into town from out there.'

'Then–'

'It appears we have something up your street.'

Renard waited.

'A suspicious death,' Chalmers said with obvious distaste. 'A murder, possibly.'

'Now?' Renard asked, aware it was an idiotic question the moment the word left his lips.

'If the roads are still passable, I advise you to make your way to Shakespeare Cliff in the morning. There's a bird hide there. I'll arrange for Kelly to meet you at the foot of the hill close to the harbour and show you the way. The two of you can investigate.'

He was thinking of the way he would have handled this in London.

'I'll need more than one officer, sir. A pathologist. Forensic. Fingerprints. A photographer.'

Chalmers laughed, a rare event, he suspected.

There was the roar of an explosion. A bomb perhaps, or an artillery position.

'This is Dover. At war. Kelly is all you have.'

PART TWO

CHAPTER 31

The Lees lived in a tied cottage a couple of miles out of Dover on Whinless Down. Two up, two down, outside toilet, no running water, just a well out back, close to the privy. It belonged to the Hollis estate, a rambling, mostly agricultural manor of more than three hundred acres. The land had been in the hands of an aristocratic London family for two centuries. They'd grown bored with the fact it was unsuitable for pheasant shoots and leased out the useful fields to local farmers. The hovel was on a peppercorn rent Frank Lee rarely paid. The land agent didn't have the courage to kick him out. The man knew there'd be consequences.

He was frying eggs from the hens out back and some bread, fuming over the sight of his son bent over the breakfast table. Harry had a black eye and scratches down his right cheek. The work of Sergeant Joe Dobson it seemed, not that the boy was talking much.

'I'll see that bastard pays,' Lee said as he brought the plates to the table.

'Forget it, Dad.'

'No one beats my boy about.'

'*You* do,' Harry muttered.

'Only when you ask for it. You asking now?'

The lad toyed with the eggs and bread.

'No...'

The night before they'd watched Dover on fire, listened to the bombers and the sirens, followed the searchlights and the planes they caught in the sky. One had gone down somewhere inland. Another time Frank Lee might have got in his beat-up farm van and gone to see. But it looked bad out there and, while he wasn't a man easily scared, something told him it was best to keep his head down.

Harry hadn't said a word all night. That was fine. It would all come out in the end.

Now was as good a time as any. Frank Lee had work to do, more training with the Cordelia people. Maybe more weapons or something else to nick and sell. He could make good money on the black market from pinching butter, bacon, other meat, anything that was on ration through the town. Military equipment though... that was like gold dust. Everyone wanted something to protect themselves from the violent times to come.

'Right. Enough of this nonsense,' he said and slammed his knife and fork on the table. 'I want to know what happened.'

Harry stared at his food in silence.

Frank Lee went to the door and took down the leather strap that had hung there since his own father rented the place. Two generations of Lees had been whacked with that, hard and thorough. The thing hurt like hell.

He slammed the buckle down on the table, right on his son's breakfast plate. Smashed the cheap china. Sent eggs and bread flying through the air.

'Now clear that up.'

Harry kept his eyes on the floor, went and got a bucket, picked up the pieces of crockery and food, sat down, shaking.

'You're next. Start talking.'

'Took... took his girl May down the bird hide,' Harry said in a low, scared voice. 'Thought she'd be impressed.'

Frank Lee banged the table with his fist.

'You did what?'

'Took her down the Cordelia place,' Harry said, close to a whisper.

'I told you that was between the two of us. *I said.*'

His son was trembling.

'For God's sake tell me you never took her down those steps.'

'That's where the beds are, Dad.'

The kid looked ready to cry.

'Jesus Christ, Harry. I don't know what Joe Dobson did, but it's nothing next to what's coming your way from me.'

Frank Lee grunted and dabbed some bread in his egg.

'Did you get inside the girl, then? How old is she?'

'Fifteen.'

'Was it worth it?'

No answer.

'Come on, son. Did you?'

In a weak, hurt voice, he whispered, 'No...'

'Never have, have you?' Frank Lee laughed. 'God, sometimes I look at you and wonder. Can't believe a pathetic weakling like you's one of mine. Your mum must have been putting it about as much as me.'

Harry shrieked, 'I didn't know there was someone dead down there!'

His old man shook his head then finished his food.

'Someone dead?'

'A woman, I think. She was under the bed.'

'Who?'

'I don't know. Didn't stop to look. May was going mad and screaming. We got out of there as fast as we could. Then her dad's all over me punching my lights out, yelling all kinds of things.'

'Well...' Lee put down his knife and fork. 'Think about it.

You're bound to be the prime suspect, aren't you? Take a young girl down there to have your way with her. Just like you did with this first tart you took there and killed—'

'I didn't hurt no one! I wouldn't. I didn't know there was a dead woman down them steps.'

He hesitated a moment and Frank Lee wondered what he was coming up with next.

'Say it then, son. Out with it.'

'It's got to be someone who knew about that place. I thought it was meant to be a secret.'

'If it was a secret, you wouldn't be down there trying to loosen that girl's knickers, would you?'

'You told me!'

'True.'

Lee went and put the belt back on the door then grabbed his jacket. Harry sighed, relieved.

'This is bad,' his father said. 'Shameful.'

'I said I'm sorry...'

'I don't want the bloody coppers here, lad. Not going over my place. Sticking their noses in where they don't belong. Can't let that happen.'

Harry stared at him from the table and said, 'What do you mean?'

'God, you're slow. I mean in a little while you're going to walk down to Dover nick and hand yourself in. If you don't, they'll be up here some time and that bastard Dobson won't pass up the chance of turning every brick of this place upside down. Which might mean your old man going back to jail and he ain't having that.'

'What about me?'

'You're seventeen years old. Not a bloody baby.'

Harry got up and said he'd be off then.

'You know what's the best way you've got of getting out there quick and easy?'

The kid looked lost.

'No...?'

'Tell them Joe Dobson beat you up real bad. That you'd nothing to do with this dead tart but if anyone ought to be up on charges it should be him. Grievous bodily harm. Shocking, a police sergeant turning on a teenage lad like you. No one likes Dobson in that nick anyway. He's a Londoner. I heard he keeps talking about how he'll work with the Jerries once they show, as well.'

A black eye. A cut cheek. Harry put his fingers up to his face and said, 'Oh, right.'

Frank Lee frowned. Then he came close, nose to nose. Harry could smell the sweat on him, his sour breath, see the grim, glad anticipation in his face.

'Trouble is that copper just left you with a few scratches. Looks like a playground scrap. You're barely hurt at all.'

His son stood there cowering, knowing what came next.

'Well, Harry lad. Best we put that to rights. Then we pay them a visit in an hour or two. Once they've got their feet under the table, as it were.'

'Dad... please...'

The first punch was to the ribs and took the wind out of him. The next ones were to the face and before he knew it Harry Lee was on the floor screaming as his father's fists flew at him, over and over again.

CHAPTER 32

Sunday morning and Dover seemed deserted. The Germans had targeted the town for hours. Bombers raining fire on the harbour, the Castle, the Western Heights. The town too, by design or accident no one could tell.

The night before, Joe Dobson had seen Beth and May safely into the cave shelter off the high street then joined the fire crews roaming the town with their engines, trying to extinguish blazes, digging through rubble and dust to recover anyone trapped inside. By dawn, hours after the bombardment ended, the teams were still working. It seemed a miracle only two torn-apart corpses lay beneath sheets in the mortuary of the Institution Hospital. A dozen more injured were in casualty, a couple serious, most minor.

Around seven, barely able to stay awake, he took a mug of tea and a bacon sandwich from the stand one of the cafés brought out for the rescue workers, then walked off to the harbour. The cloud of barrage balloons over the fleet had been ravaged by Nazi shells. Boats manned by naval crews were busy recovering grey fabric and wire hawsers from the oil-stained water. The wreck of the *Codrington* looked as if it had been hit again. That was all the serious damage he could see. Aerial bombing, it seemed, was a haphazard skill. Death and destruction might be rained upon the innocent as easily as those targets the pilots wished to hit.

A tall woman in a dark jacket was taking photos by Waterloo Terrace. He sighed, wandered over and told her to stop.

'Why?' she asked.

She sounded American.

'Because I told you to. It's not allowed. Are you a Yank?'

'Canadian.' She showed him some press credentials and nodded down the terrace. 'Don't worry. I'm not a spy.'

He nearly laughed, for the first time in days.

'I rather imagined you wouldn't be. Out here in broad daylight with a camera. All the same...' He looked at the press card. 'Mrs Marshall. Please stop.'

Instead, she took a snap of him and said, 'If Captain Shearer says I can take pictures here, I will, Sergeant...'

'Ah. Shearer. You must be new to his team.'

She didn't much like that. The woman looked exhausted too.

'I don't work for him. I just need his permission to be here.'

'May I ask where you're staying?'

'The Lord Raglan.'

'I trust they pointed you to a shelter last night.' He glanced at the harbour. 'Bad one. Don't imagine it's going to get any better.'

'Is that really any of your business?'

'I was trying to make you feel welcome.'

'I stayed in the hotel. I'm a reporter. You don't get stories hiding away in caves.'

Dobson had seen a few battle addicts around town. People who got a thrill from being close to danger. The strange thing was, most of the time they seemed to get away with it. The Nazis caught the innocent, the wary, the cautious on their way to safety, more than those who tempted fate, remaining in the room of a mediocre hotel, say, when they might have been underground in a shelter. Not that a cave would save anyone if there was a direct hit. They'd discovered that already when a German shell penetrated the roof of a hideout near the Castle two weeks before. It was a miracle no one died in that.

'I'd have thought that being in a shelter might make a good story for you. What it's like in those tunnels. How people get by. What they do. The songs they sing. The tricks they use to keep their spirits up.'

She nodded and seemed to like that idea.

'Another night, Sergeant. So, which shelter were you in?'

'I was working, ma'am. After I saw my wife and daughter safely off to a place up the high street. You might want to try it yourself tonight.'

'I might. Thanks.' She held out the camera. 'Please?'

He took a shot of her against the harbour. Then, at her request, another with the plain background of Waterloo Terrace. Perhaps Shearer might think the picture with part of the fleet in it too sensitive to use.

'Everything I file from here, words and pictures, goes through that office over there,' she added. 'No need to worry. I couldn't compromise you if I tried.'

There was a low, relentless buzz in the sky, coming from the north. Four Spitfires appeared over the town, heading out to the Channel.

'They never rest, do they?' she said.

'No. They never do.'

She pulled out a notebook and pen.

'The Hippodrome, Sergeant. Would you happen to know where the women who dance there live?'

Dawn Peacock, the one who'd muttered something that sounded German, worked there. With that memory the furious argument with May returned. The way he'd lost his temper and punched Harry Lee. The night's grim, relentless work had pushed everything to the back of his head. It was important he didn't allow it to stay there.

'I'm sorry,' he said. 'Please excuse me.'

The shelter in the high street was empty save for a couple of people sweeping up and taking out the rubbish. No one had been hurt overnight, they said. The nearest bomb damage was on the hill a quarter of a mile away.

Dobson rushed home to Priory Hill.

CHAPTER 33

It was almost ten before Dan Kelly could lead Renard to Shakespeare Cliff. There were squaddies everywhere, ambulances, fire crews dealing with a wrecked building that had partly blocked the road back to Folkestone. Kelly had turned up to meet him but nothing Louis Renard could say, no amount of waving of his warrant, could persuade the soldiers and fire crew to let them through.

When they were finally allowed past, they got up the hill and parked near the summit. The hide was a quarter of a mile walk from the road, the place surrounded by soldiers by the time they got there.

The man who came up to meet them, a sergeant, glanced at Renard's warrant and grunted, 'Yes?'

'Who's in charge here?' Renard asked.

'I am. What do you want?'

There must have been a dozen soldiers, a few armed, most carrying cleaning equipment, brooms and mop buckets. Renard watched them coming and going inside the hide and said, 'You need to stop this now. We're here to investigate a reported murder. A woman–'

'She's gone, pal. We had an ambulance pick her up first thing. You can go and take a look down the Institution morgue if you like.'

Renard didn't get angry often. This could be an exception.

'Murder's a police matter, Sergeant.'

The man laughed right at him.

'Is it now? This, *Inspector*, is a military installation. Property of the army. A place of some importance when Jerry turns up, or supposed to be.'

Then they got the lecture. If they'd wanted to be there first, they should have got there first. The air raid notwithstanding. The army had been informed by Superintendent Chalmers that their bunker had been breached and police were too busy to deal with the matter at that moment. After that, the orders came from the Castle to bring the bunker back into a serviceable state.

'We might need men in there this evening,' the sergeant added. 'I don't give a bugger about anything else.'

'We had a report that a woman had been stabbed to death,' Renard told him. 'You think that counts for nothing?'

'No. I just think it doesn't count for much right now. But...' He turned and looked at the hide. 'We're as good as done here. Go see for yourself. Feel free. Keep it short, then I want you out of there. Boys! Make way for the coppers. They think they've got a job to do.'

The hide was open. So was the trapdoor to the bunker below. A soldier was coming up the steps as they arrived, carrying a mop bucket that smelled of disinfectant. He handed Kelly a lamp and the two of them went down the wooden steps.

There was one man left, a corporal going over the radio equipment and the stores.

'Anything missing?' Renard asked from the shadows.

'Only the important stuff, sir. Guns, shells, knives and–'

He turned round, realising he wasn't speaking to the military.

'And who the hell are you?'

'Dover police,' Kelly said. 'Where was she killed?'

He was a young soldier, an engineer maybe. More a technician than a warrior by the looks of it.

'I don't know. How would I?'

Kelly had started poking around the other chambers already.

'Where was she found, then?' Renard asked.

'Through there. Didn't look too close to be honest. Medics came in and took her out first thing.'

The room had two military beds pushed up against the wall. They both looked as if they'd been recently moved. The floor was shiny, still wet, and the chamber stank of disinfectant and damp.

Renard swept his finger across the iron frame of the bed.

'Someone's wiped this whole place clean, haven't they?'

'Well, yes,' the squaddie said. 'Standard procedure if you've had a corpse, isn't it? Blokes could be living down here for days, from what I gather. Don't want them catching something.'

'A woman's been murdered.'

'Best take that up with the Castle,' the soldier said, then excused himself and legged it up the steps.

Kelly was wandering round, poking at things with his toes.

'Haven't been in one of these before. Never imagined it would be like this.'

'It shouldn't be.'

'What would you bring in? I mean, if you could?'

The list was long and entailed skills and people who were entirely unavailable. All the same Renard rattled off a few: a pathologist, a photographer, forensic officers. And constables who could get down on their hands and knees for a fingertip search.

'I can do that last bit if you like. As to the rest...'

'No point, Kelly. They've swept this whole place clean. I can't even see a spot of blood.'

The constable shrugged.

'With all respect, sir, we haven't really looked.'

He took a lamp and placed it on the tiled floor, crouched down and started to shuffle round.

'I think only one bed's been moved. By the looks of the scratches on the tiles I'd say it was over here by this wall originally. Hang on a moment.' He took out a penknife and lifted two of the floor tiles. There was a mark on them. Something dark. The same beneath. 'I'm no expert, but you tell me. Does that look like blood?'

Renard crouched down too, put a finger out to touch the damp earth revealed by Kelly's penknife. Sticky, dark, familiar.

'Am I right?'

'You are indeed, Constable. Congratulations.'

The two men stood up.

Kelly took another look around, sniffed and complained about the heavy chemical smell of bleach.

'No snapper. No pathologist. Pretty much all the evidence gone. Are we going to get one, sir? A chance, that is?'

Renard cocked his head to one side and said, 'You tell me. What *do* we know?'

'A woman got killed here. Not much more than that.'

Renard folded his arms and said nothing.

The young copper bristled.

'If you don't tell me, boss, how am I supposed to pick things up?'

It was a long time since Renard had first learned those lessons, from old detectives of the Yard, tough men, suspicious of the fact he came out of Cambridge and wanted to join their ranks.

'The first thing you do, Kelly, is try to think like them.'

'Not sure I can do that.'

'Try. If you wanted to kill someone here, when would you do it?'

Kelly thought for a moment then said, 'When it's dark. There's that gun battery down the way and if you came during the day someone's going to see you.'

'Correct. But there's a curfew. What kind of people get to move around freely at night?'

'Soldiers. Us. People doing a job.'

'Firemen, wardens, any locals stupid enough to brave the streets... not that there's many of them, are there? And if we see them, we pick them up.'

'True.'

'This is a fine and private place to kill someone. Would you leave them here to be found?'

Kelly wrinkled his nose.

'Not if I could help it.'

'Clearly, then, he had no choice.'

'Right. Maybe he was scared. He bumps her off in the dark. Then hops it. Leaves her here during the day because like I said, someone's going to see him. Then comes back at night-time and gets rid of her. Chucks her over the cliff or something.'

'When the tide is in?'

'Tide doesn't reach that close to the cliffs, so no. There are caves. Places you could hide someone.'

Renard took one last look around the bunker. It had been so scrupulously cleaned he knew there was nothing to be found. No prints. Not a shred of evidence. Just a sticky patch of blood in a gap between two tiles.

He walked to the steps and, hand over hand, climbed up, went outside. It was getting warm. Another bright hot day coming.

Kelly was right behind, squinting at the sun.

'What do we know about who we're looking for?' Renard asked.

'Probably a man. Since you don't see many women out after dark and anyway, I can't see a lady stabbing another to death.'

'Stop guessing, Kelly. The only one allowed to guess here's me. What kind of man, if it *was* a man?'

'A soldier. A copper. A fireman. A medic. Someone...'

Renard stared at him, hard.

'Someone in a uniform, sir. That's the best way of guaranteeing no one stops you in the dark.'

He patted the young officer on the shoulder.

'I could make a detective of you yet, Kelly. Given time. Who knows? Perhaps a job with Scotland Yard beckons.'

'With you, sir? You mean you are going back to London?'

Renard regretted opening that line of conversation.

'We'll see. Now what do we do?'

Kelly thought it over.

'We go up to the Castle and get the names of everyone who knew about this secret little place of theirs. Go through them one by one. Find out where they were last night.'

Renard sighed and looked disappointed.

'What did I get wrong now?'

'If it's a murder, Kelly, we need to look at the body.' The young constable winced. 'I take it you're fine with that.'

'Part of the job, isn't it?'

Renard walked to the cliff edge and gazed down at the shallow bay beneath. The military installation was obvious, even if most of the artillery there was camouflaged with netting and canvas coverings. A train was slowly making its way out of the tunnel on the way to Dover. The sea was calm, the sky clear.

Not for long, he guessed.

'Yes,' he said. 'It's part of the job.'

Chapter 34

Beth Dobson was in the kitchen spooning porridge from a pan. May sat at the table, eyes down.

'Want some, Joe?' Beth asked as she placed a dish in front of the girl.

'I've eaten.'

He took a chair, determined to stay calm, tried to catch his daughter's eye, couldn't.

'I'll do my best to keep you out of this,' he said and reached out to touch her arm. May recoiled.

'Why?' she asked in that dry teenage tone that always got to him.

'Because you're my daughter and I don't want you near it.'

'Not because you're ashamed of me then?'

'We all make mistakes, love. I'm sorry I flew off the handle.'

She shrugged and stared at her dish of porridge. Milk was hard to come by so it was watered down and she never liked that.

'All I need to know is what happened. If you tell me, I should be able to make sure you don't need to tell anyone else.'

Beth pulled up a chair and listened.

May stared at her bowl, took a pained breath then said, 'Harry wanted to impress me. He said there was some kind of special place. Somewhere they're going to fight a secret war when Jerry comes. We were just messing about, Dad.'

'What did you see?'

She winced, remembering.

'Not much. There was something, someone under the bed. I felt... skin. Then I looked at my hand and it was bloody. I couldn't see who it was. I just knew... I just felt it was someone dead. I legged it out of there. What else was I supposed to do? Harry was right behind me, scared out of his tiny mind.' She did look at him then. 'It was just as big a shock to him, Dad. He's not that bright. He couldn't... pretend. Not about something like that.'

'Did he hurt you?'

She seemed to find that funny.

'No. Maybe I hurt him. He's pathetic. A Lee. I felt sorry for him. I was bored. It was stupid.'

Joe Dobson could scarcely think straight. No sleep during the long and exhausting night. Mind spinning, full of flames and fire and the shriek of bombers overhead. Perhaps he could fit in an hour before he went back to the nick and tried to argue that May was nothing more than an innocent witness to something she barely saw.

'Who is it?' she asked. 'I didn't really see a face. It was horrible. Didn't want to look.'

He was sure it was the tart he'd picked up three nights before. Had she really muttered something in German? Or was that his imagination?

'I think she was a dancer,' he murmured, mostly to himself. 'Worked at the Hippodrome.'

May gasped. She was ashen-faced, staring at him and he couldn't work out why.

'Dad. Are you sure?'

'Yes. I picked her up one night. Took a note of her details. She was...' God, he thought. It was only yesterday that May was a bright-eyed, happy child, keen to go walking with the two of them, happy with just a picnic on the cliffs. Now she was so different, trapped between a past that was lost and a present that seemed harsh and cruel and indifferent. Say it anyway, he thought. She wasn't a kid anymore. 'I think she was soliciting soldiers. I take it you know what soliciting means. Her name was Dawn. Dawn Peacock. Or so she said.'

She wiped her arm across her face. Tears that cut him to the quick.

'May. You mean...' This couldn't be right. 'You knew her?'

'Joe...' Beth took his arm. 'We need to talk...'

'Mum!' She was shrieking. 'You said you'd never tell him! You promised!'

'You promised you'd behave,' Beth snapped back. 'Next thing we know...'

'Dammit.' Her face was wet with tears, flushed with something, shame or anger. 'I give up on this bloody place.'

Then she raced up the stairs, stamping on every step until they heard the slam of her bedroom door.

Dobson closed his eyes for a moment then said, 'I've got to go to the nick and deal with this. You need to tell me everything now.'

'You look worn out, Joe. Get some sleep. Just go to bed for a while and–'

'I don't have time to sleep.' His voice was too loud. He hated shouting. 'I don't have time...'

Beth was close to tears.

'I told you months ago we should have let her go with the other kids,' she said, and it was almost a whisper. 'I begged you.'

'You did.'

'My fault.' Beth blinked, screwed up her eyes for a brief moment. 'She didn't know what she was doing. You weren't here. Me neither.'

'What was she doing?' Dobson asked, and wondered if he really wanted to know.

CHAPTER 35

Ian Henderson came down to meet her in reception in Waterloo Terrace.

'Well,' he said, beaming from behind his brown-rimmed glasses. 'Look who it is.'

He had on the same tweed jacket with leather elbows, too hot for summer, too small for his tubby frame. A bachelor, probably older than the early twenties she first thought. A natural number two, which was perhaps why Shearer picked him.

'I hope you enjoyed a tipple from your bottle of Scotch. Only Johnnie Walker, I'm afraid, but that's about all you can buy round here just now.'

'Where is he? The boss?'

Henderson paused for a moment then said, 'Occupied. Been called out on something.'

'What does he actually do here? It's not just the Ministry of Information, is it?'

From the look on his face, it was obvious this was an unwelcome question.

'We have... broad responsibilities. The press. Security.

Intelligence. We try and take the workload off the Castle. They're busy enough as it is. How may I help you?'

She handed over the 35mm film and asked if they could process it.

'Holiday snaps, are they?'

Henderson had a forced bonhomie that could, she felt, become wearing very quickly.

'I took some shots by the harbour. Some of the town. Some of me, too. In case they need a picture byline from here.'

'I'll have to check them.'

'You do surprise me.'

He rolled the film cartridge across the desk to the secretary and told her to get it to the darkroom.

'You managed to take your own portrait too? Very clever.'

'No. A police officer did it. Dobson. Sergeant Dobson.'

Henderson nodded.

'Dobson. Not from round here but you can't have everything. Wife's a nurse at the hospital. Daughter...' He licked his lips and looked as if he was speaking out of turn. 'Well, she was at school. Who knows what they get up to now?'

'I thought they'd been evacuated.'

'This isn't Germany. We're a free country. People can make their own choices.' He placed a telegram envelope on the desk. 'This came in for you overnight.'

It was from the foreign desk in Toronto. Short as always.

```
LATEST    COPY    EXCELLENT.    FRONT    PAGE.
PREVIOUS  MESSAGE RESCINDED. WELCOME  BACK
ON   BOARD.  DO   NOT  BREAK  THE  BANK  AGAIN.
SYNDICATION    PAYMENTS    WILL    BE    HELD
AGAINST OVERSPEND. CALHOUN.
```

'Good news, I trust,' Henderson said.

She really didn't know why he wasted time pretending he hadn't read it.

'Apparently my work's being syndicated.'

'All over the Commonwealth papers. You are or will be in Australia, New Zealand, India, Hong Kong, Ceylon, Africa, places I've barely heard of. I believe the *Express* is running it here tomorrow.' He beamed ever wider. 'See what happens when you follow our advice, Jessica. Like Captain Shearer said, we can make your career.'

'But only if I write what you want.'

'There's a price for everything,' said a familiar voice from behind them.

Fred Lumsden was there with his little dog.

'I'll get that film processed,' Henderson said. 'Then, if it's all fine, we'll wire your photo to everyone who's using your copy. Can't guarantee they'll use it.'

'An attractive woman,' Lumsden cut in. 'Good chance they will.'

'In that case don't bother,' she snapped.

'Oh dear, Benny.' Lumsden was talking to the dog. 'Your dad's put his foot in it again. May I make amends? Let me be your tour guide, eh? Enough of bombs and destruction. Dover's got its sights, you know. Right back to the Romans.'

'History was invented here,' Henderson added.

'Well...' Lumsden chortled. 'I wouldn't go as far as that. Come on. Where'd you like to go?'

She pulled out her notebook and checked the pages from the week before. The idea had been nagging her for a while. It was always a good plan to reconnect with people you met. They felt flattered you hadn't forgotten them. So long as you hadn't upset them in print, they often wanted to help again.

'The theatre. The Hippodrome.'

'That's easy enough,' Lumsden said. 'Won't be a show on until later though.'

'No. I met someone there. A dancer called...' She checked the page again. 'An interesting woman–'

'I believe we spiked that piece,' Henderson said with a badly fixed smile.

'I believe you did,' she said. 'Perhaps this time I'll try to be a bit more positive.' She waved the notebook at him. 'Positive's what Captain Shearer wants, isn't it?'

'Then positive,' Lumsden agreed, 'is what he shall get. Come on, Benny.'

'Here...' Henderson held out an envelope. 'The photos you got from Edith Winter. Alf and his son. We're done with them.'

'I'll take them back,' Lumsden said. 'The lady was promised a fiver for her troubles.'

Henderson grunted, handed over a note, said ten bob would do and he'd need a receipt.

Fred Lumsden shook his head as they left. The clean-up parties in the harbour had been hard at work while she was inside Waterloo Terrace. No planes dotted the bright blue sky. No artillery sounded. There was just the rattle of machinery and the odd shout. Normality of a kind, the closest Dover got.

'That was a bad night,' Lumsden said as the dog tugged him along the seafront. 'I hope you found a nice deep shelter.'

'Did you?'

'Up near the Citadel. Edith Winter was in there too. She'll be glad of that money. I'll give her back both pictures. She can always chuck one if she wants.'

'I can find my own way to the Hippodrome, Fred.'

'Oh, I'm sure you can.'

'Are you my allotted keeper now?'

He laughed and she realised she was starting to like this genial old man, even if he did seem to have been ordered to stick to her like glue.

'I doubt you've any need of a keeper. Or that there's a man alive who could fill those shoes.'

'There was once. He didn't stick around.'

That personal detail just slipped out and straight away, she knew why. She hadn't spoken to anyone about private matters in months. It was always work, writing copy, checking to make sure she got things right because getting things right mattered more than anything. More than a deadline sometimes, however much that infuriated Mark Calhoun.

And here she was bending the facts for propaganda, inventing quotes, turning a wife-beating Blackshirt into an everyday working-class hero. Getting more space and attention for that than anything she'd ever written in her life.

War changed people. She understood that. In some idiotic way she'd believed it would never change her.

'More fool him then,' Lumsden said. 'I apologise if I offended you with that comment about your photo. I'm right, though. That's the way papers are. A picture of a pretty woman – you're very pretty, Jessica, and I'm not afraid to say it. Well, that draws your eyes to the page. Think of it this way. You get more readers and nothing's more important than that.'

'Nothing,' she agreed.

'I'm not your keeper, love. Think of me as your Benny here. A tame little terrier on a lead. Happy to go where you go.' His eyes were on her, bright and sharp. 'Ready to snap and bite if anyone gets in your way. Shall we have a cuppa first?'

'I'd rather get to work.'

'The Hippodrome?' He laughed. 'Love, there won't be a soul in that place till midday. It's not a theatre anymore. It's more a burlesque show. A rather ribald strip joint to an extent, some would say. No one starts early. A cuppa and a toasted teacake. Then I'll leave you to it.'

CHAPTER 36

The Institution Hospital was a former workhouse complex in Union Road, a narrow lane that wound behind the Citadel. The place hadn't changed much in a century and a half. Behind its prison-like walls, the wards ran through rooms and galleries where the homeless poor once knitted socks and sacking and made leather shoes to pay for their food and board.

Kelly showed his warrant card at the front desk. The young woman there seemed to recognise him. They were told to go to the adjoining block where the mortuary was located and wait for an available doctor. On the way they had to walk through two wards full to the brim. What looked like long-term patients: men, young, some amputees, soldiers rescued from Dunkirk, Renard guessed, still recuperating from their wounds.

Then others more recent. Women and children in mixed ward beds, fresh bandages, fresh blood.

'Is this where they brought you, sir?'

Renard didn't like hospitals. The look of them, the smell, the memories, confused as they were.

'No. Ramsgate. I had a head injury.'

'That where you got that scar?'

'Yes.'

They walked briskly on.

'Does it still hurt?'

Renard glared at him.

'Just wondered. I mean you're a bit of a mystery, if you don't mind my saying. One minute you're at the Yard. Next on the beaches at Dunkirk. Hospital. Then Dover nick. I wondered–'

'We're investigating a murder, Kelly. Wonder about that.'

Chastened, but not much, Kelly dawdled along, saying hello to a couple of people he knew.

'This isn't a social visit,' Renard told him when they got to the next annexe.

'I'm aware of that, sir. It's just that I'm not in the habit of ignoring people I'm familiar with, especially when they're not well.'

Duly reprimanded, Renard thought. Deservedly.

'Of course,' he said. 'I try to avoid the medical profession as much as I can. They so often provide you with more questions than answers.'

'Even pathologists?'

'Even pathologists. If I could find one.'

Back in London they had some of the finest in the country. Professors lecturing at the city universities and medical schools, only too keen to help out when it came to corpses in the hands of Scotland Yard. None of them would come down to Dover even if he begged. It wasn't just the distance. It was him.

A young woman was striding down the corridor swinging her arms and whistling. She was dark-haired, Latin-looking, about thirty, in a plain white medical jacket and a tight, dark skirt.

'Can I help you?' she asked with the briefest of smiles.

'We're looking for a doctor,' Renard said.

'Really?' That quick smile again. 'Well, this is a hospital. You seem to be in the right place.'

'If you don't mind, Nurse,' he said, rather more curtly than he intended. Renard pulled out his warrant card. 'We're police. Here about a suspicious death. A woman found on the cliffs last night. Murdered, we believe.'

'Murdered? Really?'

'Kindly find me a doctor, please. Preferably one with some experience in these matters...'

She didn't move an inch. Kelly nudged his arm and said, 'Er, sir...'

'Poppy Webber,' the woman said and held out her hand. '*Doctor* Poppy Webber. What can I do for you, Inspector?'

He blinked and muttered, 'You mean you're a doctor here?'

'No, I'm a moonlighting farm vet bored with shoving my arm up cows' arses. What do you think? Are you here to see this poor woman or not?'

'He's from London,' Kelly said by way of apology, pointing to Renard's forehead. 'Got a bang on his bonce coming out of Dunkirk. Be gentle, Doc.'

She glanced at the scar.

'Seen worse. Come this way.'

It was cold, the way morgues always were, and had the same chemical smell as the one at the Yard. Kelly, to both his annoyance and amusement, thought the mistake quite funny, and wasn't minded to disguise the fact. When they got to the door Poppy Webber said, 'If either of you happens to be squeamish stay here. The last thing I've time for is getting a porter to mop up vomit from the floor.'

'I'm not squeamish,' Kelly said. 'My uncle Larry's got a farm outside Ramsgate. He kills his own pigs. One every winter, bleeds them too. Big family party. Best black pudding you've ever tasted.' He nodded at Renard. 'The boss is a murder-squad detective from Scotland Yard. He can't be squeamish, can he?'

She cocked her head. 'Aren't murder detectives supposed to wear natty hats or something? Not...' She stared at his jacket and the worn shoes. 'Well. Are you squeamish then?'

'I'll try not to be,' he said and gestured for her to lead them through.

She went straight to a long metal table and lifted the top of the sheet there. A face below, a woman, perhaps thirty or forty. He always found it hard to tell when they were dead. Hair matted, lipstick smeared down her cheeks. There was a livid bruise on her right cheek and the eye above was purple and swollen.

'I was hoping to have an experienced pathologist's report ahead of the inquest,' he said.

'I have experience, Inspector. I was attached to a hospital in Edinburgh for a while. Your colleagues in Scotland were inclined to call on us to sweep up the pieces when required.'

'Pleased to hear it.'

'As to an inquest...' She frowned. 'If there is to be one it's months away. TAWO.'

'What?'

'There's a war on,' Kelly explained.

'There's a war on,' she repeated. 'We have no coroner and no time to deal with one if we did. The dead are, at the moment, of much less consequence than the living. Now...' She waved the sheet over the face and picked up a clipboard by the table. 'Do you want a name?'

'I think we already–'

'Dawn Peacock. Or at least that's what we've been told. A performer down at the Hippodrome. One of her fellow terpsichores came and identified her very tearfully an hour ago.'

'What's a turpsy... turpsywhatsit?' Kelly asked.

'A dancer, Constable. A dancer,' Renard said. He gestured at the doctor to take the sheet off entirely.

'Oh my,' the young constable gasped and looked away for a moment. 'Poor thing.'

There were livid marks around her throat – bruises, purple and yellow. Two obvious cuts beneath her ribcage. No attempt at autopsy, that much was obvious. Given what Webber had told them, he doubted that would happen at all.

'Cause of death please, Doctor.'

'She was stabbed,' Kelly pointed out. 'Isn't it obvious?'

'Nothing impedes a murder investigation like the obvious, Kelly.' Renard walked up and down the table, looking at the body. 'What was she wearing?'

There was a sacking bag beneath the table. She took it out and opened up a long red dress, the sides torn and stained with blood.

'She had this on?' he asked. 'When she came in?'

'She did.'

'And underwear?'

'And underwear.'

The doctor stared at him, arms folded, and said, 'Well, Inspector. You're the murder detective. What's your opinion?'

Never rush. He'd learned that early on from a Yard superintendent old enough to have been tutored by a man who'd worked the Ripper killings. Quick guesses, impetuous decisions, sudden wrong turnings rarely led an investigation in the right direction. Unless a case was solved quickly, with an obvious solution, it was often better to wait a while, to see the way the cards fell, let events take their course.

Renard asked for a towel.

'She didn't die of the stab wounds.'

He wiped away some of the blood around the entry points.

'These are shallow. Inflicted to cause pain, not serious injury.'

'I agree,' the doctor said.

Renard picked up the right hand, then walked round the table to examine her left. Both stained with clotted blood.

'There are red marks, burn marks around her wrists and her ankles. She was tied, roughly, probably to the iron bedstead we saw in the bunker. Then cut with something like a sharp military dagger around the torso.'

Kelly looked as if he couldn't believe it.

'Why in God's name would someone do that?'

'It's called torture,' Renard replied. 'I don't imagine you see it much in Dover. To be honest I haven't seen it much in London.' He hesitated then asked the inevitable. 'Were there signs of sexual assault?'

Poppy Webber nodded, as if she was impressed.

'None at all. The wounds you see are the wounds she has.'

'It was torture.'

'Just like the Nazis,' she said. 'That's what they do to their enemies. They were up to it before the war. Jews. Socialists. Homosexuals. Anyone who didn't match up to their precious Aryan dreams. They were torturing people while the British government was still indulging them. Thinking we could all be friends.'

'You sound as if you know them, Doctor.'

'I do. My father's from Frankfurt. My mother's half Scottish, half Spanish. Our original name is Weber but for the sake of convenience... And to save any awkward moments with the authorities.' She put a finger to her cheek. 'Renard's French.'

'Only if you pronounce it,' he had a good smattering of the language from school, '*Renard...*'

'His first name's Louis,' Kelly added. 'That's French too. So–'

'May we leave my names out of this? Are your parents safe, Doctor Webber?'

'Dad was a banker. They fled three years ago. Lost every penny they had. I was in medical school in Scotland already. They're up there now. They're surviving. He's not well, but...' She sighed. 'They're better off than his relatives back home.'

Renard could feel Poppy Webber's gaze on him just then. He was being judged.

'Dawn Peacock was tortured, but she died of strangulation.' He indicated the marks on the woman's neck. 'He used his bare hands. Not some kind of scarf.'

She looked puzzled.

'Why would you think he'd use a scarf?'

He ignored that and went on.

'The bruises come from fingers. Strong hands. A man's. Deliberate. There's no anger here. He set out to hurt her. Then he set out to kill her. Whether he got whatever he wanted...'

'Even a Scotland Yard detective can't know that,' she said. 'You look pale. You're not about to faint, are you?'

'No.'

'Glad to hear it. You seem very good at reading the dead. Quite a talent.'

'A cerebral one I'm afraid. Reading the living's much more difficult. Which is a shame, because that's where the answers lie.'

She rolled the sheet back over the corpse.

'Relatives?' Kelly asked. 'Are they being informed?'

'The woman from the Hippodrome said she always claimed she never had any. A bohemian lady. Went from town to town, theatre to theatre.'

'What?' Kelly said. 'None at all? Everyone's got a mum and dad.'

Renard glanced at his watch.

'Not everyone knows who they really are, Kelly. Come on. We've taken enough of the doctor's time.'

She saw them to the car park. Another fine day. The sky was busy. From somewhere to the west, around the road to Folkestone, there was the sound of heavy land traffic, doubtless military.

'If any new information comes to light, Inspector...'

'You'll tell me about it straight away.' He held out his hand. 'Thank you for your time. I apologise for the misunderstanding.'

She turned her head to one side.

'Is that what it was? A misunderstanding?'

'No. It was an idiotic presumption. Which is worse. Are there many women doctors here?'

'Just two.'

'I'm sure that will change soon enough.'

'That head wound must have been nasty.'

'You said you'd seen worse.'

'I have. Are you receiving any follow-up care?'

Renard smiled, thanked her again, and gestured for Kelly to climb in the car. Then he slipped into the passenger seat.

'Where next, boss?' the constable asked cheerily.

'The nick. And take that stupid grin off your face.'

'Quite a character, Doctor Poppy Webber. Spanish blood, eh? Exotic. I think she likes you.'

He didn't say a word.

'I don't wish to intrude, sir, but–'

'Then don't.'

CHAPTER 37

It took a while, but Jessica Marshall finally managed to shake off the persistently friendly attentions of Fred Lumsden and his little dog. They'd lingered over a pot of Earl Grey and toasted teacakes in an old-fashioned café near Maison Dieu, the "house of God", once a church, now part of the town hall. He'd grumbled about the paucity of dried fruit in the teacakes and how the butter didn't taste quite right and was probably margarine. Finally, he took the hint, glanced at his fob watch and said he and Benny had to be off for an appointment with the vet. She watched the two of them wander towards the waterfront. Perhaps Shearer did animal husbandry on the side.

Alone, finally, the way she preferred to work. The only real routine for a reporter on the road unless they'd been lumbered with a photographer as company.

Time to explore the town in daylight, dodging between military patrols and sailors on shore leave, watching the way firemen and builders were making safe some of the recent bomb damage, putting up fences, pulling down shaky, half-ruined walls. It was both ordinary and extraordinary at the same time. The stench of war – destruction, dust, even a whiff of cordite – hung over Dover. But it had for months, she guessed, and the locals had decided there was nothing to do but cope.

The theatre was in Snargate Street behind the inner harbour. Shearer's office lay a quarter of a mile away, separated from the road by a stretch of water filled with small boats, military and civilian. The Hippodrome bore a worn but elaborate façade in a terrace of everyday shops. All the front windows were blacked out and a wire dangled down by the neon sign with the theatre's name, a visible notification that it had been disconnected.

A poster by the closed front door read, "To Hell with Hitler and his bloody bombs, the Hippodrome is open". Another by its side promised organ concerts described as "the blackout blues" and nightly continuous performances at six and eight, with a comedian, dancing girls, the "cheeky but charming Francine Bird" and, on the side, readings with an astrologer, Lady Serena, "the international seer who will give you advice about relations abroad, at home or anyone missing, along with news of relatives and friends who are prisoners of war".

There was always money to be made, even from loss and grief.

She was staring at the posters when a woman staggered out of the theatre door, weeping, dabbing at her eyes with a ragged pink handkerchief. Make-up and scarlet lipstick came off her face with every stab.

'Are you all right?' she asked.

'What does it look like, love?'

'I'm sorry. I didn't mean to intrude.'

The woman shook her ginger hair, wiped her eyes again, pushed the rag into the pocket of her skimpy summer jacket.

'The box office don't open till one. I recommend the show. Francine can be a little fruity with her language, but she's funny all the same. Can't go wrong with a session in Serena's booth, either. She knows things you don't yourself. And...' Her face fell again, then came more tears. 'Why am I giving you this nonsense? I *am* Francine. I'm Lady Serena. If you'd been here an hour earlier you could have seen me sweeping up the stalls as well, getting rid of all the fag ends and beer bottles from last night.'

'Oh...'

'Apologies, love.' There was the briefest of smiles. 'Hate to ruin people's illusions about show business. The glamour and all that.'

'I never had any to be honest. Do I call you Francine or Serena?'

'Sandra, actually. Does it matter?'

She pulled out her notebook and a press card.

'I'm a reporter. Here with the permission of the Ministry of Information.'

Sandra sniffed and said, 'I didn't think real reporters needed people's permission.'

'They do now.'

'If you're here to write up the show, please be kind. It's rubbish really and filthier than we ever used to do. But we've got to put something on to cheer up the lads. Keep the old place open too. If you give up on the little things, the big things turn titties up soon after.'

There was another story idea that had never occurred to her. All the earlier work, chasing politicians, seeking interviews with the important – men always, men in control – now seemed almost irrelevant. It was, perhaps, what Fred Lumsden had been trying to tell her. The stories of the ordinary were so much more interesting, more informative too in a way, than the manufactured narratives that came from on high.

'I suppose you want a free ticket.'

'Not at all. I'll pay. If you take things for free people feel you owe them. I don't work like that.' She took out her purse.

The woman snorted.

'A ticket for one? A pretty young lady on her own? With the crowd of lads we get?'

'I can cope, I promise.'

Sandra thought for a moment.

'A box is normally three bob, but I'll let you have it for two and you can be on your own. I wouldn't recommend being in the stalls with our present clientele. The soldiers can get a bit unruly and as for the navy boys...'

'Done.'

'Six o'clock performance. The eight o'clock you'd be lucky to get out of there in one piece even if Jerry don't bring the curtain down quick.'

'Fine.'

She pushed open the door and said to come in. The foyer was dark and dusty and possessed both the look and the smell of neglect.

'Thanks,' Jessica Marshall said and took the three-shilling ticket for a florin. 'I was really looking for someone I met here before.'

'And who's that?'

'A dancer. Dawn. Dawn Peacock.'

There was a silence. Then more tears. Then anger.

'What is this? Are you some bloody coffin chaser or what?'

She shook her head.

'I'm sorry. I talked to her in town last week. On a trip from London. I just wanted to say hello. Is she here?'

Mascara was starting to streak down the woman's cheeks in thin dark rivers.

'Why'd you think I'm howling like a baby? We had the coppers round this morning. Dawn's dead. I had to go and identify her in the Institution. Some bastard killed her. I've told the girls a million times. Never walk out of here with a squaddie or a sailor unless you know them first.'

Jessica Marshall couldn't believe what she was hearing.

'Normally,' Sandra went on, 'I'd let the place go dark tonight. Out of respect. She was a funny girl. Bit of a loner. Bit strange. Had to tell her to keep a few more clothes on at times else she'd get us into trouble with the coppers. But she was one of us. All the same... I can't.'

'The show must go on,' Marshall whispered and wished she hadn't. It sounded so very trite.

'Not really. We just need the sodding money. What did you want of her?'

Nothing much, she thought. It was all just a hunch.

'To talk. She seemed really chatty. Most people aren't like that when they know who you are.' She had to ask. 'Do you know what happened?'

'The hospital wouldn't say except it seemed like murder. How we all had to look out in future. And if she had any relatives.'

'Did she?'

The woman got out the grubby hankie and started to wipe the mascara and make-up from her cheeks.

'Dawn Peacock could talk the hind leg off a donkey, but she never said a word to me about family. Anything like that. I'm sorry if I snapped at you.'

'No. Goes with the job. I'm sorry you've lost your friend.'

'I didn't say she was a friend. She wasn't. She could be a pain in the arse and never did a thing I asked unless she wanted to. Also...'

Sandra kept tidying up the ticket rolls on the box office desk.

'Also, what?'

'There was something about her that didn't ring quite right. The way she talked. Couldn't work out where she was from really, and she never said.' She grimaced. 'I shouldn't speak ill of the dead. You need to be here at quarter to six to get seated. I suggest you wait for the rabble to leave before you go yourself.'

Sandra stopped her at the door.

'That wasn't her real name.'

'Sorry?'

'Dawn Peacock. It wasn't her real name. Half of us here use stage names. She did. The thing is, we're supposed to look at their papers to get their details for tax and things. Dawn said she'd lost hers. She could dance. She could be funny. I didn't give a bugger. We could be playing to the Jerries next week. Why should I? She wasn't Dawn Peacock though. I forgot to tell the coppers that. Are you going to see them?'

'I imagine so. I thought I'd go and look up some of the girls she lived with first.'

'Go where?' the woman asked.

'It was a nice street. A big white house. Old. She was outside and I assumed...'

'Dawn never lived anywhere like that. She was in digs with a landlady in Victoria Avenue. A right old dump...'

'What number?'

'Quarter to six,' Sandra said. 'Don't be late.'

CHAPTER 38

Joe Dobson spent ten minutes in the nick and that was nine too many. The place was half empty, with the few officers on duty mostly out dealing with the aftermath of the night's shelling. No one wanted to talk to him, thank God. No one had demanded May be called in for an interview... yet.

There'd never been a murder while he was there. In peacetime it would surely have been the talk of the town. Within hours, he guessed, there'd have been detectives down from headquarters in Maidstone, muscling in on a tasty case, looking for someone to send to the gallows. In war, the death of a woman, a stranger, part of the chancy bohemian theatre crowd, was simply an inconvenience. Superintendent Chalmers in particular didn't seem to want it on his watch.

He'd given the case to the new inspector from London, Renard. A man no one really knew, any more than they understood why he'd joined the ranks of Dover, not London where he belonged. There was something odd, murky even about the way the man had appeared. All anyone knew was that he'd somehow been a volunteer during the Dunkirk evacuations, suffered a head wound, been sick for a while.

Then turned up in Dover nick, blinking at the daylight as if he hadn't seen a lot of late. Didn't talk much, didn't mix, didn't have a lot to do until the body on Shakespeare Cliff got thrown in his lap.

Renard was still out. Dobson felt ready to cycle up the hill for another day in the tedious company of Lieutenant Mortimer. Chalmers nabbed him at the door.

'You thought of anything I need to pass on to the new man, Sergeant?'

'Nothing, sir. Nothing new.'

Chalmers had a miserable, suspicious gaze, one he wore almost constantly.

'Last thing I need. Everything else we've got on. No officers. No discipline.'

Dobson couldn't understand what he was getting at.

'I'm sorry...'

'I gather you were talking to that reporter woman down by the harbour this morning. Took photos for her.'

Someone in Waterloo Crescent must have noticed.

'She asked me to take a picture of her. I didn't see anything wrong with that.'

'Reporters get left to Shearer's lot. You know the rules. We have nothing to do with them.'

'Will the inspector be wanting statements?' Dobson asked, heart in mouth.

'That's up to him. It's a dead tart down a hole,' Chalmers replied with a scowl. 'Doubtless some squaddie thinking he wasn't getting his money's worth. Not worth our time. Renard can bury it quick. I've enough on my plate already.'

That was it. Dobson got his black police bike and made his way, sweating and grunting in the heat, to Nissen huts A and B up the hill.

Mortimer was at his desk, signing off documents. He didn't look up as Dobson walked in.

'Morning, Lieutenant.' It was a job to sound cheery. 'Much to do?'

'Too much.' Mortimer lifted his head from the papers and glared at him. 'Too bloody much, thanks to you.'

The army had been to deal with the body. He should have realised.

'Do you have any idea of the work you've caused us?'

He wasn't taking that.

'Not really, sir. I found a dead woman down the Shakespeare bunker. I thought–'

'No, Dobson. You didn't think. You should have come to me first. Not the police. That bunker's mine. Sovereign Cordelia territory. It's no one else's business–'

'A woman was murdered down there,' Dobson retorted. 'The law still works here, *sir*. Don't try and tell me it doesn't.'

Perhaps it was the oh-so-refined accent, but Dobson hadn't thought about it before. Maybe Mortimer could be trouble in a fight.

'When Hitler is here, Sergeant, how much use do you think your laws are going to be then?'

'I've no idea. Perhaps I'll ask him.'

Mortimer threw the team log files across the table.

'You sound as if you're looking forward to it. A whole unit spent most of the morning cleaning up the mess down there. Dumping that damned tart, whoever she is, down the hospital. Now I discover your colleagues have put some detective from London on the case. As if I don't have better things to do...'

'I can deal with Inspector Renard.'

'You're going to have to. He's asked for the name of every man on Cordelia who's been given details of that bunker. Every engineer who's worked down there. Every technician we've had putting in the radios. Every armourer on the guns and equipment.'

Dobson glanced at the filing cabinets. Mortimer's brief was to deal with the members of Cordelia. Not the engineering or supply sides.

'I only have the names of the recruits...'

'Then you're in for a long and boring few days, aren't you? He wants a statement from you as well, I gather. And your daughter.' Mortimer pulled a mock-puzzled face. 'I gather she was down there with a boy. What were they up to, I wonder?'

'May's got nothing to tell him. She's very upset. I don't want anyone to talk to her.'

'Best you explain that to him. Now...' He checked his watch then rapped his fingers on the desk. 'I have an appointment.'

Dobson's head was spinning.

'What should I say if anyone wants you?'

'You should tell them I'm out. Think twice before you decide to throw a spanner in my busy works again, Dobson. Once is infuriating. Twice, unforgivable.'

'I didn't ask for this job,' he replied. 'The law is the law and–'

'I really am wasting my breath here, aren't I?'

'And what would you have done? If I'd come to you instead? Do tell me, Lieutenant? I'd love to know.'

Mortimer shrugged.

'I would have had options. Thanks to you I was left with none.'

He picked up his cap and marched out, slamming the door behind him so hard the flimsy Nissen hut shook with the force.

Dobson went to the desk and stared at the mound of papers there. Almost forty men attached to Cordelia knew about the bunker beneath the Shakespeare Cliff hide. Scores more must have been involved in its construction and fitting out. Then there was the gun emplacement not far away along the cliffs, the one he'd spoken to the night before when he was out looking for May. And the old sound mirror installation further along towards Folkestone, which had once been continually manned.

The men based on both those sites must have seen what was

going on when it was being dug beneath the hide. The birdwatchers themselves had to have known their little hut on the cliffs had been requisitioned by the military. The place might have been a secret to the Germans, but a hundred or more locals had to know about it. There was no way he could provide Renard with a meaningful list of names.

No way he could let the man near May.

CHAPTER 39

There was a commotion when Renard and Kelly got back. It was Frank Lee holding forth while his son sat head down on a hard bench seat, dabbing at his bleeding nose.

'Mr Lee,' Kelly said as they walked in. 'You're making a racket, I must say.'

'He's here to raise a complaint,' Jones, the desk sergeant said.

Kelly laughed.

'There's a turn-up for the book. Frank Lee complaining about us.'

'I want that Dobson bastard charged. I want him out of a job. Can't go around beating up kids for no good reason.'

'We can't go around beating up kids for any reason at all,' Renard said. 'I take it...' he looked at the desolate figure on the bench, '...this is Harry Lee. The young man who had the misfortune to find a woman's body in a bunker on Shakespeare Cliff yesterday. And you're his father.'

'They all know me here. Don't you?'

Kelly shook with laughter.

'Truest word you ever said, Frankie boy.'

Renard glared at him.

'Thank you for coming into the station, Harry.' He glanced at the father. 'Saves us coming to fetch you.'

'He knew you'd want to talk to him, so he came in,' Frank Lee said. 'What's wrong with that?'

'Nothing, Mr Lee. Put Harry in an interview room, Constable.'

'I want Joe Dobson done for this!' the father roared.

Renard ignored him.

'Would you like a cup of tea, Harry? A biscuit or something? This may take a while.'

The lad looked up. He was in a state.

'Please... I don't know much.'

'Do you need a doctor?'

'What he needs,' the father cut in, 'is Sergeant Dobson in a cell.'

'Does he now?'

Kelly got the nod and took the lad by the arm towards an interview room.

'Is anyone listening to me?' the father demanded. 'Your sergeant beat my son black and blue–'

'If you want to join us for the interview,' Renard told him, 'you're most welcome.'

The man hesitated. He didn't want to be in the nick any longer than he had to.

'Do you want your father with you, Harry?' Renard called out.

'I'll come,' the man said, before his son could answer. 'You can bring me tea and biscuits as well.'

CHAPTER 40

Jessica Marshall found out where the woman who called herself Dawn Peacock had lived through the oldest journalistic trick in the book: knocking on doors. It only took two. The police had been out, and Victoria Avenue was a grim and narrow street of shabby terraces, the kind of place where nothing went unnoticed.

An elderly woman with an old and overweight cat in her arms opened the door and before she could say a word, announced, 'You're in luck, love. A room just came free. Move in this afternoon once I've cleaned it out. It'll cost you–'

Marshall pulled out her press card.

'Thanks, but I'm not looking for a room.'

'Strop me,' the woman said. 'That's quick. Only had Lily Law round an hour or two ago saying she was dead.'

'Can I come in?'

'I don't like reporters.'

'Understandable.' She stood her ground. 'Did they say what happened?'

'Just that she was dead, and did she have any friends I knew about. No. I didn't. She'd only been here eight or nine weeks and I hardly ever saw her.'

The place looked dingy and there was the smell of boiling cabbage wafting past an old bicycle half blocking the shabby hall.

'I didn't realise she lived here. I thought... I met her last week. When I was wandering round...' When she'd thrown off the Ministry drones for an hour, something they hadn't liked at all. 'I thought she lived somewhere different. A big white place...'

'Effingham Terrace.' The cat yawned. The woman patted it. The creature's fur looked brittle and over-combed. As if there was nothing else in this mean boarding house to love. 'I know nothing about that place. Don't want to, either. Can't help you. Sorry.'

The door slammed in her face. It wasn't the first time. She just wasn't expecting it in Dover right then.

———

Back down the street, a woman with a young girl and a baby in a pram gave her directions. It was a ten-minute walk away, a smarter area, more of what she'd first expected of the town. The street was broad and lined with trees, the houses old and substantial. A couple of boys ambled past in uniforms – the extravagant, colourful kind she associated with minor public schools. It seemed an oasis of quiet and rare affluence in a place that was mostly chaotic and on its uppers.

She stopped outside number twenty-one. It had been close to dusk when she was here the week before. By then she was exhausted, barely taking much notice, going through her notebook. Perhaps Dawn Peacock saw her first. Thinking back, she wasn't sure. She'd spent the whole day being shepherded around town being told who she could speak to, getting the cold shoulder from any suspicious local she approached who wasn't on the list. Then Dawn Peacock appeared here, Jessica Marshall felt sure. Only too keen to talk.

The house was detached, Georgian probably, a medium-sized

rich man's mansion lately gone to seed. Bow windows, a low tiled roof in need of repair. White walls, the paint peeling, a garden of neglected shrubs, flowerbeds and sprawling hydrangea bushes rambling everywhere in profligate bloom. Two dustbins stood by their tumbling blossoms, both overflowing, spilling beer and whisky bottles onto the broken bricks of the drive. All the ground floor and upstairs windows were blacked out.

No one answered when she rang the doorbell. She wasn't even sure it worked so she hammered on the giant brass lion knocker on the red front door. Still no answer so she walked all round the house, looking in the windows. There was a basement flat, the curtains open unlike the rest of the place. No sign of anyone.

Marshall was about to go and ask next door when a long, black car pulled up. David Shearer poked his head out of the window.

'Are you lost, Jessica?' he asked.

'Are you following me?'

He laughed.

'Don't be so silly. I'm on my way back from a meeting. What on earth are you doing round here?'

'The woman I spoke to last week. The one in the story you spiked...'

'What about her?'

She didn't move.

'What bothered you about that? Really?'

He rolled his eyes.

'Oh, surely that's obvious. She made the town sound sleazy.'

'It *is* sleazy. In parts.'

'That doesn't mean we need to advertise the fact. Can I offer you a lift back to the Raglan?'

'I gather she's dead. I talked to someone at the theatre. They're very upset. The police have been. It was... violent.'

He didn't look in the least surprised.

'Not my field I'm afraid. I heard there was a suspicious death or something. These are wild times. If the woman was propositioning drunk soldiers–'

'Who said she was?'

He gave her a hard, cold stare.

'Look. The papers come across my desk. I can't go into details. Nor could you write about it if I did. The police are investigating. What I can tell you is she didn't live here. I don't know where you got that idea. What I can also tell you is you're right. It's sleazy. Nothing your readers around the world would be interested in.'

She pointed at the house.

'I got that idea because I saw her outside this place. She was going in. I'm... I'm sure.'

He popped open the passenger door.

'When people insist they're sure, it's usually a sign they're not. Do get in. You look wiped out. Did you sleep last night?'

No answer. He was on that straight away.

'Did you go to a shelter after the sirens sounded?'

'You know I didn't. I was working. That's why you got your copy.'

He nodded.

'Very good it was, too. It went down well. You should be proud.' He beamed. 'You should be grateful.'

'But–'

'One last time. The police are on the case. An inspector from Scotland Yard, no less. It's a sordid little murder. Beneath you, honestly. They happen. As of now they signify nothing. You're not some lowlife crime reporter for the *News of the World,* are you?'

She climbed into the passenger seat. The car was very shiny, very clean.

'And tonight, my dear, you will go down to a shelter if the sirens sound.'

'Yes, *sir.*'

He laughed at that. For once the mask dropped and she saw

another man. A pleasant, handsome one who perhaps stayed hidden because he sometimes got in the way.

'Then tomorrow, Hitler willing, I will purloin the finest chef they have in the Castle and he can cook us dinner in the Raglan. Lobster, Dover sole, a good Chablis. You do like fish?'

She didn't answer.

'God knows,' he said, 'we all need a little light in our lives.'

CHAPTER 41

Harry Lee had precious little to offer. What he did say was punctuated with him wincing as he felt at his bruised and swollen face. He'd gone to the cliffs with May Dobson because they were both bored. They'd come across the bird hide and decided to go inside. Then found the trapdoor open and decided to look down the steps.

'Inquisitive sort, aren't you?' Kelly observed. 'Amazing how you and your dad find yourself on other people's property that easy.'

The lad said nothing.

The father was still mad.

'He didn't break any laws. Just out for an innocent lark and along comes Joe Dobson and beats him up.'

Lee was a sorry-looking lad, probably even without an obvious beating. Scruffy clothes, didn't wash much, unkempt hair. That port stain on his cheek. Renard knew how cruel kids could be. A lost, impoverished boy like him must have got hell at school.

'Was it your idea to go up to the cliffs, Harry? Or May's?'

He nibbled at a biscuit. Hungry, by the looks of it.

'Bit of both.'

'But you knew what was in that hide, didn't you?'

'Shut up, Harry,' Frank Lee barked.

'You knew because your father told you. He's on Cordelia's team.'

'What?' Kelly asked. 'They let him in there? With that record?'

Lee glared at the pair of them.

'Hitler don't look at your record, does he? What I do with Lieutenant Mortimer's between me and him. None of your business, chum. Coppers come second in this town right now, in case you never noticed.'

'You weren't meant to mention it to Harry, though, were you?' Renard said. 'I wonder why you did. Lots of valuable material down there I imagine. Guns. Knives. Food. Equipment–'

'Who told you that, then? We're not supposed to talk about it.'

Renard made a few notes.

'You told me, Mr Lee. Just now. So, Harry, your father let you know there was a secret place down there? And you thought young May might be impressed?' All that got was silence. 'It's all right. No law against trying to chat up a pretty girl.'

'We didn't do anything.'

'I'm not interested in what you did, lad. Just what you saw.'

'There was a body. Underneath the bed. May spotted her and screamed. Then we legged it. And Sergeant Dobson turned up–'

The father started squawking again until Renard told him to be quiet. Teasing more details out of the lad was hard, but he got there after a while. The hide was unlocked. Someone had been inside and left it disorganised. Cordelia's masters would surely find that infuriating.

'The dead woman was a dancer at the Hippodrome,' Kelly said. 'Dawn Peacock. Ever meet her?'

'No.'

Kelly wasn't giving up.

'Ever hang around with some of the women you see

downtown at night, Harry? You know. The ones who'll do you a favour for a bob or two–'

'Don't have to answer that, son.'

'I was asking him, not you, Frank.'

'No,' the lad said in a soft, slow voice. 'I only wanted to be near May. She was nice to me. Kind. She's...' He was speaking so quietly it was hard to hear. 'She's beautiful.'

Not much is for the likes of you, Renard thought.

'And what did you want to do?' Kelly asked. 'As if I don't know.'

Harry Lee glared at him.

'Most of all I wanted to stop her crying. Stop her being miserable. And mad. It was like she was mad at everything. Not just me. Her dad. This place. The lot.'

'And why would that be?' Kelly wondered.

'That's something we should ask her, Constable,' Renard interrupted. 'And we will.'

Kelly bent over and whispered, 'Had a quick word with Chalmers before we came in. Joe Dobson says the girl's real upset today. Thinks it would be best if we talked tomorrow.'

'Does he?'

'She's a nice kid. Used to come in here with his sandwiches before the war.'

'Tomorrow then...' Renard shuffled his papers together and announced, 'We're done here, Harry.'

Frank Lee stood up, outraged.

'I want Joe Dobson charged. I want to see him in the dock. Grievous bodily harm, this is...'

'You should know, Frankie,' Kelly nodded and gave him a wink, 'done enough of it yourself.'

'Sodding coppers, you always stick together. You don't get to go round beating up kids. Also, you want to be looking at that Dobson fellow. Some of the things he says. Tell them, Harry.'

The lad looked round the room, as if there might be some escape.

'Tell us what?' Renard asked.

'May said her dad wasn't that worried about the Jerries. Said we'd have to work with them when they turn up. Can't just fight them like we're supposed to.'

'There.' Frank Lee looked triumphant. 'How about that for evidence?'

'Of what?' Renard said, then bent down in front of the boy and tried to catch his eye. 'I won't ask who did this, Harry. You can go now.'

'Dobson did this,' Lee cried. 'I want him nicked.'

'Mr Lee.' Renard opened the door. 'Sergeant Dobson last saw your son more than twelve hours ago. If he'd inflicted those injuries, they wouldn't be swollen now.' He patted the man on the arm, came close, face to face. 'If you like we can resume this conversation with you in the chair. And you can tell me how Harry wound up this way. When. And by whom?'

Frank Lee looked shifty and didn't say a word.

'Alternatively, I can let you out of here. You choose.'

'Bastards,' Lee snapped. 'All the same. You think you bloody own us.'

He stormed out, spitting threats as he left.

'Sir...' Kelly was looking uncomfortable.

Harry was still in the interview room, head down, slumped on the chair.

'What is it?'

He came over, and said quietly, hoping the lad wouldn't hear, 'Aren't we missing something here? Harry knew about the place. What's to say he didn't kill the woman? What's to say he didn't bring May Dobson back there, planning to do the same?'

Renard dragged him outside the door, sighed and cocked his head to one side, waiting for more.

'It's worth considering, isn't it?'

'Oh, Kelly. And I was starting to feel the faintest tremor of hope for you.'

'What...?'

'Look at him! The kid's crushed. The father's given him a thrashing this morning trying to put the blame on Sergeant Dobson.'

'All the same...'

'She wasn't sexually assaulted, Constable. She was tortured. To get something out of her, one assumes. Do you believe Harry Lee is capable of that?'

Kelly thought about it and said, 'Oh.'

'Harry?' Renard popped his head around the door. 'The way you went at those biscuits I don't think you've had much breakfast. Are you hungry?'

The lad perked up.

'A bit.'

'Take him down the canteen, Kelly. Get him a bite to eat.'

'What canteen? We don't have a canteen. This isn't Scotland Yard.'

Renard had never thought to check. His aunt always had Danvers make him a packed lunch.

'Well...' He pulled out a shilling and handed it over. 'Give that to the desk man and tell him to buy the boy something to eat.'

'A bob? He's a Lee...'

'He's a sad little kid, with a thug for a father. Oh, to hell with it... Harry!'

Renard went and told the desk sergeant himself and didn't wait to hear any objections.

'That'll get around,' Kelly said.

'Good.'

'Where are we going now?'

'Wish I knew... Where was Dawn Peacock living?'

'A flophouse in Victoria Terrace. Turned up from London six weeks ago. A couple of lads checked it out while we were on the cliffs. The landlady's got no idea about relatives. Or friends. Same at the theatre when we sent someone round. Bit of a mystery woman.'

'From London? You're sure of that?'

'That's what she told everyone.'

There was only one thing for it.

'Right. Go and see these Cordelia people in the Castle and tell Sergeant Dobson I want his daughter in here for interview first thing in the morning. Sniff around. See if they saw anything while they were so busy cleaning up there.'

Kelly didn't look happy with that.

'What's wrong?'

'Superintendent Chalmers says he needs to clear any visits there with the man from the Ministry. All those suits down Waterloo Terrace. Shearer. They don't like being disturbed.'

'Well call them, then.'

'What are you going to do?'

Harry Lee had wandered over to the desk and was asking about a pork pie.

'I've some calls to make. Don't take no for an answer from Sergeant Dobson. I want that girl in here first thing.'

He propelled Kelly to the door.

'Feel free to go home afterwards. Your shift's going to be over anyway. I don't imagine it will be long before the sirens start.' There was, he realised, a question he'd never asked. 'You do live in Dover, don't you?'

'No. With my mum and dad in Walmer. They're dead impressed I'm on a murder case with a bloke from Scotland Yard.'

'Walmer's the other side of Kent, isn't it?'

That amused Dan Kelly.

'Not quite. Six and a bit miles along the coast. Just before Deal.'

'How long does it take you to drive?'

'Don't have a car. A motorbike.' He grinned. 'Got a new 500cc

BSA Gold Star last year. Does nearly a hundred if I belt her. Record from nick to home is eleven minutes.' He put his hand to his cheek and whispered, 'But don't tell the traffic blokes, will you?'

'Are there any left?'

'Fair point.' He delivered a light and playful punch to Renard's chest and from the look on the man's face, immediately regretted it. 'See you in the morning.'

'With May Dobson!'

A salute, then Dan Kelly was gone.

CHAPTER 42

In London, Louis Renard had an office to himself. Access to the finest intelligence and research service in British policing. Specialists he could call on. As many junior officers as he wanted. All Dover had to offer was a desk, a telephone and a keen subordinate in the form of Dan Kelly.

He knew he needed time to himself to think. The nick offered it in the form of a CID office no one else wished to use during the day.

First off, he called back to the Yard, one of the few old friends he could still talk to. After the preliminaries – how was he and was there any chance he'd ever return? – the officer agreed to search out any files they had on a woman called Dawn Peacock, early thirties, supposedly a theatrical dancer.

It might take days and turn out to be a dead end altogether. When he came off the telephone he sifted through the general paperwork in the tray, messages for all the officers on duty. Most were routine notes about troop deployments and the names and details of suspects to be detained on sight. Among them was the round robin about the Canadian journalist in town, Mrs Jessica Marshall. It said any police officer making contact with her was to report the fact to the Ministry of Information immediately. That was it. No address for her. No specific reasons why the Ministry might be interested.

An unusual instruction, Renard thought. He'd yet to meet Shearer, the officer pulling so many different strings from the Ministry offices in Waterloo Crescent. The way Kelly had spoken about the man it seemed best to avoid him altogether. He appeared to have a remit which ran far wider than controlling information in and out of the town.

The story Jessica Marshall had written was still in his bottom drawer. Renard took it out and read the typed pages again. They had to be in Chalmers' office for a reason. Perhaps, he guessed, because the Ministry had pulled the story somehow. It didn't chime too well with the mood the mandarins in London were trying to impress upon the country and the world just then.

There was still something odd there he couldn't put his finger on.

He called Waterloo Crescent and asked for Shearer. A young and upper-class female voice announced that the captain was busy.

'Tell him it's Inspector Renard from Dover Police and I'd like to talk to him about Jessica Marshall.'

The line went quiet for a while then a calm man's voice said, 'Renard? We've yet to meet. Welcome to Dover. How's your aunt?'

'You know her?'

'I know of her. Who doesn't? A classical beauty. If you don't mind my saying. Those films. Never saw her on the stage, sadly. But I hear…'

'I need to talk to Jessica Marshall. Where's she staying?'

'Why's that?' Shearer asked.

'I'm investigating a murder. A woman found in a bunker on the cliffs. You may have heard.'

'I may indeed.'

'She interviewed the dead woman last week.'

'Did she now? How do you know?'

'Because I'm a police detective. Finding things out. It's what I do. This is very minor. I'd just like to clear up a couple of points. If you could tell me where she's staying, I'd be most grateful.'

'The Lord Raglan. There can't be many attractive Canadian journalists in town. I'd have thought a Scotland Yard detective might have found that out for himself.'

'I have now. Thank you, Captain. I trust we'll have the chance to meet in person soon.'

Jessica Marshall, he guessed, would be working during the day. No point in going round until later.

He got himself a pot of tea and opened the sandwiches Jessie Danvers had made. Brown bread and potted crab, which for once didn't taste as if it was out of a jar. After that he jotted down some notes in the private pad he kept, not the official police pocketbook that might be called as evidence in court. The typed-up story, he put in his jacket pocket.

Scotland Yard had a summer aroma of its own, too many sweaty men crammed into too small a space, heavy petrol fumes from cars and buses, the stink of burning coal when the wind was wafting smoke from Battersea Power Station across the river. Dover's aroma was more complex: dust and the dank smell of extinguished fires, but a tang of marine salt too and now and then fresh, sharp country air blowing in from the farm fields that stretched off in every direction once one was free of the grubby town.

He hadn't heard much from any of his old colleagues in the Yard since the perilous adventure in Dunkirk and his stay in hospital, a time that still seemed bleary and vague. His old colleagues' duties would have changed too, while he convalesced in Aunt Veronica's pleasant country mansion until the day she decided he needed mental stimulation and talked the Chief Constable, no less, into giving him a desk in Dover nick. And now there was an unexpected murder, an intrusion, an annoyance during Dover's preparations for the invasion everyone thought inevitable. Chalmers had handed it over to keep him occupied. He felt sure of that. A stranger, imposed from above for reasons none of them knew, he lacked the local knowledge to be of use to the military, who, it seemed, had come to run the town.

Perhaps Chalmers and his like wouldn't mind in the least if he failed at the task.

There was a copy of the *Daily Telegraph* on the desk, not the usual kind of paper coppers read. Renard flicked through the news, such as the paper saw fit to print. The slant was surely obvious to all. Gung-ho stories about how brave British pilots were bringing down enemy aircraft by the score. Tales of heroism still trickling out from the troops evacuated from Dunkirk. Exhortations from Churchill down, all the familiar calls for civilised and courageous British stoicism in the face of the Nazi threat. Someone, he guessed, had taken the decision to paint the entire German nation as monsters, inhuman, beyond evil. He could appreciate the necessity, up to a point. Still, it wasn't so long ago that some of the British papers were lauding Hitler as a patriotic politician to be emulated, and the streets of London were thronged with uniformed thugs from the British Union of Fascists intent on bringing their tyrannical ideology across the Channel.

It might have happened, too. There were more than a few police officers in the Yard who were Mosley supporters, vocal ones until the war began. Had they gone quiet because they'd changed their minds? Or simply to save their own skins now the climate had changed so radically? What would those men do if the Nazis were victorious? Go about their jobs under their new masters as if nothing had really changed?

No one knew. No one wanted to ask. The intelligence agencies had done their best to assemble lists of known Fascist supporters, as James Mortimer had said the evening before. Still, Renard doubted they knew the worst of them. A drunken, mouthy local bank manager with extremist leanings was unlikely to be much of a peril to the realm. Hitler had been preparing for war with Britain for years as Churchill, from his political wilderness, had warned. The real threats would be well-hidden, perhaps buried deep within the agencies of state from top to bottom.

The men hunting those traitors doubtless thought they had good reason to believe the grim torture and killing of a solitary woman paled in importance next to the battles to come. Louis Renard hoped they would not voice that opinion in his presence. Dawn Peacock – if indeed that was her name – had her life snuffed out bloodily in an underground cavern built for a covert war against the Nazi invaders. For once there were no signs of a sexual motive. Nothing to make him believe she was the victim of robbery. Murder was rarely cryptic in Renard's experience. It stemmed from base and predictable human emotions – hate, love, lust, disgust, envy and betrayal. Something about the death of a dancer from the Hippodrome, hidden beneath an iron military bed like a discarded piece of baggage, did not fit. He also found himself wishing he could have a lengthier discussion of these matters with Poppy Webber, the intriguing doctor with foreign connections now working the corridors of the Institution Hospital.

Another time, he thought. First, he needed to talk to Jessica Marshall.

Jones, the uniform sergeant, was still on the desk when he went out.

'That was a generous thing you did for the Lee lad, sir,' he said.

Renard almost laughed. A shilling. It scarcely seemed much at all.

'He'd taken a beating from his father and God knows what else over the years. The poor kid looked starved. And terrified. Not a lot to give. Did you get him a pork pie?'

'Two for that money and a dripping sandwich.'

'Thank you.'

'In case you don't know... Frank Lee's a real villain. As was his father before him. God knows what he gets up to. I wouldn't put him past murder. Not for one second.'

'That doesn't mean the son has to turn out the same way.'

Jones cleared his throat then flicked through the diary in front of him.

'Say it, Sergeant.'

'You're not from round here, sir. People like the Lees don't have many choices in life, it seems to me. And people with very few choices tend to take the ones they're offered. Or that offer themselves.'

'Perhaps the war will change that. What about Sergeant Dobson?'

The officer closed the diary with a very certain slap.

'A decent chap, I'm sure, but he's never gone out of his way to make friends.'

'Has he ever spoken about the Nazis?'

'Labour man from what I can gather. His father was a trade unionist. A pacifist. Lot of use we have for one of them.'

Perhaps, Renard thought, that was what Frank Lee was talking about when he said Dobson was easy on the Germans. The man simply hated war. He wasn't alone.

'The daughter?'

'May? Lovely-looking girl. Used to be a real charmer. You have children yourself, sir?'

'I'm not married.'

'Well, take it from one who is. All your offspring go through phases. One day they hate your guts. The next they love you to pieces.'

He left it at that.

'And?'

'I don't think May Dobson's quite reached the next day bit yet. She gives Joe and Beth the runaround day and night.' He winced. 'Like I said. Lovely-looking girl. That only makes it worse for a dad, I reckon. You never know when to stop worrying.'

CHAPTER 43

Dan Kelly walked into the Nissen hut wearing his usual cheeky grin, clapped his hands and said, 'Blimey, Sergeant. I thought you were living the life of luxury up here. Not stuck in a tin can. This place makes the nick look like the Ritz.'

Dobson wasn't even a quarter of a way through the names of those associated with the Shakespeare Cliff bunker. It was going to take another day or two at least.

'If it's the list you're after, it's going to take ages.'

'In your own time,' Kelly said. 'Inspector Renard wants May in the nick in the morning. He needs to hear her side of things.'

Something fluttered inside Dobson's chest.

'She told me everything that happened. I can pass it on.'

Dan Kelly sat down and grinned at him.

'Come on, Joe. Are you having a laugh?'

'Sergeant...'

'Come on, Sergeant, then. May found a body. We went to see it this morning. Some dancer from the Hippodrome. Cut about something rotten. Strangled. Tortured.'

'What?'

'Tortured, the inspector says. He's from the Yard. He knows these things. I thought you'd seen her down there.'

'I just... only briefly.'

Kelly whistled, long and low.

'Yeah. And then the army only came along and snatched her away. Cleaned up every last thing in there before we could take a shifty.' He ran his fingers over the papers on the desk. 'Is this that list of names you're giving us? Everyone who knew about the place?'

'It's not easy. I said. It'll take a couple of days.'

Kelly felt the lapels of his cheap suit.

'I'm a murder detective now, me. Working with an inspector from Scotland Yard. How about that, then?'

'I'm so pleased for you.'

'We've heard Harry Lee's side of the story.'

'And you believe him?'

'His dad said you beat him up something rotten. The boy's face is a right old mess.'

Dobson sighed.

'I didn't do much. Just... apprehended him.'

Kelly tapped his shoulder.

'Don't worry. We know it's not true. Inspector Renard bawled Frank out. It was him, trying to nail you. Renard's a good bloke, even if he is from London. And a bit scruffy and strange. If anyone's going to get to the bottom of that poor woman's murder, it's him. Relentless. Knows all the questions to ask, too.'

He started rifling through the papers on the desk.

'Any of our regular customers in your private army then?'

'Just Frank Lee. The rest are mostly old blokes who think they ought to be doing something. If Hitler knew...'

He stopped. It was the wrong thing to say.

'If Hitler knew... what?'

'You'll get your list in a couple of days. I'll take a statement from May tonight and drop it off at the same time.'

Kelly stared right at him.

'Knock it off, will you? The inspector wants to see her. I'm sure he'll be okay if you want to sit in on the interview. But you're not just popping a statement through the post box like it's a birthday card. He won't be happy with that.' He rapped his finger on the desk. 'Me neither. Get her round the nick first thing in the morning. Otherwise, I'll come looking.'

Dobson glared at him.

'You being a murder detective now?'

'That's right. Your girl's an important witness. The inspector wants to hear what she's got to say. I'm amazed you think he doesn't. Well...' Kelly got to his feet and looked around the bare office. 'Till tomorrow then.'

Dobson watched him head off to his motorbike. He'd no idea when Tobias Mortimer would be back. He didn't care, either.

Once Dan Kelly was out of sight, he called the hospital. It took ten minutes to get Beth to the telephone.

'You need to leave, love,' he said. 'It's important. Go home. I'll be there as soon as I can.'

'What do you mean... leave?'

'You and May. I want you out of Dover tonight.'

'Joe! I can't just walk out of here.'

'Is she still home?'

'How would I know? She promised.'

'As if that means something.'

'Don't start–'

'You've got to make an excuse. Get out of there. We need to talk. All three of us. Please.' She didn't say a word. 'It's important.'

Beth Dobson hesitated for a moment. He wondered if she was about to argue.

'I've got rounds to do. An hour, maybe two. All right?'

It'll have to be, he thought.

CHAPTER 44

A woman, early thirties, tall and striking, was walking out of the Lord Raglan. She looked out of place in Dover. Elegant, confident, neat brown hair. As Kelly had said the day before... a looker.

'Mrs Marshall?' He took out his warrant card. It was still for the Met. Kent hadn't got round to issuing a new one yet.

'You're a long way from home, Inspector.'

She had an easy smile but a pale face, narrow, prominent cheekbones, a little drawn, he thought. Signs of the times.

'On attachment to Dover,' he said. 'I'm investigating the death of a woman here. Murder, I'm sorry to tell you.'

'Dawn Peacock. I know. I interviewed her last week. I went round the Hippodrome this morning to see if I could find her again.'

'May I ask why?'

'The woman was willing to talk to me.' A frown then. 'Not that the piece I wrote made it into the paper. I thought... I hoped she'd be willing to chat again. People don't tend to be well disposed to the press at the moment. She was different.'

He nodded at the hotel.

'Perhaps I can buy you a drink. Or a coffee?'

'Not now. Sorry.'

'This is a police matter, madam.'

'I've a ticket for the Hippodrome. All booked and paid for. The six o'clock show.'

'All the same...'

She smiled again and touched his sleeve.

'A box. You could join me, Inspector. I'd appreciate the company. I was warned the clientele can be a little fresh with the opposite sex. Oh, please... I hate going to the theatre on my own.'

'Then why are you going?'

'I thought it might make a story. We can talk afterwards...'

Renard hesitated for a second then asked her to bear with him. He went back into the Raglan and called Temple Ewell.

'Well, that's the food right out of the window, thank you very much,' Veronica declared in a highly theatrical manner. 'Danvers snared four trout this afternoon. Four! Those brown buggers really work if you know how. We're having *truite au bleu.* You can try it cold if you like. With cold potatoes.'

His aunt's nagging was only half serious.

'You got me this job, Veronica. I may just stay in the police station overnight. Or a bunker. It feels wrong being away from all of this.'

'No one likes a copper with a conscience, Louis.'

'Was that a line from one of those bad crime capers you and Maurice made in Barnet?'

'Very possibly. I'll keep your trout until ten. If you're not home by then I'll give it to the feral cats.'

'Too kind...'

But she was gone.

'You look as if you needed to get permission,' Jessica Marshall said when he got back.

'Did I? I'd really appreciate it if we could talk right now.'

She waved a ticket for the Hippodrome in his face. Somewhere, miles away, there was the rattle of artillery.

'Very well,' Renard groaned.

Thirty minutes later, after he'd paid two shillings at the box office of the Hippodrome, they were in their seats. The stalls were packed, mostly raucous soldiers and marines in uniform, men desperate to let off steam. A small band began playing loudly and barely in tune. Then a scantily dressed woman took to the stage and began singing a risqué song, giving back as much filthy abuse as she got from the seats.

'Is this a long show?' Renard whispered. They sat side by side in the tiny box above the stalls, one with uncomfortable chairs that appeared to date from Victorian times.

'Two hours, I believe. Dancing. A comedian. A magician too, I think. And singing. Lots of singing. I do hope you'll join in.'

'Will you?'

'I'm Canadian. I doubt I'll know the words. But you lead and I'll try to follow.'

Jessica Marshall took out a notepad and pen and began to scribble something.

'Cheer up, Inspector Renard. Everyone needs a little entertainment.'

CHAPTER 45

Beth was back by the time Joe Dobson got home. May was upstairs. She'd checked, she said. The girl had been there all day long, as they'd asked.

'What's wrong, Joe? You look terrible.'

He'd been to the bank and got out all the money they had. Just under two hundred pounds. Years of savings.

'Here.' He handed it over in an envelope. 'Take this. There's a train going to London at seven. I want the two of you to catch it and stay with your mother until this is over.'

His wife was still in her nurse's uniform. There was dried blood on the apron and her hair had come astray from the pins beneath her hat. To him, she didn't look much older than when they married seventeen years before. He was a young constable in the Met, Beth going through nursing school. The world was fast recovering from another war, one he'd just managed to miss though his father, a pacifist and ardent trade unionist, would surely have tried to stop him volunteering. Everything about the future had seemed bright, especially when May came along. The move to the coast – promotion, more money, a better house – was supposed to be the icing on the cake.

'You've spent months telling me it's not safe for May to leave here. Now you want us both gone just like that. I'd like an explanation.'

That morning's cryptic conversation, half argument, half confession, still left him confused. So May had been a regular at a house in Effingham Terrace, led there by the woman who called herself Dawn Peacock, a friend, or so she thought. A woman who was now dead, murdered in a bunker up on the cliffs.

'Not now, love. Just get packed, will you? Please…'

Beth folded her arms and stared at him. Matron material, he used to joke with her back when there were joking times. Made to boss people around when she wanted.

'When are you coming?'

'I don't know. Not straight away.'

'Then what…?'

'If you stay here, the Germans… We could have Jerry on the doorstep any moment.'

'Been like that for weeks, Joe.'

Fine, he thought. Then say it.

'If you stay here a murder detective from Scotland Yard's going to drag May into the police station tomorrow morning and ask all kinds of questions. I've no idea if he knows about Effingham Terrace yet but it won't be long before he finds out. You need to get out of here.'

'And that's it, is it? Joe Dobson's decided. So we're off.'

She always wanted detail, facts, corroboration. It was the nurse in her, he guessed.

'There's something funny going on. Not just Jerry round the corner. Or a murdered woman up on Shakespeare Cliff. The woman who ran that house. Someone May knew. I don't want you two around here getting dragged into it.'

There was movement on the stairs. She'd been there all along and they'd never noticed.

'Anyone going to ask me?' May said.

Dobson had to remind himself he'd barely had any sleep for twenty-four hours. It was hard thinking straight, hard keeping his temper too.

'Right now, I think not,' he replied. 'You're fifteen. You'll do what your parents say.'

Red-faced, arms flying, she came at them.

'Nice of you to take an interest, Dad. Finally.'

'Not now...' Beth murmured.

'Why not? The two of you have hardly looked at me since school packed in. All summer, day and night, you're out of here. Suddenly now it's all about me. All my fault.'

Dobson told himself to stay calm.

'May, love. If you stay here, they're going to take you into the nick tomorrow morning. They're going to put you in a room, and they won't let you come out until you've told them everything. I mean... everything. Every last detail. I've checked this copper out. He's only been here a week. He's a different kettle of fish from our normal blokes.'

'Worried I might embarrass you?' she asked with that same teenage sneer he'd come to dread. 'Terrified they might find out your little daughter takes her knickers off when she feels like it?'

Beth closed her eyes, hurt, and he felt that pain too. Felt May wanted to inflict it on both of them for no other reason than she could. They'd abandoned her. She had a point.

'No.' He took her by the shoulders, gently, a gesture of love. 'I'm terrified what you might have got yourself into. The woman you knew from that damned place has been murdered. There's something going on here I don't understand. I don't want you mixed up in it more than you are already.' He put one arm round her, one arm round Beth, pulling the three of them together and Joe Dobson wondered if he was about to cry. 'You two are all that matters to me. All that ever will. I know I've been bloody awful at showing that. I know I got things wrong. But please. Listen to me now. You need to get out of here before the balloon goes up. Not just Jerry. Or maybe... I don't know.'

He felt exhausted. The words wouldn't come.

'Gran will love it having you both there,' he whispered. 'Peckham will be safe. Safer than here, anyway. When things calm down...'

When the case of the woman on the cliffs was finally closed one way or another. However long that took. When the Germans had turned up. Got beaten back. Or else...

'One way or another I'll get us all together again. Not here. Not Dover. I know that was a stupid idea of mine now. Maybe back to Bermondsey. Or the countryside somewhere. You tell me.' He hugged them. They were crying. So was he. 'We belong together. We will be too, as soon as I can manage it. Just give me time.'

He closed his eyes and wondered how much longer he could stay awake. Lieutenant Mortimer would doubtless be moaning about the fact he'd left the Castle without permission, probably calling Chalmers to complain. He could go hang. It was Dover police that Dobson joined, not some funny secret outfit in Nissen huts A and B.

'We'd best pack,' Beth said finally.

May sniffed and said yes.

He kissed them both.

Forty minutes later they left the house to buy tickets at the station.

Joe Dobson watched them go, wondering when he'd see his wife and daughter again.

Chapter 46

'Don't you know the words, Inspector?' The entire theatre had risen to bellow chorus after chorus of an old music hall song, 'Roll Out the Barrel'. 'This is the grand finale. You're supposed to join in.'

The showgirl had been joined on stage by an accordionist and four women in skimpy costumes, all beaming broadly while dancing their hearts out.

Jessica Marshall looked ecstatic and was belting out every repeated line.

'Renard! I don't even know your first name...'

'Louis. Look. Can we please–'

'The show's nearly over!'

'Thank God for that.'

'Sing, Louis, sing!'

'It's the same damned thing repeated over and over. Just raised a tone every few bars. I mean... really...'

The magician had joined the gang on stage and was now flourishing paper flowers from his sleeves. Then came the unfunny comedian, a brash Cockney purveyor of crude innuendo and puns. Renard had sat through almost two hours of solid, very amateurish entertainment, mostly from a tiny cast, all performing multiple roles, with barely disguised multiple identities.

'This is insufferable,' he shouted over the racket.

'They'll be doing it all again in a little while,' she yelled back. 'The second show. If you'd like–'

'No, I would not!'

'You don't seem a very musical fellow.'

'Show me some music and–'

'You're in Dover, Louis. Cheer up.'

He refused to respond to that, so she sang the lines yet again, then tapped him on the shoulder, hard.

'Stand up and sing or I'm going straight home to work afterwards. So there.'

He sat ever more tightly on the uncomfortable chair and folded his arms. She got to her feet, waved her arms around with every line. Renard couldn't help but smile and hoped she didn't notice. Not that Jessica Marshall seemed a woman who missed much.

It wasn't a lot to give. Finally, in a bored and tuneless voice, he went through the motions alongside her.

'There. That wasn't so hard, was it?' she cried, eyes glistening as they took their seats again, released from something, he thought. The war, naturally. Renard liked to think he was good at reading people. He'd failed miserably with the charmingly cryptic doctor at the hospital that morning. Perhaps Jessica Marshall was simply easier to fathom.

There'd been at least four key changes to the same damned tune already. The squaddies and the sailors in the stalls were on their feet, bellowing, cheering, waving Union flags.

Morale, he thought. There was no practical reason why a theatre should stay open on what was effectively the frontline in a battle about to be launched. Except to keep up the spirits of the men, which amateurish productions like this appeared to do.

The accordionist signalled another shift up another tone, another round of choruses.

'Will this never end?'

Then a deafening noise filled the theatre and the music stopped on the instant. They had to have a siren close by. There was no other explanation for why it sounded so loud that it rattled the walls.

'I have to go back to the Raglan to work,' Jessica Marshall said when the racket ceased.

Renard picked her jacket off the free seat and handed it over.

'The sensible thing is to go down to a shelter.'

'I told you. I have to work.'

The siren sounded again. The men in the stalls began to file slowly out of the hall.

Then the artillery started up. Loud, incessant, so close the walls shook hard and dust began to rain down from the ancient ceiling.

The theatre was rocked by an explosion, close too, one that sent the crowds below scuttling for the doors.

'Very well,' Jessica Marshall said. 'The shelter it is.'

CHAPTER 47

Harry Lee didn't dare go home. He'd no idea what kind of mood his father might be in and feared that just his presence might earn him another beating. High summer still lingered, the nights hot enough to sleep out on the hills if he wanted. Something he did from time to time. Frank Lee never minded, never said a thing. Usually he was out somewhere himself, boozing, seeing one of his women, up to things his son didn't want to know about. The one time his father took him thieving, breaking into a farmhouse near Martin Mill, Harry had been so clumsy the owner had woken up, come out with a shotgun and loosed off some pellets in their direction. No burgling for him after that, his father had said, before he went for the belt on the door.

The months Frank Lee spent in jail were some of the happiest in Harry's life. He'd cooked for himself, worked on the local farms, got eggs for free, bacon too. Dreamed about May Dobson, waited for her when she came out of school just to stare. He'd listened as the locals talked about the war and how it wasn't quite real. Just a phase the country was going through and soon Chamberlain and Hitler would make up, be friends again, with just a few readjustments on both sides. The Jews wouldn't like it, or so Billy Lennon the butcher said. But who gave a damn about them?

By the time his father was out of the chokey, the mood was different. Bill Lennon was dead, blown to pieces taking a basket of illicit sausages, beyond the rations allowed, to his bit of skirt. Dunkirk was happening and Dover was suddenly a different place. The war was no longer a joke, a passing phase. Then the bombs started to fall, and the sky was full of planes. Harry Lee still dreamed of being in the cockpit of one of them someday, which was why, as that strange day was coming to a close, he found himself in the recruiting office near the town hall, praying they'd enlist him on the spot, give him a uniform, somewhere to stay.

The man behind the desk wore an army uniform, three stripes on his shoulder, had a greying moustache and the florid face of a drinker.

'I'd like to join the RAF really,' Harry said, squirming on the hard seat. 'Fly a plane.'

'No idea how many times a day I hear that, sonny.' He had an accent. Welsh maybe. 'We're all heroes, you know. Whatever uniform you wear. All fighting Adolf to the end.'

Not you, he thought. You're sitting on your arse in a nice office full of posters, not even a weapon on your belt. Deciding the future of lads who come and sit opposite, hoping for the best.

'I've always been interested in aeroplanes. I can join up right now, mister...'

'Sergeant.' The man patted the stripes on his sleeves. 'You got to recognise these for starters, boy.'

'Sergeant. Sorry.'

'Army it's going to be. Don't argue.' The man pulled out some papers. 'How old are you?'

'Eighteen.'

He scribbled something on the page.

'What's that funny thing on your face?'

'Just a mark, sir. That's all.'

'I can see the mark. I meant all the bruises. Looks to me like you've been in a fight.'

'Fell off my bike.'

The sergeant glared at him in a way that said he was well versed at reading liars.

'Had a bit of a fight as well,' Harry added. 'You should see the other lad.'

'Very good. Fill in your name and address. Let's see if you can write.'

He could. Not joined up, but that was okay, or so the school used to say. So long as people could read. He put down his name, the cottage, his father as nearest of kin.

'Wait here,' the sergeant said and stepped outside.

The posters on the walls made signing up sound so exciting. Soldiers with rifles, posted to exotic locations like India and Hong Kong. Lots of different planes for the RAF. Sailors in uniforms smiling on ship decks. None of it fitted well with his memories of the wounded, bedraggled men getting off the ships back from Dunkirk. They had to sell the idea of joining up, he guessed. Though not at that moment for him.

The sergeant came back in, bent down, glared in his face and said, spittle coming with his fury, 'I should kick your sorry arse from here to hell and back, you lying little prat.'

'What's wrong...?'

'Harry Lee. Local toerag. Dad's a villain and you are too. You think no one knows you round here?'

'Didn't realise being a villain stopped you signing up.'

Cheeky, he thought. But sometimes the words just came out. He'd seen plenty of roughneck squaddies around town. It almost looked like there was a special regiment for villains on occasion.

'It doesn't, you idiot. But being seventeen does. I just called the nick and they told me. Had you in today, didn't they? Think you can run from what you've done by hiding out with us?'

He should have seen that coming.

'Haven't done nothing. I just want to sign up. Army. Navy. Whatever you've got.'

The sergeant balled up the form and chucked it into a bin by the door.

'Come back when you're eighteen, sunshine. If you're not in jail by then. Maybe I'll be generous and find you a hole to fight from. That way no one need look at your ugly bloody face. Now stop wasting my time and piss off out of here.'

He didn't move an inch. The fellow was a thug, a bully, and the only man like that he feared was his dad.

'Not eighteen till December. Jerry might be here then. You want me on your side or not?'

'It's not a fucking billiards match, son. This is war. A man's game. Not for little idiots like you. Now scram before you feel my boot up your arse.'

The light was fading in that gentle, velvety way it did by the sea. Squaddies were rushing round looking as if they thought something was about to happen. There was the smell of smoke in the air, and the dust that came with bombs. More air raids on the way. More fire in the night sky.

He wandered up towards the station, thinking maybe he'd kip out on the hills that night.

Then he saw them. Two figures with suitcases, hats, coats. Walking along the platform, getting into a carriage.

'May! *May!*'

He ran up to the iron railings, but the train was moving already. Her mother was sitting by the window, staring out, sad-faced, crying as they pulled out of the platform.

Harry Lee ran round to the entrance. A man in uniform was there, shutting up the ticket box.

'Where's that train going, mister?'

'Good question, lad. Exceptionally good one, that.'

He grabbed the man's sleeve.

'Where, please? My girlfriend's on it.'

The railway fellow shook him off and laughed in his face.

'What, that lovely young thing's yours, is she?'

'Sort of...'

'Why are you asking me where she's going then?'

Lie. That was always easiest.

'We had an argument.'

'A lover's tiff.' The chap seemed so amused. 'Well, the answer is I've no idea. I told them. That's the London train but there's problems on the track before Folkestone. Hard enough running this line without Jerry messing things up.'

'They're going to London?'

'They bought tickets for London, sonny. Not the same thing. I told them. They'd get as far as Shakespeare Halt and have to wait there for a while. Maybe a long while. Maybe they'd never get past Folkestone at all tonight. But do people listen? Do they hell...'

Harry wasn't taking his words in anymore. If the train got stuck at Shakespeare, he could find a path down the cliff there and try and see her. Say he was so sorry. Make amends somehow. Maybe even climb on the train and go with them. He'd never been to London. There could be a new life there. A different one.

It was getting dark already. There were a couple of bikes in a rack outside the station. He looked round, picked the one that had a light on the front, grabbed it, and started to pedal.

The railway bloke had seen him and was yelling stuff about how he'd call the police.

Do it, Harry thought. Do what you like.

'Thieving little bastard,' the man cried, trying to run after him.

Harry turned, grinned, stuck up two fingers just like Churchill, only the other way round. Then he pedalled for the hills as hard as he could.

Chapter 48

There was an air raid shelter not far from the Hippodrome, a tunnel that ran from Snargate Street to Durham Hill, cut through bare rock, lit by strings of weak bulbs. It was hot and busy already by the time they got there. Families and servicemen and women crowded together, queuing for cups of tea and biscuits. Many had brought pillows and sheets with them, the parents had toys and books for the kids. The atmosphere, it seemed to Renard, was patient, resigned... bravado with an undercurrent of fear.

They sat down against a wall near the entrance. He asked her if she wanted a cup of tea. She gave him a wry glance and pulled a flask of Scotch out of her handbag along with two small silver cups.

'Always be prepared,' she said and poured a couple of shots.

He must have winced when he sipped at the drink because she looked at him and asked if it was all right.

'More of a wine man really,' Renard confessed.

'That's a shame. Don't think there's going to be much coming from Bordeaux for a few years.'

He thought about his aunt and the people he'd seen at the

reception for the vicar. Kent's upper class. They, he guessed, would manage and doubtless had their cellars well stocked in preparation.

'What are you doing here?' she asked.

'Trying to avoid Hitler's bombs.'

'Very funny. I mean… what's a Scotland Yard detective doing in Dover?'

He finished the whisky and declined a top-up.

'Investigating a murder. Dawn Peacock's.'

'You're sure she was murdered?'

'That is one thing I do know.'

'The woman at the Hippodrome seemed to think she might have been with a soldier. Or a sailor.'

'Does she indeed?'

'Do you think she might be right?'

'I really don't know, Mrs Marshall.'

He still had the article she'd written in his jacket pocket. Renard pulled it out and showed it to her.

'What in God's name are you doing with that?'

'I found a copy in the police station.'

'What's it doing *there*? Someone spiked the piece. Apparently, it was bad for morale.'

'Then I imagine that's why there was a copy in the nick.'

'You mean you're all keeping an eye on me?'

There was a boom nearby. British military more than a Nazi shell, or so he guessed. A cloud of sooty dust fluttered down from the ceiling. Quite casually, Jessica Marshall brushed some off her jacket, then, when he didn't move, did the same for him.

'One always has to keep up appearances,' she noted.

'Crumpled. That's me. I'm staying with my aunt at the moment. She tells me all the time. Crumpled suit. Shirts rarely troubled by an iron, let alone bleach. The wrong ties.' He waggled his brown shoes which did, when he thought of it, clash with the dark-blue trousers. 'The wrong footwear.'

'You didn't answer my question.'

'I'm not keeping an eye on you. Though I rather imagine a foreign journalist loose in such a sensitive town, at such a sensitive time, would warrant attention. Dawn Peacock.' He brandished the story. 'You met her last week. May I ask why?'

She seemed untroubled by the question.

'I was doing my job. I threw off the minders from the damned Ministry of Information and went looking for real copy. A local who'd talk to me. Most wouldn't give me the time of day. Then I struck lucky...'

It seemed a straight and believable story. How she'd wandered around the town on her own with her camera taking photos when Dawn Peacock came up to her in the street and asked what she was doing.

'What was she like?'

'Very forward. Very friendly. To be honest, at first I thought she might have been one of Shearer's plants. I told her straight out. She found that very funny. She was a dancer. Very theatrical. I told her I was a reporter from Canada looking to interview someone. We talked. Then...' She tapped the pages. 'I wrote this, and some jerk killed it.'

'You met her at the Hippodrome?'

She picked up her notebook and went through the pages.

'No. That's the funny thing. When I went there this morning, they said she lived in digs in Victoria Avenue.'

'She does.'

'That's not where I saw her. It was a street called...' She checked again. 'Effingham Terrace. Much smarter. I walked round there this morning. Seems it wasn't her home at all. The place was empty.' She frowned. 'Shearer drove past. A coincidence, he said. Told me I was barking up the wrong tree.'

He took out his own notepad.

'Number twenty-one,' she said. 'A very smart place. Once upon a time, anyway. Georgian or something. It really didn't seem as if anyone was at home. Then Shearer gave me a lift back.'

'Why did you think she lived there?'

There was a racket down the tunnel. A bunch of men began singing a bawdy song. A family nearby was begging them to be quiet.

'She had bags of shopping with her. Drink, it looked like. I thought perhaps she was about to have a party.'

'But she didn't go in?'

From the look on Jessica Marshall's face, she was thinking it through again.

'No. The place was all blacked out. I didn't hang around. I wasn't supposed to be wandering round on my own. I'd just finished talking to her when one of the minders from the Ministry popped up and in the nicest possible way told me to get back to the Castle or else.'

'Name?'

'I don't remember. He was a minion from London. Not local. Is this of any use?'

'Who's to know?'

She rifled through the pages again.

'Now I think of it... she really wanted to talk. I mean... she came over to me. Couldn't wait to chat. I thought...' She screwed up her nose, thinking. 'I could be wrong, but I thought she had a funny accent. As if she might have lived abroad for a while. Or come from somewhere they talk differently.'

'Like you?'

She laughed.

'You think I've got an accent?'

'Definitely. Not quite American. There are sounds, vowels mainly.'

'You are an observant man, Inspector Renard. Crumpled. But with the eye of a hawk, I suspect.'

'Too kind. You should meet my aunt. You'd get on.'

She was barely listening. Jessica Marshall was rifling through the pages again until she found the one she wanted.

'Here. I should have mentioned this. It was curious. Never had it before.'

The writing was different. Slanted, almost artistic. They were the same words he'd read in the story.

The devil's favourite piece of furniture is the long bench.
We're not good at putting things to one side. If there's a job to be
done, folk get on with it. Anyway, the closer you get to the grave,
the more you seem alive.

'I don't understand.'

'She said if I was going to use what she said, I had to get it right. Every word. It was important. She didn't want to be misquoted.'

'"The devil's favourite piece of furniture is the long bench..."'

'Me neither,' Marshall said. 'But I promised I'd put it in, and I did. Not that a word of it ever got into print.' She cricked her neck towards the door. 'I can't hear any bombs. I'm going back to the Raglan to write this up.'

'You're supposed to wait for the all-clear.'

She smiled at him.

'Are you going to arrest me? I've a story to write. A pass from the Ministry of Information. Captain Shearer hungry for my copy.'

'Not a story about Dawn Peacock, I hope.'

'If that was her name. Theatricals. Never believe a single word they say. No. A tale about a wonderfully patriotic theatre show performed with skill and enthusiasm in the face of Hitler's *blitzkrieg*. Then a spell inside a tunnel hiding from his bombs. With a charming if crumpled Scotland Yard murder detective.'

'If you wish to quote me,' he said, 'use this.'

He scribbled on her pad two words: *No comment.*

'And keep my name out of it.'

'Only joking. I rather thought that might be the case.'

Renard walked to the mouth of the tunnel. It had turned quiet outside. He could see her back to the hotel if that was what she wanted. Then drive to Temple Ewell for a late-night supper of cold trout.

———

The night smelled of diesel, cordite and smoke. The Raglan looked deserted behind blacked-out windows, but the landlord had given her a key.

'That was an interesting evening,' she said as she let herself in. 'If you'd like a nightcap...'

Renard stayed where he was.

'That's very kind, but I'd better be getting back.'

'To your aunt?'

'Cold trout waiting for me.'

'That's not a very nice way to talk about her.'

He laughed.

'Very good.'

'Do you never get lonely, Inspector?'

'Does it look as if I do?'

'I don't know. I haven't quite worked you out yet.'

She came back and stood in front of him.

'I'm not in the habit of inviting men for nightcaps, if that's what you think. And it was just for company.'

'I didn't think anything, Mrs Marshall. I need to get home.'

Sometimes he wished he wore a hat. There were occasions when it seemed one was needed.

By the time he got back to the car, the sirens were howling again. The all-clear this time.

All-clear for Dover, anyway. Somewhere else then feeling Hitler's wrath for sure.

CHAPTER 49

The train hadn't moved from the short platform called Shakespeare Halt for an hour or more. From what May could make out in the blackout, the place was more a military encampment than a stop for everyday travellers. Soldiers were bustling round, tending to what looked like gun emplacements under tarpaulins. As they watched from the carriage, one of them lit a fag and got bawled out by an officer. The lights had been off in the train ever since it got dark. The carriages seemed pretty much empty too, apart from the guard who wandered up and down the corridor sucking on a stinky pipe.

'You were warned,' he said, the one time her mother complained. 'Trouble on the track at Folkestone. Can't go into the tunnel ahead until we know we can get out of it, can we? Wouldn't want to be stuck there in the dark.'

'Is it just us?' Beth asked.

'Got three sailors up front. Nice lads but they're full of drink, ladies, so I suggest you stay here.'

'We're stuck then?' May snapped, and that drove him off.

They had two small cases with them, heavy with clothes, not much else apart from the cash in an envelope buried deep in the biggest inside some underwear. May couldn't quite believe how much money her father had turned up with. Maybe he was a secret saver. Maybe it was something a child – and she always was a child in his eyes – wasn't supposed to know about.

Barely a word had passed between them since they left the house. It was agreed. Peckham to stay with Gran, a kindly old bird, not quite right in the head, especially since the war began. For how long, no one seemed to know.

May Dobson wouldn't miss Dover, that was certain. It felt good to be leaving everything behind, even if she'd no idea what might lie ahead. It was a place she'd visited often enough over the years, staying in Gran's modest terrace in Peckham, half the size of the house in Priory Hill. Life was going to be different, she guessed. No father around for one thing, at least for a while, though whether that was good or bad she'd no idea. No school either. They'd closed in London, with most of the kids evacuated.

'Want a mint?' her mother asked, holding out a packet.

The things people said to try and start a conversation. They were always so insignificant. As if you could hope to make something meaningful out of something so small.

'No thanks. Are we ever going to move?'

'You heard what the guard said. The line's blocked.'

'We should have waited till tomorrow. We always do what he tells us.'

Voices outside. Men somewhere, arguing. The night had turned darker. Clouds scuttling over the moon. There was the sound of artillery fire from Dover, the beams of searchlights just visible round the corner of the shallow bay. The air was rank with the smell of spilled fuel. It was hard to work out what the army was hiding under all those sheets. Long guns pointed seawards. Some kind of armoured boats too, she guessed.

Finally, the guard came back.

'Sorry for the delay, ladies,' he said with a cheery grin. 'Trains, eh?'

'Are we going to go now?' May asked.

He shook his head.

'I wish. What I came to say is we're stuck here for another hour at least. If you want to get out on the platform and stretch your legs that's fine. The navy lads are happy with their bottle of rum, so you won't get any trouble from them. Just remember the blackout.' He pointed to his pipe, now extinguished. 'The soldiery out there are very keen we don't do anything to let Jerry know we're here.'

He went off whistling a tuneless tune.

'Come on,' her mother said. 'It'll make a change of scene.'

Away from the guns and the tanks of diesel the night was fresh with the breeze from the sea. The bench seat felt hard and they had to sweep dust from it before they sat down. Soldiers and a few men in boiler suits kept moving through the forest of weaponry on the pebble beach.

'Go on then,' May said. 'Ask me.'

Beth Dobson leaned back on the hard bench and closed her eyes.

'We're leaving all that behind, love. What's the point?'

Typical adult, May thought. Didn't have a clue.

'If the bad's in me, Mum, we're not leaving it behind at all, are we? You're just shifting it somewhere else.'

'Oh love...' She was near crying again, then hugged her, cheek to damp cheek in the dark night. 'Don't be so hard on yourself.'

'What I don't understand is... if men are meant to like it... why can't we?' She tried to peer into her mother's eyes. 'I'm not wrong, am I? Liking it? It doesn't feel wrong when you're doing it. Only...'

The hoot of an owl cut through the black night. Then came a splash of what smelled like petrol followed by the curse of a squaddie.

'Stop this. Stop it now.'

May barely heard. She was thinking, hard and straight, in a way that never happened in Dover because something there stopped it. Something that made her tell herself not to ask those awkward questions.

'Dawn said we did it for lots of different reasons. It felt good. Felt great. Made men want you and who doesn't need that?'

'May...'

Her mother's voice was getting whiny. May couldn't stop thinking about Effingham Terrace and what went on there.

'I wonder who killed her. I wonder why...'

CHAPTER 50

As Harry Lee pedalled the stolen bike to the foot of the hill, darkness fell, a swift and inky swamp. A war night, pierced by searchlights, the rat-a-tat of tracer fire, red-hot bullets streaming into the high, patchy cloud. The ground artillery seemed to be shooting at grey and fluffy cotton wool as far as he could see. When the sky cleared a little, a quarter moon cast a weak silver light over the blacked-out town and the hump of the cliffs ahead.

Sirens were shrieking everywhere, not just Dover, a distant wail from Folkestone too. He couldn't wait to get away. Try and find May if she was still in the train stuck at Shakespeare Halt. Say he was sorry and he'd do anything to make up. Girls... he'd never had the experience. Never thought she knew what all that was about, either. Stupid wasn't a big enough word. Sorry, neither.

Pedalling up the steep hill, then across the dry and bumpy grass, he tried to picture Shakespeare Cliff in his head. It was meadow on chalk, the rock face running a sheer several hundred feet down to the sea. But there had to be a way to the shore somewhere, past the hide where they'd made that dreadful find. A path down. A train stuck below. Maybe she wasn't mad at him anymore. He could make it up to her. Get on the train with them.

Go all the way to London, start a new life there. Together. Forgiven. May putting what she'd done with all those men in Dover behind her. Him forgetting about the stain on his cheek and a town where the name Lee was a mark on your character.

After a while the field levelled and he found the path, bone dry and potholed. Twice he fell off the bike, banged his bruised face hard against the coarse summer grass, felt like crying, wondered what May would say.

In the end he left the bike behind, walked, half ran, still trying to picture what the cliff was like, where the way down to the halt might lie.

There was a gun battery up front, pumping fire into the sky. He backed off inland, made a long circling detour to avoid it. The squaddies manning the artillery wouldn't appreciate company on a night like this.

It wasn't far off an hour after he left the station that he finally saw the faint silhouette of the bird hide break the horizon above the cliffs, between the hazy sea and sky. Just the sight of it made him feel sick. Then something moved.

Another silhouette.

A man, he thought, not far from the hut where he'd got so close to May it hurt.

A man standing close to the edge, looking right over, down to Shakespeare Halt, something shining in his hand.

CHAPTER 51

'For God's sake,' Beth Dobson begged, 'I don't want to hear this, May. *Please.*'

The soldiers had gone into a huddle by a small hut. One was on the radio. She could hear him grumbling about someone or something, not that she could make out the words. They were smoking there, the walls not quite hiding the tiny red lights of their fags. The smell reminded her of Effingham Terrace. The blokes there always had a fag in their traps, usually stank of booze too, not that it stopped them wanting what they'd come for.

No lights out to sea. No lights in the sky above, just the fading edges of the searchlight beams along the coast. A stiff breeze coming onshore and the distant wail of sirens like angry insects begging for food.

'Dawn said it was all right. Not just all right, but proper. Kind of helping. Patriotic.'

'I don't want to know.'

'That's a shame. I want to tell you.'

She gripped her mother's hands.

'It wasn't just me being a complete tart like you think. There was a reason. The men who came into that house...'

Beth Dobson tried to put her hands over her ears. May dragged them away.

'Listen, will you? Dawn said we had to get them talking. We had to ask them questions. About the Castle. The tunnels. See if they got all talkative with a bit of drink and...' She didn't want to say it. 'You know. The rest.'

Her mother closed her eyes and bent her weary head to one side.

'Because it all went back to blokes who needed to know. People in charge. Churchill's people. Helped them spot squaddies who were mouthing off. Dawn said maybe we'd trap–'

'I wish that train would do something.'

'Nothing special about letting a man have you, is there? Girls do it all the time. Men think it's what we're here for. Anyway, we could all be dead next week. Why not? Who's to bother?'

'You're fifteen...'

'So what?' May was getting mad again, her voice going higher. 'Fifteen and dead's worse than fifty and dead, isn't it? At least you got to have a life. What have I had? Stuck in that dump on my own. You and Dad out all the time. What do you expect me to do? Read a book? Do a jigsaw? *Play with my toys?* I'm not a child.'

'No,' Beth Dobson snapped. 'I can see that.'

'Dawn said we had to be nice to them and that way they'd talk–'

She put a hand over her daughter's mouth.

'I don't want to hear, May. None of it. Your father's given us the chance to get out of that damned place and that's it. What happened there's buried. You won't say a word about it to anyone. Me neither.'

May wasn't listening. Stiff and upright on the hard station bench she was staring up at the cliff.

'Not a word,' her mother repeated. 'Have you ever thought for one moment what they'll do to your father tomorrow?'

May snatched her mother's hand from her mouth.

'Why will they do anything?'

'Because he's got you out of there! Before they can chuck you in a room and ask a load of awkward questions.'

'Dad's a copper. They never get into trouble.'

'I stand corrected,' Beth snarled. 'You *are* still a child.'

And there it was. The coldness between them back again.

May got to her feet, arms round herself. The wind had picked up so much she was starting to shiver.

'Someone's up there,' she said and pointed. 'Look.'

At the very tip of the ghostly rim of the chalk cliff, the edge just visible against the grey sky, was the dim shape of a figure. There was a lamp too, big and bright, and he was waving it side to side, out to sea.

A beacon. One that would surely be visible for miles.

The soldiers in the hut had noticed. One was on the radio again, voice loud and urgent, calling someone.

A snatch of what he said came to them.

'There's some bastard on the cliff, Sarge! He's got a lamp.'

The two of them fell quiet and May shivered again, a shaky nervous movement this time, like a spasm. Soldiers seemed to be starting to move everywhere. Shakespeare Halt, so empty, so quiet, was coming to anxious life.

The train guard came along looking worried, sucking wildly at an unlit pipe.

'Best get back on board, ladies. Stoking up the engines now. Driver thinks it's maybe best we pull into that tunnel after all.'

CHAPTER 52

They were in the study, a schooner of dry sherry each, and Veronica was being stern.

'Danvers has done his best to polish the lumps of battered leather you call shoes. His sister has ironed what passes as shirts and pressed the rest of your wardrobe. We waited a week for you to ask, Louis, but I decided I could wait no longer. You are supposed to be a serving police officer so at least make an effort to look like one.'

She was in her scarlet dressing gown, hair in a towel, straight from the bath. A plate of Turkish delight was fast diminishing next to the glass of *fino* she kept reaching for.

'You haven't seen what the rest of Dover nick look like.'

'Rather smarter than you, I'm sure. Also, if you don't get yourself a haircut soon, Danvers will do the job. Since his experience is limited to shearing sheep, I'd advise you to arrange something. There are standards to be upheld in Temple Ewell, you know.'

He'd never really thought much about clothes, even before Dunkirk. They always seemed of little account.

'This place is very quiet,' Renard said. 'You were such a social creature when you and Maurice lived in London. It seemed to be one long dinner party, from what I recall. Don't you miss it?'

She took a sip of her sherry.

'What I miss no longer exists. Either the war took it, or fashion. It's a sign of growing old. How was your cold trout?'

'Lovely, thanks.'

She growled at him.

'Don't patronise me. It was muddy. The fish were too large. Food and drink are beyond you too, it seems. If you'd really be happier going back to Scotland Yard there may be someone I could call...'

He shook his head. The fish really had tasted fine.

'No. Not London. Not yet.'

'What worries me is you look more troubled since you went back to work.'

'No.' That was wrong. 'Less. It's just...'

The sherry was good, flinty and bone dry. He wondered how much of it was left. When the world might turn again and find some kind of normality. How long that much-needed peace might last.

'Just what, Louis?'

'I seem to be embroiled in a case. That's all. A puzzling case. Very.'

'A murder, I gather. A woman.'

'How do you know?'

'Jimmy Mortimer told me when he called and asked the two of us round to dinner sometime. I told him, not now. He was only being polite after I invited him to the do. Murder. It's the talk of the town apparently. Had enough of those in London, didn't you?'

'Not like this. Not in these circumstances.'

'Don't let that man suck you in. The lord lieutenant likes to create acolytes around him. Followers. Devotees.'

This interested him.

'Don't you like the chap? As you said... he is the king's representative in Kent.'

Veronica was discreet and tactful around strangers, while anything but reticent with her opinions among family. All the same, she seemed to take stock before going further.

'Look. This isn't London. Kent's a glorious piece of England, but in all honesty it's still feudal at heart, little changed since that horrible Norman popped over the Channel and put us all under his thumb. He was a Viking really, you know, and it still shows. Every last one of us is meant to know our place. You'll never begin to understand this strange county until you appreciate that. We're not civilised. At least not in the accepted sense in which that term is applied to what I believe they still call the Home Counties.'

His aunt had dropped the odd political, even republican sentiment from time to time, especially in theatrical circles in London. There was a rumour that she and Maurice had come out on the side of the miners during the General Strike.

'And I must wear shiny shoes,' he added.

She slapped him lightly on the wrist.

'That's just good grooming.' The slap turned into a grip. 'And you are highly amusing company, nephew. Your old aunt's grateful for it.' A thought, and she turned very serious. 'Are the Germans really coming, do you think? The idea's so odd. I still can't get it straight in my mind.'

No, said a voice in his head. *They're already here.*

'I think we'll find out soon enough.'

'And if they do...'

'There'll be hell to pay. For a while, anyway.' He got up. 'Do excuse me. I need to make a call.'

Constable Kelly, to his surprise, had a home telephone number, a luxury that came with his father, a criminal solicitor in Deal who, in peacetime, occasionally received clients of an evening. The young constable answered, sounding sleepy.

'How's it in town tonight, sir? Keep hearing a lot of banging out your way. Lots of red on the horizon but it's damned dark out there. That always makes it seem worse.'

Walmer lay beyond the cliffs, on an open bay that had to be a primary target for any Nazi invasion plans. There was a huge barracks in neighbouring Deal, or so he'd heard, one dating back to Napoleonic times. The place had a strong naval tradition too. Kelly and his parents must have known they were as much in Hitler's sights as anyone in Dover.

'You told Dobson I wanted the girl in tomorrow morning?'

The young man chuckled.

'Oh yeah. He didn't like it. Not one bit. Got no choice, has he? Funny bloke. Almost...'

'Almost what?'

'Almost like there was something fishy going on. Like he had something to hide.'

'Most of us do. Effingham Terrace. Number twenty-one.'

A pause, then Kelly asked, 'Is that meant to ring a bell or something?'

'Obviously not. We'll bring the Dobson girl in later. First thing, eight thirty, I'll meet you there, outside.'

'Any particular reason?'

Veronica wandered out with the sherry decanter. He put a hand over his glass.

'Eight thirty,' Renard repeated. 'On the dot.'

CHAPTER 53

May and Beth scrambled into the carriage. The soldiers outside were yelling to one another. It looked as if two were on the radio, dimly silhouetted against the gentle tide. Boots dashed noisily across shingle, metal clashed against metal. Among the artillery emplacements gunners were racing to remove the tarpaulins from the long barrels of the weapons there.

'Christ...' May muttered.

At the end of the platform, looking up towards the cliffs, a bunch of squaddies had formed a kneeling line, rifles raised like a firing squad. With a sudden, shocking burst of noise they released a volley of shots up towards the cliff, the weapons bucking against their shoulders, bullets flying like tiny fireworks up the white chalk.

The guard came and sat with them. He looked scared.

'When are we moving?' Beth asked.

'Fool engineer let the fire down, didn't he? Can't just flip a switch. We need some steam.'

Shapes were beginning to appear out to sea, just visible above the watery horizon. Fast-moving, bobbing like gigantic stiff-winged black birds. Then they heard it. Two smaller planes, unseen and much closer, the outriders of the pack, skimming the surface of the bay, perhaps fifty feet above the sea. With a sudden roar of their engines, they soared above them, over the straggly encampment by the beach and the stranded train, climbing to clear the clifftop.

Tiny pale-white parachutes were falling from their bellies. There was a brief moment of near quiet as the planes rounded the heights above. Then it was like bonfire night come early, a crazy one where the fireworks rained down from the sky, not up towards it. Flares, scores of them. White, bright beacons that turned night to day and revealed in cruel detail the little bay beneath Shakespeare Cliff: the rock face, the artillery, the figures scattering around. A small army of men trying to bring their weapons to life. A bustling nest of uniformed ants scared out of their nest, faced with an approaching fleet of predators racing out of the blackness, scattered across the horizon, wingtips almost touching, the steady drone of their engines getting louder, closer by the second.

May stood up at the window and peered out at the strange and unimaginable scene in front of her. After a moment she thought she could see the propellers turning on the silhouettes of the fast-moving bombers bearing down on Shakespeare Halt.

'We're going to die,' she whispered, then flew to the seat and buried her head deep in Beth Dobson's arms.

CHAPTER 54

By the time Harry Lee reached the bird hide the sky was alive with fire. First, the white and incandescent searing light of flares, so harsh they made his eyes water and ache and still he couldn't stop staring straight at them till they floated down towards the bay. Then came the sharp outlines of tracer bullets, raining like red-hot spears from aircraft flying low and fast, sparking as they met the ground below.

Most of the stuff he'd told May about recognising planes and fighting Jerry he'd made up. His dad had shown him the hide the week before, told him it was a bunker meant for men who'd go undercover, armed to the teeth and deadly when Adolf showed his face. Knowing his father, he was probably planning to use the place to nick something. The rest of the nonsense he'd told May about the invasion to come, he'd invented. Looking at what had to be a fleet of German planes bearing down on the White Cliffs now it struck him straight away, this could only be the beginning.

A first wave. One that moved so fast, so low, the leaders had to pull up quick, engines racing, to crest the clifftop, sending Harry flat to the ground as the machines roared over him like angry metal beasts.

Then there was a gap and he thought, hoped, this was the end.

He stumbled to the edge of the cliff and looked at the bay below. The flares were still falling. Men raced round in panicked anticipation of a coming fire. There was a train too, trapped in the open line between the two tunnels that ran between the cliffs. No flames. No sign of anyone.

'Oh May,' he whispered. 'Please be all right.'

The night began to fill with noise again – a deeper, deadlier roar.

He knew what he'd see when he lifted his head and peered for the horizon. The first group of aircraft *was* just the beginning. Lone fighters softening up the target for what was to come.

These were bombers, ugly black leviathans lumbering through the air, so huge it was hard to believe they belonged there. Below, by the shingle, a few artillery positions looked to be opening up on them already.

Too few. Too late. A massive plane passed over him, leaving in its wake what looked like the iron droppings of a terrifying bird.

Harry Lee watched as they fell to earth, watched as the shells burst across the little bay, raising smoke and flame, screams and the shriek of torn metal.

A second bomber came and its droppings fell in a perfect shower over the trapped train carriages stuck by the platform in Shakespeare Halt.

He was crying by then and it wasn't because she was the most beautiful thing he'd ever seen. It was for her. Damaged, miserable May, who'd taken pity on him when no one did, only for his cack-handed stupidity and ignorance to ruin it all.

There was another plane behind the others, lower than the rest. He could hear its engine stuttering, and in the red glow from beneath, he saw that it could surely never clear the cliff.

The thing was coming right at him.

There was nothing he could do. No one he could save.

Harry Lee turned and started to run.

PART THREE

CHAPTER 55

Dan Kelly was outside the house in Effingham Terrace, taking off his black waxed motorcycle outfit to reveal a smart double-breasted suit underneath. It was just before eight thirty. Renard was getting used to the morning smell of Dover. Smoke, smouldering timber and the distinctive aftermath aroma of artillery fire, chemical and acrid.

'You look smart, Constable. And punctual.'

Kelly grinned.

'Got to start the week proper, boss. Bright-eyed and bushy-tailed. Came straight here.' He felt his lapels and grinned. 'Mum got me this for Christmas. Made to measure in Burtons. Was keeping it for a special occasion. Which this is. You like it?'

'It's possible you'll have to go down a sewer shortly.'

The young copper looked terrified.

'Mum wouldn't like that.'

'Just joking,' Renard said. 'I may need a new suit...' The look on Kelly's face voiced agreement. 'Where do you recommend?'

'Canterbury. Only decent tailors here got bombed out a month ago. You heard the news?'

'What news?'

'Jerry got a right kicking by our fighter lads yesterday. Sixty of their planes gone down, the BBC said. Feels like maybe a turning point. Hope so.'

Renard murmured his agreement then headed for the front door. The house was as Jessica Marshall had described: large, white, run-down but almost palatial, a minor merchant's mansion he'd have guessed, probably dating back to the end of the eighteenth century, around the time The Pantheon was built. Some architect in East Kent clearly had a taste for the Palladian.

He walked round the place. The garden was a mess. Stacked next to the back door were three commercial-sized bins with bottles, beer mostly, a few Scotch, spilling out of the open tops.

'Someone who lives here's got a bit of a thirst,' Kelly said. He picked up a couple of empty beer bottles. 'Truman's. Shame they don't have any taste.'

'Snobbery about ale, Constable?'

Renard had banged the brass knocker on the front door and got no response. Like a side entrance and what looked the way into the kitchen, it was locked.

'Picky about my beer, sir. There are few good local breweries round here. Ramsgate. Margate. If you want a guide–'

Renard wasn't listening. He had his skeleton keys out and was feeding one into the kitchen door lock.

'What are you doing, if I might ask?'

'Breaking in. What does it look like?'

'Are we...?' Kelly sounded nervous. 'Are we allowed?'

Renard smiled quickly.

'I believe you've already supplied the answer to that. TAWO.'

'But how...?'

'I once arrested the finest cat burglar in Kensington. A charming fellow. Old Etonian who hit hard times and discovered a talent for entering without breaking.' He rattled the skeleton inside the lock and got nowhere. 'Do you ever talk to your customers after you've arrested them?'

'Other than saying, "Consider yourself nicked, chummy"? No. Why would I? They're criminals.'

'They're also people.' Renard tried another skeleton from the set. 'There but for the grace of God. Little tip. Always pick their brains before they learn their sentence. They tend to be less obliging after.'

'Most of my customers are very much along the lines of Frank Lee, sir. I suspect you have a better kind of clientele up in the Smoke.'

Something clicked then turned. Renard opened the door and said, 'After you.'

The kitchen was a mess. Dirty plates in an old Belfast sink, dirty glasses on an ancient oak dining table. There was a coat stand with a jacket, a man's, military-looking, and a pair of muddy soldier's boots at the foot.

'Just a thought, sir... What if someone's here?'

There was a ventilated door to what had to be the larder. Renard went over and threw it open. Not so much as a bottle of milk inside. Or a slice of bread.

He walked out of the kitchen into the hall. There was a dining room on the left, with a dusty chandelier over a walnut table. Glasses everywhere. A gramophone stood in the corner. He walked over, switched it on and placed the needle on the vinyl. A raucous piece of American jazz blared out, nothing like the music hall he'd been listening to in the Hippodrome the night before with Jessica Marshall. This was more like party fare. All the same, it made him wonder again about the woman and the story she'd told. Of how Dawn Peacock had scribbled down the exact quote she wanted in the paper.

'You reckon this dump was some kind of nightclub?' Kelly asked, following him into the room.

'One word for it. And no one at the nick ever knew?'

'I didn't. This isn't a part of town where we get much business. The likes of Frank Lee smashing a window and helping himself to some jewellery maybe. Not against the law to have a bit of a shindig if you're blacked out though, is it?'

Renard picked up a glass tankard. There was lipstick smeared over the rim.

'Where's the place to look after someone's had a party?'

Kelly thought about it.

'Upstairs?'

The house had eight bedrooms on two floors. Four large, the rest smaller, though they'd all been provided with what looked like recent, cheap double beds. The sheets were all over the place, some stained with drink and coffee. Ashtrays were scattered around randomly, overflowing onto ancient, frayed carpets.

'What exactly,' Renard asked, 'is Dover's policy on brothels?'

'Houses of ill repute, sir. That's what we tend to say here.'

'Where I come from we call them brothels. You clearly had a highly active one here, not more than a mile from the nick.'

Kelly glanced round the room, scowling.

'Don't get me wrong. I'm not defending it. But you look at all the squaddies we've got here. Navy men. All kinds. They want their entertainment. We'd be making a rod for our own backs if we didn't turn a blind eye to some of what goes on. Even if we did have the officers to do much about it. Which we don't.'

True, Renard thought. Perhaps he was being pompous. He'd always hated the way prostitution was tolerated in Shepherd Market back in London. But that was Mayfair, where the customers had money and class, or so they thought. And the women were invariably beautiful, often quite in control of their own lives. It wasn't the same further down the social ladder. Places like Effingham Terrace attracted the damaged, the needy, and the desperate.

'Oh my,' Kelly said with a sigh. He was going through the sideboard. Boxes of cigarettes and army rations of prophylactics. More tools of the trade. 'This isn't good.'

It was a photograph. Two women outside the house, smiling,

arms round one another. Judging by the state of the garden and the trees it must have been taken recently. This was summer.

One of them was Dawn Peacock.

'That's Joe Dobson's girl,' Kelly said. 'Here. She's fifteen, for God's sake.'

'Doesn't look fifteen.'

An adult dress, theatrically elegant. She had a lovely face, a lovely smile too, fair hair tied back, too much lipstick, make-up she surely didn't need.

'Joe's going to go mad when he finds out.'

'What makes you think he doesn't know already?'

'I can't imagine he would...'

Renard wasn't listening. There was a lamp on a small table next to the bed. Twisted cable fed into it, but when he looked more closely there were three threads there, not the usual two. He followed it round. One led off behind the iron bedstead. At the end was a small metal disc attached to the frame.

Without a word he went into the adjoining bedroom. The same apparatus was hidden behind the headboard.

'Check all the others,' he ordered, showing Kelly the wire and the disc. 'Look to see if there's a microphone hidden in the frame.'

The wires ran under the carpet, into the floorboards. Same on the floor below. In the hall there was a small metal conduit fitted from the ceiling to the floor, freshly painted.

'Every room,' Kelly said, rushing down the stairs. 'Every bed's got one. They were bugging these lads then?'

There was a door in the middle of the central corridor. Locked. Renard reached for his skeleton keys.

'Can I know what we're looking for?' Kelly asked.

'Where all those wires go. It seems the place has a basement apartment. You can see the windows from outside. Blacked out.'

'I never noticed that...'

Renard simply gazed at him.

It took three different attempts then the door was open, a dark set of steps going down beyond it, steep, narrow but recently carpeted. Renard found the light switch and went ahead.

At the bottom was a single door. As they stopped, they heard a sound behind. Someone moving.

'Don't think we're alone here after all,' Kelly whispered. 'Allow me the pleasure...'

'No need,' Renard said, and walked in.

The room was in shadow, all the curtains closed. Then a light switch flipped, and they were blinking at the sudden brightness.

A woman stood by a desk at the window, stocky, middle-aged, stern-faced. She wore the khaki jacket and skirt of the Auxiliary Territorial Service and there was what looked like a service revolver in her hands.

'*Guten Tag meine Damen und Herren!* You bastards finally made it here then,' she cried. 'I ought to shoot the pair of you right now.'

CHAPTER 56

Joe Dobson turned up at the nick half an hour late, hungover, dishevelled and miserable. Chalmers was there with a handful of uniform men. They all seemed more harassed than usual and wouldn't look him in the eye.

'Office,' the superintendent said, and nodded at his lair.

There were papers stacked in tidy piles on his desk. Neatness, for Chalmers, seemed stand-in for actual work.

'Sit down. You look bloody awful.'

'Thanks.'

Half a bottle of cheap Scotch had gone down his throat the night before. There seemed nothing else to do, alone in the house on Priory Hill for once, trying to think through the future. Beth and May were never coming back to Dover. He felt sure of that. Perhaps there was the chance of a transfer to the Met and a police house somewhere. Forces everywhere had started complaining about a shortage of experienced officers. Which doubtless meant Chalmers would fight to keep him, however much the two had never got on. Anyway, it wasn't just about a job and somewhere to live. There'd been a breach in the family, something ripped apart between him and Beth, May as well. He'd played the head of the household, laid down the law, told them what to do, not listened for a second to what they wanted. The war was the excuse, but not a good one. They deserved better. He was meant to protect them. He'd tried as best he could. Tried and failed.

'I got drunk. One of those days. Felt like it.'

Chalmers looked even more unamused.

'I tried to call you. Last night. Eight or nine times. Didn't get an answer.' He leaned forward and said, 'Where were you?'

An odd question. It almost sounded like an interrogation.

'At home. Dead drunk, like I told you.'

'Too far gone to answer the telephone?'

Dobson wasn't in the mood.

'Seems so. Free country. So far. A man can drink himself stupid in his own time, can't he?'

Chalmers grunted something under his breath, then said, 'We had a big one last night. Jerry was on top form.'

That didn't sound right.

'How come? I didn't see much at all when I came in to work.'

'Not Dover. Outside. Shakespeare Halt.' He rifled through his papers. 'Got a call from the army just when I was knocking off. They were squawking like mad.'

Dobson said nothing.

'They've got a big camp down there by the railway line. All manner of stuff waiting on the invasion. But you know that already. Lieutenant Mortimer told us. That operation you were working on for him. They've got a place, haven't they?'

'What is this?'

Chalmers waved a page at him, too quickly for Dobson to read.

'The call said there was someone on the cliffs waving a light. Directing Jerry straight to those poor sods below. They did a good job, too. Bombed the living daylights out of the place. The Castle's going ballistic. The army is doing its best to recover what they can.

Lot of good men dead. Wouldn't want to be that chap with a torch when we find him.'

'Take me out of the Castle. I'll do it. Wouldn't mind some real police work for a change.'

Chalmers rifled through the papers, not that he was looking at them, just trying to avoid Dobson's eye.

'You knew Renard wanted your daughter in for questioning this morning. About this murdered woman up on Shakespeare Cliff. You knew about the bird hide too, didn't you?'

It felt hot in Chalmer's office. Dobson wondered if he was going to be sick.

'Yes to all that. I still don't understand...'

'So why did you put her on a train to London? Her and her mother? Were you going to hop it too? After...'

'After what?'

Chalmers didn't say anything. There were voices outside. A woman, screaming, shrieking curses. He knew that sound of old. It was the racket people made when they were told someone was dead.

'I can explain.'

'If it was you with that lamp on the cliffs, they'll shoot you. I'll pull the trigger myself.'

'What? *What?*'

'Where were you?'

'Home!'

'Stinking drunk?'

'As I said. Why would I do Jerry a favour?'

Chalmers glared right at him.

'You've been coming up with the surrender talk here for weeks, Dobson. People have been telling me. Telling Shearer's lot too and that comes back to my desk as well. How you said you'd work with the bastards if they showed up. Sounded as if you couldn't wait.'

Dobson wished he didn't feel so rough.

'Balls! I was just telling the truth.'

'The truth, was it?'

'Yes. Are you saying you wouldn't work with them either? You'd leave our people here to a bunch of Nazi thugs? Going round locking up who they liked? When they show up, we're going to have to swallow our pride and deal with it. Like it or not.'

'When? Not if?'

His head was pounding, his mouth dry.

'I mean if. If they come. If they win.'

Chalmers lit his pipe and blew the smoke across the table. Dobson choked and wondered again about puking.

'You still haven't told me why your wife and daughter were on that train.'

'I didn't want May here. Not with Jerry on the way and some nasty murder case hanging round. I should have let her go with the other kids when they were evacuated.'

'And your wife?'

'She couldn't be on her own. They were going to her mum's in Peckham.'

'You put an important witness on a train out of town so we couldn't do our job and talk to her?'

'I did,' Dobson said. 'She'd told me what she saw. I can write out her statement now.'

'Statements need signing, Sergeant. If they're to mean anything. You know that.'

'I'm...' He was struggling. 'I thought it was for the best. She saw a body in the bunker. That's all there is to it.'

'And last night you were on your own? No one to confirm where you were?'

'This is ridiculous. Why in God's name...?'

Chalmers ran his fingers across the table, didn't look at him when he said, 'There's never any easy way to say this, is there? But you're a copper. You know that.'

'Say what?' Dobson whispered.

'They never got to London.'

That was it. Just a few words. But the way Chalmers said them...

His head began to throb, his stomach to churn.

'What do you mean?'

'The train got stuck at Shakespeare Halt. Couldn't move. Another couple of minutes and they'd have fired up, or so I'm told...'

Sweating from the booze and the fear, Dobson struggled to his feet.

'I need to be there.'

Chalmers got up and stood in front of the door.

'You don't. I'd have sent a man round to your place during the night if we'd had anyone to spare.'

'Are they all right?' he asked and from the look on Chalmers' face he knew the answer.

'Only one poor bugger came away alive from that train and that was the driver. He's got no legs now. Maybe won't make it through the week.'

Joe Dobson found he was crying, with rage and guilt and grief. Shaking too and he didn't know what to do, to say.

'You're telling me they're dead?'

Chalmers looked a touch embarrassed then.

'No other way to say it. They're in the morgue up at the Institution. You don't need to identify them. The matron there's done that. Are you a religious man?'

'Do I look it?'

'I don't know what you look like, Sergeant Dobson. I never have all the time you've been here. Too quiet, too much thinking going on in my opinion. There's a vicar from Temple Ewell been hanging round this morning looking for business. I can arrange for him to have a word if you like.'

'I want to see them...' Dobson murmured.

'From what I've heard, I very much doubt that.'

He opened the door and called to Hawkins, the duty sergeant, to come over.

'Sorry, Dobson,' the man said, eyes on the floor.

They knew. All of them. Knew too that someone had been spreading rumours about him being missing the night before, telling tales of how he'd talked of working with the Germans.

'Put Sergeant Dobson in the custody room,' Chalmers ordered. 'Renard can deal with him. I want his belt removed. Leave him nothing he can harm anyone with, himself and you lot included.'

He pointed Dobson towards the battered green door of what was, to all intents and purposes, a cell.

'I do so hope that wasn't you out there on the cliffs last night,' said Chalmers. 'Bound to prey on a man. Bad enough betraying your own country. Killing your own wife and kid by accident into the bargain...'

Dobson didn't move. Couldn't think. The idea Beth and May were gone seemed unreal, even though it weighed on him like a nagging physical ache.

'I didn't do anything,' he whispered and knew the moment the words came out how weak and pointless they sounded.

Hawkins groaned.

'Jesus Christ, mate. You're a copper. You know they all say that. You heard the super. Off with that belt now.'

CHAPTER 57

'On balance I'd rather you put the gun down,' Renard said, scratching his chin. 'Oh, and while my German may be skimpy at best, I believe it's just *Herren*. Not *Damen*.'

The woman didn't move.

'Don't try that funny business. Name, rank, serial number. That's all you'll get out of me. You'll never quell the British bulldog, you know. Jerry doesn't have it in him.'

'I fear you've rather misread the situation.'

The gun performed a perfect circle to each of them and back.

'You speak English then?'

'Doing our very best,' Kelly said and took a step forward, beaming. 'It's Miss Perkins, isn't it? Dan Kelly. I was in your form at Deal Junior. Didn't know you'd signed up.'

'Daniel Kelly?' Finally, the gun went down. 'The lawyer's boy?'

'You were a grand teacher, Miss. Bit fierce at times to be honest, but–'

'If you're a policeman, why aren't you wearing a uniform?'

Kelly felt his lapels again.

'CID. Plain clothes. Working with Inspector Renard here. He's from Scotland Yard. Murder squad.' He winked then did a theatrical sniff. 'Ooh, is that bacon I can smell? Nothing better than nice bacon.'

The two men showed her their warrants. She slammed the revolver on the desk, picked up a pack of Navy Cut cigarettes and lit one. Tarry dark smoke mingled with the smell of frying.

'I've been stuck here for days waiting for someone to come!' she grumbled. 'Couldn't answer the door. Curtains closed night and day. Heard nothing but bombs and guns.' She jabbed a stocky finger at Kelly. 'You're not touching my bacon.'

'I'll put the kettle on,' Renard said.

A few minutes later they were sitting round the table with mugs of tea while Maud Perkins tucked into three rashers of bacon, two fried eggs and a couple of tinned tomatoes.

'I still don't understand why you've been stuck here all this time thinking Jerry had come,' Kelly said, eyeing her breakfast.

'I have no telephone, Daniel. My orders are to stay out of sight. No one's meant to know I'm here. When it went quiet... apart from all that damned noise and bombing, I assumed... well...' She glared at them. 'Instead, it appears they forgot about me. What a cheek.'

Renard eyed the desk in the adjoining room. Next to the listening station with its headphones – two sets – was a pile of lined notepads.

'How did you file your reports?'

'Didn't they tell you?'

'We're just Dover plod,' said Kelly. 'Menials.'

'One of the girls took a transcript round during the day. It's not as if they have customers here then. While I...' she blinked and waved her arms quite theatrically, 'stay trapped down here, no sign of daylight, like a flaming mole.'

Renard asked, 'How often did that happen? That you heard something of importance?'

She glared at him.

'Not my job to tell you that. Is it?'

He shrugged.

'When did you last have customers?'

'Good question. What day is it today?'

'Monday,' Kelly said.

'Right. Tomorrow I would have been relieved, then. I do one week on, one week off, with a lady from Alkham.'

'Customers,' Renard repeated.

'Thursday. One squaddie. Worse for wear. Said nothing of momentum so I never bothered to file a report. Waterloo Terrace get grumpy if they feel you're wasting their time.'

Renard was adding up the days.

'Nothing on Friday night?'

'I just told you...' She picked up his warrant card from the table and checked the name. 'Inspector. Nobody. Not till you two bounced down the stairs.'

'How many women worked here?'

He got the icy stare again.

'Is that really any of your business?'

'It is. I know one of them was Dawn Peacock.'

'Ah.' Maud Perkins put down her knife and fork and tapped some cigarette ash into an old teacup, still half full. 'The boss. Perhaps you should ask her.'

'I can't. Dawn Peacock's dead. Someone murdered her, probably on Friday night or the early hours of Saturday.'

There was a long silence. Then she put down her knife and fork and murmured, 'Oh my God.'

'You didn't hear anything like a fight here then?' Kelly asked.

Renard scowled at him.

'Did you see the slightest evidence of violence upstairs, Constable?'

'Well, no, but... maybe someone snatched her.'

'Mrs Perkins...'

'Section Leader if you don't mind. And it's Miss.'

'How many women did you have working here?'

'I didn't have *any*. My job was to eavesdrop. What went on upstairs was for them to deal with, not me. As you'd know if you'd spoken to Captain Shearer before blundering in here.'

Renard got up and went back into the office. There wasn't a single note on the desk. No sign of any recent activity.

'You shouldn't be here,' Perkins said, coming to join him.

'May Dobson. Was she one of your girls?'

The woman went pale.

'What about her?'

'She found Peacock's body,' Kelly said. 'In some secret bunker on Shakespeare Cliff.'

'My job...' she picked up the headset, '... was to listen to the men when they visited. Running the place was down to Dawn.'

'She's fifteen,' Renard said. 'A fifteen-year-old girl in a brothel.'

Maud Perkins got out another cigarette, lit it and sat down at the desk.

'I said to Dawn I thought she was very young. She was having none of it. She insisted the girl wanted to be here. She liked it.'

'How many other women?' Renard insisted.

'There were six a couple of weeks ago. They all left, except for Dawn and May. Back to London, mostly. I only talked to one. She said there was more money to be made up there, and a better class of clientele. They were street girls, weak little things. Scared about what might happen when Jerry came. They...' She hesitated, wondering whether to say it. 'The idea was we'd be stuck here behind lines, servicing the bastards. Me listening in. Sending it north. They were going to give me a radio when the balloon went up. This was a dry run to pick up any soldiers who yapped too much. Maybe even a spy. We never told them, but I think they guessed.'

'Did you find a spy?' Kelly asked.

'You need to talk to Shearer. I've said too much already. I'm going home.'

She went into the bedroom and came out with a small suitcase. They followed her up the stairs.

'Who do you think killed her?' she asked as they reached the front steps.

'The more pressing question is why,' Renard said. 'Until we understand that... When did you last see her?'

She thought for a moment.

'Now I think about it, Dawn did come round Friday afternoon. Looked a bit drained, to be honest. Tidying things up, she said. She wasn't in the Hippodrome show that night. I wondered if she was expecting company. She said she wasn't, but I listened anyway, didn't hear anything. Though sometimes...'

'Sometimes what?'

'Sometimes I think she put a pillow over the microphone. Or disconnected the wires. Dawn was only human. I imagine she needed a bit of privacy now and again. I wasn't going to argue. This was her caper.' She glanced down the road. 'I'm sorry she's gone. Funny woman. Never quite knew where you were with her. And this...' She glanced back at the house. 'Well, it was dirty work in a good cause. Still didn't make it any less dirty. If you've any more questions, ask them of Shearer. I think you've got company, by the way.'

CHAPTER 58

A uniform constable was cycling up the street in their direction as Maud Perkins stomped off towards the town centre.

'What is it, Bill?' Kelly asked when the copper turned up.

'Been looking for you all over. Chalmers is going mad.' He caught his breath. 'All went belly up with Jerry last night. Someone stood on Shakespeare Cliff and waved their bombers right in.' Another gasp. 'Got thirty dead, lots more injured. Whole camp's gone. There was a train stuck out in the open between the tunnels. Killed everyone on it except the driver and he's as good as.'

'Oh, my goodness...'

'Thing is... May and Beth Dobson were on it. Dobson was rushing them out of town for some reason, even though he knew you two wanted to talk to her this morning. Chalmers blew his top. He's chucked him into custody and says it's for you to sort out what's been going on there.'

'They're dead?' Renard asked. 'His wife and daughter are dead and the super's thrown him into a cell?'

'That's right.' He shuddered. 'Horrible just thinking about it. Dobson's gone half crazy. Can't blame him, can you? Funny bloke. Never did fit in. Don't know what's gone off, but he didn't want you talking to his daughter. Couldn't say where he was last night either, not for sure.'

Renard got out his car keys.

'We'll come right now.'

'Haven't finished,' the copper said. 'They've seen a body out at Shakespeare Cliff. Trapped halfway down. They think it's the bloke who had the lamp. He fell off from the top. Got shot by one of his own or something and–'

'I'll deal with it,' Renard said.

'Superintendent Chalmers sent me round here to say you're to leave it to the army. It's down to them.'

Kelly shuffled from one foot to the other. A habit he had when he was nervous.

'Sort of makes sense, sir. I mean a bloke on the cliffs waving a lamp...'

'I've caused the army enough work already,' Renard said with a smile. 'It's only polite we offer a hand.'

The uniform stayed where he was, hanging on to his handlebars. He waited till Renard was behind the wheel of the Hillman Minx then said to Kelly in a low and worried tone, 'Listen, Dan. I don't know what's going on round here anymore, but I don't like it. Bad enough having Jerry on the doorstep. Your bloke don't seem to be making life easier for anyone.'

'What's that supposed to mean?'

'I mean people are starting to talk. There's something funny about him. Don't pin your colours to the wrong side, pal.' He looked Kelly up and down. 'You and your fancy suit. This is Dover. We don't do airs and graces. Chalmers don't change, either. He's always looking to pass the blame on to some poor mug down the line. Dobson's in a cell, one outsider in the doodah already. Your smart arse from London's going to be next in line if he keeps on like this, you with him.'

Kelly pulled a sarcastic smile, walked off and climbed into the car. Renard had the engine idling but still hadn't put the car in gear when he said, 'If a man's just lost his wife and child, who'd throw him in a cell?'

'Joe Dobson knew you wanted to talk to May this morning. He didn't look happy when I told him up at the Castle. He had to have a reason to want her out of here.'

'She was fifteen. Someone put her in a shady, wired-up whorehouse to try to squeeze some intelligence out of the locals.'

'You heard the woman. Miss Perkins. That was all a dry run for when Jerry comes.'

'And now May Dobson and her mother are dead. What did she teach at your school?'

'PE. Sports. Used to play, too. Rugby. Seen her with boxing gloves on sometimes, in the ring with some big lads. You wouldn't mess with Miss Perkins, not if you had your head screwed on right.'

CHAPTER 59

David Shearer's office in Waterloo Crescent felt as if it was home to an editorial conference of old, one dedicated to Jessica Marshall's work alone. He sat behind his desk, swinging the chair from side to side. Ian Henderson was by the window, red pencil over her copy. Fred Lumsden perched awkwardly on a stool next to him, reaching down every few seconds to pat his dog. She took the seat opposite Shearer, like a suspect there to be interrogated.

The piece she'd written the night before about the evening in the Hippodrome had failed to make the grade for reasons she couldn't begin to understand. It was bland, atmospheric, short on detail, almost chirpy. She'd no idea what she might have done to offend Shearer's delicate sensibilities this time.

'Is someone going to tell me why you didn't wire that? I spent quite a lot of time on it. I'd really like to know.'

Shearer nodded at Henderson.

'We don't need you identifying targets, Jessica,' the young officer said. 'That's just asking for trouble.'

She was lost for an answer.

'The Hippodrome,' he went on. 'You named the theatre. You

said it was full of servicemen. May as well paint a target on the roof.'

'They only perform at night. I don't think that would be much help.'

'Very funny,' Henderson retorted.

'I wasn't trying to be funny. The Hippodrome advertises its shows in the local papers. Everyone in town must know about the place. If the Germans have spies here, and I assume you believe they have, they know what goes on there already. They've no need of a piece by me to tell them.'

'Good point,' Shearer said with a nod. He aimed his pencil at Henderson. 'I have to be honest. I only found out about this just now. He spiked it last night. I was busy elsewhere. Not my decision.'

'We have a rule about locations.' Ian Henderson didn't look pleased. 'I was following them.'

'You could have just knocked out the name,' Lumsden suggested.

'And then we'd be putting a target on the roof of every theatre and burlesque show in town.'

Shearer sniffed and told him to call the place the Theatre Royal and put the story on the wire.

'There is no Theatre Royal, is there?' Marshall said.

'No. But who's to know?'

'Anyone who's familiar with Dover and reads my copy. If I make one thing up, they'll think I'm making up the rest.'

He tapped the desk with his pencil and said, 'Another good point.'

'You really don't have any journalistic insight, do you, Captain? How on earth did you get a job with the Ministry of Information?'

He smiled.

'I wear a number of hats, Jessica.'

'I followed the rules!' Henderson protested. 'What's the point of rules if–'

'You did the right thing,' Shearer told him. 'You ticked the boxes, line by line. I, on the other hand, have discretion. Go...' He waved at the door. 'Get it out there now, leave the copy exactly as it's written. If we're to make Jessica a star she needs to file daily. To establish her name and her credentials. Wire the photo of her, too. The one that doesn't have the harbour in the background.'

The young officer left in a huff.

'He didn't like that,' she pointed out.

'It's not my job to make him happy.'

Lumsden raised a finger and said, 'What about this murder?'

'Murder?' Shearer replied.

'Knock it off, Captain,' the old man snapped. 'Some woman up on the cliffs. Cut about, from what I heard. In normal times, that'd be a story and a half.'

'Where did you hear this?'

'Good lord. Do you think people don't talk? There's the hospital. Coppers chasing things. You got all these soldiers dealing with that hut up there. Neighbour three doors down from me's a birdwatcher and he's not happy you stole their hide from them. You can't keep a secret in a place like this.'

'We need to right now.'

'You're not doing a great job of it then. Any other time, we'd have the nationals down here chasing everyone.' Shearer lit a cigarette. 'Maidstone would be sending down a team of detectives to look into what happened to that poor woman. Not leaving it to one bloke from London and a young constable.' He waved away the grey tobacco smoke that came in his direction after that. 'A woman got killed. I don't care if she was a bit loose with her social habits like they reckon. Could be an outright streetwalker for all I'm bothered. We're still owed law and order.'

'I can't write it, Fred,' Jessica Marshall said with a wry smile. 'There's no point in having this argument.'

'What made you think I was having it for you, love?'

There was an awkward silence. Shearer closed his eyes, leaned back in his chair. She checked her notebook, thinking about what story she might turn to next. The piece the night before had been just about the Hippodrome and the show there. She still had the tunnel to write about too.

'You were in the Hippodrome with Louis Renard,' Shearer said.

How he knew that she'd no idea.

'Yes. He wanted to talk to me about the Peacock woman. The one who was killed. I spoke to her briefly the week before. As you know, since you spiked that copy.'

'What did you make of him?'

It wasn't an easy question to answer.

'A nice man. Not what I'd think of as a Scotland Yard detective. A bit dishevelled if I'm honest. Almost... almost as if there's something fragile about him. I gather he was in Dunkirk. He was wounded. Why would a Scotland Yard detective find his way there?'

'Apparently he doesn't want to say,' Shearer said. 'Does he have any idea who killed this woman?'

'If he did, he didn't tell me.'

'Did he tell you anything?'

No, she thought. But there was the odd fact she'd passed on to him. About the strange way Dawn Peacock had written out her own quote for the story the Ministry had killed. Not that she was in the mood to mention that now.

'Nothing. I don't think he's a very forthcoming sort of person, except when he feels like it.'

The silence again. Then he said, 'Do you know what happened last night?'

'Just the usual, wasn't it?'

Shearer and Lumsden were silent. Whatever it was, they both knew.

'Jerry took out an entire installation in a bay along the cliffs,'

Lumsden said eventually. 'A whole squadron of them bombed the hell out of Shakespeare Halt.'

'Lots of casualties,' Shearer added. 'Lots of damage.'

'I don't know why you're telling me this, Captain. You surely won't let me write it.'

'A train was hit. The London service. Three civilian passengers, a dozen servicemen. They were all killed, along with the guard. Two of them were a mother and daughter from here. She was married to a police officer. Would you like to interview him?'

'Wait.' She didn't understand. 'Why are you asking? You'd let me run that?'

'Depends what you write. You need to talk to him first. See what he has to say. I can help with some questions.'

'You,' she said straight away, 'want to help me with some questions?'

'They might come more easily from a reporter than me.'

Enough, she thought, and got to her feet.

'I am not your property, Captain. I may let you do what you want with my copy. But I won't play these games. Nor am I interviewing a man who's just lost his wife and daughter because you want to pry into something quite beyond me.'

'Shame,' he said with a shrug. 'It's a great story.'

'I'll write about being in the tunnel. Brave Brits singing through the bombing. Bulldog spirit. All the usual rubbish.'

'Was it really like that?' Lumsden asked.

'Most people were terrified and didn't want to show it. That's not what I'm supposed to say though, is it? Oh, screw this...'

———

She grabbed her bag and marched down the stairs, stood outside by the harbour, watching the activity on the waterfront. Some boats were coming back from the west carrying what looked like mangled artillery, black and bent. The faces on the men there told their own story. They looked lost, downcast. Defeated.

Something nudged her leg. It was Benny the terrier pulling on his lead as usual.

'Must have been quite something last night,' she said as Lumsden turned up.

'Whole bunch of men got trapped round the corner. Seems someone guided the Jerry planes right in. Waved a lamp and they bombed the living daylights out of everyone.'

She wondered if she'd heard him correctly.

'They were guided there?'

'The lads below saw the light first. Called here. Called the police. They must have known they were sitting ducks.'

Jessica Marshall found the strange scene in the harbour depressing. It was all about the war: guns and men, wreckage and the forest of barrage balloons rising over everything. The Channel must have been lovely once. She wondered when it might be again.

'Why on earth would he ask me to interview a bereaved policeman? Knowing I couldn't run a single word he said?'

Lumsden chuckled.

'One thing I've learned about David Shearer over the months. There's no point in asking why he wants something. Funny, isn't it?'

'I'm not finding anything funny right now.'

'What I meant was... here are three of us. One retired reporter. One still working. One recruited to be by David Shearer's side. We all used to think our job was finding out the truth and telling people. Now it's propaganda. What he wants. Lies, if need be.'

She shook her head.

'I don't think I can do this anymore, Fred.'

He nudged her elbow.

'Oh, come on. That twerp Henderson binned your story because he's jealous. You've got a career ahead of you he could only dream of. Now fate's given him the chance to run a red pencil across your copy. Little man can't wait to do it. Nothing sadder than ambition in a chap of meagre talent promoted above his station. We've all met them. Let's go for a cuppa and a bun, eh?'

That got a laugh, anyway.

'Is that your answer to everything, a cuppa and a bun?'

'It's a start. Don't go mad on the buns though. Captain Shearer asked me to remind you he's bringing a chef and some fancy food round to give you dinner in the Raglan tonight.'

'I didn't say yes.'

'Well, you tell him that when he turns up. In the meantime, he says write your tunnel story. He'll go over it with you tonight and bring it back and wire it straight away.' His smile faded for a moment. 'Best leave Inspector Renard out of it.'

'Why?'

'Well.' Lumsden could look shifty at times. 'Never good to name names when it comes to coppers, is it? Do you reckon he'd want it, this Londoner?'

She thought about that.

'No. I'm sure he wouldn't. Why would a Scotland Yard detective be on the beach at Dunkirk?'

'Can't imagine. You'd have to ask him.'

Lumsden was grimacing at the harbour. There was something else he wanted to say.

'What is it, Fred?'

'If Joe Dobson, the copper who lost his family, wanted to speak to you? Would that make a difference?'

She felt cold.

'Dobson? He was here. I talked to him yesterday morning. It's him? His family?'

The sergeant she'd met the day before had been exhausted, but quiet and decent, or so he'd seemed.

'It is, love. I only met him a few times. Polite. Not your usual Dover copper if I'm honest.' He shook Benny's lead. 'Come on. Let's get out of here and find that cup of tea.'

267

CHAPTER 60

Renard had to leave his car close to the top of the hill after an army checkpoint blocked the way. Their warrants got them through, but only just.

'They don't want us here,' Kelly grumbled. 'Chalmers don't want us here. And these blokes have got guns.'

'Oh yes. Guns. Have you been offered one?'

The question surprised Kelly.

'No. They're like gold dust. Don't think anyone in the nick has.'

'Do you know how to use one?'

'I can learn.'

There was a busy group of figures by the bird hide. Further along towards Folkestone was the burnt-out wreck of a plane, wings folded back like those of a broken blackbird. A Nazi cross was just visible on the side.

On the clifftop an army sergeant was watching a team of eight or more heave and tug at thick ropes running over the edge as they turned up.

'Well at least that one didn't make it,' he said, nodding at the downed aircraft.

'We shot him down?' Kelly asked.

A scowl and a curse under the breath.

'Seems not. The buggers came in low and that one didn't pull up soon enough. You can see where he hit the cliff and bounced. Never knew Krauts could be such lousy drivers.' He looked at their warrants. 'What do you two want? This is an army operation.'

'We call it a murder investigation,' Renard said and walked past him to get a view of the bay below. Kelly joined him there and let out a few curses himself. The gentle curve beneath the white chalk cliffs was a scene of devastation. The tortured remains of gun emplacements, craters of pebble and brick and torn iron. A small flotilla of boats was moored along the shoreline, two with red crosses on their side, the rest taking off what equipment they could salvage.

'There's the train,' said Kelly, pointing to the right of the blackened, mangled camp. 'What's left of it.'

A sudden summer breeze rose up from below, bringing on its breath a flurry of flecks of ash, some black, some pale grey, along with the acrid smell of the incinerated. The locomotive had stopped just short of the Folkestone tunnel and now lay there on its side. What looked like four carriages were scattered behind, no longer the malachite green of the Southern Railway company, more the burnt ember of fallen branches from a tree caught in a forest fire. All the doors were open, sides torn apart, strewn across the railway lines, uprooted from the ground and twisted like a child's toy.

'Poor sods.' Kelly went right to the edge and peered over. 'To think Joe Dobson's wife and kid were in there. Why are we here exactly, sir?'

'Because someone mentioned the magic word "body" and for once I'd like to see one before the army whisks it away. And besides...'

Besides nothing, Renard thought. He knew when people were

hiding something. He'd felt that had been happening ever since this strange affair began.

A team was hauling up a body sack, hemp webbing, strapped to a military stretcher. It looked a slow and painful job, six men at the edge and three brave souls clinging to the chalk face below, every one of them roped for safety. Mountaineers, it seemed, saved from the deadly plummet to the carnage below by khaki harnesses and hemp.

An argument was going on close by – one loud voice, one quieter, upset, a woman. Renard thought he recognised it and walked over to look. A group of men in uniforms were trying to pack off a diminutive figure to a military wagon parked next to an ambulance behind the hide.

'Dammit,' he said and marched off in their direction.

'Sir...' Kelly followed, sounding worried. 'Superintendent Chalmers said quite specifically we weren't to dabble in army matters. I mean...'

There were six squaddies there: five privates who looked embarrassed and a florid-faced sergeant with a salt and pepper moustache, the one making all the noise. Poppy Webber was his target. She looked damp-eyed and exhausted in a blood-stained medical jacket.

'You're getting in the van, darling,' the sergeant yelled. 'Do it now or these lads will pick you up and throw you in there. Name's on the list and that's all that matters. I don't care who you are or what you've been doing...'

Renard stepped quickly between them, warrant card out. Kelly, to his surprise, did the same.

'Dover police,' he said. 'What's going on?'

The privates were all staring at the ground. They clearly wanted no part of it.

'Army business,' the sergeant barked. He held up a sheet of paper, four names on it, three of them crossed off. 'We've got standing orders to pick up suspect aliens and turns out this woman's on our list.'

'I'm a British citizen,' she said through clenched teeth. 'I've been working all night on the wounded and dying down on the cliff below. I am not a suspect and I'm not an alien.'

He tapped the page.

'Suspect alien. All that matters is your name's here, love.'

'Don't talk down to me.'

He held out a finger. Renard pushed his arm to one side and got a filthy look in return.

'She's coming, one way or another.'

'No. She isn't. Doctor Webber is a member of the police team in this town, Sergeant. A much-valued member. As she's already told you, she's been working all night trying to save the lives of your comrades.' He pointed to the men working the ropes on the cliffs. 'When you people finally manage to recover that cadaver, Doctor Webber here will be the only professional pathologist anywhere near East Kent who may be able to help us identify it and tell us what the hell happened here.'

He snatched the list from the man's hands and tore it to pieces in front of his face.

'If you want to be responsible for preventing that, I will happily pass on your details to Captain Shearer.' He cocked his head to one side. 'What is your name, by the way?'

One moment's hesitation. That was all Renard needed to know he'd won.

There was a shout at the cliffs. The hemp sack was there, in the arms of the team at the top. The climbers scrambled over the edge, breathless.

'Please take him to the ambulance,' Poppy Webber cried.

'Ma'am,' said one of the squaddies, with a salute. 'And thank you for your kindness down there at the Halt.'

It only took two of them to lift the sack. Renard watched,

feeling, as always, the curious mix of dread and prurient curiosity that accompanied an unexplained corpse. The cause appeared obvious. The man had seemingly slipped over the edge of the cliff in the dark and fallen a good forty feet or so onto a hard outcrop. As always, Renard regarded the obvious with the deepest of suspicion.

The sergeant seemed deflated, which was heartening to see. Renard hated bullies, always had.

'I apologise, sir, if I seemed abrupt. I didn't realise you were a colleague of Captain Shearer's.'

'Now you know.' Renard slapped him on the shoulder, gave him a hard stare. 'But perhaps it's Doctor Webber you should say sorry to.'

'Of course. I...'

She was marching over to the ambulance already. Duty always called, Renard guessed. Except there she sat down on the back step, head in hands, shaking. The sergeant sloped off to the team on the cliffs. A couple of the privates glanced at Renard. One winked and mouthed, 'Thanks.'

'Go ask around, Kelly. See if you can pick up any bits of information.'

'About what?'

'About how two corpses a couple of days apart connect with this place. I don't believe in coincidences and nor should you.'

He sat down next to her at the back of the ambulance. The sacking with the cadaver was inside, covered up.

'Doctor.'

'Poppy, please.'

'Louis.'

He held out his hand and they shook, which seemed odd. Renard had lost his touch with women and he knew it.

'Men in uniform do as they're told,' he said. 'They rarely question orders. That may be a good thing. It may be bad. The trouble is, you rarely find out which until later.'

That didn't seem to impress her.

'I've been down there at the Halt all night. I've never seen anything like it. People torn to pieces. There were... there were two women. Civilians.' Tears began to shine in her eyes, like liquid pearls. Soon they ran in sluggish streams down her cheeks. He didn't think she cried much. But then, he didn't know her. 'They were in each other's arms. They died that way, as if they loved one another.'

'They did, I'm sure. They were mother and daughter.'

She wiped her face with the sleeve of her bloody medical jacket. 'You know who they are?'

'We do. The father's a police sergeant. There's still a lot we... I... don't understand.'

Poppy Webber was glaring at the soldiers.

'When they kept saying my name was on their stupid list... all I could think of, all that went through my mind, was I might have been in Germany. That's just what the Nazis do. Or Spain under Franco. God, you never get away from them, do you? They just pull out a piece of paper. Say, "You're ours now". Then you're gone. God knows where.' She gazed right at him. 'I've got relatives that's happened to. Friends as well. I never thought I'd see it here.'

It was a mistake, Renard told her. Some bureaucratic civil servant had probably discovered her father was German, her mother half Spanish, and added her name to a detention list without a second thought.

'I imagine they'd have pulled you in, questioned you, then, when they found out who you are, let you go.'

'You imagine that, do you?' she replied, quite cross. 'How do you think I imagine it? A bunch of uniformed heavies demanding I climb into their truck with them or else?'

Kelly was at the cliff edge talking to the climbers.

'I'm sorry. There are few niceties in war, it seems. And the few we have may be disappearing rather quickly.'

She grimaced and said, 'I shouldn't be taking this out on you. But you chose to be the nearest. Your fault entirely.'

'The body...?'

They'd take it back to the morgue at the Institution. She needed a few hours' sleep. After that she'd take a serious look.

Poppy Webber looked up at the bright blue sky.

'It was very dark last night. Hardly any moon. We had to bring in lights to deal with the injuries down there. I suppose it would be easy to slip off the cliff.'

'It would help to see a face.'

She got to her feet, grumbling about feeling creaky and tired. Poppy Webber looked ready to fall fast asleep. All the same, she was inside the ambulance before him, pulling back the sacking.

The body was badly mutilated. Bone as visible as blood.

'He must have taken a battering when he fell,' Renard said.

'I'll let you know later.' She bent down and took a closer look at the face. 'He had previous. This isn't all fresh. He's just a boy.'

Renard nodded.

'Just a boy.'

Kelly came racing across.

'Sir, sir.'

'What is it?'

'From what they said,' Kelly climbed into the van, 'it sounds like the blighter waving his torch to bring in all them Jerries, it was...'

Renard pointed at the body, the face, battered from Frank Lee's fists. Bruises from Joe Dobson somewhere, too.

'Harry Lee?' Kelly cried. 'Harry Lee, a kid, causing all that mayhem below?'

'What on earth do you mean?'

'I mean this. It was slung round his neck on a strap. They took it off to get him in the bag.'

In his hands was a tall black metal can with what looked like a closed eye on the front.

'Lamp Electric Number One,' Kelly said. 'Everyone in the nick's got one.'

'I haven't.'

'Well, you're new, aren't you? It's a torch. Good kit as well. You can lift that flap up the front and get maximum light. Or keep it half shut and walk along with just a little beam on the ground. But I mean... Harry Lee waving in Jerry...'

Renard ushered him out of the van.

'We should leave this to the doctor. Time to go back to the nick. Oh...' He smiled at her and she smiled back too, a little. 'Poppy. Please forget about that nonsense with the list. Consider it dealt with.'

Five minutes later they were in the car headed down the hill.

'Can you do that?' Kelly asked. 'Tell that lady doctor they won't come for her again?'

'The magic of the name "Captain Shearer" seems to have escaped you. As long as we can keep throwing that at people it seems we can get away with murder.'

'Harry Lee. Has to be that father of his behind all this, I reckon. Harry wasn't a bad lad. Just easily led.'

'You think, Constable Kelly?'

'I do, sir. What about you?'

No answer.

Kelly leaned back in the passenger seat and put his hands behind his head.

'It's Poppy now, is it?'

Renard said nothing, just kept driving down the road.

CHAPTER 61

There was a black Bentley in the police station car park. It took up the space of two police saloons. A man in a Homburg hat was sitting in the driving seat, another in khaki uniform next to him. They both got out as Renard parked along the way.

Kelly was on it in a flash. The young copper was turning out to be smarter and more alert than he'd first appeared.

'Oh bugger,' he murmured. 'That...' a finger straight ahead, '... is Sir James Mortimer. Lord Lieutenant of Kent. The king's–'

'The king's representative in the county. Yes.'

'You know him then?'

'We had drinks two nights ago at Temple Ewell. A garden party for the new vicar.'

'You do move in the right circles. He doesn't show up here without a reason.'

'Who's the other one?'

'Lieutenant Tobias Mortimer. His son. Runs the Cordelia show from the Castle.' Kelly scratched his head. 'Joe Dobson's boss. Or, well, the chap he answered to up there.'

Renard said he'd see him inside the nick and waited. It was obvious who they'd come for.

Mortimer Senior smiled when he saw them. His son didn't. He must have been a late child. Mortimer Senior was a widower, Veronica said, and had been for some years, content in a house on the bay of St Margaret's with a spectacular view across the Channel. Tobias Mortimer was a product of military college, now married to the army. The two were all that was left of a line that ran back centuries, to the Norman invasion, Veronica had said, though whether she was joking he'd no idea. Still, Renard remembered what she had told him about the county being essentially feudal. Both had the appearance of lords of the manor.

Renard walked over, was introduced to the son, and the two shook hands. Mortimer Junior looked as if he'd rather be elsewhere.

'Lieutenant. Sir James. How can I help?'

'Oh, for God's sake drop the titles. It's James. This is Tobias. Well, Louis. How are you enjoying Temple Ewell?'

'Very much. It's good to be near my aunt. In times like these...'

James Mortimer laughed, a deep, pleasant and throaty sound.

'As I believe I said, you don't need to worry about your aunt. If Hitler should turn up, I'm sure she'll put him in his place. People worry too much about the future. The only thing that should concern us at the moment is the present. Do you agree?'

Renard could not read this conversation at all.

'How can I help?' he asked again.

'You can find out if your man Dobson's jeopardised months of my hard labour,' Tobias Mortimer said. 'And why this damned police station sent me someone I couldn't trust.'

'Sergeant Dobson lost his wife and daughter in the attack last night. I doubt he's going to be making much sense for a while.'

'He knows everything. Every bunker. Every weapon and munitions store. The name of every last man we've recruited. I now learn he's been speaking favourably about the Germans!'

James Mortimer intervened.

'I had a word with Superintendent Chalmers this morning. He

was wondering what to do about Dobson. The man sent his wife and daughter out of town when he knew you wanted to interview the girl. He's been saying some odd things of late.'

'It seems that way,' Renard said.

'I suggested it would be wise to detain him for interview.'

If Chalmers had wanted advice from anyone it would surely be a senior officer in Maidstone, the chief constable even. Not the lord lieutenant, holder of a position that was meant to be largely honorary.

'We'll do our best to get to the bottom of what's happened. A woman's been murdered. My priority–'

'The death of some tart from the shows is scarcely a matter of priority,' Lieutenant Mortimer said. 'We're expecting Jerry at any moment. My father here virtually lives on his landing point.'

James Mortimer looked less than pleased.

'This isn't an argument to have in front of others, is it?' He turned to Renard. 'My house happens to be just above the beach. It is quite exposed...'

'Exposed? When they land, Father, they'll come straight through you.'

'Then I'll get my shotgun and wait for them at the top of the cliff. With you. We are taking precautions, Tobias. Rest assured. You're not the only one fighting this war.'

The lieutenant swore, glanced at his watch and said he had to be off. There was a meeting back at the castle. He was expecting to be hauled over the coals about the breach in security over the bunker on Shakespeare Cliff. And much else besides.

'The young,' James Mortimer said as his son marched off towards a racing-green two-seater sports car, a Morgan Roadster if Renard wasn't mistaken – one of the flash boys at the Yard owned one too. 'So much impatience. I gather you have no family of your own.'

'I have Veronica.'

'I meant children.'

'I'm not married.'

'She did say. I forgot.'

Mortimer Junior roared out of the car park, spinning his wheels on the asphalt for no reason Renard could imagine.

'I apologise for my son's abruptness. The uniform's gone to his head. He'll be in terrible trouble if it turns out your man Dobson is behind any of this.'

Kelly had poked his head out of the back door of the nick and was waving at him.

'I think I'm wanted. As I said, my job is to find who murdered a young woman called Dawn Peacock.'

'I know, Inspector.' Not Louis anymore. 'But if you come across anything that can help my son understand if Cordelia has indeed been breached, and if so by how much, you would be doing your duty to let us know.'

'You or him?'

Mortimer scowled.

'I think you'll find my place more amenable than a Nissen hut. Pop round for a drink. I get bored on my own. Bring Veronica. It's ages since she came over.' He smiled. 'I can show you where Jerry thinks he'll turn up. Quite a view.'

He reached forward and patted Renard on the jacket.

'That gun I gave you. You don't seem minded to wear it.'

'As far as I'm aware, most of our men are still waiting on their firearms. I don't want it to appear I'm boasting.'

Mortimer bit his lip, thinking.

'If you believe you're getting near one of these bastards...'

'Then I'll carry it.'

'Good man! Jerry knows nothing of manners. And remember what we do to traitors these days. It's either the firing squad or the rope.' He kept looking at Renard. 'Do you own a hat?'

'In London.'

'I believe you can still buy them here. Hitler hasn't closed down the millinery trade yet.'

'Fair point,' he said, then smiled and walked inside.

A tall man, handsome, almost like an actor, was lounging against the reception desk. He wore a sharp dark suit and was smoking a cigarette. Renard listened to the conversation between him and the duty sergeant.

So that was what Captain David Shearer looked like.

CHAPTER 62

Fred Lumsden and the dog took her to a different café. One near the station, more local, rougher, a few squaddies there. One of them made a coarse remark and with that Lumsden was up on his feet, berating the man.

All he got in return was a mouthful of foul curses.

He came back, somewhat subdued.

'I know it's not easy, love, but try and ignore them. You get this with blokes in uniform, thinking they might have to fight for their lives before long.'

'You sound as if you're speaking from experience?'

He shook his head.

'No. Observation. That's what reporters do, isn't it? Look at people. Try to work them out. I was too old for the last one. Being a reporter meant I was in a reserved profession anyway. They wanted the papers running. We were part of keeping people's spirits up.' He scowled at the teacake crumbs in front of him. 'Bloody stupid, that whole show was. This time round I can see we're up against a monster. That first one though...' Fred Lumsden gulped at his tea. 'No real reason for it at all. Just toffs playing a game with people's lives. I lost my kid brother and a nephew, all for nothing.'

She touched his hand and said she was sorry.

'Their fault. They fell for it all. Couldn't wait to get to the frontline. I'd understand that with Hitler. Not back then. Also...' He looked upset for once. 'It was what we put the Germans through after we won it that made him. Hitler. We kicked them so hard they couldn't wait for the opportunity to kick back.'

That, she knew, was true, not that anyone was supposed to say it. Living in Berlin she'd met plenty of decent locals who hated the Nazis but understood it was the economic depression after the first war that gave them a path to power.

'People told me that in Germany, too. Not that they thought it was an excuse.'

He grimaced.

'Too late for excuses. War, it's a disease. An epidemic. It doesn't just kill people. Pulls the living apart, too. I mean... look at us. Doing Shearer's bidding. Twisting things. Forget about going to talk to Joe Dobson. Seemed a nice enough chap to me. Came from some rough bit of London. Thought that house they gave him in Priory Hill was a palace next to what they had. Poor bugger's just lost his wife and young girl.'

She'd never seen him so upset.

'Beth Dobson was a lovely woman. A nurse up at the Institution. We'd run pictures of her in the paper. She was always doing things for charity. Looked after my wife during those last few months. So kind. Unbelievable...'

'And the girl?'

He didn't look her in the eye.

'May. Fifteen, I think. They should have let her go with all the other young 'uns when they were evacuated. Beth moaned at me when I met her shopping a few months back. Joe wouldn't hear of it. He wanted to keep her in town.' He shut his eyes for a moment.

'She was so pretty. God knows what she was getting up to. You hear all kinds of stories...'

'Like what?'

'Hanging around the wrong places. Wrong people. Theatre folk. Squaddies.' He rapped his teaspoon on the table. 'Can't leave kids to themselves in times like this. They need protection. Guidance. And anyway... what would you say to a man like Joe Dobson when he's just seen his whole family wiped out?'

She'd no idea. That wasn't her kind of reporting, as the awkward conversation with Edith Winter had shown. Without Fred Lumsden's help she would never have made a story out of that. Even one that was in part fictitious.

'Inventing stuff...' he grumbled. 'That's not what we're about.'

'Aren't we?' She stirred the dregs of her tea. 'I always thought we invented our own lives. Either that or someone else does it for you. I've been inventing mine for as long as I can remember. Not sure I know how to stop.'

'Well...' He got up, and the dog too. 'I'll be going then.'

She'd embarrassed him. It was obvious.

'Thanks for your help, Fred.'

'Not sure I have really,' he muttered, then went off to the counter to pay.

CHAPTER 63

The streets were busy. The usual army vehicles everywhere, soldiers marching round with their rifles. No police anywhere as far as she could see.

One story a day. That was the rule from now on. If she was to use Shearer's link to the outside world, to Toronto and the syndication feeds to the other papers in the Commonwealth, she had to deliver regularly. That had been her mistake in the interim between Paris and London. Thinking she had time to write, to produce the perfect finished piece. But she was no Ernest Hemingway, a novelist with a sideline as a war correspondent, however much she longed for that. The necessary literary talent was elusive if it existed at all. Just as importantly, Toronto wanted something that passed as news, not an exercise in fine writing.

The night in the tunnel was a story, one she had in her notebook, in her head too. But the tone and the spirit of it – another paean to English stubbornness and sparky courage in the face of imminent invasion – was identical to the piece she'd filed the night before about the atmosphere in the Hippodrome. She needed to vary the timbre of these dispatches from the front. They couldn't all be jingoistic stories about the legendary British stiff upper lip.

The piece about Edith Winter had gone down well. A lost husband, an injured son. But the tragic death of the wife and daughter of a serving policeman in an attack on a civilian train... that had more drama, more tragedy, more promise. As did the murder of a showgirl, if only she could find some way to get the story past David Shearer.

Something about Dawn Peacock nagged at her too. Louis Renard's reaction had made her think about the brief encounter in Effingham Terrace again. What happened there – the woman's insistence she write her own quote in her notebook – was extraordinary. If asked, she'd have written down the words in longhand and showed them to her. Though perhaps scribbling them down herself hammered home the point that they were supposed to be used.

There was also the quiet interest Louis Renard had. He was not a man who showed his feelings easily, but she could sense there was something in what she said that caught his attention. Perhaps it was the way Shearer had turned up so conveniently just when she went back to the house where she first saw the woman.

It was a short walk away. There wasn't a soul around as she trudged up the slight hill towards the dilapidated mansion. The weather was cooler, the smell of smoke and gunpowder less marked than usual. The night had been quieter than any she'd spent in the town. Attacks on military encampments like Shakespeare Halt apart, perhaps Hitler was shifting his anger somewhere else. Odd if he really was about to storm the southern coast.

The rubbish had gone. The windows were still blacked out, even the basement ones now, so perhaps someone was at home. Half hoping, she went to the front door and banged the giant brass lion knocker.

All this was prevarication, surely. A way of avoiding the truth that she still didn't have a worthwhile story to file. The more she thought about the tunnel and the time she'd spent with Louis Renard, the more she began to think that was a piece to be saved for a later date. Perhaps written now but tucked away in the pocket of the typewriter case, stored for when it was needed. A reporter on the road never knew when the foreign desk might come on, demanding copy, anything to meet an editor's demands. Not that she seemed to be under the thumb of Calhoun in Yonge Street anymore. David Shearer appeared to have taken over that role.

One more try with the knocker. No answer. She turned round and almost jumped out of her skin. A hefty, middle-aged woman with a short, mannish haircut stood in front of her, blocking the path to the road.

'Who the hell are you and what do you want?'

'Nothing. I mean...'

'This is private property.'

She pulled out her press ID.

'I'm a reporter. *Toronto Inquirer.*'

The woman checked the card and handed it back.

'What are you doing here?'

The woman retrieved her own ID out of her burgundy cardigan and brandished it like a weapon.

'Section Leader Perkins,' said Jessica Marshall. 'Very good. Is this your house?'

'It's not yours.'

'The ATS. That's like women soldiers, isn't it? *There's* a story for me. Even Captain Shearer will be happy with that.'

The name got some kind of reaction, though what precisely, she wasn't sure.

'What do you know of Shearer?'

'I'm here under his wing, as it were. You don't think we can run around Dover unchecked, surely?' She nodded at the house. 'Is anyone home?'

'Why do you want to know?'

She wasn't going to give this pushy, aggressive woman what she wanted.

'I was trying to work out how this place connects with someone called Dawn Peacock. I talked to her here. Outside, anyway. A week ago. Now she's dead. Murdered.'

Perkins looked a touch shaken.

'You can't write about that. You can't write about any of it.'

'No... *Section Leader*. I can't. Because I don't know what happened.'

The woman was on her, mouth full of curses, beefy arms wrapped round Jessica Marshall's slight frame, dragging her to the pavement. It was a furious, unprovoked outburst. It hurt too and Maud Perkins was so powerful there was nothing she could do to prevent it.

'I don't give a rat's arse what piece of paper you're carrying from Shearer,' Perkins spat at her when she was almost in the road. 'Get lost, you prying little cow, and don't come back. There's nothing for your kind here.'

Half an hour later, Jessica Marshall was back in her room in the Raglan listening to the planes, high overhead this time, headed elsewhere. The last of Shearer's Scotch spilled from the brim of the glass in her left hand. The typewriter sat in front of her, two sheets of paper separated by a battered carbon rolled through the carriage.

The page was quite blank.

CHAPTER 64

Joe Dobson sat at the table in the interview room, no tie, no jacket, trousers loose, no belt it seemed. His head was down as he shuffled about on the uncomfortable metal chair the nick reserved for interviews.

Chalmers was lurking at the desk while Renard and Kelly waited by the door, ready to start.

'They're out looking for Frank Lee,' Kelly said. 'No sign of him at the cottage. Lieutenant Mortimer says he was supposed to show for more training up at the Castle this morning. Nothing.' He ran through the pages of his notebook. Very tidy writing, Renard thought, much better than his own. 'Seems Harry nicked someone's pushbike from the station last night. Told the platform man there his girlfriend was on the train pulling out.'

'Why would he do that?'

'The bloke let him know the train was going to be stuck at Shakespeare Halt. Problems on the line. Maybe Harry thought he could get down and see her or something. Little idiot.'

'Love. You'd be amazed what it makes men do.' Renard hesitated for a moment. He hadn't been sufficiently generous towards Kelly, who seemed a decent, intelligent young fellow. 'Well done, anyway. Go and check out Lee's place for yourself.'

'They've been there already! He's not around.'

'That doesn't mean there's nothing to be found. Get on your motorbike. See if you can find something uniform missed. That's what we do in CID, Constable. Fill in holes. Join the dots. Go and find some. They're not in this place, I assure you.'

'Inspector...' Chalmers called him over as a grumbling Kelly walked out of the door. Shearer was with him now.

'Sir?'

'This is—'

'Captain Shearer. I've heard much about you.'

'The good parts are true,' Shearer said with a quick grin. 'The rest is invention. Given the security implications here, I need to sit in on your interview. I trust that's not a problem.'

Renard opened the door.

'Superintendent Chalmers?'

There wasn't the least chance the man was going to take part, but he wanted to make the invitation all the same.

'This circus is all yours, Renard. Every last piece of it,' the man said with a scowl, then marched back to his office.

Just the two of them then, with the miserable Dobson across the table. He'd have to make his own notes and hope he could still read them afterwards.

Renard went straight over and bent down in front of the man.

'I'm deeply sorry to hear about your family, Sergeant. There are no useful words in circumstances like these.'

Dobson looked up, face full of grief and anger, eyes pink.

'They took my belt off me. My tie. They threw me in a cell. My wife and daughter are in the hospital and they won't let me see them.'

'I'm sorry to say this,' Shearer interrupted, 'but the injuries from what happened last night do not make a pretty sight. The whole of the bay was wiped out.' He stared straight at Dobson. 'With the help of someone local.'

The sergeant stared right back but kept quiet.

'Tea,' Renard said. 'I think it's time for tea. Have you eaten, Sergeant?'

'I don't want anything.'

'Well, let me get some tea anyway.' He stopped at the door. 'Harry Lee. I believe you had an altercation with him.'

Dobson sighed.

'That I did. Lost my rag. Stupid.'

'He's dead. We found him halfway down the cliff above the Halt. He had a lantern on a strap around his neck. It's possible he fell in the dark.'

The sergeant blinked.

'Harry? Dead?'

'Very.'

'Are you trying to tell me that little idiot waved Jerry in?'

'No,' Renard said, satisfied. 'I'm not.'

He went and got a pot of tea, a plate of biscuits and three cracked mugs then brought them back on a tray.

It didn't look as if a word had passed between the two men while he was out.

'I brought some digestives too,' he said, handing round the plate. 'Not chocolate, I'm afraid. Hard to come by these days. Tell me about Dawn Peacock.'

'I picked her up,' Dobson said. 'A week, ten days ago. Warned her for soliciting. Wrote a report. Never got looked at, for some reason.'

'Why?'

'I heard her cursing. She'd had a few drinks. It was German, I swear. Then she's dead...'

'I believe Dawn Peacock is the least of our worries,' Shearer said with something close to a yawn. 'We had an attack on an important installation last night. Given two teenagers were found trying to spoon one another in one of our bunkers, there's every reason to think Cordelia has been breached. Next to that–'

Dobson flew at him. Straight over the table, hands going for Shearer's throat. Renard was there in a flash, between them, prising the two men apart. One elbow to Dobson's chest sent the man sprawling to the floor.

'You put my daughter in your bloody brothel,' he yelled, slumped against the wall. 'Fifteen, she was. *Fifteen.*'

'I want him handcuffed,' Shearer said, straightening his tie. 'The man's out of his mind.'

Renard walked over, picked Dobson up, helped him to his seat.

'Do that again and I will cuff you, Sergeant.'

'He made my daughter a whore!' An accusing finger, spittle flying from his mouth. 'She told me why she did it. That Peacock woman and her lies...'

'This isn't why we're here,' Shearer said. 'I want to know where you were last night, Sergeant. I want to know why you were so keen to get your family out of Dover. What knowledge prompted that event.'

Renard let the room go quiet then passed around the tea and biscuits again.

'All in good time,' he said eventually. 'First, I'd like to know about Dawn Peacock. In particular, why a report by a sergeant here of someone speaking German, well...' He took a sip of tea. 'Why it was never acted upon.'

'Anything else?' the captain asked instead.

'Yes,' said Renard. 'I'd also like to hear why you killed a rather anodyne article by Jessica Marshall, which mentioned Miss Peacock in harmless, it seems to me, terms.' He smiled. 'And why a copy of that article was sitting on Superintendent Chalmers' desk for some reason.' He held out the plate. 'May I interest you in a digestive?'

The man in the dark suit said nothing.

CHAPTER 65

Dan Kelly lifted his pristine, polished BSA Gold Star onto its stand outside the hovel that was home to the Lees. The machine was his pride and joy. Another two years and seven months and it would be paid off. Three generations of Lees had lived in this primitive tied farm cottage, Frank being the worst, more violent, more crooked than even his own jailbird father. Harry might have escaped the family habits if only he'd lived. There wasn't much bad about the kid, from what Kelly had seen on his occasional appearances in the nick. He just kept poor company: his father's.

The place bore the illusory name of Swan Cottage, but it was little more than a tumbledown red-brick wreck stranded at the end of a dead-end earth track out of sight from the narrow lane, a quarter of a mile away, the only way to reach it. It was surrounded on all sides by fields of wheat and barley, a golden host of ripe ears waving in the brisk late-summer breeze. Somewhere nearby a tractor was out harvesting. Kelly could hear an old, asthmatic engine and the air was hazy with the miasma of harvest, dust settling everywhere and with it the rich, warm smell of threshing. As always, that gave him the start of a sore throat. Growing up in

Walmer had made Dan Kelly a seaside man. Salt air was more to his taste.

This was a part of the countryside behind Dover he barely knew. There was no reason to come out here, unless they were chasing the Lees, something he'd never done in person. But as he walked round the place, wondering how long its tumbledown catslide roof was going to last, he realised he wasn't as far from the coast as he expected. The wreck of the downed Nazi plane was visible, a blackened corpse on the distant green clifftop. The bird hide where Dawn Peacock had been murdered stood no more than a mile or so away, an easy walk defined by the hedges leading to the Folkestone road. It occurred to him that it was little more than twenty-four hours since he'd stood with Louis Renard in the hidden bunker beneath that place, looking at bloodstains, starting to think like a detective, something that had never happened to him before. He wasn't sure what to make of the man from London. There was a reticence, a distance about the chap's manner, as if there was something he didn't want others to know. Or perhaps to acknowledge himself. But he seemed pleasant enough, genuine too and with a keen and intelligent insight Kelly hadn't noticed around Dover nick before. Something to be learnt there – and that was a first in a police station usually given over to routine crime, drunks and violence, larceny and the petty motoring misdemeanours of the magistrates' court.

He stopped outside the front door and took a good look down to the coast again. There were planes in the sky, heading over from France. No aerial battles at that moment, but they were surely Jerry's on their way to create mischief. He could only hope the Spitfires and Hurricanes would meet them soon and give the Nazis a bloody nose. A couple of ships lay close to mid-Channel, whose he'd no idea. These were common sights now, ones he scarcely thought about. The war was strange. In a way it had become almost mundane over the past few months. Explosions day and night, shells from across the water, bombs from the air. People rushing for the shelters, some with lunch packs of sandwiches and bottles of beer to keep them going during those long hours underground. Dog fights in the blue summer sky. Aircraft ditching in cold grey waters where the freezing sea might kill you as easily as the bullets. Nightly sorties by unseen aircraft met with deafening artillery rounds from the emplacements dotted in and around the town. This was normality now, an extraordinary one taken for granted after a while.

If he'd learned one tip from the new inspector, it was to challenge the idleness that came from repetitive experience. To approach the routine as if it was all new. Renard's challenge to him, barely spoken, was to be more observant, more questioning about everything he saw, however uninteresting it might appear. A Dover detective of old, one of the grumpy plain-clothes squad who once ruled the roost, put villains in court on the basis of history. If there was a burglary, a Lee did it, so you pulled Frank in and found out where he'd been. That worked, to an extent. But there were times when evidence was manufactured, statements dictated, police notebooks forged. All to put the guilty away, of course, even if you had to con the courts to do so.

What never happened was the kind of policing Louis Renard seemed to prefer: deduction, detection, the creative distillation of truth out of a combination of research and, on occasion, imagination. This was a different kind of police work, one that interested him greatly.

'Stop thinking, chum, start doing,' he said to himself and walked to the front of the cottage.

'Frank! Frank Lee! Are you home or what? I got news for you. Not nice news either, but you've got to hear it.'

It must have been a couple of hours since the uniforms were out here. Lazy pair, too. He was sure they'd probably just have banged on the door, hung around for a minute or two to see if there was an answer, then sidled off back to the nick. No one liked doing death knocks, telling people their relatives had copped it. It was still part of the job.

'Frank!'

From what he remembered, Lee ran an old and probably unsafe farm van with an enclosed back, useful for stuff he'd nicked. There was no sign of it anywhere, no tyre tracks either. Perhaps the thing had finally conked it.

One last time he called out Lee's name. Then he walked all the way round once more, ticking off what was there. The kitchen door was ajar. He went in anyway. Frank Lee was the last man in the world to start screaming about warrants.

The place had a sweaty, evil smell about it. The sink was full of dirty plates. A frying pan thick with congealed fat and bacon rind was on the wood-fired stove. Two bedrooms upstairs, both with unmade mattresses and dirty, dishevelled sheets.

'Mr Lee!'

Nothing. He came back downstairs. Went into the last room, a tiny hole with a single dingy window, an empty fireplace, one big chair. It was hard to believe a teenager lived here. There couldn't have been much for Harry Lee at all.

'Well, Daniel,' he said to himself, 'that was a right old waste of time.'

He thought about taking a different route back to town. Maybe go across the fields. They were dry and the BSA could cope with anything.

Then he looked outside again. There was a primitive separate privy round the back, the door open, a filthy toilet pan behind it, a stack of torn newspapers by the side. Beyond that a ramshackle shed, too big for a private garden, more the kind of outbuilding found on a smallholding or a modest farm. Details were what mattered and that was one he noted. There was a padlock and a chain on the door. Something farmers never bothered with.

Kelly looked around, called Frank Lee's name one last time.

The wood on the double doors was rotten. The chain and the lock came off with three good kicks.

He stuck his head inside. The place was barely lit. He should have brought a torch. Never go anywhere without one, they used to say when he was in uniform.

He shouldered the double doors open. Inside lay crate after wooden crate, stacked two high, all with army markings on the side. The lids on the nearest were open. Dan Kelly peered in and let out a long, amused whistle.

'Oh, Frank. You are a naughty boy. Me and my mates down the nick getting fobbed off with stories about how there aren't enough guns to go round...'

Here they were, aplenty. Revolvers. And as he worked round the other cases there was ammunition, daggers too, the military kind he'd seen up at the Castle, slender, scary-looking things that gave him the shivers.

He walked further inside. One case had helmets. Another, boxes of rations. The next...

The wooden lid was half open when a voice behind made him jump.

'And who do you think you are?' said a hard, low voice out of the shadows.

Automatically, he reached for his warrant card.

'Detective Constable Kelly. I think we need a chat, Frank. Don't you? And not just about–'

He didn't get to finish. Something hit him. Dan Kelly fell to the floor, whimpering under a rain of blows so hard, so fast, so relentless, that even the lessons he'd learned at Deal Boxing Club failed him.

The next thing he heard, how long after he'd no idea, was the sound of an engine. A familiar one. The deep and rhythmic thump of a BSA 500cc single cylinder getting kicked into life.

CHAPTER 66

'Do you know what *Unternehmen Seelöwe* is, Renard?'

That threw him.

'I have very little German, Captain Shearer.'

'Sergeant Dobson?'

No answer.

'*Unternehmen Seelöwe*. Operation Sea Lion. It's the name of Hitler's plan to invade England. Starting here.' He gestured at the window. 'Right here. Along the coast as well, of course, but from what we know Dover will bear the brunt. The place could fall in a day or so. Heavy casualties. Within a week, the Nazis could easily be halfway to London. This town, the people who survive, will be the first in England to find themselves living beneath the jackboot.'

Dobson lifted his head and said, 'And what the hell has that to do with my daughter?'

'Because we all must play our part.' He picked up a biscuit and took a bite. 'Dawn Peacock's real name was Anna Schmidt. Born here to Austrian parents. Talented at languages. Could speak English like a Brit, German like a German. We recruited her in Berlin seven years ago. She was a dancer, an actress, a woman not reluctant to sleep around if we gave her reason and the right rewards. Good at getting men to talk. Showy, talkative, attractive if blowsy. A perfect spy in many ways. Just before war broke out, we had reason to fear the Nazis knew what she was up to. Out of caution and loyalty we spirited her away here.'

He stopped, as if remembering something.

'A very brave woman, if a little spontaneous at times. She loathed Hitler. She told me she'd do anything – *anything* – to fight them. I trusted her completely.'

'My daughter!'

Shearer looked vaguely apologetic.

'I'm sorry. I realise that's a terribly inadequate thing to say in the circumstances. I'd no idea Anna had taken your girl into Effingham Terrace. Frankly, I'd no knowledge of what went on there, nor did I wish to be told the details.'

'You like to keep some distance, I imagine,' Renard said.

'Results interest me. Not how they are gained. It was important for security reasons that the woman be allowed to do whatever she wanted without having to report directly to me. We had an officer hidden away in the basement listening to conversations in the bedrooms. The girls offered what they could as well. Anything incriminating said there came back to me. The means, I didn't know about and I didn't want to. We needed the place to appear nothing but a discreet, private... enterprise.'

'She was fifteen,' Dobson said.

'I didn't know. I told you I was sorry, Sergeant. There are only so many times I can repeat it.'

'You bastard...'

'If being a bastard keeps this nation free, I'll live with that.'

'The article,' Renard said.

Shearer hesitated, as if wondering whether to go on.

'I need to know, Captain.'

'You don't. All the same...' There was the sound of a low-flying aircraft somewhere. Then a volley of artillery. Shouts in the street. A distant explosion. Truck engines getting revved. 'There were specific rules. Anna... *Dawn* was not to contact anyone in my team directly. I wanted to make sure no one could track the operation back to us. We agreed a series of code words. Phrases she could use in some way, in a note, say. Or a letter. Seemingly innocuous. But they would have a meaning to me.'

Renard pulled the folded-up article out of his pocket.

'This quote. She wrote it down for the reporter. Directly in her notebook.'

Shearer took the pages from him, flicked through them, then stamped his finger on a single sentence.

'"The devil's favourite piece of furniture is the long bench". She came up with it. If I got that message, it meant she believed she was in danger. The ring had perhaps been compromised. It was a cry for help. By the time I heard it, she was dead. The whole elaborate enterprise scuppered, and perhaps Cordelia with it.'

He turned to Dobson.

'Sergeant. You were up there in the Castle. How many men knew about that bunker?'

'Scores. I told them all that already. There were the volunteers Mortimer recruited. Engineers to build it. The quartermaster and his men who put in the stores.'

Shearer looked gloomy.

'As I thought. I've lost an operative to God knows who. While we must assume Cordelia's dead, too. So, Inspector... can you tell me who's responsible? Who murdered poor Anna? Who was on the clifftops last night waving that lantern, inviting in the bombers that killed this poor man's family and scores of servicemen too?'

Dobson cursed and said, 'That idiot Chalmers seems to think it's me.'

Shearer leaned forward.

'I can't help but wonder, Sergeant. I received reports of some of your comments around here. About what you'd do in the event of an invasion...'

'I'd do my job,' Dobson snapped back. 'A decent one. Not dirty, like yours.'

Renard intervened.

'Anna Schmidt probably died on Friday night or early Saturday. Where were you then?'

'Home. With my family. Who are dead now. So that won't help me, will it?'

'And last night?'

'Same place. On my own. Getting drunk on cheap Scotch. Couldn't think of anything else to do. Unfortunately, a bottle can't talk.'

'There must be someone...'

'There isn't! I know! I know! I'm a copper too, remember. I've got no alibi for either. I gave the Lee kid a good hiding. Now you say he's dead. And you really think I called Jerry down to kill my own? Well then...' He held out his hands, clasped together, ready to be taken. 'Charge me. Put me up in court. Do you think I care?'

Shearer glanced at Renard and said nothing.

'You knew I wanted to talk to May this morning. You made very sure I couldn't do that. Would you care to tell me why?'

The man was pink-eyed, choking up, struggling to find the words.

'You don't have children, do you? Neither of you do. You're looking at me like I've got something to answer for. Apart from sending my wife and kid to their graves. You've no idea.'

'Just tell me, Sergeant.'

'This unfeeling bastard put my daughter, a child, in a brothel. I don't give a damn what justification he thinks he had. I don't give a damn about this stupid war. All I cared about was my family. All I wanted to do was protect them. What more can a man do? And you two don't even have that.'

Renard let Dobson simmer for a while. Then he said, 'All I wanted was to hear May tell me about the woman we knew as Dawn Peacock. Nothing more–'

'That bitch talked her into going to bed with anyone who paid! Anyone that damned woman sent her way! She let them do whatever they liked and tried to get them talking. Because that's what that cow asked of her. Get them to blab. About who they were. What they did. What rank they held. What they knew about the Castle. The plans...'

'And thanks to that,' Shearer cut in, 'we managed to put three mouthy soldiers in a cell to teach the fools a lesson.'

'Was that it?' Renard wondered aloud. 'Some tomfool soldiers? Not spies? No traitors? It seems scant reward for so much effort.'

Shearer closed his eyes, hesitated, then said, 'A man can be too inquisitive, Renard. The value of intelligence can only be assessed in hindsight. All we know is that if we have none, there's nothing to assess.'

'Everything May had to tell you, she told me.' Dobson was sweating, furious. 'Every last disgusting detail. I made her do it and God knows that hurt us all. Me. Beth. Her. I *made* her. I sat there writing down all the filth so you'd have it. Here...' He pulled three sheets of balled-up paper out of his pocket and threw them on the table. 'Take them. A dead girl's confession. She shagged old men for England. Not enough though, is it? You need to see the pain yourself. I did and I didn't want to put May or her mother through it anymore. Not that it matters now. Do I get to see what's left of them, or not?'

'Did she name names?' Renard asked.

'You don't think they told her real ones, do you?'

'Dobson. I'm trying to help.'

For a moment he looked guilty.

'She wouldn't tell me any names, no. It wasn't the easiest of conversations, not that I imagine either of you two will appreciate that.'

All the same, Shearer picked up the balls of paper, put them in his jacket pocket, then stood up.

'Renard,' he said. 'May we speak outside?'

CHAPTER 67

Dan Kelly came to on the grubby floor of Frank Lee's shed, realising he must have passed out trying to get to the door when he heard the bike start up. He stumbled outside, let loose a stream of curses. The shiny BSA motorbike was gone. It was getting on for four o'clock. He must have been out for half an hour or more.

The sky seemed emptier than it had been in weeks. No planes, no artillery. Just the lazy, asthmatic throb of the tractor putting up a cloud of straw into the summer afternoon. A battered red tractor that was towing a threshing machine. By the looks of the field, the harvest was almost done. Kelly marched over, waved at the driver to stop, and showed his warrant card. The farmer killed his engine, munched on an old meerschaum pipe and said, 'Well what can I do for you then, Constable?'

'Tell me where I can find Frank Lee. He whacked me over the head and stole my bike.'

The man pulled a grim face.

'No one ever knows where a Lee will show up, son. Just that they'll do it when you least want. Anything else?'

'A lift into town? I need to get to the nick.'

'Hop up then.'

Kelly looked at the battered old machine.

'How fast can this thing go?'

'Faster than you can walk. But I have a car down by the road. I'll drive you.'

Kelly climbed onto the side. The thing was so rattly he had to shout to make himself heard as they set off.

'What do you know about Frank Lee?'

'He's a bad 'un, like his old man before him. That's all I need to know.'

'That shed of his...'

The farmer stared at him and raised an eyebrow.

'You went looking in Frank Lee's outbuilding? Brave fellow. Rather you than me.'

———

The car was smart and recent. Comfortable, too. On the way into town, trying to get his detective mind in gear again, he asked if the man had any idea whether Lee had other places to go to. Somewhere to run to.

'Got a sister somewhere. Nice woman, couldn't wait to get away from here. That's all I know. Sorry. We weren't exactly on speaking terms and–'

'Stop! Stop!' Kelly banged the dashboard. They were coming up to the station. There it was, his bike, on the stand. Unharmed.

'Thanks, mate,' he said and ran for the BSA.

A railway man came out and looked him up and down.

'You're not the one who parked it, son. Had enough people nicking things round here.'

The warrant card again.

'Dover CID. I'm the one who had it thieved. Did you see what happened to the bloke who took it?'

'I did. He took the train to Victoria.'

'Where will he be now?'

He checked his fob watch.

'About twenty-three minutes outside Canterbury, if everything's on time. Which it won't be.'

'I need to use your telephone.'

The desk sergeant was Hawkins. He answered straight away. Kelly didn't offer any explanations.

'Frank Lee's done a runner. He's on the Dover train coming into Canterbury in twenty minutes or so. Brown jacket, ugly mug, corduroy trousers, farm boots. Gingerish hair that looks like it last got a wash years back. I want him grabbed, on or off the train.'

'What's he done now, Dan? Spot of burglary again?'

'Nicked my BSA, the bastard. Oh...' Wrong way round, he thought. 'Spot of murder by the sound of it, too.'

The bike started first kick.

'Well done, my beauty,' he said as he pulled away from the forecourt, tapping the tank. 'Inspector Renard's going to be well pleased with us.'

CHAPTER 68

Chalmers marched out of his office the moment he saw Renard and Shearer had left the interview room.

'Well?' he said. 'What did he say? Dobson's been a pain in the arse ever since he came here. Thinks he's better than the rest of us. Talking out of turn...'

'I'm letting him go,' Renard told him.

'What?'

'I'm letting him go.'

'I have a dinner appointment. You must excuse me,' Shearer announced and slipped out of the door.

'May I ask why?'

'Because he's done nothing wrong,' Renard went on. 'He's a bereaved husband and father. He wants to see... to see what's left of his family. We owe him that.'

Chalmers shook the wad of papers in his hand.

'He can't answer for his movements last night.'

'Or the night the Peacock woman died. All the same, we've no reason whatsoever to think he was involved in either case.'

'He stopped you interviewing that girl of his! That's obstruction.'

'Possibly,' Renard agreed. 'He was ashamed for the girl. He wanted to remove his family from the source of that shame. I find that entirely understandable in the circumstances.'

'Obstruction!'

Renard shrugged.

'I have nothing to keep the man in custody. If you feel differently, Superintendent, I'm happy to hand the case over to you.'

'You're CID.'

'Quite. And this is my decision.'

'Some bloody genius from Scotland Yard you are, aren't you? Let him go then. I'm still suspending him until further notice. No pay. I'll put it in writing this minute.'

Sure enough, he marched back into his office and started tapping away at the typewriter. That seemed to be the man's definition of real work.

Renard opened the interview door and told Dobson he was free to go. Then he went to the desk and told the officer there to call a car to go to the Institution Hospital.

'I can find my own way,' Dobson muttered as he came out into reception. 'Tell Chalmers he can stick his job up his backside. I'm done with Dover. Now... I would like my jacket, my tie, and my belongings.'

One of the uniform men went into a back room to fetch them.

There was a figure in black on the bench seat by the window. Renard had to think for a moment then he remembered where he'd seen the fellow before.

He went over.

'Reverend Partridge, isn't it? This is Dover. Not Temple Ewell.'

'After I heard about what happened last night, Canterbury felt it only right I should come over to offer my services. Your colleague...' He nodded at Dobson. 'He seems distressed.'

'The man lost his wife and daughter.'

Partridge nodded.

'If you think I could offer something by way of comfort...'

Dobson had his police jacket over his arm and was putting on his belt. The tie, he threw in a waste basket. That was one way to end a career, Renard thought.

'I'll leave that up to you,' he said, as the sergeant stumbled out into the street.

CHAPTER 69

Chalmers was still typing away. Renard thought about going in and asking the man to be a touch more generous. Dobson was leaving, surely, but he could be persuaded to resign, to stay at home on sick leave, at least get paid for a month.

Before he could do a thing, Dan Kelly came in from the uniform section. He looked different. Busy, engaged. There was a bruise on his cheek.

'Constable Kelly...'

'I went to Frank Lee's like you asked. The bugger only whacked me on my head and stole my Gold Star.'

'Your what?'

'My bike. I told you.'

'Oh. Are you all right?'

'I am. I got my bike back too. Thing is...'

Kelly rattled it off so quickly Renard had to make him calm down and tell it all again, in greater detail. Then one of the uniforms came out.

'Sorry, Dan,' he said. 'Just off the telephone. They missed Frankie boy at Canterbury. He ran off.'

'Don't Canterbury coppers run then?' Kelly yelled.

'No need to bite my head off. Just passing on a message.'

Renard made him go through what he'd found in Lee's outbuilding again.

'Big stash of weapons. Army marks on the side of the crates. All ready for Jerry when he comes.'

Renard called the Castle and got through to Lieutenant Mortimer. The man sounded in a hurry, as if he wanted to go home. He swore vividly when told what had been discovered outside the remote home of one of his recruits.

'I think you need to see this for yourself, Lieutenant. It would be useful if you could bring along a quartermaster. Someone familiar with your inventory.'

Mortimer cursed again.

'You think the creature stole all this from me?'

'That, sir, is what I'd like to know.'

Chapter 70

One page, double-spaced, in need of corrections. That was all Jessica Marshall had and the piece felt dull and clunky. If she could have brought Louis Renard into it then there would most certainly have been more colour. A wry, interesting, perhaps mysterious Scotland Yard detective added spice to any story. But Shearer would never let it through.

The telephone rang on her desk by the window.

'Dinner.'

It was not a question.

'A meal generally taken in the evening. Next?'

'Can we make it six?' Shearer said. 'Early for someone of a continental nature, I know. But needs must. Work...'

'You really don't have to–'

'On the contrary, I do. I've been rude, abrupt, unthinking. It's the job, I'm afraid. Forever dealing with the men. Their brusqueness rubs off. I should never have suggested you interview that police officer, not when he's been so recently bereaved.'

There, she thought, he was wrong. A good few reporters back in Toronto specialised in the death knock. They could go out into the night, face an angry reception on the doorstep, talk their way inside, come out with a story and photographs of the lost, vanished, murdered, run down in the street. Children sometimes, too. It was a strange, and to her uncomfortable, kind of talent. Mike, her estranged husband now with his girlfriend in Seattle, seemed to possess it almost naturally. He could charm anyone given the chance. One time, after a particularly brutal murder, he even got a letter from the victim's parents thanking him for the way he'd listened so kindly. Jessica Marshall knew she could never be that kind of hack. All the same, she'd rejected Shearer's idea not so much out of principle but because it was the kind of story she felt beyond her. Too personal. Too close. Telling herself it was Shearer's insistence on control that stopped her taking the story was just an excuse.

'I'm still working.'

'Then stop. For pity's sake, Jessica, we can't fight the war twenty-four hours a day. I've stolen a chef from the officers' mess in the Castle. The best they have. He's purloined two Dover sole from the stores, a bottle of champagne, lobster bisque and summer pudding. Kent is the garden of England, or so they say.'

Hardly rationing, she thought.

'Sounds delicious.'

'It will be. The man's due in the Raglan kitchen in half an hour. We dine at six. Just the two of us. The hotel business is scarcely booming at the moment. Your host will be grateful for the business.'

It was hard to imagine the sour-faced, miserable Eric being grateful for anything.

The page in the typewriter stared back at her.

'I really need to write something. I have this demanding bastard for a boss.'

'Calhoun's that bad?'

'I wasn't talking about Calhoun.'

The line went quiet. Perhaps she'd gone too far.

'Six,' Shearer said in the end, pleasantly too. 'I look forward to it.'

CHAPTER 71

The tractor was still working in the adjoining field, the late-afternoon air hazy with grain and dust from the thresher. Renard decided to leave the outbuilding to the last. Instead, he went into the two-bed hovel that had been home to the Lee family for decades.

No photographs anywhere. No ornaments. No memorabilia to say the place was once occupied by a woman. The two bedrooms were tips, dirty clothes strewn on the floor. In the one he assumed to be the father's, three grubby beer glasses stood by the bed next to a couple of bottles.

'Whitbread,' Kelly said and sniffed. 'Typical. No taste.'

'I don't think Frank Lee is concerned much about taste.'

Renard went through all the drawers and told Kelly to do the same in the room they assumed belonged to Harry. There was nothing of any interest.

'The attic,' he said, pulling a chair up to the small door in the ceiling of the hall.

'In my new suit?'

He just pointed. Kelly grunted and groaned and got up there

on hands and knees, took out a torch and vanished. A minute later he was back covered in dust and cobwebs.

'Fine day this is. Get knocked on the head. My bike nicked and now I've clambered through all this muck.'

Nothing there, he said, except evidence of an owl that had taken to disembowelling mice of late.

'Be grateful they don't have a sewer,' Renard told him and went downstairs where they went through every drawer, every nook and cranny.

'Well,' said Kelly, as they watched a racing-green sports car park by the grass track, 'that was a waste of time.'

'Why?' Renard asked.

'Because we found nothing.'

Renard sighed and walked outside.

Mortimer had changed into civilian clothes, tweedy sports jacket and slacks, and was accompanied by an officer from the stores in khaki uniform and cap. The lieutenant looked furious, the other embarrassed.

Renard introduced Kelly and let him explain what had happened as they went inside the shed. The boxes were still there. The quartermaster swore as he went round checking them.

'Do I take it they're yours?' Renard asked.

'Looks like it.'

'How is that possible?'

Mortimer glared at his man.

'I would like to know that too.'

'Can't tell you, sir. I'll have to do an inventory when I get back. Look at the books.'

'Clearly,' said Renard, 'Frank Lee had access to the stores.'

'If he was on the Cordelia list,' the quartermaster said, 'then he'd have been inside to get his gun and stuff.'

Kelly opened the nearest crate. It was full of military knives. He pulled one out, an evil-looking thing, sharp, slender, like a stiletto only larger.

'That's a commando knife,' the quartermaster said. 'We issue one to all of them and tell them how you can kill a bloke with it.'

Another crate was full of handguns. Webleys and Enfields.

'Lucky he didn't kill my constable,' Renard observed.

Kelly brushed down his smart suit again and still the dust and the cobwebs stuck to him.

Mortimer pointed at the cases.

'I want this man found. I want him found, delivered to me and–'

'We're looking for him,' Renard interrupted. 'It seems he took a train to London and hopped off at Canterbury. Currently he's on the loose.'

'I'll hang the bastard when you find him.' The lieutenant nodded in the direction of the cliffs. 'You think he's the one who led Jerry in last night?'

'Twenty-minute walk from here at most across them fields,' Kelly said straight off. 'We know Harry was there...'

'Looking for his girlfriend,' Renard pointed out.

'Well...' Kelly was struggling. 'Maybe he bumped into his dad and his dad pushed him off the cliffs. Maybe poor Harry found his dad had kept a munitions store here for Jerry when he comes. Lots of reasons to think so.'

Mortimer glared at the quartermaster again.

'Get a detail here. I want every last item back in the stores this evening and an explanation tomorrow of how they got out.'

'Sir...'

'Can you still proceed with... what's it called... Cordelia?' Renard asked.

'My business, Inspector. Yours is finding Frank Lee and delivering him to me. After that, the military police can take over.'

'They can go and look for him if you like.'

'We have other things to do. Good evening.'

The Morgan was a noisy beast, especially the way Tobias Mortimer drove it. They watched the sports car vanish down the rough track back to the road, the quartermaster miserable in the passenger seat.

'Fancy wheels our lieutenant's got,' said Kelly.

'True.'

'Our blokes in Canterbury had better find old Frankie.'

'I'm sure they will.'

Kelly blinked and said, 'Why are you so sure?'

Patience, Renard told himself.

'Do you really believe Frank Lee is a German agent?'

'He's got all that stuff here! Weapons and things. Waiting for them to turn up.'

Silence.

'We know he's a bad 'un, sir! Been like that all his life. He's got his weapons. All he has to do is walk to the cliffs over there and shine his light.'

'And murder his own son?'

Kelly looked exasperated.

'You said yourself he beat the poor kid black and blue to make it look like Joe Dobson did it. Too many things staring us in the face here as far as I'm concerned.'

Renard shrugged and walked back to his Hillman Minx.

'Is your motorbike still working, Kelly?'

'Yes.'

'Why do you think he left it at the station? Instead of riding off?'

'Because he knows damned well I'd put my number plate out and the first patrol car that spots it pulls him in.'

The machine was on its stand next to the car.

'Fast bike,' Renard said. 'He could outrun our cars, surely.'

'True, but... all the same.'

Kelly looked lost for a moment.

'One last question, Constable.'

'What?'

'When the Germans come... *if* they come... why do you think they'd have need of a crooked farmhand's weapons store he kept in a shed? Do you not think they'd bring their own?'

Dan Kelly stood there open-mouthed.

'Then... what?'

'Occam's razor, Constable.'

'What's that?'

'When you see the obvious, assume it is the obvious. When you see the handiwork of a thief... assume it's the result of his thieving.' He checked his watch. 'Time for us to leave this for others to pursue.'

Kelly climbed on the saddle of his BSA.

'I'm rubbish at this, aren't I? Maybe you should find someone else, sir. I could go back to uniform and picking up drunks outside pubs after they've been scrapping.'

'You,' Renard said, pointing a finger, 'are a sight smarter at all this than I was at your age. Chin up, Constable.'

'Do you have any idea what's going on here? I mean... any?'

Renard opened his car door.

'I'll see you in the morning,' he said.

CHAPTER 72

The dining room of the Lord Raglan was the only part of the place that felt like a hotel. It was bright and airy with Georgian bow windows looking out onto a patio with three falling apart tables and a sad rosebush that sat wilting and unwatered, dropping rotting petals into its terracotta pot. In normal times, Eric explained, the doors would be open, and guests could choose to eat outside if they wished. But the war had seen to that, and his regular clientele. Now there was no normal restaurant service, only cooked breakfasts and sandwiches served throughout the day, usually made by him or the woman who came to clean.

'Long time since I've seen lobster served here,' he muttered as he brought out the soup. 'Or champagne.'

And the same when the Dover sole arrived, complete with a garnish of boiled potatoes, peas and tartare sauce.

She'd expected Shearer to talk business throughout, but he didn't. Instead, he told of his life in the services, which seemed to have involved travel all over the world, to Hong Kong and Australia, South Africa and the Caribbean, the very outposts of empire. Doing what, he never quite said but she got the idea.

David Shearer was a master of clandestine services, their organiser, the man who told his spies and informers where to go and what to look for. Being leader of the Ministry of Information in wartime Dover was simply a title, a cover for his real job. Pulling the levers of a secret world beholden to him alone.

Then came the "enough of me" moment and he invited her to talk about her own life, which Jessica Marshall found quite difficult. Until she'd arrived in Dover the pace had been pell-mell, moving from one city to another, trying to master what she could of the language, filing copy endlessly, hoping to make it unique and interesting, a body of work she could look back on with pride. When she'd first fought her way onto a job on the *Inquirer* city desk, she'd had no idea the politics of the 1930s would cast her as the biographer of a world falling apart, descending into a fast-spreading war that, with hindsight, seemed inevitable, but nonetheless shocking for that.

After the failure of her marriage there'd been men. A few, none that mattered, not that she was going to tell Shearer that. More than anything there'd been the desperate need to conquer the job, to file stories that meant something, to succeed and become a foreign correspondent who would one day be recognised beyond provincial Toronto. War meant opportunity, the chance to shine, to beat your rivals to the story, to defeat them with your journalistic prowess.

In the years she'd spent in Europe she had, she knew, done none of these things. At best her copy was routine – competent, never outstanding, tending to the slight, colour pieces destined for a few columns inside, rarely the front page. The story she had in her head was never quite the one she managed to set down with the keys of her Remington. Transcribed, it became dull, predictable, hovering on the edge of cliché. Even her photos all too often had a stilted and obvious quality. She was doing her best. It was just that her best was unremarkable. Though not now.

Captain David Shearer had somehow found her a wider audience. Perhaps that was all she needed. A break. Friends on high who could grease the wheels of her career. That, in her naivety, had never occurred to her. She'd always tried to convince herself journalism was a meritocracy, dependent on talent alone. There, it seemed, she was wrong.

'Where would you like to go next?' he asked as the coffee – real coffee, from the Castle mess – arrived.

It seemed a strange question.

'Next? I haven't even thought of it. Mostly I've been wondering how I might cover the Germans getting here. I presume your wire will work.'

'The moment the wire was down you'd be out of here. I'd make sure of that. No point in having a reporter who can't deliver the copy.'

'And you? Would you stay behind?'

From the silence she understood that was a question too far.

'What's your next piece going to be?'

'The night in the shelter.'

'If it's finished, I can take it back with me tonight. Get it out there straight away.'

There were barely two hundred words on the page. A fifth of the length she required.

'It still needs some improving.'

He finished his coffee and offered her a cigarette. For once she accepted. She didn't smoke much, but there were times...

'The best reporters I've met write something straight off the top of their heads. The longer it takes, the worse it gets.'

'I'd no idea you were a journalism tutor now.'

'Touché,' he said with a quick salute. 'Perhaps I can help.'

'How?'

'I don't know. Show me what you have. Just a thought.'

'It's in my room.'

'So? We're adults, aren't we?' He glanced at the champagne, still half full. 'We could finish this. And your story.'

It was getting dark. She liked writing at night. If the air raid sirens didn't sound, and so far they hadn't.

'Very well,' she said and picked up the bottle and the two almost empty champagne flutes.

CHAPTER 73

The vicar stuck to Joe Dobson like glue all the long time he spent in the Institution Hospital, waiting mostly. Not that there was much to do or see. After more than an hour, the paperwork for the deaths of Beth and May was produced, condolences offered by staff so busy they barely looked him in the eye when they said the familiar words. Everywhere he walked along the white tiled corridors he met the sick, the wounded, the dying. Some looked defiant. Some simply in despair. With every footstep, every predictable anodyne comment from the Reverend Partridge, Dobson found he was withdrawing inside himself, trying to find a solitary, lonely place where all feeling was absent, all regret and grief and pain.

When they showed him the bloody remains in the morgue, he could think of nothing at all. There was no response to being told this was all that was left of the wife he'd loved for twenty years since they were teenagers in London, coming out of the horrors of another war, finding peace in the arms of one another. Bringing the miracle of new life into the world in the form of a daughter a decent interval after they'd married, too. The closeness of family was something they'd left behind in the grim terraces of Bermondsey, all because he had thought promotion and a bigger house on the coast would make them happier.

Flesh and blood and bone had no part in those memories. The torn pieces they showed him so reluctantly might have belonged to anyone. Even what was left of their faces was quite unrecognisable. Their physical presence was gone, replaced by hazy pictures in the memory, taunting and accusing, wondering what they'd done to deserve such a fate.

Finally, he walked beyond the chemical smell of those white corridors. The last of the day's German fighters were heading back over the Channel, chased by hungry Spitfires. A military ambulance was rushing a wounded pilot into theatre, a Polish man, the stretcher carrier said, one who was probably going to die on foreign soil.

'Serves him right,' said the other medic. 'He shouldn't have sided with the Jerries.'

'They fight for us,' Dobson called out, suddenly furious. 'The Poles. The Czechs. The Belgians.'

The pair looked blank, embarrassed.

'They fight for us, you ignorant bastards,' he yelled again. 'They're on our side.'

'He speaks foreign,' the first stretcher-man said.

'Because he is, you fool. Do you think...?'

Do you think we'll win this on our own? That's what he wanted to say. But it was pointless. When this was all over, if the Nazis lost, it would be a story of British bravery they told each other of a night. Everyone else who fought and died would be peripheral. Spear-carriers, invisible on a stage dominated by the English, forgotten, ignored.

The pair swore and carried the wounded man inside, barely conscious.

'You shouldn't get cross with the ignorant, Sergeant,' Partridge said. 'They can't help themselves.'

'They can read, can't they? They can listen. They can learn. God knows I did. Though where it got me...'

The vicar looked as if he regretted being there.

'The Bible teaches us love and grace and forgiveness.'

'Don't think it quite reached that pair, do you?'

There followed more sanctimonious prattle and an offer to join with him in prayer.

'I never believed before,' Dobson said, barely looking at the man. 'Why should I start now?'

'I was trying to help.'

The vicar seemed impervious to offence.

'You want to help? Here's one way. I've no money. I gave it all to Beth to help them settle in London.' Not a penny of that had been recovered from Shakespeare Halt. Some squaddie had probably pocketed the lot along the way. The spoils of war, Dobson thought, guilty to be consumed by such selfish and bitter bile. 'Can the church pay for an undertaker? Two funerals? That would be good.'

He knew the answer but wanted to ask all the same.

'The business of dying,' the vicar sighed, 'and it is a business. Such burdens to bear even when the end is not unexpected.' He handed over a card, an address and a telephone number in Canterbury, with a local one for Temple Ewell added in blue ink beneath. 'It's hardly appropriate to use our scant funds when those sadly affected aren't part of any congregation. Outside the club as it were... If there are other ways in which I can assist. Counsel. Comfort. We could pray together. There's solace in the Bible.'

'Not for me.'

The man looked unimpressed.

'Well, I offered. I apologise if my presence here was unwelcome.'

'I didn't ask, did I?'

Partridge's bland face spoke ingratitude as he headed for his car.

Chapter 74

She sat at the desk by the window and fiddled with the paper in the Remington. Shearer pulled up the spare chair next to her. The story looked even worse now she'd come back to it: lifeless, forced, marred by the occasional cliché. Unoriginal and hackneyed, the kind of thing she hated.

He read the few words she had on the page and said nothing.

'I know it's no good,' she said.

'Why's that?'

'I said already, didn't I? It's too close to yesterday's piece. Feels like I'm cranking out the same tune just in a different key.'

He offered her a cigarette. She said no and asked him not to smoke. She hated the smell in the room, even though it had the faintest aroma of stale tobacco from whoever had stayed there before her. Perhaps it was him, she thought, when she saw the way he was looking round.

'You had this room before, didn't you?'

'Until they found me a place in the Castle. Yes. Why do you think you're here?'

The travel agent in London, the one who'd told her it was the best place in town. He'd taken two days to come back with an offer of accommodation. Obviously, he had to check with the Ministry first.

'Have you been... managing me from the start?'

'In war one must exercise control. You're very perceptive.'

'Comes of staring at people and wondering if I can turn them into words.'

He got up, put the cigarette case away, and walked round the room. There was a picture on the wall. A watercolour of the cliffs, white chalk, green meadow dotted with flowers. He took it off and showed it to her.

'See this?'

'What about it?'

'It's perfect. Exactly what we're fighting to defend.'

The picture was cheap and badly executed. Something bought from a gift shop. He surely knew that.

'I'll work on the story tonight,' she said. 'Then bring it round in the morning. I'll get there in the end.'

'I doubt that,' he said, placing the picture back then turning to face her, close again. 'Once something has the feel of failure about it... well. If only there was something else.'

She knew exactly what he was hinting at.

'I don't like the idea of disturbing a man who's just lost his wife and daughter.'

'I understand.'

'So why do you keep pushing it?'

'If you had an alternative...'

She kept quiet.

'There's also this, Jessica. What if he would *like* to talk? What if he wants to say something? To have it reported? How would you know if you didn't ask? You've my credentials, you know. You may come and go as you please. Curfew. Air raids. You're as free here as you wish.'

He was very skilled when it came to planting ideas that would grow and nag at you.

She said she'd think about it.

'Good. Do please report back to me everything he says. Before you write it.' He didn't move even though she thought she'd given him an obvious invitation for him to leave. 'Do you like it here, in Dover?'

'I'm not sure what you mean.'

'I mean... do you like the feel of the place? For once, you know, we're liberated in a way. That's what war does. All the old rules, the strictures, the boundaries that civilisation, or what passes for it, places around us. They're gone. This little world is ours, to do with as we see fit.'

She laughed.

'Your world, you mean.'

'No.' He came and sat next to her at the desk. 'I mean ours. You must have ached for that freedom. You've left your home. Your husband–'

'He left me.'

'More fool him.'

'And Mrs Shearer?'

'Ah.' He paused for a moment. 'Much the same, really. Eleanor is now in Cheltenham. She walked out on me at Christmas. For a dentist. It appears dentistry retains nine to five hours even during war. I do not. We correspond infrequently about when we might fit in the divorce. I'm rather too busy for inconsequential matters like that. There are no children, in case you're wondering.'

'I wasn't.'

'The point I was trying to make is that we are, for once, without shackles. We can be ourselves. Our true selves. Do what we like. With whomever we wish. No consequences–'

'There are always consequences.'

'Not now. Not here. This town's a sinkhole. A dump. A sweating, heaving mass of military humanity. No one cares a damn about anything except Jerry and when he's going to come. Didn't that woman say something like that when you talked to her last week? The closer you get to the grave, the more you feel alive.'

'She also said she'd never been happier in all her life. And now she's dead.'

He winked, the deliberate, almost obscene way men did at women sometimes.

'Exactly. We won't have these freedoms for long. One day Hitler will be defeated. Dull normality shall return. And we'll be back to being our mundane selves.'

He reached out and touched her, then ran a finger down her cheek. After that his hand slipped to her back and nimble fingers found the zip behind her neck, pulled it down an inch or two and she felt his smooth and rhythmic touch against her naked back.

It would have been so easy to give in. He was an attractive man. She was, in some ways, lonely. There was a release in sex, mindless, physical, thrilling, that she missed.

All the same she pulled back from him and said, 'I want to work, Captain Shearer. I think it's time for you to leave.'

'We haven't finished the champagne,' he said, pointing at the glasses.

She picked them up and poured the contents down the little sink by the bed. Then handed the bottle and the flutes to him. He seemed amused.

'Another time,' he said and very quickly, before she could move, kissed her cheek. 'Priory Hill. Number seven. It's a police house. Dobson's. For now, anyway.'

———

Even after a further hour of struggle the page didn't look any better. She needed to write. There was nothing to work with. Shearer had given her a window onto a world of coverage, bylines in papers and places she'd barely heard of. The taste of that was sweet. The idea of losing it unconscionable.

The moon was slight, the night black stroked with silver. No sirens yet, only the growl of unseen planes.

Priory Hill. Number seven.

She grabbed a pen and her notebook, the credentials Shearer had given her, and went downstairs.

'Nice meal, was it?' Eric asked. He was lounging alone in the saloon, a glass of stout in front of him.

'Very, thank you.'

'I don't normally allow visitors to the rooms. We're not that kind of place.'

She thought of telling him it was only work.

Instead, she smiled and said, 'Perhaps you'd better raise the matter with Captain Shearer.'

That brought out a gloomy and resentful look.

'Go careful out there, Mrs Marshall. It may sound quiet right now. But you never know.'

CHAPTER 75

Joe Dobson couldn't begin to think about what lay ahead. Not just funerals and undertakers. He'd have to try to explain what had happened to Beth's mother in London, an elderly woman, already on the edge of a breakdown because of her fears about the war. There were only a few pounds left in the bank. Enough for a train fare to London, not much else.

As he wandered back into town a young uniformed copper cycled past on his bike near the shops, spotted him, looked away, embarrassed.

For a moment Dobson stood outside the house in Priory Hill trying to believe they might still be there inside, quietly bickering as always. The place was twice the size of the terrace they'd had in Bermondsey, with a fraction of the memories and the love.

There was something on the doorstep. A bottle it looked like, wrapped in old gift paper, bells and holly and a grinning Santa Claus. That was a dark time ahead he'd never thought about. Christmas without them, living alone, God knows where.

A simple card was tucked beneath. Blank except for the handwritten message, "*Condolences, Joe. From your colleagues.*" Nothing more. Maybe they weren't all bad in the nick.

He went inside, wondered if he could still detect the smell of them, Beth's perfume, a birthday special every year. May and her love of a floral soap she bought from Boots. But all he got was damp from the walls and windows kept closed during a hot and humid summer.

With a grunt he sat at the kitchen table, aware he'd barely eaten since breakfast. Just a couple of digestives served up by the curious detective from London, a man as out of place in Dover as himself. One who'd probably pay for it too, before long. Dobson recognised that look in Chalmers' eyes. Renard's days were doubtless numbered already.

There was a bottle of Johnnie Walker inside the wrapper. Just as well. He'd finished the one from the night before.

Joe Dobson went and got himself the last hunk of tasteless cheddar lurking in the larder, some bread, some butter.

And a glass. He poured the whisky, didn't even smell it, just chucked it down his throat.

The food could wait. This was a time to drink.

CHAPTER 76

Renard was finishing a solitary supper at the ornate iron table next to the gazebo. He could hear the gentle voice of the river at the foot of the garden, imagine the trout there, idling in the sluggish current. Tired, still struggling to make sense of the day's events, he'd taken a bath then put on his ancient, blue-striped winceyette pyjamas, tartan dressing gown and a pair of leather slippers that were falling apart. His hair was still wet, which only made him realise he was long overdue a visit to the barbers. In the pocket of the dressing gown was the crumpled copy of Jessica Marshall's rejected article, read yet again, still a source of puzzlement.

Veronica had taken one look at him, made a mildly caustic remark about how she loved men who took the time to dress for dinner, then deposited the food. Cold ham, a quarter of a cucumber, a single tomato, two sticks of celery in a cut-glass vase, a small pool of homemade mayonnaise and a glass of local cider. The price of missing the meal with her, which was taken on the dot at six every night, al fresco of late. The English summer, she said, was so brief and its chance of sun so rare one had to make the most of things. Then she ordered him to savour the mayonnaise since the Tuscan olive oil was down to its last dregs and she'd no idea when the next might arrive. In future, she'd said with a shudder, they might be reduced to salad cream made with dried eggs, vinegar and Colman's mustard powder.

Renard had explained on more than one occasion that police work rarely made for punctual meals at any time, not that she'd listened. Though he decided not to mention he'd never much noticed any great difference between salad cream and mayonnaise in the first place since they both seemed much the same colour. Veronica left the bottle of cider on the table and went off to doodle on the piano in the study. He was sitting by the light of a candelabra, listening to the distant mumble of sporadic artillery from the coast and Veronica's feeble attempts at Chopin, dabbing the remaining celery into the mayonnaise, when he heard a car scrunch across the gravel drive. Veronica, naturally, was there first, beaming as she guided Poppy Webber to the house with the torch she used for blackout, then out to the table in the garden.

'A visitor, Louis,' she cried. 'Try to remember what it's like to be a host.'

Poppy Webber was still in her hospital gown, which was white and stained, and she looked exhausted.

'I won't take much of your time,' she said.

'A visit is a visit,' his aunt declared, doing her best to hide the bottle of cider behind her back. 'I was about to open a bottle of wine. Excellent Chablis and we won't be seeing that again once it's finished.'

'I'm driving.'

Veronica looked bemused by that answer.

'I'll fetch cheese and biscuits then. I don't think the Dover coppers care much about the odd tipple behind the wheel.' She looked Renard up and down. 'Any more than they care about evening wear.'

'Not if they know the chief constable,' Renard replied with a sharp smile. 'Who can get you off a charge of driving under the influence.'

'I wasn't under the influence. Merely swayed by the odd glass or two.'

Still, she looked sheepish as she went to fetch a plate of crackers and some cheddar before retiring to the house. Then a bottle of wine and two glasses in any case, after which she deftly removed the cider.

'I've seen her at the pictures,' Poppy Webber said when she was out of earshot. 'Can't remember what.'

So many, Renard thought. None of them destined for immortal fame.

'Veronica's my last living relative,' he said. 'My aunt.'

'She seems... formidable.'

'You could say that.'

'Mmmm.' Half a glass of Chablis went down very quickly. It looked as if she needed it. 'Lovely wine.' She looked around. 'Lovely place. And a river.'

'I keep meaning to learn fly fishing. There are trout. Veronica's bought me all the tackle.'

'Really? My father's a keen fisherman. I've been out on a salmon river with him in Scotland.'

'Caught some?'

'A few. I do hope I'm not keeping you up or anything.'

'Ah.' He laughed and looked at the dressing gown and the old pyjamas. 'If I'd known I was expecting company...'

'No matter. What I came to say first of all was thank you. For saving me from being interned. If you hadn't been there–'

'Then someone would have intervened and freed you later. War is about paperwork and bureaucracy. As I said, you were simply a name on a list. They'd no idea who you really were. When they found out, they'd have let you go. You're needed, aren't you?'

'Thank you all the same,' she said. 'What I also wanted to tell you was–'

'Harry Lee was murdered.'

She gulped, spilled the drink, laughed and said, 'Look what you made me do.'

'Sorry.' He passed her a napkin. 'It was kind of you to come.'

'Needlessly, it seems. How did you work that out?'

He frowned.

'It was obvious. He had a torch strapped round his neck as if he was the one who'd stood there guiding in the German planes.' Renard shook his head. 'A ridiculous idea. I saw him that morning. Harry was little more than a terrified child. He got a mild beating from a police officer on Saturday. A thorough thrashing from his own father yesterday. He looked lost. I wish...'

His words drifted off. Renard cursed himself again for not doing more. Though what...

'He was on the cliffs,' she said. 'Perhaps he was a part of it.'

'No. Harry stole a bike at the station. He knew the train would be stopped at Shakespeare Halt. He was chasing someone. His girlfriend, he told the stationmaster. Not that she was. She died on the train. You have her too. And her mother.'

'Oh dear...'

He remembered now. She'd seen them. What was left. Poppy Webber had been taken aback by what she'd encountered in the mayhem and slaughter in the shallow bay, and on the railway line below the White Cliffs. Damn, he thought. He was shockingly thoughtless sometimes.

'I'm sorry, Doctor Webber. I'm talking as if all this is just business.'

'Poppy, please. It's an investigation for you. It is business really, isn't it?'

'It's people dying for reasons I fail to understand.'

She raised her glass and gave him a curious look.

'If it wasn't you there on the cliffs, knowing what you do, they'd probably have believed it was that young man.'

Yes, Renard thought. He was aware of that too.

'Possibly.'

'Do you have any idea who you're looking for? I'm sorry. I know. I shouldn't ask. If you did you wouldn't tell me.'

True. All the same, she was easy to talk to. Someone he could share thoughts and ideas with, perhaps. In a way that was impossible with the young constable, Kelly.

'I have a single firm dot on the horizon. That's all. Nothing to join it. To draw a line from here to there. The line is what you look for. Dots mean nothing on their own. Or to use a different analogy... I can glimpse the summit of Everest. I'm completely without a map or waypoints to take me there.'

'Sounds like being a doctor. Looking for the diagnosis of an asymptomatic disease.'

That was a parallel he'd never considered.

'Harry Lee was seventeen. I should have done something.'

'Such as?'

He'd no idea.

'The least I can do is find who pushed him off that cliff.'

She took another sip of the Chablis, then retrieved a plain brown envelope out of her handbag, placed it on the table and lifted the flap.

There was a bullet there, mangled and bloodstained.

'That wasn't what killed him. This did. He was shot in the back. The shell lodged in his spine. Given the injuries he'd suffered in the fall, it wasn't obvious.'

'Poor Harry,' he murmured.

'Is it any use to you?'

He picked up the envelope and, through the paper, turned the shell round in the candlelight.

'I can send it to London. There's no real forensics here. Whether they'll have the time...'

She seemed disappointed. Once again, he'd failed to sense the mood. Poppy Webber wanted to help somehow. He pulled the typed pages out of his dressing-gown pocket.

'See what you make of this. The week before she died, Dawn

Peacock insisted on being interviewed by a reporter here. Seemingly for a reason.'

She read slowly, carefully, he thought. Perhaps that was the doctor in her.

'Wait,' she said suddenly. 'This. "The devil's favourite piece of furniture is the long bench".'

'An odd expression, I agree.'

'Not if you're German. *Des Teufels liebstes Möbelstück ist die lange Bank.* Procrastination is to be avoided.'

He nodded. 'She was German. Dawn Peacock wasn't her real name. She was a kind of spy, working for Shearer. Or someone in the Castle. I don't know the details. I doubt I ever will.'

'But–'

'She was afraid someone had discovered her real identity. That was a message. A plea for help.'

A plane flew overhead. Perhaps two. Headed north. Luftwaffe aiming for London. British aircraft returning home. There was no way of knowing.

'It is strange. That's all I can say.'

'Never mind,' she said. 'I've taken up too much of your time already. You've two murders to deal with. A newcomer to Dover, I gather. I shouldn't intrude.'

'No, please.' He put out a hand to stop her, briefly touched hers. 'You're not intruding.'

She gazed at him, the way doctors sometimes did, trying to work something out.

'Why are you here, Louis? You seem London all over. Your manner. The way you go about things. I've been in Dover for two years now. If you don't mind my saying, you stick out like a sore thumb.'

He raised his glass and said thanks.

'Well.' She looked ready to go. 'If you don't want to talk about it...'

More than anything he was reluctant to lose her genial, pleasant company.

'It's to do with a man who called himself Morven Graves. Among other things,' Renard said. 'If you've heard of him.'

She let go of the wine glass. It shattered on the stone floor of the patio. Her dark-brown eyes gaped at him.

'Ah,' said Renard, regretting the slip immediately, knowing now he had no choice but to go on. 'I see you have.'

CHAPTER 77

Damn Eric, she thought. If he hadn't uttered that low warning when she left, she wouldn't have felt spooked about being out alone at night at all.

Damn Shearer, too. Except he'd only confirmed what she knew already. The piece set in the shelter wasn't right. She needed something hard, tough, shocking. Like the interview with the widow of the dead fisherman, the one killed by the very men he half admired.

A police sergeant who'd just lost his wife and daughter to a Nazi air raid fitted the bill. If she could get him to talk. And if not, she'd discuss the matter with Shearer anyway and see if there wasn't something to be invented. No one seemed to complain about that in Dover. The place was living on its dreams, the British bulldog standing up to the German monster. Myth fed on myth and before long became as tangible as anything the real world, such as it was, had to offer.

A squaddie with a scarred face and a surly northern accent stopped her in Mill Street. When she pulled out the pass Shearer had provided, he shone his blackout torch on it, swore, and still asked what she was doing.

'Working,' Marshall said.

'A working girl, huh?'

'Do I have to ask your rank and name and number? Do I have to give that to the office down by the harbour and see what Captain Shearer thinks?'

'Women.' He spat at the dark ground. 'This isn't your war. You should be home in bed with a lucky man. While you can.'

She took back the pass and walked on. Priory Hill was five minutes away, past the site of what must have been a massive explosion. A terrace at the end of Mill Street stood in ruins, brick and rubble, broken glass, rope round the public side to keep people out. The artillery was busy on the Castle, shafts of fire and deafening explosions breaking the night every few minutes. But nothing seemed to be raining on the town and the blackout torch she'd brought, with its downturned beam, was good enough to find the way.

Then she rounded a tight corner and found herself bumping straight into a figure in the dark. He was moving quickly, breathless, stumbling. She barely saw him and apologised even though he was the one who had almost bowled her over.

All she caught in a brief glimpse was a pale face, worried, maybe scared.

He said nothing, not a word of apology, then was gone into the darkness towards town.

'Don't mention it,' she cried after him, and threw a curse into nothing but shadow.

Her shoulder bag had fallen to the ground. She picked it up and the notebook, the pen stuck in the spiral, tumbled out. It felt as if everything was going wrong. Letting Shearer come to her bedroom, an invitation. Then kicking him out, getting that icy smile in return, the one that said, "Perhaps not now, but soon." There was something about saying no to him that made her feel stupidly guilty, more willing to do what he wanted next time round. Gratitude and a kind of weary submission, all in return for spreading her work around the world. Making her name. Promising her she'd be a star. While she sat in her shabby room in the Lord Raglan, staring at a blank page, knowing it was never going to work.

If you can't go back, and she couldn't, there was only forward, whatever lay there. She'd make Sergeant Joe Dobson talk, one way or another. She'd deal with Shearer too, even if there was a compromise to be made. Dover lay at the end of a long and tortuous road, two turnings ahead only. Obscurity and failure or the kind of artificial fame a man like him might offer, at a price.

Priory Hill was in darkness and as luck would have it the battery in her blackout torch began to fade as she walked up the road.

Like all the other houses, number seven was in darkness. There were steps up from the pavement to a door, white-painted, she could just make out.

Jessica Marshall took a deep breath, reminded herself of what one of those English death-knock merchants back home once said. The tougher the story, the more you need to promise yourself you're not leaving till you've got it. Then placing your foot in the door and refusing to remove it without the tale you were painting already in your own head.

Slaughter on an English beach: the wife and daughter of an English bobby.

There. The headline popped into her head so easily she wondered where the words came from. "Slaughter" not plain "death" ever. The dividing line between being prolific and a hack was shockingly slender. Though doubtless the sub-editors around the world who handled her copy would come up with versions of their own.

She rapped on the door. Under the gentle pressure of her knuckles, it gave. The place was unlocked, open. Unusual, she guessed, in a town where burglary was not uncommon even, or perhaps especially, at the height of war.

'Sergeant Dobson,' Jessica Marshall called, then, in the waning light of her torch, she stepped inside.

CHAPTER 78

Renard had been given the case in the spring of 1939 after the previous inspector on the job was moved elsewhere for a lack of progress. Soon it had come to take up all his time in the Yard, and much of his leisure, too. A fixation, Delia Martin always said, only half-jokingly. One that would get in the way of the wedding if he wasn't careful.

The date was set for St. Martin-in-the-Fields, October 1940. It had been a long courtship, she said, so why not a long engagement? They both had work on their hands. Delia supervised the telephone switchboard in the War Office, just round the corner from Scotland Yard. An efficient, loyal, conscientious woman who never talked about her job, even with him.

Then, when the conflict began, she dropped the bombshell. Along with twelve other telephonists in Whitehall, she'd volunteered to join the administration unit of the British Expeditionary Force headed for France to take the fight to Hitler. It had never occurred to Renard that war needed telephone operators in the field. He was naive. He was also appalled. They argued, for the first real time ever. The engagement, while not cancelled, teetered on the edge. Nor did the mysterious Morven

Graves help. That was the principal name the Yard had for an individual suspected of a series of rapes and murders across London, mostly carried out in the busy streets of the centre. Graves was slippery, cunning and ruthless. Seven women were known to be dead. Two had lucky escapes when he was disturbed in the act. After a particularly savage killing – a woman left in a side street behind the Foreign Office – some of his *modus operandi* reached the press. Morven Graves was sensational front-page news until war with Germany took his place.

The case was the strangest Renard had ever worked. The man seemed able to change his name, alter his appearance, his papers, his job on the instant. There was little in the way of geographical logic to his whereabouts. An attack on a wealthy victim in Mayfair might be followed by the murder of a hotel cleaner in Shoreditch. He seemed able to travel freely at will, never short of money or opportunity. Three times Renard had raided boarding houses where he'd been staying. Three times he'd missed him, only to be left a note, addressed to him personally. A taunting message, written in good handwriting, articulate, with perfect spelling. The work of an educated man, not the itinerant salesman Graves was meant to be.

By the time Delia left with the BEF for France, he was under intense pressure from an unsympathetic Met hierarchy. The press was still hounding the commissioner about the lack of progress. As if to taunt the police further, Graves chose for his latest victim a young secretary at the Yard, stalked her as she went to travel home from Charing Cross, raped her and left her for dead in the grim railway arches where the tramps lived on the way down to the Embankment. Graves, it seemed, was somehow tracking people across the government offices of central London. Boasting to Renard, in letters postmarked from around the capital, that no one was safe anymore. Hitler wasn't the only beast at large. There was another, a domestic monster, one who might take anyone he pleased whenever he liked. This, he said, was his world now – one of blood and death and chaos. A private war to match the public one.

For two months everything went quiet. No letters. No attacks that they knew of. Since the man loved publicity, Renard was convinced he would never have hidden his work. Perhaps, he hoped, Morven Graves was dead himself.

Then, that May, as Hitler drove the bedraggled forces of the BEF back towards the coast and Dunkirk, came another letter. This time it had an army postmark, one that indicated it originated from within a British camp in France itself, the very one where Delia worked. The message had taken three weeks to arrive. Renard could still remember the chill, the shiver that ran down his spine when he opened it in his office that Tuesday.

> *Greetings, Inspector Renard.*
>
> *You will be wondering why your old chum has been quiet of late. It is not for want of activity, that I promise. Being a dutiful Englishman I am with our forces over here in France. It would amaze you what a man can achieve when in His Majesty's uniform. I am labouring steadily, you'll be pleased to hear. Though since they be mainly Froggies you have no need to add them to your list.*
>
> *I trust this letter finds you well and employed with more successful ventures, though none so interesting as mine, I imagine. Oh, and before I forget, I must tell you that your beloved Delia is well and dutifully manning our phones here with great courage and tenacity in circumstances most pressing.*
>
> *She wears fine stockings on fine legs. But that you doubtless know.*
>
> *Your faithful friend,*
> *Morven Graves Esq.*

He'd gone inside to fetch the letter from his room. Stained with water and dirt, it sat in Poppy Webber's trembling hands.

'I walked right out of the Yard the moment I read it.' He shrugged. 'Didn't stop. Didn't talk to anyone to ask for permission. I went straight to Charing Cross and caught the first train to Dover. The papers were full of Dunkirk. The evacuations were underway. I used my warrant card and talked my way onto the boats. That, in itself, was a breach of discipline.'

'Louis.'

'I know. I know. It was stupid.'

'Foolhardy. I think that's a better word. This man's obsessed with you. Why?'

'Perhaps because he feels I'm obsessed with him. I don't know.'

Three months on, the memories still burned. The Channel crammed with boats, large and small, defenceless against air attacks, focused on one thing only, rescuing the teeming ranks of soldiers on the beaches. Dead and wounded everywhere, on the sand, on the decks, men fighting to get onto the constant and chaotic flotilla that kept braving fire from air and land to reach them.

'Somehow, I found her unit on the beach, waiting on the boats. The women were fierce. They didn't want special treatment. They'd wait their turn. They...' He'd told this twice before only, to a doctor in the hospital who'd barely listened and to Veronica who'd broken down in tears. 'They said Delia had gone missing five days earlier during the retreat. No one understood why. They weren't under attack. She should have been safe. It wasn't the Germans.'

'You think he was there? Graves?'

Renard blinked and wondered if this was a good idea after all.

'I kept looking. Couldn't stop. In the end there was a mortar attack on the beach. The blast knocked me out.' He touched the scar on his forehead. 'I had some shrapnel in here, but it stayed in the bone, not the brain. I was lucky. Others weren't. They put me on a fishing boat from Ramsgate. The next thing I knew I was in a ward ranting and raving. About Delia. About a man called Morven Graves. About how I needed to get back to France and find her and nothing was going to stop me.'

'That,' she said, 'is entirely understandable.'

'Not from an inspector from Scotland Yard. I'd abandoned my desk without permission. Lied to get onto the boat. Betrayed everything I'd worked for. They demanded my resignation. It was either that or I'd get fired. I was out of my mind. So they said. Headed for an asylum.'

She swore beneath her breath then waved a finger at him.

'Utter rubbish! It's called shock. It can affect someone for months. Years even. Doctors understand it even if generals and a bunch of idiots in Scotland Yard don't.'

'Thank you.'

Perhaps he didn't sound convinced, because she glared at him.

'I mean it. I've been treating men off those Dunkirk boats. The damage isn't just physical. They're scarred inside by what they've seen and what they've been through. They're not mad, they're shaken. And you know what? The moment they can walk they'll be sent back to fight. Their generals won't be questioning their sanity when they need them at the front.'

She looked at the grand country house behind them.

'This isn't an asylum, is it?'

'No,' he agreed. 'Veronica, being Veronica, drove to the hospital outside Ramsgate where they were keeping me under lock and key. She can be fierce-'

'I can imagine.'

'She took me in. I stayed here. Doing nothing except trying to think straight.'

Three months, it must have been, not that he had counted. The early part was a blur, a mist of lethargy and blind fury. Veronica persisted, taking him for walks, reading him books and poetry, bringing him back into the world.

'My aunt decided what I needed was work. Activity. A

challenge. She called the chief constable and he agreed to find me a job in Dover. I believe it was supposed to be a gentle sinecure. A ruse to keep me out of the way until... whatever happens.'

Too much, he thought. Too far. Poppy Webber was still a stranger, although in a way that meant he could speak more freely.

'I'm sorry to have burdened you with all this, Doctor Webber.'

'Poppy!'

'Poppy. I'm sorry.'

'I was working at Barts when all those stories about that dreadful man came out. Every woman in our accommodation block was terrified. The administration warned us against going out in London alone at night. I was outraged. What was the point of living in London if you couldn't go out? There was something he did that was horrible. Vicious and squalid. I don't remember. I think I pushed it out of my mind.'

He hesitated and asked if she really wanted to know.

'That's why I asked, Louis.'

'An officer at the Yard told the papers. For money, I imagine. I had the man fired when I found out who he was. Morven Graves had some kind of fetish. The first two women were prostitutes he'd paid for. He strangled them with a pair of silk stockings pulled tight like a rope. Fine stockings, always. They had to be silk. If they were wearing anything cheap, he wouldn't use them. He brought his own in case.'

'The woman in the bunker. Shakespeare Cliff. She was strangled. That's why you asked about the scarf?'

'Exactly. But there were thumbprints. He used his bare hands. No sexual assault. Also...'

He went quiet.

'Also what?'

'After he killed them, he wiped himself with the stockings and crammed them into the woman's throat. That, thank God, never made it into the papers.'

Somewhere outside there was the sound of screaming.

'It's just a fox,' she said.

'There were no fingerprints, of course. Not on silk. And there's nothing can be done with his semen.'

A long silence followed, punctuated by a further shriek from the distant vixen.

'He could be dead,' she said.

'He could be. I'm sorry. I just blurted all this out. I don't know why.'

'Well.' She glanced at the watch pinned to her jacket. 'It's done now. I need to get back to the Institution. Patients. And meetings. The meetings are more difficult than the patients sometimes.'

She stood up, smiled, held out her hand. It was warm, the skin hard, calloused in places. The job of a doctor was difficult and physical, he guessed.

'You asked,' he said.

That seemed to amuse her.

'Are you glad I did, Louis? I don't think you've talked like that to anyone before.'

He was. He was also embarrassed. It was hard to shrug off the feeling that there was something to be ashamed of. Abandoning his desk in the Yard in an instant, without a second thought. Lying to get on the flotilla. Coming back to England unconscious, taking up space on vessels that were meant for fighting men and a few brave women. Then those weeks in the hospital, being treated as if he'd lost his mind.

'I am glad.'

'And are you well now? Head wounds don't mend overnight. The damage they can cause...'

'I believe so,' he said and left it there.

She picked up her bag, smiled quickly and took out her car keys.

'Do say goodnight to your aunt and thank her for the food and drink. I doubt there's anything else to discover about Harry Lee. But if I come across something, I promise I'll let you know.'

CHAPTER 79

'Sergeant Dobson?'

Three times she called him as she walked gingerly along the hall. No reply. There was the faintest light ahead so she aimed for it and found herself in a kitchen that spoke of the busy chaos of domesticity. Unwashed dishes. Jackets on hooks behind the door. A half-full basket of what looked like dirty washing stood by a copper tub and a mangle, poised by a large, cracked Belfast sink. A couple of feet along, the flyscreen door of a larder was open, revealing what looked like little more than a pat of butter, some cheese in white paper, and half a dry loaf. There was a clothes horse in the corner, pegs on it and a washing line. The room had the feel of a still life, a picture that trapped the mayhem of family in a single frame and cut out the noise and bustle of reality.

A strong and unmistakable smell of cheap whisky hung around the sink. The bottle stood on the table, quite empty. No glass next to it. Or anywhere. But there was a man's wallet there, with a few pound notes, and by its side a stack of coins. That was what they did when they went to bed drunk. Emptied their pockets then shuffled off to the sheets.

Given what had happened to Dobson, she could hardly blame

him. Still, it made the chances of a meaningful interview yet more remote. Full of drink meant full of remorse and anger. It certainly had with Mike, the man she'd married in a whirl, on nothing more than a passing whim, stupidly, with barely a thought for the future.

She went back into the hall and shone the failing torch around. There was a large living room with a settee and a tall mahogany wireless by the window. When she moved aside the curtains, she could just make out in the gloom a tiny courtyard garden, a dustbin, a greenhouse and a tidy vegetable plot. Someone so wanted this house to feel like home.

Next to it was a smaller room with a single armchair, a desk with schoolbooks on it, and two sets of bookshelves, all full, something she somehow didn't expect in Dover.

'Sergeant Dobson?'

Then she waited, listening to her own breathing, the whine of a siren some way off followed by the roar of a burst of artillery.

There was someone on the floor above. She could hear movement, faint but clear.

'I'd just like to talk,' Jessica Marshall said and, in the dying light of the torch, found the stairs.

CHAPTER 80

Renard saw Poppy Webber to her car, a modest Ford, plain black, practical. He waved as she drove off down the drive, just one headlight working, taped to a slit, the way the authorities demanded.

His aunt was waiting at the front door when he got back. She was in her billowing scarlet dressing gown, smoking a cheroot.

'I like that young woman, Louis. Who is she?'

'A doctor at the Institution. You barely met her.'

'I saw what she did to you. Invite her round for dinner sometime. I'll get Danvers to wait on you, then make myself scarce.'

Renard growled and made for the cognac decanter in the study. It was her favourite room, his too, now. Three leather armchairs, a desk, the piano, bookshelves and photographs everywhere covering Veronica's career from the stage to silent films then the Talkies. The people she worked with, some he recognised, a few doubtless long gone. Her favourite was a signed picture from a production of *Private Lives,* the stars, a beaming Noël Coward, a handsome Laurence Olivier and Gertrude Lawrence with a long cigarette holder, toasting one another. It was a reminder of a happier age, not so distant.

'No more drink for you,' she said, grabbing the decanter before he could get there. 'Busy day ahead tomorrow. That young lady...'

'I'm not in the business of inviting women round for dinner just yet.'

'You talked a long time.'

'True.'

'Did you tell her? About Delia? About London?' A pause and then, 'About Dunkirk?'

Renard shook a playful fist at her.

'Have you ever thought of getting a job with the Secret Service? They need interrogation specialists, I'm sure.'

'Not till now, but if you know of an opening... *Did* you tell her about Dunkirk? That beast of a man?'

'Yes. And I don't know why.'

'Oh, my poor nephew.' She took his arm and guided him to the large leather wingback armchair by the shuttered window. 'For a man so perceptive when it comes to others, you're remarkably blind when it comes to yourself.'

Renard fell into the chair, which was so old and saggy he thought it might consume him.

'I still–'

She pulled up the matching footstool, perched on it. Veronica was right, as usual. He didn't need another drink.

'You've been itching to talk to someone for ages. Tell one person and you're just passing on a secret. Tell two and it's a burden shared. It's like when you've eaten something bad, or... or mixed champagne with Guinness and Pernod or some such thing. You can walk around forever and ever trying to keep it down. The only real cure is to stumble off to the smallest room and have yourself a damned good chuck.'

Sometimes she came out with the most extraordinary

statements. He'd heard any number of wild stories about her antics with her theatrical friends over the years and believed every one.

'Thank you for those sympathetic sentiments, so elegantly put.'

'You're welcome. Elegance is for strangers. Frankness for family. There was a telephone call for you. Jimmy Mortimer.'

'Sir James.'

'He's invited you round for breakfast. Seven thirty tomorrow. His house is called Agincourt Lodge, ridiculous I know, but he claims one of his ancestors fought there. An unusual place. He lives on his own now. Down near the bay in St. Margaret's.' She handed over a sheet of paper. 'I've drawn you a map.'

'I'm in the middle of a murder investigation.'

She raised an eyebrow.

'He's the lord lieutenant, Louis. This is Kent.' Veronica poured herself a small glass and raised it. 'You should be flattered. When the feudal master calls, the peasants must obey.'

Chapter 81

The damned torch was dying, growing fainter, a fading waxy yellow with every step. The stairs were steep, short, narrow.

Jessica Marshall kept calling Dobson's name as she crept up, listening, trying to analyse what she heard.

Movement certainly, the creak of wood.

One minute looking round when she got to the top of the stairs, she told herself. Then, if Dobson was unwilling, it was back into the street, struggling through the dark, home to the Raglan, probably pounced on by a couple of nosy squaddies along the way.

'I'm a reporter,' she said into the endless shadows. 'I know you probably don't want to talk to anyone right now. I understand that. But if you'd like to have a chat then...'

Nothing. Just that random squeak and creak.

She edged forward, dashing the light from side to side, wondering where the bedrooms were.

Something cold and clammy brushed up against her cheek. With it came a drip, a stink, an unmistakable smell.

There was a dead man in front of her, and as her eyes grew used to a new source of faint illumination from the skylight ahead, she could make him out. A hanged man, a corpse dangling from a rope, swinging side to side, his cold and icy legs brushing against her face.

Jessica Marshall was not a woman given to screaming.

It was only when she was outside, listening to the distant roars of the night sky, that she realised her throat hurt from all the noise she was making, that tears were running fast and hot down her face.

PART FOUR

CHAPTER 82

They were in what Sir James Mortimer dubbed his "philosophers' grove", a shady bower with a view over the shallow bay of St. Margaret's. It was a fine clear morning. Wanting some exercise and time to think after the confession with Poppy Webber the previous night, Renard had parked at the top of the village and walked down. The French coast was visible across a Channel dotted with warships. Somewhere, Hitler's great guns were being trained on the coast. None of this seemed to disturb the Lord Lieutenant of Kent. Smoked haddock kedgeree, homemade, toast and marmalade and a pot of fresh tea were on the table along with a copy of *The Times*.

'You like my little sanctuary from our busy world?'

The alcove was ringed by a flowery hedge dotted with classical busts, bearded men mainly, familiar from museums.

'It's beautiful, sir.'

Mortimer nodded towards the line of grey marble heads.

'I come here to read with my mentors.'

'Which is your favourite?'

He frowned.

'Hard to say. Plato's quite the chap. Socrates too. But...

Aristotle. Now, he tutored Alexander the Great. A man who went on to conquer most of the known world. A fellow like that deserves a hearing.' He glanced across the table. 'Is that the weapon I gave you I see around your shoulder?'

Agincourt Lodge was a detached Edwardian mansion dominating the shoreline. Large for one man, Mortimer said, but he was too lazy to move now. His son occupied a bungalow at the top of the hill. The two of them dined together once a week on Tuesdays, always at six.

'It is indeed.'

'You have someone in your sights?'

He'd got the weapon out the night before and given it a second look. Renard knew rather more about firearms than he'd let on when Mortimer handed him the Webley. There was, he believed, no point in offering up a surfeit of information and opinions to anyone. Nevertheless, James Mortimer appeared the kind of man who would expect gifts to be acknowledged. It was only polite that Renard wore the holster beneath his jacket.

'I believe you can't be too careful.'

'Ah,' Mortimer poured some tea, 'careful when it comes to idle talk too. Even with the lord lieutenant. Quite right, Inspector. I should never have asked.'

The house was quite eccentric, the features built to resemble those of a ship. The dining room represented the cabin on the first floor, long bow windows looking out onto the sea. Above was a tower, the Union flag fluttering from a long pole, with a crow's nest at the top. The lookout was built for astronomy and had a large telescope for stargazing built into the roof. Another smaller scope sat on the table by the front window along with several sets of binoculars. In the event of an invasion, Mortimer said the head of the local forces would use the place as his primary forward base to try to monitor any local attack on the coast.

'A dancer's dead, I gather,' the lord lieutenant said, raising his teacup. 'All those poor people down in the bay. Soldiers. Civilians.

Some bastard's responsible for that. I wouldn't expect you to say if you had any ideas. I hope someone has.'

'I'm a detective, sir. Not an intelligence officer.'

'I gather from my son Chalmers believed one of his own sergeants might be responsible. Such times.' Mortimer shovelled some haddock to the side of the plate. 'Tastes old. Don't feel the need to eat it. Nothing's quite right at the moment, is it?'

Renard said it was fine, which was true, or so he thought.

'How do you find Superintendent Chalmers?'

War surely meant Mortimer had little opportunity to visit the rest of the county, a sprawling fiefdom, running from the Channel to the mouth of the Thames and inland to the borders of London. He seemed an active, inquisitive man. Renard could understand how that might translate into an excess of interest in local matters.

'He seems a very competent officer from what I've seen.'

Mortimer spread some Oxford marmalade on his toast and took a bite. Spitting out a few crumbs he said, 'He's a cheerless pen-pusher promoted beyond his talents. Dover's never been a posting for officers looking for careers. You need to be closer to London for that. Or Canterbury. What few bright and competent senior officers we had have gone elsewhere.'

'I barely know the man.'

'No need. I should talk to the chief constable and suggest they promote you. Put you in charge *pro tem*. Chalmers couldn't spot a villain if he walked into that place wearing a striped jumper, an eye mask and a bag over his shoulder marked "swag". Also...' He shook his head. 'The man was a member of Mosley's crew. The damned Union of Fascists. Half that police station was for a while. One reason it's so understaffed. Cyril Simpson had to break the whole gang up and send them elsewhere. God knows Dover's not the most welcoming of places for foreigners at the best of times. Didn't need a bunch of goose-stepping policemen as well. I'll talk to Cyril.'

'I'd rather you didn't bother the chief constable.'

'Why, Renard? Do you think you're not up to the job? I was told you'd recovered from your problems.'

'I'm new here. The situation is complex, to say the least. If–'

'I understand you're somewhat discomfited about Dunkirk. I rather imagine Chalmers knows too. He's an inquisitive bastard. But we're beggars here and beggars can't be choosers. In any case, it was your business and yours alone should you choose to keep it that way. If by some miracle we get through this summer without Hitler on our doorstep the town needs to be brought back into some kind of order. Dover's like the damned Wild West at nights. Drunkenness. Whoring. God knows what's going on. Now murder, for pity's sake.'

All true, Renard thought.

'Without the men...'

'The *right* men, Inspector. That's what's needed. The right fellow at the top most of all.' He sat back and folded his arms. 'I understand your position. You wish to be loyal. You also know full well Dover police station is crying out for a new broom. I have no need of your permission to organise a small coup, Renard. What I do require is your assurance that, once the smoke clears, you'll still be around to help me pick up the pieces. Not scuttling back to Scotland Yard and the comforts of London.'

The thought of returning to his old office seemed quite ridiculous.

'I rather doubt they'd welcome me back with open arms.'

'In that case you are, for once, quite misinformed. I happen to know different. Good policemen are like gold dust at the moment.'

'This is hardly the time–'

'This is *exactly* the time. We can't stand on precedent. A firm hand is needed there. Not that of a lickspittle pedant whose experience goes little beyond beating seven bells out of the odd burglar now and again. Serious times require serious men.' He leaned forward and tapped the table. 'And don't think for one moment Chalmers doesn't know you're the obvious chap for the job. He's a sly sod. Didn't get where he is without being able to cut the brake pipes of better men around him. It may...' he waved the toast, '...be a matter of survival.'

The telephone rang, for which Renard was grateful. Mortimer got up and answered.

'It's for you.'

Dan Kelly was on the other end, sounding breathless and worried.

'I've had the devil of a job finding you, sir.'

'You should have called me at home.'

'I did. No one answered. In the end your aunt came and gave me a right rollocking for getting her out of the bath.'

Mortimer was back at the table, staring at the unsatisfactory kedgeree. The man didn't appear to be eavesdropping. Doubtless he thought that beneath him.

'What is it?'

'Joe Dobson. He's dead. Hanged himself at home last night. Chalmers is going ballistic. Saying you should never have let him out of here. That it was him all along.'

'What's the address?'

'Seven Priory Hill.'

'Don't touch a thing. I mean not a single thing.'

Silence.

'What is it, Kelly?'

'Chalmers told them to cut him down already. He wasn't a pretty sight. And we had that reporter woman all in a state. She found him.'

'Whatever they're doing, tell them to stop. I'm on my way.'

He put the telephone back on the receiver.

'Trouble, Inspector?'

Renard smiled.

'Thank you for breakfast. It's a beautiful home you have here.'

'Too big for an old widower. I'm simply far too attached to it

363

to leave. Nor am I about to hand it over to Jerry. I've got more guns where yours came from. Lots, I assure you.'

'Understandable,' Renard said.

'Oh,' Mortimer stopped him at the door, 'I nearly forgot. Age, you see. My son asked me to pass on a message. It seems the military police have been busy overnight.'

'Doing what?'

'They've arrested one of the supplies johnnies up at the Castle. Seems he was selling goods on the quiet to some black-market villain you've been looking for.'

'Frank Lee?'

'I believe that was the name. The army fellow is up on charges shortly. I gather the MPs picked up Mr Lee in Canterbury in the early hours, drunk and punchy. Never a wise way to approach a military policeman. He is recovering in the medical section of the barracks there I believe.'

'Lee's a civilian. He needs to face civilian charges.'

'I merely pass the message on. What you do with it is up to you.' He glanced back at the bay. 'Don't get distracted by minutiae. Men like you and I have more important matters on our plate. Such as who's going to run Dover police in a time of peril.'

Renard said his goodbyes and walked up the hill.

There was a large bungalow at the top with "Crecy" on the gate. A green sports car sat in the drive. Mortimer's *fils*. Lots of money, like his father. A love of old English victories over the foreigners too, it seemed.

It was a short drive back to Dover. He went straight to Priory Hill.

CHAPTER 83

Dan Kelly was in the house with two bored-looking uniform constables. Dobson's body had been cut down from the skylight where they found him hanging and was now in the Institution Hospital. According to Kelly nothing else had been touched.

'Topped himself, sir. Doesn't look good.' He took Renard to one side. 'I'm not saying it with those two around because it'll go straight back to Chalmers. But he's blown his top. Says we should have charged Dobson with something and kept him in custody overnight.'

'Charged him with what?'

Kelly scowled.

'Super Chalmers can always come up with something. That's never been a problem.'

He ran through what he knew. Jessica Marshall had come round to the place the night before, hoping to persuade Dobson to give an interview about the loss of his wife and daughter. The door was open. She walked round and found him upstairs. Electric cable wound round the skylight. Chair kicked away underneath.

'Topped himself, like I said.'

Renard went round the ground-floor rooms first. The front

two seemed uninteresting. In the kitchen there was a whisky bottle on the table, empty.

'Where's the glass?'

Kelly pointed to the draining board by the sink.

'He washed it up.'

'How do you know?'

'W-well...' Kelly stuttered. 'Who else could it have been?'

Renard grunted something under his breath then said, 'We need fingerprints. Who do you call for that?'

'Now, sir? We don't have anyone in the nick handling that. We'd have to call in someone from Canterbury or Maidstone. Everyone's tied up. And well...'

Renard sniffed the bottle then took a good look at it. He went to the larder and found a bag of flour. Then he bent down and blew a fine mist of grains towards the bottle. They settled on the surface as a thin film.

'That's clever,' Kelly said.

'No, it isn't. It means I can't get proper prints that I could use as evidence.'

'Oh.'

'Not that there are any.'

There was a food bin by the sink, the lid half open.

'Have you looked in there?'

'No. Why would I?'

'Because it's a place people discard things. Sometimes objects of interest.'

Renard opened the top. There was some Christmas wrapping paper, scrunched up, in the middle of it a label that read, "*Condolences, Joe. From your colleagues.*"

He showed it to Kelly.

'Know anything about that?'

'Um. Seems a bit rum. I don't think Joe Dobson was the most popular fellow in the nick. Especially not after yesterday.'

He told Kelly to ask the uniforms if they'd heard of a whip-round for Dobson while he poked around.

'You're saying there aren't any fingerprints then?'

Renard picked up the bottle and told him to sniff it.

'Can't smell anything.'

'That's because it's been rinsed out,' Renard said. 'Then wiped down. Tidy man, Sergeant Dobson, it seems. Even when he was about to hang himself.'

He walked upstairs. The cable was still there, and a puddle of foul-smelling excrement on the bare polished wood of the landing. A chair was overturned by the door to what looked like the main bedroom.

'There,' Kelly said. 'He must have got up on the chair, looped the cable round that skylight and stepped off.'

'You should have left him here.'

Kelly looked exasperated.

'I wasn't around. They got a call last night. Couple of uniform blokes turned out, took a look and didn't know what to do except bring him down. I got into the nick and Chalmers was screaming blue murder about you. Wondering where you were. By the time I got here Dobson was in an ambulance and they were taking him off to hospital.'

'Did you see what he was wearing?'

'Pyjama top and underpants. There was a lot of, well... poo around.'

'Happens when people are hanged.'

'I didn't know that.'

His voice had gone quiet. Renard had to remind himself Dan Kelly was doubtless a stranger to such events. A shocked one. The first time was always a blow.

'Was there any sign of a note?'

'Not on him. Not anywhere obvious. It would be somewhere obvious, wouldn't it?'

'If he left a note, he wanted people to read it.'

Renard walked into the bedroom. There was the shape of a head on one pillow, what looked like Brylcreem staining the cotton. The sheets were ruffled as if someone had been underneath them.

'So, Constable Kelly, what do you think?'

'Well, pretty clear really. The poor bloke lost his family down at Shakespeare Halt. We saw what he was like yesterday. Devastated... That was partly why Chalmers didn't want him released, wasn't it? He took his belt and tie off him to make sure he didn't harm himself.'

'Which I duly returned and let him go.'

'You did.'

'On the grounds we had no reason to detain him! It wasn't Dobson on the cliffs, waving in the Germans. He didn't kill Harry Lee.'

'You seem very sure of that.'

'I am.'

A set of drawers stood by the window, old, cheap, a line of photos above it. Dobson, his wife and daughter, by the beach somewhere, years back. Happy.

'And after I let him go, he came back here. Found the gift of a bottle of Scotch, seemingly from the nick. He drank the whole bottle, washed it out, wiped it down, and the glass too. Then came up here. Went to bed, half in pyjamas, half out. Woke up and decided to hang himself.'

Kelly was wavering.

'Put like that it sounds a bit fishy.'

'A bit?'

'I have done a couple of suicides, sir. When people are on drink they do funny things. There's no point in looking for logic in them. A farmer I dealt with shot himself because his pig didn't win best in class in the Kent Show–'

'We're not talking pigs, Kelly. We're talking about a police officer who apparently downs a whole bottle of Johnnie Walker then washes it out, wipes it down and puts it on the table. Why?'

That, Kelly said, he couldn't explain.

'Have you looked in the chest of drawers?'

'You said to touch nothing.'

The top one was already ajar. Renard pulled it out further, peered in and pulled out a pen. Then he retrieved a handgun, the pen through the guard, and placed the weapon on top of the bed.

'Bloody hell, sir. That looks a nasty piece of hardware.'

'Enfield No. 2. Standard army issue. You've not seen something like this in the nick?'

'I told you. Haven't seen any guns being offered to us lot yet. Isn't that like some of the stuff Frank Lee had in his stash?'

Renard didn't answer. But it was. The envelope Poppy Webber gave him the night before was in his jacket pocket. The bullet she'd recovered from Harry Lee's corpse. He took it out, held it in his fingers. There was no point in pretending forensics would ever come to his aid in Dover. The place was too far gone for that.

There were three shells in the revolver. He shook them out onto the top of the drawer. Kelly came over and said, 'They're just bullets.'

'They're not just bullets. They're unjacketed shells. Soft lead. We're not supposed to use them.'

'I didn't realise you knew a lot about guns.'

'I didn't realise I needed to advertise.' Renard looked at the shell in the envelope. Same calibre. Soft lead too. 'I rather suspect we've found the weapon that killed Harry Lee.'

'Hold up. I thought he got pushed off the cliff. And you said Joe Dobson couldn't have...'

Renard glowered at him and Kelly shut up.

One drawer down was just shirts and socks.

The bottom one had sheets, a lot of them.

Renard handed the bedclothes over to Kelly then took out what they were hiding.

It was a brown leather shoulder bag, shiny and new. He flipped up the catch, took out a black box and placed it on the bed. The thing had dials, a rotary tuner, a set of headphones, a small Morse key, what looked like an antenna and two power cables, one with a British plug, the other he assumed foreign. In a separate cardboard box with the name Telefunken on the front was a large glass electrical valve, tiny filaments bobbing around as he held it up to the light.

Renard had seen something very similar in a briefing at the War Office when the war began. The session was about the methods used by German secret agents to go about their business. This was a suitcase transmitter that allowed the man or woman concerned to communicate with the German military intelligence service, the Abwehr. The equipment they were shown had been confiscated from two Nazi spies posing as refugees who'd been shot in the Tower after a brief trial.

'Is that what I think it is?'

Renard couldn't stop looking at the valve. The unit in London had been deliberately stripped of all German connections. No words, no instructions, nothing visible. The War Office specialists knew they could quickly detect its source, either by checking it against known secret radio devices or simply taking the thing apart and examining the structure and manufacture. But leaving the valve in the original German manufacturer's box almost advertised its origins.

'It's a Nazi transmitter.'

'What the hell was Joe Dobson doing with one of them?'

'I want to talk to Jessica Marshall. Let's get her in an interview room.'

Kelly looked nervous.

'I was going to tell you about that. She's round at Captain Shearer's. We need to talk to her there.'

'Why?'

'Because he says so. Chalmers agreed.'

'Did he?' Renard packed the radio back into its case. 'Take this back to the nick. Check with the military to see if they can tell us more about it. And find out who had a whip-round for Joe Dobson.'

'Asked downstairs about that while you were looking round. No one did. I said. They didn't like him.'

Renard grunted something under his breath.

'I'm going to the Institution to talk to Doctor Webber.'

A grin and Kelly said, 'Oh, really?'

'Yes. Really. I'd like her opinion on how Dobson died.'

'It's obvious, isn't it?'

'Yesterday it was obvious Harry Lee fell or got pushed off a cliff. Now we know he was shot first. Oh. That too. Call the military in Canterbury and tell them we want Frank Lee brought to the nick for questioning. He's a civilian case. Not one of theirs.'

Dan Kelly took a deep breath and said he'd do his best.

'Superintendent Chalmers isn't going to like any of this. I have to tell you.'

'On your way out,' said Renard, 'inform the uniforms I want one of them to stay here and make sure nothing's disturbed.'

'Anything else?'

'One last thing. When you're done at the nick, I want you to go round to Captain Shearer's office and tell Mrs Marshall she's required for interview. CID office.' He glanced at his watch. 'No later than twelve thirty.'

'Superintendent Chalmers–'

'I don't give a damn what Chalmers thinks. I want Jessica Marshall in an interview room on my territory. Not Shearer's.'

He looked around the landing. The chair. The cable. The bed. Then, followed by Kelly, he went downstairs back into the kitchen, sniffed the bottle again, and finally the sink.

Kelly came and did the same.

'Smells like he poured it down there, doesn't it, boss?'

'Someone did,' said Renard.

CHAPTER 84

Jessica Marshall was breathing in Shearer's cigarettes again, the hazy tobacco smoke clouding his office like a grey autumn mist. He'd sent Henderson round to pick her up from the Raglan. No arguments. Everyone else could wait.

It was midnight before they let her out of the police station, not that any of the uniform officers there knew what to do. A suicide, one of their own. A troubled man who, a couple of them said, should have been kept in a cell, no tie, no belt, to save himself from himself. Except Louis Renard, the London detective no one much liked, had overruled the local superintendent and let him go.

The hours passed mostly awake and she'd barely touched Eric's badly cooked breakfast when Shearer and Henderson turned up. Shearer had been observant enough to spot this and sent for coffee and pastries. In one of those odd quirks of fate a bakery round the corner was run by an expatriate Frenchman and produced near-perfect croissants. The crumbs spattered her skirt as she sat there listening to him tease out of her the story of the night before.

For a while she went along with this then a little voice inside objected, and she said, 'Shouldn't I be telling all this to the police? I imagine Inspector Renard will be interested.'

He rolled his eyes.

'Jessica, Jessica. Have you not noticed by now?'

'Noticed what?'

'The police are largely here for a show. Dover's a place where they no longer serve much purpose beyond checking papers. We're waiting on unwanted guests from abroad. Nothing counts except preparing ourselves for their arrival.'

'Not the murder of a woman called Dawn Peacock?'

He opened his arms.

'In the great swing of things... at the moment...'

'Then why are you interrogating me about Sergeant Dobson?'

She remembered meeting him not far from Shearer's office that first morning. He had seemed a pleasant, ordinary man. Perhaps out of place in Dover, judging by his London accent, so very different to the local almost rural tones. But in that he was hardly alone. Louis Renard appeared much the same.

'I need to know what's going on. It really is as simple as that.'

'In order for you to control it?'

'If I can.'

'So you can control me? You're doing that already.'

He sighed, picked up the coffee pot, pulled his chair closer and refilled her cup.

'Real coffee,' she said, sipping it. 'Not foul chicory. The idea we're all in this together is rather rich, don't you think?'

'I never said we were. There are those of us made for times like these. Most aren't. That's why they rely on the likes of me. We are... essential. We need to be fed. With information. Support. The truth.' He smiled. 'A little affection wouldn't go amiss at times.'

She closed her eyes. It had occurred to her in the sleepless hours that she was trapped here now, imprisoned, with Shearer as a kind of authoritarian muse. There was no alternative freelance work she knew of in London. Calhoun in Toronto had been talked into taking her back. Shearer was now syndicating her work around the world, even to a national in Fleet Street. To walk away from him would be to turn her back on the chance of a career she'd long dreamed of. Famed foreign correspondent. A new Hemingway. Perhaps he'd recognised that need and set the trap – one she'd been so ready to trigger.

'I went round to see Sergeant Dobson because you nagged me.'

'I simply pointed out the story you needed.'

'I wondered if he wanted to talk. As you demanded.'

'Suggested, Jessica. I've never demanded anything of you. If you wish you can leave Dover right now. I'll pay your train fare. Some expenses.'

He knew damned well she wouldn't take that offer.

'There's really nothing more to say,' she told him. 'The door was open. I went in. He was upstairs. Dead. Hanging. It wasn't...' She wondered how long it would take for that picture to leave her head. 'It wasn't pretty.'

'Death rarely is. Except in paintings. Did you see anyone close by?'

'No. I ran right out of there. Straight to the police station. Where they seemed... embarrassed. As if I'd created a problem for them, or something.'

'Who did you talk to there?'

'I don't know! I'd just seen a dead man hanging. Half-naked. Shit on the floor. They left me sitting there for hours then one of them walked me back to the Raglan and said I'd have to talk to Renard sometime today.'

He was quiet.

'What is it?' she asked.

'I was wondering if there's a story in this for you.'

She laughed at that and immediately felt ashamed.

'What? You've been nagging me to write something uplifting. Good for morale. Bulldog spirit and all that. A police sergeant who hangs himself–'

'After his wife and daughter are slaughtered by the Nazis.'

'If I'd managed to talk to him.'

'You could make up the quotes. You did for that dead fisherman.'

'I spoke to his wife and *altered* the quotes. Reworked them. That's not the same as pure invention.'

He frowned.

'A fair point, I suppose. There is a shortage of material. Leave it with me. I'll come round again tonight.' He thought. 'Steak. North Americans love steak, don't they?'

'Not many people eating steak in Dover.'

'If you like steak then steak it is.'

'Are you the king of this strange little kingdom?'

He thought for a second then said, 'More... its temporary governor. Until we see what comes next.'

She stayed quiet.

'I'll try to be there for six,' he added. 'Work permitting. We'll eat. Then we can work on your article.'

'In my room...'

It didn't come out as a question.

There was a rap on the door. The stern-faced young woman from reception popped her head round.

'There's a police officer downstairs,' she said. 'He'd like Mrs Marshall to come to the station for an interview. By twelve thirty at the latest.'

'They agreed to interview Mrs Marshall here,' Shearer said.

'I told him that. He said Inspector Renard wants her in his office. He insists.'

He shrugged.

'Well. What difference does it make? Fetch more coffee, Valerie.'

'I can go to the police station right now,' Jessica Marshall said.

His hand came out to stop her.

'One should never be early for the police. Twelve thirty will do.

Let me run you through some of the feedback we've been getting from the syndication people. Mostly positive.' He rifled through the pages on his desk and finally found the one he wanted. 'Mostly.'

CHAPTER 85

Something was going on at the Institution. There was a line of ambulances parked randomly at the back, some still discharging people on stretchers, an air of panic all round. Young and old, male and female, shocked, bloody, injured on stretchers, in wheelchairs.

Renard made his way through the crowd. Poppy Webber was where he expected, in the thick of things, dispatching nurses right and left. She looked just as exhausted as she had out on the cliffs the day before. He waited until there was a pause in the people trying to talk to her, then barged in.

'What happened?'

'Some kind of attack in Folkestone.' She brushed the hair away from her eyes. Perhaps she'd been crying. 'I don't know any more than that. They can't cope down there so we're helping. I'm sorry, Louis. Not now...'

'There was a corpse brought in during the night. A police sergeant. Joe Dobson.'

'Dobson?' She blinked. 'Isn't that the name...?'

'Yes. The father.'

'My God. What's happening to the world?'

A cry went up nearby. Someone in pain. Then another voice

began, a long, agonising wail, a man crying, 'Don't let me die. Don't...'

'Your people probably thought it was suicide. That he hanged himself.'

'What?'

'I need to see the body. It has to be examined. I need you to take blood samples and look at them. I don't believe it's suicide. I think he was drugged. There was this empty bottle of Scotch in the kitchen and...'

She stared at him in shocked silence.

'I know... I know you're busy, Poppy.'

'Busy?' she said, pulling a face. 'This isn't busy. It's insane.'

'If you could just let me see for myself. The blood sample can wait an hour or two–'

'An hour or two?' Anger flashed in her dark eyes. 'Are you blind, man?'

'I think it's murder.'

'Jesus, Louis Renard. Death does seem to follow in your shadow, doesn't it? Look at this place. *Look at it.*'

Another ambulance had turned up. Two more bandaged and bloody victims were being lugged out of the back.

'I'm sorry but–'

'But nothing. I indulged you before because you look like a man who needs indulging. This is a hospital. We're here for the benefit of the living. Not the dead.'

'I'm among the living, in case you hadn't noticed. I now have three murders on my hands.'

Poppy Webber waved a clenched fist at him.

'Your aunt's right. You are a damnably infuriating man.'

She turned to go.

'When did Veronica say that?'

'When, out of the kindness of my heart, I came to see you in Temple Ewell last night. Now kindly bugger off.'

The curse was so unexpected he was speechless. Renard stood

in the midst of the chaos for a moment, wondering if he might badger one of the nursing staff to take him into the morgue.

'Move it, chum,' said an ambulanceman at the front of a stretcher, a young girl lying on it, eyes blank with disbelief, moaning, bandages round her chest.

No chance to see the corpse. No blood test. Nothing but his suspicions without a single shred of hard evidence.

The dot on the horizon was still there. The line to it quite invisible.

CHAPTER 86

Chalmers was on him the moment he set foot back in the nick. He gestured to his office. Renard could see Frank Lee in the adjoining interview room. The man looked as if he ought to be in the Institution himself. Black eyes, purple bruised face. He sat handcuffed, two military policemen in uniform with him.

'What are you charging Lee with?' he asked as he took the seat opposite Chalmers.

'Every damned thing I can find. Collaboration with the enemy.'

'I'm not sure that's an exact offence, sir. Even if it was, Lee wasn't collaborating with anyone. He's a thief. A black marketeer.'

Chalmers sneered at that.

'What do you know? Lee had a stash of weapons stolen from the Castle armoury.'

'To sell. Why would the Germans need our arms?'

'To put them out of commission?'

Fair point perhaps, Renard thought, not that he was going to say it. Instead, he looked right at Chalmers and asked, 'Was he a member of Mosley's crew?'

Colour rose in Chalmers' cheeks.

'How the hell would I know?'

'It's just that I gather there were... there are a lot of them in Dover.'

The superintendent reached beneath his desk and pulled out the spy radio they'd found in Dobson's bedroom. He placed it on the desk then took the Enfield revolver out of his drawer and set the weapon by its side.

'I'm more interested in these.'

'Yes,' Renard said and folded his arms.

'Well?'

'It's a German transmission set issued to their agents. I've seen something like it in London.'

'And this?'

'Standard British army-issue handgun. The sort we ought to be receiving here, I imagine, unless they want to give us their old Webleys.'

'The same as the guns you found at Lee's place?'

'The same,' Renard agreed.

'Do you think they were working together?'

It was hard not to laugh.

'Dobson gave Harry Lee a mild beating. We all saw what the father thought of that when he came in here.'

'An act, Inspector. It could have been an act.'

'I don't believe Frank Lee has a theatrical bone in his body. Or, from what I saw, Sergeant Dobson either.'

'What do you believe then, Inspector Renard? What wonderful insight do the talents that saw you rejected by Scotland Yard have to offer us poor yokels here?'

They'd never had the conversation about his past. He'd no idea how much the man really knew. Veronica had organised all this through her friendship with the chief constable, Cyril Simpson. It was the kind of back-door deal Renard normally hated. But she was probably right. He did need the work, the intellectual stimulation. Dover had, to his surprise, provided a surfeit of the latter.

'As I said, Frank Lee is a thief. Of no interest to me in my enquiries. I suggest you charge him, get him remanded in custody to Canterbury or somewhere, and let the courts do their job.'

Chalmers rapped his knuckles on the desk.

'And what of Dobson? You let him go, against my wishes. If we'd kept him here, he'd still be alive to answer charges. If you'd done that and searched his house, you'd have found this damned Jerry stuff.'

'We had no reason to keep him here. Nothing to charge him with.'

'There's always something to charge them with, Renard! That's what being police means.'

As Kelly had said, Chalmers was the kind of copper who could always find the evidence to fit.

'Not in my book, sir.'

'The book of a failed detective from Scotland Yard.'

That, he thought, did not merit a response.

'You let Dobson out of here instead of keeping him, searching his house and finding...' he banged his fist on the radio suitcase, 'this. If you'd done as I asked, we could have had him in front of a court in the morning. In a noose before long. Where he belonged.'

Renard shook his head and kept quiet.

'Say something,' Chalmers demanded.

'It's not as simple as that.'

The superintendent rolled his head back and swore.

'Good God, man. The evidence is there in front of your eyes. We know Dobson had no alibi for where he was the night he waved the planes in. And killed the Lee boy. For all I know he saw that message from the damned Peacock woman when Shearer passed it on. He knew his time was up.'

Renard asked, 'Then why did he put her name down in a report? Only for it to be ignored here?'

'Covering his tracks.'

'But why?'

'You're the smart one. You tell me.'

Was there any point? Renard wasn't sure.

'I don't believe we would have found the radio and the weapon if we'd searched Dobson's house yesterday. I don't think they were there then.'

'Really?'

'A spy who leaves such incriminating evidence in a bedroom drawer? Along with a stolen weapon?'

Chalmers waved at him.

'Carry on, Inspector. It sounds as if your mental problems have yet to go away.'

'Joe Dobson didn't kill himself. Someone left him a drugged bottle of whisky, supposedly as a gift from his colleagues here. Not that any of your men appear to know about that. Where it really came from...'

The man opposite sat silent, stony-faced.

'Dobson drank the whisky. It knocked him out. Then someone came in, dragged him out of bed and hanged him. Put the transmitter and the gun in the drawers. Emptied the whisky bottle down the sink, washed it out so we'd have no easy way of finding what was really in there. Then walked away. And still he's walking.'

'Do you have the least piece of evidence for this fantasy, Renard?'

'Given time I'll assemble it. A man in possession of a handgun would surely kill himself with that rather than struggle to put his neck in a noose made of electrical cable then jump off a chair.'

'He was drunk.'

'I know. Which makes me doubt the little performance left for us even more. I have a witness to interview, sir. Mrs Marshall. She found the body. If I may get on with that task, then I would hope to clear this up shortly.'

'Psychic powers, Renard?'

'I have none.'

Chalmers smiled.

'Did you enjoy your breakfast with the lord lieutenant?'

Renard's focus was briefly broken.

'I wasn't aware that my table habits were public news.'

'Mortimer rang me afterwards. Told me you were a good man. Someone to be cultivated. Indulged if need be.'

'I know nothing of that. The lord lieutenant invited me to join him. It would have been impolite to refuse.'

'Doesn't invite the likes of me to that mansion of his, does he?'

Renard glanced at his watch.

'Did I get a mention?' Chalmers asked.

'Only to say that he has the utmost confidence in the way you're running the station in the most difficult of circumstances. I concurred with that, naturally. These are... strange times.'

'What the hell am I supposed to do with this?' Chalmers said, glaring at the radio.

'I'm sure Captain Shearer will know. May I...' he looked at the door, 'continue with my interviews?'

'I want this wrapped up by the end of the day, Renard. I want a name. A guilty party. Someone to blame. This nonsense has gone on long enough. If you can't come up with a better explanation the name will be that of Sergeant Joe Dobson. He never fitted in here. Now I think of it, he was always ambivalent when it came to the Germans.'

'Well,' said Renard with a quick smile, 'ambivalent is better than being their admirer, I believe.'

Chalmers nodded at the door.

'Clever bastard, aren't you? You heard me. By the end of the day. I want it done.'

CHAPTER 87

Jessica Marshall looked different. Not just exhausted, but defeated too. Renard sent Kelly to get her a cup of tea. She didn't want anything to eat. When he was back the three of them sat down, Kelly to take the notes that would, if there was time and the need, be part of a formal statement. Renard had seen how the bureaucracy of investigation was falling apart under the pressure of war and the paucity of manpower. Perhaps her comments would remain scribbles in Kelly's notebook for good.

'I enjoyed the story about the theatre,' he said.

That brought a brief, bright smile.

'I banged the thing out in thirty minutes. Didn't even reread it properly. What was the point? A true hack at times.'

Veronica had Danvers deliver two papers. *The Times* to check who she might know in the obituaries. And the *Daily Express* to see what people at large had been fed. Marshall's piece about her night in the Hippodrome covered much of an inside page of the *Express*, next to an advert from the government exhorting the public to be wary of loose talk.

'My aunt thrust it at me over breakfast. I'm grateful you didn't mention me.'

'I said I wouldn't.'

'What a reporter says and what a reporter does are sometimes very different things,' Kelly chipped in. 'I've been stitched up by them before.'

'I'm only responsible for me, Constable Kelly.'

She said it so sweetly and with such a hurt expression he blushed and apologised immediately.

'You have been busy,' Renard said. 'What's your next story about?'

The smile vanished.

'I'm not sure. I've been looking. Struggling.'

There was a notebook in her bag. She pulled it out and went through the pages.

'Yesterday I went back to that place in Effingham Terrace.'

'Why?' Renard wondered.

She shrugged.

'Idle curiosity. I got chased off by a very fierce woman.'

'Section Leader Perkins?' Kelly suggested.

'Yes. How did you know?'

'We got an earful when we went round there. She used to be my PE teacher at school. Always a bit of a dragon. She was living in the basement all the time.' Kelly laughed. He was in full flow and didn't notice Renard staring at him. 'Thought the Jerries had come. Thought *we* were Jerries.'

Marshall shook her head.

'I saw the basement curtains were blacked out. They weren't the week before.'

'They were open then?' Renard asked.

'I think so. Is it important? I'm rambling. It's Sergeant Dobson you want to know about, isn't it? I'm just trying to avoid the... the nasty memories.'

All the same, she told it in a plain and linear fashion, much as he'd expect of a reporter. Shearer had been pressuring her to get an interview with Dobson, one that would prove the basis of a moving story about personal loss due to Nazi savagery.

At first, she'd been reluctant. It was an intrusion on a newly bereaved husband and father. Then Shearer persisted and asked... What if the man *wanted* to talk? What if he had a story he wished to share?

'Does that happen often?' Kelly said.

'It's not my usual line of work, to be honest. But yes. Sometimes. My husband... reporters I knew used to be very good at that kind of thing. Not me.'

'Would you have reported it all back to Shearer before you wrote your story?' Renard asked.

'What do you think?' she said with a scowl. 'Look. The door was open. I went in. Shouted out. The kitchen stank of whisky. There was an empty bottle on the table. I imagine the man must have got drunk and gone upstairs. I... I went up and...'

She stopped, pulled a hankie out of her bag, came close to crying. 'I'm sorry.'

'No need to apologise,' Renard said. 'Do you want another cup of tea?'

'Do you have any idea how very English you sound?'

'We are English, Jessica.' Kelly picked up her teacup and saucer. 'If you do—'

'No. I don't want any more tea. I went upstairs and... bumped into something at the top. After that, it's all a bit blurry. I ran out. Came here.' She screwed her eyes tightly shut for a moment. 'I think someone offered me a cup of tea then.'

Renard asked if she'd touched anything in the house or moved any objects.

'Why would I?'

'Do you think there might have been someone else there? While you were inside?'

For a moment she thought about it then said, 'I think I'd have heard. There was just this creaking from upstairs. I know what that was now.' She dabbed at her face one more time, then put the hankie back in the bag. 'I'm not much use, am I?'

'You can only tell us what you saw.' Renard nodded at Kelly. The notebook went away. Interview ended. 'There was no one around outside when you left? Watching, say?'

'I doubt I'd have noticed. Sorry.'

'And on your way in?'

She stayed quiet.

'Jessica?'

'There was someone. When I was at the bottom of the hill. It was dark and I was struggling with the torch. These damned blackout ones. It's hard to see. The battery was on the blink and–'

'Forget about the battery,' Renard said. 'Just tell me what you saw.'

'Not much. As I said, it was very dark. He was rushing round the corner and bumped straight into me.'

'He?'

'Yes. He. I didn't see a face or anything. It happened so quickly. A man barged right into me as if he was in a rush. And then he was gone.' She took a deep breath. 'Not a lot, is it?'

'Did anything stand out? Think. Please.'

Her hand went to her neck.

'Yes?'

'There was something odd. I barely saw it. It was around here. It was...'

Renard thought back to the previous day.

'White?'

'Yes.'

'Could it have been a dog collar? Like a vicar wears?'

Jessica Marshall paused.

'It might have been.'

Renard got to his feet, thanked her and opened the door.

'Do you need me to sign anything?'

'No. Do you have plans?'

'I don't but I believe Captain Shearer has them for me.'

He couldn't work out how she felt about that. Worried or grateful.

'If you need anything, Mrs Marshall, you can always reach me here.'

Kelly watched her go.

'We're off to see the Bible-basher then?' he said when she was out of the door. 'The one who was hanging round here yesterday looking like a travelling salesman hunting for a customer?'

'Well remembered, Constable.'

'What's his name?'

'The Reverend Jolyon Partridge. The vicar of Temple Ewell.'

Chalmers watched them go. When they were out of the building, he called Shearer.

'We need to meet,' he said.

'I'm busy.'

'So am I, Captain. The usual place. Ten minutes.'

CHAPTER 88

The usual place was a small café near the town hall, twelve tables, a simple counter, a tea urn, a gas stove little used, a modest selection of cakes and buns from a nearby bakery. The posters on the wall were pre-war railway advertisements. The castle at Walmer where Wellington died. Another for the five Cinque Port towns: Hastings, Rye, Hythe, Dover and Sandwich. And beaches, Broadstairs and Dymchurch, Folkestone and Camber, children playing with buckets and spades while their parents sunbathed in deckchairs. Ancient monument or golden beach, everything was now given over to the military.

Four buildings along was the wreck of a haberdashery store, destroyed by a shell from across the Channel. The owner had died in the attack. The elderly couple who ran the café had closed after that. Then, a week later, they returned, washed off the dust, repaired the shattered windows and reopened as if life was normal. Shells could land at any time, from across the Channel, from the air. There was a good trade usually, especially from squaddies and civilians who wanted a break from their secret work up the hill. A little money to be made and everybody needed that. The couple reasoned they could die at home, bored and impoverished, or behind the counter where they'd worked most of their lives. It was not a difficult choice.

Chalmers walked there, trying to still his fury. Before the war Dover police station was well-staffed, mostly with men chosen locally. Obedient, loyal officers who knew their place. Then came the clean-out after someone – Sir James Mortimer, he felt sure – tipped off Maidstone about the number who'd been talked into signing up for Mosley's British Union of Fascists. The message Mosley had been spreading – about law and order and the need for a patriotic national identity – had struck a chord. Coppers liked to hear that kind of thing, and a few, a good few he suspected, smiled when the man talked about the Jews as well.

He'd gone along with the crowd without much thought and only escaped the ensuing purge by making a grovelling apology in front of Cyril Simpson, the chief constable himself. The head of the police force for the whole of Kent was no fool and perhaps didn't believe Chalmers' plea that he erred more out of stupidity than conviction. But others stuck to their guns and said their political views were theirs, private, nothing to do with the force. They were the first out. Simpson was aware he couldn't purge the whole of Dover nick, even during that quiet period they called the Phoney War. A real one was on the way, and no one knew what that might bring. Even with Dover as a kind of Wild West frontier outpost waiting on Hitler, the public face of a police presence was required alongside the military and the shadowy intelligence creatures under Shearer's thumb.

The captain was waiting alone at a table by the back, a cup of muddy-looking coffee in front of him, nothing else. Chalmers ordered tea and a Chelsea bun, and the two men made small talk until they were truly alone.

'Well, Superintendent?'

'You need to get Renard off my back. Out of the station altogether. He's a pest.'

Shearer sipped at his coffee and said nothing.

'Are you listening?'

'To every word. Inspector Renard is an employee of the Kent Constabulary, over which I lack the power of hire and fire. As you must surely know.'

Chalmers had come to loathe the man opposite him. Shearer could squirm out of any tight corner and leave others holding the blame. A talent he'd acquired himself in thirty years of police work in Dover, but not with such artful skill and determination.

'Kindly do not talk down to me. I know full well you can do what you like in this town. And beyond. It's one reason we're in this mess in the first place.'

The other man put his coffee down, pulled a pained face and said, 'Why am I here drinking this nauseating filth? Do please explain.'

'Renard will not stop. The man is downright obsessive.'

'I believe that's why the Yard were unwilling to have him back after his odd escapade in Dunkirk. Did you ever get to the bottom of that?'

Chalmers had asked around everywhere, but the answer always came back: no one knew why Renard had crossed the Channel, not even his superiors in the Yard who'd come to interview him in Ramsgate.

'You know I didn't. Any more than you did. He's got friends on high.'

'Wrong,' Shearer said. 'His aunt does. She called in a favour and got him a chair along the corridor from you. Perhaps you should have put him in a corner to count paperclips. Not hand him real police work.'

'I don't have the officers for real police work! Or paperclips to count, for that matter. We're going through the motions while you and your people on the Castle call the shots.'

'I still don't know why you called.'

'He had breakfast with the lord lieutenant this morning.'

From the look on Shearer's face that was a surprise.

'Oh,' Chalmers said, with a sudden brightness. 'I've told you something you don't know. How strange. Mortimer invited him round for a chat then, just to let me know I was under some pressure, rang to tell me. A social visit, supposedly. My arse. I know what it was about. Getting me moved elsewhere and asking Cyril Simpson to put Louis Renard in my seat.'

'You appear to have a persecution complex.'

'Far from it. I've stitched up men myself over the years. I can smell it in the wind.'

'That's ridiculous,' Shearer snapped. 'The fellow was nearly confined to a mental hospital only a few months back. There's not the least chance they'll let him run a frontline station like Dover.'

'Then why–?'

'You're seeing conspiracies where there are none.'

There was no alternative. He had to say it.

'I can't stop him.'

'Doing what?'

'I can't stop him digging.'

Shearer took out his silver cigarette case and lit a Du Maurier.

'Thanks for the offer but I'll pass,' Chalmers muttered.

'What about the Lee man? You have him in custody. He's got a record as long as your arm. Throw the book at him.'

'Frank Lee's a common thief. A thug. I've nothing to connect him to the Peacock woman. Even with the stupidest of solicitors we'd never get past a remand hearing.'

'Then find something. Invent it.'

'He'd hang.'

'This is war. People die. Is a man like that much of a loss?'

Chalmers had bent plenty of cases in his time. But always for a reason, jailing men he believed guilty of some crime even if it wasn't the offence that sent them down.

'I'm not putting a noose round a man's neck for a murder I know he didn't commit.'

'Oh,' Shearer smiled, 'you have a conscience now. Will that

conscience serve you well when Hitler's knocking on your door? Or will your previous affections for your goose-stepping friends come to your aid?'

There wasn't a thing the man didn't know. He was an encyclopaedia of secrets, especially the ones men wished to forget.

'I can't build a case against Lee for any of this.'

'Dobson it must be, then.' Chalmers had to wave away the smoke between them. 'Your man was in possession of a German radio. A stolen gun. I know this may be embarrassing for you–'

'It's not as simple as that. Renard believes someone framed Dobson.'

'Affairs are as simple as we choose to make them. We have spies amidst us. If indeed they framed your sergeant then I want them to think we've fallen for it. That way, they drop their guard. Either way Dobson's dead and won't complain. Do you comprehend now? Or is this too complex for a mere policeman?'

Chalmers took a deep breath.

'You don't seem to understand. Renard–'

'Then *I'll* tell Inspector Renard it's Dobson. He can go and chase shadows elsewhere.'

Chalmers tried to convince himself that would work. It was impossible.

'You don't know the man. He's tenacious. Straight as a die. Or thinks himself that way.'

'In that case, take the matter over yourself. You run what passes as a police station there. You say what happens. The woman's dead. The boy. Dobson too. Just do it.'

A single artillery round sounded from somewhere above in the grounds of the Castle. It shook the windows. The woman behind the counter closed her eyes and seemed to be mumbling a quick prayer.

'If I can...' Chalmers said.

Shearer rose from the table.

'You'd better. Or I'll be the one throwing you out of your comfy seat. Not Louis Renard. Not Sir James Mortimer. Me.'

CHAPTER 89

'Morose. That's what Chalmers called you.'

The Minx was edging its black nose up the snaking, narrow lane to the Temple Ewell vicarage.

'What? I'm not morose.'

'Never said you were, sir. Chalmers did. Talking to Hawkins. I heard him.'

'This may come as a shocking revelation, Constable. But it is possible to keep a thought to oneself. Not blurt it out the moment the words pop into your head.'

That small epiphany seemed lost on Daniel Kelly as they pulled into the drive of the Temple Ewell vicarage.

'Can't have a dodgy parson, can you?' he said instead. 'Not right.'

It was not unlike a smaller, smarter version of the run-down former mansion in Effingham Terrace where the woman who called herself Dawn Peacock ran a bordello that spied on its customers. Only with much tidier gardens and no dustbins full of empty booze bottles.

'Why not?' Renard wondered.

'Well, I mean... man of God and all that.'

'He was hanging around the nick enough.'

'Looking for business?' Kelly said as they got out. 'Even a vicar's going to do that.'

Partridge's wife was bustling over a trellis of roses with a pair of secateurs and appeared not to have noticed them. Then the front door of the vicarage opened and the man himself peered out. Meeker than he'd been at the garden party, scared almost.

Even from a few yards away it was clear to see he had a shiner of a black eye. The right, yellow and blue and swollen above the brow.

'Oh,' Kelly said with a broad grin as they walked over.

'We need to talk, sir,' Renard said. 'Don't we?'

'I don't feel so well, Inspector. Could we perhaps arrange an appointment for tomorrow?'

Renard shook his head.

'It's either here or we're taking a drive to Dover police station and an interview room. I'll leave the choice to you.'

Five minutes later they were sitting in the rectory dining room at a polished walnut table. A vase of freshly cut roses was on top. Linda Partridge had brought them tea in a silver pot with delicate china cups and a plate of Garibaldis.

'Dead fly biscuits,' Kelly said, picking one up and munching on it. 'Don't suppose you've got any fig rolls? Haven't seen a fig roll in months. Maybe Adolf's snaffled them all.'

She gave him a filthy look then walked out.

Partridge's hand was shaking as he raised his cup.

———

'Tell me about Berlin,' Renard said. 'Did you enjoy it there?'

'A fine city,' Partridge muttered. 'Beautiful. Though some of the...'

'Not a fan of Mr Hitler, then?' Kelly asked, halfway through his second Garibaldi.

'The man's a heathen. He'll close every church that doesn't agree with him.'

'Then Brussels,' Renard said.

'Briefly. After that, Canterbury. Temple Ewell.'

'Then last night, Priory Hill. And a dead man called Joe Dobson.'

Partridge looked more scared than ever when Kelly pulled out his notebook and started to write a few words.

'What?'

'Sergeant Dobson. The officer you left the station with. He was found hanged from his skylight last night. I've every reason to believe he was murdered.'

The man's pale, sweaty face turned whiter.

'Good God.'

'The way you were lingering round the nick yesterday, sir,' Kelly said, 'I rather imagined you'd have been on top of that one. Another funeral booking, eh? Nothing like a few burials to keep the coffers turning.'

Partridge glared at him.

'I find that deeply offensive.'

'Then I'd apologise if only I was sorry.' Kelly was getting into his stride. 'Just come out with it and–'

'Constable?' Renard silenced him. 'The reverend is going to tell us everything, I'm sure.'

The vicar glugged at his tea and stared at the table. Then it started to come out.

It was true, he said, that he'd been hanging round the police station looking to see if he could offer some assistance. Canterbury had called and started asking questions about what he'd been up to since he took over Temple Ewell. Very little, as far as they were concerned. There was also the question of money. He had targets for weddings, funerals, christenings. No idea how he could meet them.

'It's hardly my fault half the parishioners fled before the Nazis turn up. Most of the places here seem to be weekend cottages for the wealthy of London anyway. I am available for personal advice. There'll always be a Sunday service, even if my wife's the only one in the congregation.'

'You left the station with Sergeant Dobson,' Renard said. 'What happened afterwards?'

Partridge hesitated for a while.

'We could discuss this elsewhere—'

'The bereaved are never easy to deal with, Inspector. One wrong word and you can make the situation worse. Sometimes they turn quite furious even, for no reason whatsoever.'

'What was the word?' Kelly asked.

'I didn't need one. The man was there already. Quite livid with himself. With the police. With everything, I suspect. We went to the hospital. They were busy, a little offhand. He was allowed to see... the remains. I demurred.'

'Should think so too,' Kelly observed.

Again, Renard stopped him with a glance.

'Dobson got into an argument with some ambulancemen who were dealing with a Polish pilot or something. He was cross they thought the man was an enemy just because he was foreign. Quite incandescent. I told him. There was no point in getting angry with the ignorant. If you did that around here, you'd end up in a state of perpetual fury. The man...' He shuddered. 'He revealed himself as quite godless. Possessed of extreme political opinions as well, from what I'd heard. And after that he had the impertinence to ask me for money.'

'Don't sound like the Joe Dobson I knew,' Kelly cut in. 'He was a proud man. Never asked anyone for anything.'

'He said he was penniless. He'd given everything he had to his wife when they left for London. All missing.'

'And you said?' Renard wondered.

'I told him it would be quite inappropriate to use what scant funds we had on someone who wasn't simply outwith our congregation but the Church itself.'

They waited. Nothing more.

Renard leaned across the table and stared at that big bruise.

'That's not when you got your black eye though, is it?'

'I really...'

'You went back. You went to his house on Priory Hill. Someone saw you running away from there that night.'

Partridge got up and closed the door. His wife might have heard outside.

'The funds are scant, Inspector. I could have got into terrible trouble with this if the wrong person in Canterbury heard. But the Lord's will is that we show mercy to all, even the ungrateful and the ungodly. I couldn't get the sorry man out of my mind when I came home. I informed Linda I had an important appointment in town.'

The tea was cold, the biscuits gone.

'There was someone inside. I could hear them moving about. Then... then the door suddenly burst open. Before I knew it, he punched me right in the face. Very, very hard too. Well...' He pointed to the eye. 'You can see. I fell backwards onto the steps. It's quite a miracle I wasn't badly hurt.'

'Was the light on, Reverend Partridge?'

He shook his head.

'I don't recall, Inspector. I don't think so.'

'There was a blackout. How did you know it was Dobson?'

'Who else might it be?'

'Can't see Joe Dobson sucker-punching a vicar,' Kelly cut in. 'Punching anyone like that, if I'm honest. He was a gentle kind of bloke. Didn't even give the local toerags a leathering when they asked for it.'

Partridge glared at him.

'You weren't there. I was. It was him.'

'Did he say anything?' Renard asked.

'No. Not then. He'd said enough at the hospital. Quite fierce and unpleasant things. He came across as quite a bitter man, to be honest.'

'Maybe,' Kelly said, 'because he'd just lost his wife and daughter.'

Partridge looked a little taken aback.

'If I'd suspected he was suicidal I'd have gone round to the police station. As it was, I didn't want him charged for assault. He'd had trouble enough in his life, poor man. Oh dear...' He dabbed at his weeping eye with a hankie. 'I feel so guilty now. Sometimes it's impossible to do the right thing. Canterbury won't need to hear of this, will they?'

Kelly rolled his shoulders and said, 'I think you went in that house, sir. I think you had an argument with Sergeant Dobson and got into a fight. That's what happened, isn't it? You want to tell us the rest?'

Renard sighed.

'Are you serious?' Partridge asked. 'Do I look like the kind of man who'd willingly get into a fight?'

'You never know...'

'Constable Kelly.' Renard pointed at the pen and the notebook and told him to put them away. 'We're done here.'

'What about my statement? I want it on the record what happened, Inspector. I don't want any doubt on that front. I require it remains confidential. No word of this sad episode to Canterbury if you please.'

'Doubt, sir, seems to run through everything.'

'But...'

Renard left it at that. The interview, he said, was over, for now at least.

On the way to the car Linda Partridge watched them every step and didn't say a word.

'He's about to get an earful by the looks of it,' Kelly said. 'Shouldn't we have got him to sign something?'

'Such as what?' Renard asked. 'A statement that he recognised the man who briefly attacked him even though it was dark, he barely saw anything and ran off afterwards? What use is that?'

'May be no use but it's what he said...'

'And kindly spare me the heavy-handed "I know what really happened so out with it, chum" act in future. It never works.'

'It does at the pictures.'

Renard cast a sceptical gaze in his direction. Kelly smiled.

'It was a joke, sir.'

'Dobson didn't kill himself. I'm sure of it.'

'I know you are.'

'I don't have a scrap of hard evidence to back that up. Or, it seems, the resources to uncover it.'

Kelly kept quiet.

'You know that too, don't you, Constable?'

'Tell me what to do and I'll do it.'

'Can you think of anything we've missed?'

Renard started the leisurely drive back to Dover, barely more than twenty miles an hour all the way. The countryside was beautiful around Temple Ewell. True England. Green fields. Hawthorn hedges. A couple of hop fields with trellises covered in rampant vines. Wild flowers everywhere. From somewhere there was the fragrance of a freshly mown lawn, and not long after, the scent of cut hay.

'Sorry, sir,' Kelly said. 'I can't.'

CHAPTER 90

They drove the rest of the way in silence. When they got to the nick the uniform shift was changing. A handful of men Renard barely knew. His fault, really. He'd been almost bullied into joining Dover police by Veronica. He'd gone along with the idea. It was hard to fight his aunt's wishes at the best of times. All the same he'd felt an outsider from the beginning, regarded with suspicion, from the point of view of Chalmers, unwanted. Perhaps Dan Kelly, mouthy, inclined to insolence and insubordination at times, was handed him as a punishment for both of them. A plain-clothes pair in the understaffed CID rooms of Dover, waiting for a fall.

'You all right, boss?' Kelly said as they pulled into the nick car park. 'You've gone all quiet.'

'I'm quiet most of the time, aren't I?'

'A different kind of quiet, then. Just thought I'd ask.'

Kelly dragged his notebook out of his pocket.

'Maybe that vicar's lying. Could all be a pack of porkies. Dog collar don't mean you don't tell them, does it?'

'He wasn't lying.'

'How do you know?'

Renard wondered how much to explain, what to leave

unanswered. He'd learned the job himself as much from observation as instruction. Looking at people, men and women, trying to see the world through their eyes. That was the starting point. Separating the wily from the innocent, the liars from those simply nervous and troubled at being close to a darkness they'd always hoped to avoid. Some people had that insight, perhaps because they'd been there themselves. Others could never learn it and relied on the rote and mechanical process of logical investigation. There was something to be said for both, but he knew on which side of the dividing line he lay.

He stopped Kelly getting out of the car. This was important.

'Did he look like a man capable of poisoning someone, dragging Sergeant Dobson out of bed, stringing him up with electrical cable? Then planting a gun and a German radio in the place?'

'I didn't say he did any of that, sir. I just thought he wasn't telling us everything.'

'People don't. Especially when they're ashamed of what they've done. Worried, in Partridge's case, that we'll tell his superiors and they'll disapprove. A man like that...' This he was sure of. 'He craves the approval of others. It gives him power. Position. A chance to climb the ecclesiastical ladder. Like Jacob on his way to heaven.'

Kelly thought about that, then said, 'He wasn't bothered about Joe Dobson at all really. Just himself.'

'He was concerned about Dobson enough to go back to the house. Don't damn the man entirely. We're complicated creatures. Part of our job is unravelling that complexity. Often in cases where the men or women concerned fail to recognise the entanglement they're in themselves.'

That was enough, he thought.

Kelly opened the door, didn't turn to look at him as he said, 'Sounds like you're talking about yourself there, Inspector Renard. If you don't mind me saying...'

The afternoon was still hot. September continued to think it was August. But again, the day was quieter. The aircraft was distant overhead. The town seemed to escape bombardment yet again.

'What do we do now?'

Chalmers was at the door already.

'Ask around.'

'About anything in particular?'

Renard simply smiled. Kelly caught the figure at the door, latched on immediately.

'Righto, sir,' he said.

CHAPTER 91

Chalmers' office was tidy in the way that the working spaces of those who laboured little often were. Neat papers. An organised desk with a diary and a couple of trays, in and out, equally balanced. It was the lair of a man who left real labour to others.

There was a long shrieking whistle outside and a crash somewhere distant. A shell from across the Channel. Chalmers had blinked at the moment of impact. A man, Renard thought, under strain.

'Anything new to report, Inspector?'

'Not at the moment. As I said earlier, my enquiries are in flux. It may take a few days to get to the bottom of all this. It's possible – unlikely, I believe – but possible I will *never* succeed. Such is the work we do.'

Chalmers looked unimpressed. He took out an old pipe, meerschaum, much used, and a tobacco pouch. Then, without a word, he packed the thing and lit it. A foul, dense smell filled the office.

'I told you earlier I wanted this matter wrapped up today, Renard. It's hanging over this place when we have better things to do.'

'I'm investigating what I believe to be three murders. What better things?'

'There are reasons this needs to be closed down.'

'Such as?'

'Captain Shearer would like it done. That's as much as you need know.'

Renard hesitated before answering. Then he said, 'If I'm confident I have the right man in my sights then I will charge him. If I'm not, I won't. That is my understanding of how policing works.'

Chalmers glared at him from across the desk.

'Did you discuss your theories of policing with the lord lieutenant when you had breakfast with him this morning?'

Renard was surprised by that. It took a moment for him to answer.

'No. We mainly talked of the weather and the prospect of dealing with the Germans if they come.'

'Such a clever man.' His eyes were sharp through the pipe smoke. 'Always with a clever answer. A great shame your mental state ended your career in the Yard. Is it hard to fall so far?'

Renard smiled.

'Not at all. I found it quite easy. Do you wish to talk about me? Or a woman called Anna Schmidt? Or Dawn Peacock? Whichever you prefer.'

'So very clever.'

'A deprived young man called Harry Lee, perhaps. Or even one of your own. A bereaved sergeant by the name of Joe Dobson.'

'Dobson was a spy for the Nazis. Right here in this station. He murdered both of them, then killed himself. It's plain.'

'It's anything but. All the evidence points to another party in his house last night and–'

'Be quiet, man,' Chalmers snapped. He picked up a sheet of paper from his desk. 'Just before you returned, I took a call from the vicar of Temple Ewell. Reverend Partridge.'

Renard sat back in his chair, folded his arms and waited.

'He had no kind words to say about you, Inspector. He said you and your constable attempted to bully him into making a statement that he'd seen some other party at Dobson's home, when he went round to offer charity.'

'He said he saw someone. It was dark. The man's terrified of becoming involved in this affair in case it affects his standing with the Church.'

'Partridge is laying a formal complaint against you for intimidation. A vicar, against a fallen detective from Scotland Yard, struggling to make a case. With no success.'

'Did you advise him to do that, sir?'

Chalmers kept looking at his notes.

'The Reverend Partridge is dictating a statement to one of my uniform men in which he makes plain it was Dobson who attacked him at his house. That he was so frightened, indeed, injured, he declined to raise this with the police. Since he'd no idea here who he might trust. With good reason, it appears.'

'The man is mistaken.'

'Then who was it at Dobson's house? Who killed the Peacock woman? Who was on the cliffs that night? I see only one possible name. The fact Dobson's treachery led to the deaths of his own family clearly drove him over the edge and–'

'He didn't kill himself. He was drugged then murdered.'

'Evidence, Inspector? A suspect? Just a name will do.'

This was all done and dusted. He knew it.

'If you would allow me one more day.'

'I want you to go out of this room. Write the case as I told you. Everything will be put down to Dobson. I want your report finished before you go home this afternoon. After which, you will take a few days' leave.' He rapped the pipe into the brimming ashtray in front of him. 'Perhaps a little longer than that. I need to find you a different role. One that doesn't cause so much trouble.'

'I can't do that,' Renard replied.

'You mean you won't?'

'I mean I will not sign off on a case with findings I believe to be wrong. Seriously so. The person responsible for these deaths, and this treachery, is still with us. I believe you may still be enough of a police officer to know that yourself.'

Chalmers almost rose to the bait.

'If I asked you to take it on trust that I am offering you sound advice? Would you do that?'

'Not for a second, Superintendent. Not unless you tell me why.' Renard waved a hand through the pipe smoke. 'And it's clear to me that is something you fear to do.'

Chalmers smiled then. A rare event, and not a pretty one.

'Well done. Was that the kind of thing that got you rejected by the Yard?'

'To be honest I can't remember. I was... unwell then. I'm not now.'

'You're suspended. Go home. You'll face disciplinary proceedings in due course, when events allow us to deal with you. Till then, stay out of my hair and keep your fantasies to yourself.' He pointed. 'That is what we call a door. Walk through it.'

Renard didn't move.

'Goodbye, Inspector.' Chalmers was on his feet. 'If you set foot inside this place again, I will find some means or reason to place you in a cell.'

CHAPTER 92

He was about to get back into his Hillman Minx when Kelly caught up with him in the car park.

'What happened in there?'

'It seems I'm suspended,' Renard said, climbing behind the wheel. 'And to face a disciplinary enquiry.'

Kelly's face fell.

'Why?'

'Because, Daniel, I won't sign off an invented casefile blaming all this on Sergeant Dobson.'

'Not sure I like you using my first name. If you must, it's "Dan".'

'I'm just another civilian now. Don't worry. This is my problem.'

Kelly grunted.

'Knew something was up. Desk sergeant told me to take a few days off and have nothing to do with you. May be back in uniform after that. With a bike. Nothing to do but cycle round town checking people's papers.'

He glanced back at the station and muttered a low curse.

'I've had it with this dump. Half the time we're doing nothing that matters. The rest, when we have a real crime on our hands, they don't want to know.'

'Dan...'

'Mind's made up. I'm going to sign up for the army. At least I might get to do something useful then. I'll tell my folks tonight and head off down the recruiting office tomorrow. Shouldn't take long.'

Renard hadn't meant to involve Kelly any further. Now it seemed unavoidable.

'Give it a couple of days. We need good coppers as much as good soldiers right now. You're going to make a very able detective. I promise.'

'Not with Fred Karno's army here.'

Renard started the car.

'You'll be at home tomorrow? First thing in the morning?'

'Where else would I be? Chalmers don't want me here.'

'Then I may call. Do nothing rash. At least not for a little while. Which is the best way to Guston?'

'Why do you want to go there?'

'Just tell me, please.'

'Miss Perkins lives in Guston. Cottage by the church. She was the warden. Maybe still is. Quite religious for a dragon.'

'Directions?'

'Up Castle Hill Road and take a left when it gets steep. Marked for Guston and Connaught Barracks. Keep right on till you get to the little church. I can show you, if you like. Not far off my way home really...'

Renard was edging the car gently out into the road.

'Tomorrow. Till then you're off duty. Go home. Await further instructions...'

'Sir! *Sir!*' He was following the Minx out of the car park. 'I can't wait instructions from you, can I? You're suspended.'

The roads were clear. So, for once, was his mind. Freed from the need to keep matters sweet with Chalmers, and the unseen but ever-watching eye of Shearer, the cheerful but intrusive presence of Kelly too, Renard found himself able to think for once.

There was always something you missed. It had occurred to him earlier that day. Now it seemed more important than ever. There was a faint line to that distant dot on the horizon, perhaps the last he'd ever see.

CHAPTER 93

Shearer turned up at five thirty with a fragrant bouquet of lilies and chrysanthemums. He was in a new suit – dark-navy barathea – white shirt, scarlet tie with what she assumed to be a military or club insignia on it. Steak was in the kitchen in the hands of a Castle chef. Foie gras with Chablis to start, then the beef with boiled potatoes, red cabbage and a bottle of claret. They ate at the same table by the window, the flowers in a vase between them. Eric served as waiter, baffled, grumpy, subservient.

There was, she thought, something different about Shearer now. The air of anxiety she'd noticed from the start had mostly dissipated. In its place was a quiet charm, with a smile that seemed genuine. He made small talk about the area he grew up, a semi-rural town in Hertfordshire, a place of farms and markets and genteel affluence. Then he prodded and probed about her own childhood in Canada, what she'd loved, what she'd hated. Nothing about the marriage at all.

Jessica Marshall rarely talked about herself. Rarely thought much about herself, if she was honest. There was always work ahead: a ladder to climb, a deadline to meet, a story to be delivered, one better than her rivals'. All the same, he teased out of her a story about growing up in Oshawa, a manufacturing town on the shores of Lake Ontario, a place where almost everyone worked for the automobile trade in one way or another. Her father was an engineer, her mother a secretary at General Motors. They'd assumed she'd follow in their footsteps.

But Oshawa was tedious and even Toronto, less than forty miles to the west, seemed, like Canada itself, insular, small-minded, unambitious. She'd grown up an avid reader, drawn to Hemingway, Jack London and John Buchan, to tales of adventure and exploration and risk. A line attributed to London – "*I would rather be ashes than dust*" – had haunted her from her teens. It was hard clawing her way onto the *Inquirer*. Hard talking them into letting her work the tough city beat instead of writing soft and insulting women's features. Had it not been for the marriage break-up and the sympathy of one of the senior editors, she'd never have got the break to travel to Europe. That was a perk Calhoun had been saving for one of his male protégés, another reason he loathed her.

Still, she was there now, where she wanted to be, at the heart of the biggest story anyone had seen in years. A war that was spreading round the world like plague. One she'd make a career of documenting with all its twists and turns. Though what might happen to a Canadian hack once Hitler was in England, she couldn't begin to guess. In a way, that didn't even matter. Reporting was about being there. Getting the words down. Telling the story. Truthfully, and as accurately as she could manage.

And there, amidst the rubble and defiance and fear of Dover, was the rub. As Fred Lumsden, a wily old man had said. His words had resonated then, even more so now. "Among the calamities of war may be numbered the lessening of the love of truth, by the falsehoods which interest demands and credulity encourages."

'Jessica?'

'Sorry. I was thinking about something.'

'Anything in particular?'

'Not really. Thank you for the flowers. Thank you for the opportunity.'

He raised his glass. The wine was good. They'd finish the bottle easily, before going upstairs to work on the story. She knew that was coming. She felt differently about it somehow, too.

'Thank you for making my job so much easier,' he said. 'My life too. I've spent too much time in the company of men.'

'I imagine that's a rarity for you.'

He took that well.

'You imagine wrong. We were a happily married couple till the war came along. As happy as one gets, I suppose. I was away a lot. Postings. Eleanor is a woman with a career as well. The law. I'd never want anyone who'd stand in my shadow. Then...'

He hesitated, put the glass down, thought of lighting a cigarette until he noticed the displeasure on her face.

'These things change us,' he said, putting away the silver case. 'In ways we never notice until they're done.'

'You said yourself last night. You found yourself liberated. Free. In this, our natural state. No rules, no laws, no boundaries. At least for you.'

'For us. You're a part of it now. An important part.'

'I'd rather be ashes than dust.'

He squinted across the table.

'I'm sorry?'

'It's an old saying. One I learned when I was starting out.'

He chinked his glass against hers.

'No ashes or dust for either of us. Not now. Not for a long time.'

She found that amusing.

'A Jerry bomb could come through the roof of this place at any moment.'

'I doubt that.' He shook his head and seemed very certain of this. 'Truly.'

'But–'

'I need another story from you. What's it going to be?'

'Oh, I don't know. How about me going round to see a distraught police sergeant who'd just lost his family? At the insistence of my boss. You *are* my boss, aren't you?'

'Only if you see it that way.'

'Going round to see a bereaved police sergeant. And bumping into his shitty legs when I find him hanging above the stairs.' She touched his hand. 'I do apologise for the brutal language. I hope I didn't put you off your steak.'

'Not at all. I've perhaps eaten enough anyway.'

'Going round and finding a dead police sergeant. Destroyed utterly by the war. Devastated by the loss of his family.'

He carved off a morsel of meat anyway and began to chew on it.

'You won't let me write that, will you?'

'Of course not.'

'Well.' She sighed, pushed away her plate and poured them more wine. 'I guess it's back to the night in the tunnels.'

'Are you fine with it now? Seeing a dead man like that?'

A question she'd asked herself, over and over.

'I don't know. It still seems unreal. Maybe... maybe...' It was worth a try. 'If I was to write it all out. There'd be a kind of catharsis. A release. No nightmares.'

'I don't think you're going to have nightmares, Jessica. Truly I don't.'

'You don't know me. You may think you can look inside my head. You can't.'

Eric came out and took away the plates. Then he returned with two desserts. Tiny pastries topped with slices of apple.

'Your man from the Castle didn't bring any pudding, Captain,' he said. 'I ran this up myself. House speciality. Canterbury tart. Sorry but you can't buy lemons for love nor money right now, so it might be a bit sweet.'

It was delicious, to her surprise. Eric, it seemed, had hidden talents.

'The reason you can't write the story,' Shearer said when they were alone, 'is that you've got it wrong. Sergeant Dobson was not the man you think.'

'In what way?'

He offered her his tart. She declined.

'In what way, David?'

He looked conflicted and she wasn't sure whether it was an act or not. 'I think there may be a way we could use this.'

'We?'

'Yes. We. Don't worry. Your name will be on it. I'll merely offer guidance and support.'

Shearer checked his watch.

'We should go upstairs now,' he said. 'Don't you think?'

CHAPTER 94

Renard was not a religious man. It ran in the family. The Huguenot tradition was to do with lineage, no longer faith. There was only one church that stuck in his memory and that was St. Martin-in-the-Fields, the Palladian temple by Trafalgar Square where he was supposed to have been married. One recommended by Aunt Veronica because she loved the place and its proximity to the theatres.

But there was no wedding. No Delia for a wife. Here, down a narrow country lane in the verdant Kent countryside, was one more reminder of his loss. He'd parked on the verge next to the tiny church in the hamlet of Guston. It was a lovely one, Norman he guessed, with crusader crosses on the door, carved by knights returning from slaughter, theirs and their enemies, in the Holy Land. Guston's tiny house of worship was dedicated to St. Martin of Tours, just like its far grander namesake in the heart of London. A tribute to a former Roman soldier who'd supposedly torn his cloak in two and given it to a beggar before becoming a bishop in France.

Lines and dots. They seemed to be everywhere. If only he could make them join.

Maud Perkins' cottage was next door, a tidy, tiny home, the door open, no one inside. But there was the faintest light visible behind the old stained-glass windows of the church, so Renard thought he'd try there. The graveyard all around was picturesquely overgrown, leaning headstones set against open fields, rotting flowers on what looked like a recent burial marked by fresh brown earth.

When he passed through the stone arch, he found himself in a tiny nave, poorly lit. Only a single bulb glowed above the altar, with it a few candles. Someone sat in the pew at the front, a large figure, shoulders slumped, head down.

Renard walked along the cool and shady interior towards the chancel, the only sound his footsteps on old stone. Conscious that once more he had no hat to remove. Life had been too strange of late to think of preparations. He sat in the pew on the other side of the aisle, waiting for her to notice.

'I'm sorry,' Perkins said after a while. 'There won't be a service on Sunday. Or the Sunday after that. The vicar has to come from Temple Ewell, and he has other commitments.'

'Does he now?' Renard replied. 'He never mentioned those when I asked him if he'd seen Sergeant Dobson swinging from the rafters.'

There was a quick intake of breath from across the aisle and then her eyes were on him, dark and accusing.

'What do you want?'

Renard shuffled round to face her.

'I've always envied people who have belief. A little, anyway.'

Maud Perkins glared at him then said, 'Why's that?'

'Because it places certainties in life. Whereas I always find myself surrounded by doubts, suspicions, caveats. About people. Whether they're telling me the truth or lying. And if it's the latter... do they know the reason themselves? Does their belief extend that far?'

She moved into the shadows and kept quiet.

'You lit candles, Section Leader. Here on your own. An offering? A prayer for forgiveness?'

'What... do... you... want?'

'What a man in my position always wants. To peer into the darkness and find some light.'

It was hard to read her face in the shadows. But this was not the woman he'd seen in the basement in Effingham Terrace, fierce, confident, determined. Something had happened to change her.

'I'm not Section Leader anymore. I've been moved at my request. They'll find something for me in the auxiliaries in Deal, or so they say.'

'And still you serve.'

There wasn't the drone of aircraft overhead at that moment. Just early evening birdsong, blackbirds perhaps and from somewhere the far-off hoot of a waking owl. The place had the smell of flowers too, not that he could see them. And incense perhaps. He had only a passing knowledge of the ways of the Church of England. Still, something told him this was one of the outposts of the wing known as 'High', where the air of Catholicism still lingered four hundred years after it was supposedly dispersed. History, the Tudors in particular, was his subject at Cambridge, part of an education meant to prepare him for a life in academia. It was a fascinating period – bloody, cruel, filled with executions carried out in the name of faith, though in truth it was usually politics that swung the axe. There, in the university libraries, in tutorials and on the bookshelves of Blackwell's, he'd discovered an interest in the forensic, the unravelling of mysteries, often ones others wished hidden. An obsession sometimes which, through strange byways, led him to join the Metropolitan Police, to his father's frequently voiced horror. Perhaps, he sometimes thought, the old man had been right.

'First,' he said, 'I wish to deal with the fantasy of your stay in the basement of Effingham Terrace. The idea you were locked there for days on end, thinking the Germans had landed. Waiting on them to discover you.'

Perkins glared at him.

'Am I under arrest then, Inspector?'

'Not unless you killed someone, Miss Perkins. Which I don't believe you did. You were, I imagine, only following orders. We both know whose.'

'What makes you think I made that up?'

It was simple, and simply explained. He told her what Jessica Marshall had said earlier that day. When she first went round to the house the basement curtains were open, the place empty. When she returned later, they were closed, as they had been the morning he and Kelly had arrived at the house.

'You were sent back to greet us, since Captain Shearer doubtless knew we'd turn up before long. The question is, why?'

Silence.

Then she gave in.

'He told me he didn't want you hanging round the place. That Dawn's death was... dealt with. The last thing he needed was the police poking about.'

'That sounds rather vague.'

'It was all meant to be under the covers! What Dawn did there. The other girls. No one was supposed to know.'

He remembered what Dan Kelly had said. The woman had been a teacher once. Perhaps hoped she would be again one day.

'How did you feel about a fifteen-year-old girl being used as a prostitute on behalf of Captain Shearer's machinations?'

That hurt. He could see it in her face.

'What kind of question is that?'

'The kind her mother and father might have asked.'

'I didn't know! I'd no idea how old she was. If you'd seen her... Dawn did her make-up, gave her a fancy dress. She looked special. More than pretty. Glamorous.'

'The men must have loved her.'

Maud Perkins stayed quiet again and he felt that little shiver of expectation that came when he detected an interesting change in the mood.

'They did, didn't they?' he went on. 'Love her? If you could call it love.'

'Dawn did her best to look after the girl. It was never any Tom, Dick or Harry. She was a cut above the rest.'

The church was so quiet, so peaceful, the smell of the incense quite soporific.

'Special goods.'

'Don't rub it in, Renard. I know we were playing dirty. It made me sick to my stomach sometimes. This is war. We don't get to be picky. Hitler isn't.'

He closed his eyes and leaned back on the pew.

'I don't believe you,' Renard said.

CHAPTER 95

The typewriter was on the desk, the usual blank sheet of paper staring at her from the carriage.

Shearer sat down on the bed, took off his jacket and loosened his tie.

'David. I've absolutely no idea what it is you expect me to write. I never spoke to the man except briefly when he was down by the harbour that first morning. He seemed pleasant. Unexceptional, if I'm honest.'

'Seemed,' he said. 'Sergeant Joe Dobson was anything but.'

She ran a finger across the old, familiar keys. Still nothing came.

'I don't know what you want me to say. What you'll *allow* me to say.'

'Do you mind if I smoke?' he asked, taking out the silver case.

'Yes, I do. Put that away and tell me how I'm supposed to start this piece.'

He relented, quite pleasantly she thought, given the crabby way she'd spoken to him.

'David–'

'I'm thinking. A moment please.'

She wished there was more booze. Anything to take away the doubts. Then he said, 'We can't use his real name. Let's call him... Sergeant B.' He waited. 'You're not typing.'

'That's because I'm not a secretary. You're going to dictate this for me?'

'Just suggestions...'

She pulled out a notebook and her favourite pen.

'Talk. As fast as you like. I do shorthand.'

'Like a secretary.'

'Don't push it, mister.'

He laughed, then declared, in a tone that was almost theatrical, '"The Salutary Tale of Sergeant B". How's that?'

'I'd say someone losing their wife and daughter, and then their own life... salutary's not quite right word.'

He seemed unimpressed by that objection.

'You don't know the real story.'

'If this is going to take a long time, I need another drink.'

He went downstairs and came back with two glasses and a fresh bottle of wine from the Raglan cellar. Cheap French red. All they had, it was old, dusty, characterless, but it would have to do.

'"The Salutary Tale of Sergeant B".'

'I've already written that down, thank you.'

He uncorked the wine, poured her some, then just a little for himself, and began.

'He seemed an ordinary man. Unexceptional, those who met him said. Yet Sergeant B, a serving police officer in one of the south-coast towns in Hitler's sights, had a life *sub rosa*, a covert existence that would haunt him to the end. His devastating secret would turn him from a seemingly humble officer of the law into a murderer. A secret that would result in the death of his innocent family and ultimately lead to his suicide, riven with the guilt and shame of a traitor.'

She finished the shorthand scrawls and looked up at him from the desk.

'This is a tale of treachery and its cost,' Shearer continued. 'Of a man lured into Hitler's grip by delusion, ambition and greed. Of how a lack of caution and observation on the part of ordinary citizens may allow the canker of treason and duplicity to poison the pristine heart of British decency.'

'Jesus,' she muttered, 'that purple prose is coming out. And the Latin. No one understands *sub rosa*.'

He got off the bed, came over, pulled up the little chair by the side of the desk and put an arm around her shoulder.

'Write it how you like. So long as you tell the story.'

He was a good-looking man when he relaxed, when he smiled. Something was different about him now too, not that she could put her finger on it.

'Is this true? Really? I can barely picture the man. You're saying he was a German agent?'

For a second he looked offended.

'Of course it's true. I may demand you elaborate a little from time to time. Even invent some small, important detail. The essential verity will always be there. Propaganda that's pure fiction rarely works. Plausibility is everything.'

He sipped at his wine, declared it poor stuff, and carried on.

Jessica Marshall went back to her notebook and jotted down his flowery ramblings in the Pitman she'd learned so patiently what seemed like a lifetime ago at night classes in Toronto. Shearer told his tale in a histrionic, overblown fashion, with a style that was downright ridiculous at a few junctures. But the story came out in a fashion she found logical and well-structured, all the twists and turns in the right places, all the dramatic moments there, right up to the conclusion.

A good tale it was, too. Perhaps the best she'd ever come across, ever written, ever thought might appear under her name. A tale that combined tragedy with deception and ended the way her readers would want, with the villain dead and vanquished, ruined, made to pay for his misdeeds.

When Shearer was done, he went and lay on the bed. Patiently, fluently, she went through her shorthand and transcribed his purple prose into something more constant, calmer, convincing. The generals and the politicians she'd interviewed over the years had come to talk constantly of the "theatre of war". It was a kind of stage too, a vast one, for the English always a variation on Henry V, the proud and high-born warrior of the sceptred isle defeating the ignoble foreigner. A bloody, deadly tragedy about the struggle for victory in the teeth of the storm. The narrative of Sergeant B worked on a smaller scale. There was no need to shriek for effect. It contained sufficient drama of its own.

She'd learned to work quickly on the *Inquirer*. A daily paper had fixed deadlines. Printers and delivery vans waited on no one. There was no place for the lazy or the late.

Forty minutes or so was all it took to get a finished version, just over 900 words she guessed, the perfect length for a piece that sat between news story and feature – unmissable, uncuttable too, which was always a boon.

Shearer stayed on the bed when she told him it was finished. All the same she went through it again, corrected a couple of typos with a pencil, went over and placed the pages on his chest. He opened his eyes, didn't even look at it and said, 'I'm sure it's perfect. Every word. You're a natural at this, you know.'

She ran through the piece one last time, amazed and said, 'This is quite a story. You don't even want to read it?'

'Not at the moment.'

'What do you want then?'

'I don't *want* anything.'

'David.'

'I need...' His hand found its way to her leg, reached beneath the skirt, touched her silk stocking, toyed with her suspender. 'I need you.'

CHAPTER 96

Renard leaned over the aisle, bent down, put his hands together as he spoke to her.

'Someone murdered Dawn Peacock. The same man shot a young and unfortunate boy called Harry Lee, who disturbed him while he was calling in the Luftwaffe to bomb Shakespeare Halt. May Dobson and her mother were killed in that conflagration. Joe Dobson died last night, hanged from his rafter with an electrical cord. Murdered, I'm sure.'

She seemed shaken.

'No, no, no. That doesn't mean it's all the same people, does it?'

Another interesting response.

'Did May have any one... customer in particular?'

Perkins took a deep and nervous breath. A hit, he thought. There it was.

'I told you. Sometimes Dawn put a pillow over the microphone. All I heard was... well, you know.'

'I don't. Tell me.'

'The bed, Renard. The bed. The... cries. You know what happens there, I presume.'

'This special someone...'

'I never asked.'

'Miss Perkins–'

'If you think I've done anything wrong, arrest me. See what Captain Shearer makes of that.'

He stuffed his hands in his jacket pockets, got to his feet and looked around.

'It is a beautiful church.'

'Are you finished now?'

'I think so. The man who was May's special customer. He was, I assume, the one you believed Dawn Peacock was meeting the evening she was murdered. Perhaps you even saw him.'

Her face was caught in the evening light from a stained-glass window. There was embarrassment, fury perhaps, or both.

'I know you think you need to protect him, Miss Perkins.'

'Don't you have a home to go to?'

'But you're wrong. He didn't just kill Dawn Peacock. As I said, he waved the Germans into Shakespeare Cliff and shot a young boy there. He drugged and strung up Sergeant Dobson to make it look as if it was all that poor man's work. He–'

'No! This can't be true!'

Perkins rushed for the door. Renard followed. A soft fading sun was casting gentle gold on the fields of wheat all around.

'I admire your faith, Miss Perkins. But does it ever occur to you that it may be misplaced? Misused? That you were being duped, just as much as May Dobson was upstairs, while you were listening to her in bed?'

She turned and he caught a look in her eye.

Maud Perkins looked ready to weep.

'I never wanted to be a part of all that. I never understood what they were asking...'

'But you had a bad feeling all the same. That Friday, you knew Dawn Peacock met someone.'

Doves were cooing somewhere and far off, a tractor was working the fields.

'You need a name?' she asked.

'Not really. But for May's sake. Her mother and father. Dawn Peacock, even. It might be best.'

She glanced back at the tiny church of St. Martin of Tours, as if something there might protect her.

'I just listened,' she whispered. 'I just did as they asked.' Her voice faltered. 'I hated every damned minute of it. They said it was my duty. Things felt wrong. Sounded wrong. I couldn't talk to anyone, could I? Couldn't trust anyone. We're all meant to be in this together, aren't we? Every one of us. All the same.'

'A name,' Renard repeated.

She stayed quiet, so he said it anyway.

The silence that followed was enough.

CHAPTER 97

There was something about David Shearer, an arrogance with a touch of shyness. It felt natural for her to take the initiative. To undress him more than he did the same for her. To mount him on the creaky hotel bed that must have been home to the activities of frantic lovers for decades. Then stay like that, watching him, fingers straying to his mouth, his hair, his neck as the heat grew and the world beyond the window – Dover with its violence, its noise, its fire – vanished into the shadows, a darkness without words, without thought, only sensations, physical and so very real.

When she sensed he was close she rolled off, lay back, waited, intent on making this last. Then he was in control, in his element above her, hard still, relentless, pushing, sighing, sweating. This was the place she longed to be, mindless, joined with another, lost inside the pulsing moment, feeling his excitement, hearing the roar of him at the height.

It didn't happen for her. That was rare and required work, practice, a frame of mind she'd yet to reach in Dover. Perhaps he was the rarity of a man who could deliver that magic. If she gave him time.

Afterwards he was gentle, kind, thoughtful. A man of

experience she didn't doubt. He stayed above her, inside her, for longer than most. Then he rolled to one side on the thin, old sheets, and lay there, not smiling, just looking at her, his fingers entwined in her hair, reaching down to her breasts, caressing the fading firmness there.

She knew she would be first to talk. He was waiting.

'I've only ever felt good about going to bed with two men in my life,' she said. 'Both, I loathed with a vengeance when I first laid eyes on them.'

'I started well then...'

He kissed her slowly, lightly on the lips and then she laughed.

'Doesn't matter, does it, David?' They'd found their way to one another. The world outside was in retreat. 'You don't need to use a rubber, by the way. I can't have kids.'

He seemed shocked. Perhaps even disappointed.

'I'm sorry to hear that.'

'I'm not.'

'You mean... how can anyone bring a child into a world like this?'

She couldn't work out if he was serious, sarcastic, or something of both.

'Up to a point.'

'Jessica, darling. We can live through this. We will survive. We will, one day, win. The world ahead is ours. I promise.'

'What's that world going to be like?'

'I don't know. We haven't built it yet.'

He sat up, slid over the side of the bed, began to dress.

'You could stay here,' she said. 'I doubt miserable old Eric dare mind. Though perhaps he'll put an extra breakfast on the bill.'

'Impossible.' He went over to the desk and picked up the story. 'This is too good to wait. I want it on the wires tonight. I could still get it into tomorrow's *Express*. Perhaps I can persuade them to use your picture.'

'The picture doesn't matter. What's one day?'

He brandished the pages.

'A day wasted.' He got his jacket, stopped, turned to her. 'Come to the office tomorrow. I'll get Lumsden to call with a time.'

'Because?'

'I may have some news.' He blew a kiss. 'Good news. Can't promise. Fingers crossed.'

Then he was gone. Not long after, a siren struck up and she thought about going to one of the shelters. On her own it didn't feel right. If the bombs were coming, let them. She'd been with a man for the first time in months. An interesting one, different, a man who'd stirred her and that didn't happen often.

Jessica Marshall stepped over to the suitcase, still only half unpacked by the wall. The old dressing gown that had followed her all the way from Toronto across a disintegrating Europe was a flimsy thing. One she kept for the memories, nothing else.

She put it on, poured more wine, winced as it went down.

A minute or so after that there was the staccato rattle of artillery fire. Not long behind the sound of an explosion, a bomb it had to be, echoing across the night.

For the first time in months, she felt alive. That was a gift David Shearer had brought her, a precious one.

What if it came at a cost?

CHAPTER 98

It was getting dark by the time Renard arrived back at Temple Ewell. Veronica was in her study, glass in hand as usual. Cognac this time, by the looks of it. She seemed downcast and for a moment he thought perhaps she'd been weeping. A photo album was on her lap, one she looked at from time to time. Not the pictures of her stage shows and films. She rarely returned to them. It was a personal album, snaps of her at home in London and Kent, larking around in the studios in Barnet too.

Maurice Sallis, her late husband, was quite a character, outspoken, flamboyant, extravagantly dressed for the part of film director, one he'd invented for himself after a career producing stage shows. The films were popular with the English public, but they flopped in America and were mostly hated by the critics. He'd never minded. Veronica was a star, the money rolled in. Then, after a lengthy illness, he'd died of a heart attack. Widowed in her early sixties, she'd never set foot on the stage or a movie set after, retiring instead to Temple Ewell.

'Get yourself a drink, Louis. You look as if you need one.'

He poured himself a small glass and took the leather chair

opposite, Maurice's favourite, she always said. Veronica closed the album and put it back on the sideboard.

'I'm so glad he's not here to see this. For all the bluster he was a sensitive little butterfly at heart. This would have destroyed him.'

'I'd never have guessed. The two of you looked as if you'd sail on through anything.'

'Maurice never spoke to you about the Great War?'

Renard shook his head.

'Not once. We used to talk about the places he'd been. All the films he wanted to make if only he could break into Hollywood. The stories he hoped to buy. How he craved to have Graham Greene murdered over some review he gave you.'

'That review was cruel but quite justified. *The Buccaneers of Dymchurch*. I still try to blank out the opera scene with the sheep. Comic indeed. Not that it was intended. God, what a catastrophe. Maurice was an officer in the Guards. The all-seeing eye was their motto. A very stupid one, it seems to me. He was ordered to lead an attack during the final advance on Picardy, just a week or two before the whole disaster came to an end. I was still on the stage then. In Stratford, *Julius Caesar* at the Memorial. Maurice knew the thing would end in disaster, but he had no choice, of course. He woke up in hospital. Gas. A leg wound. Most of his men were dead. He never really spoke of it much. He didn't need to. The point is...' She blinked and he saw now her eyes were pink. 'The point is young men go into war thinking it's some kind of game. That they're brave warriors in some great theatrical production about honour and glory. And it *is* all those things, Louis, especially this time round. But it's much more besides. There's a darkness around, even in the best of men. And women. War brings it out. They do things they'd never countenance, never dream of, in a time of peace. Then, when the lights come on again, they try to pretend those things never happened. That they're not changed at all.'

She blinked again.

'Hitler was already rattling his sabre when he took ill. I could see that cast a shadow on him even then. We had such a wonderful time during the twenties. No one believed we'd be stupid enough to go back to all that horror again. Almost in the blink of an eye.'

It was rare to see her brought low by anything. He'd no idea what to say except, 'I don't suppose you know how to cut hair?'

She looked up with a start.

'What on earth are you talking about?'

'I've decided I need to smarten up a bit. I've rather let myself go.'

'You don't say? I never noticed, not for a moment.'

'The hair. The hair's a start. Can you cut it?'

Veronica appeared offended by the suggestion.

'Dear boy, I spent years on the road with repertory companies. Of course I can cut hair. I can also stitch wounds. Change flat tyres. Gut and skin a rabbit. Nothing teaches you life better than treading the provincial boards pretending to be someone else.'

He tugged at his long, unruly locks.

'I don't suppose... now? And if you had an iron...'

'Good God, Louis. Do you need a cure for the vapours, too?'

'They suspended me today. Seems I put someone's nose out of joint.'

'Not literally, I hope.'

'Of course not. It was a question of...' How to put it? 'Policy. I'm not quite done yet.'

'You never are.'

'You don't want the details, do you?'

She got up from the chair.

'Since you obviously don't want to share them, no.'

Two minutes later she was back with a set of hairdressing scissors and a black cotton cape for his shoulders. He sat by the bookcases while she snipped carefully around his head. It was very long. Soon the Persian carpet was covered with his curly brown locks.

'Is sir planning a holiday this year?' she asked halfway through.

'No. Sir doubts he'll have time for holidays for a while.'

'Poppy. Such a lovely name. You know I've never met a miserable or unenthusiastic Poppy in my life. Never.'

'Have you met many?'

She ignored that question and asked, 'Would sir like to buy something for the weekend? If, say, his doctor friend should come to call?'

He turned a very icy look on her and, for the first time in as long as he could remember, Veronica apologised.

'A little too personal. Very well. Is sir capable of using an iron on his own? Or does he need his ageing aunt to do that as well?'

This was too much.

'I'll have you know I've been living the life of a bachelor ever since I left Cambridge. Quite successfully, for the most part. I'm perfectly capable of ironing my own shirts, and pressing a suit, thank you very much.'

'Shame you're not perfectly capable of holding down a job for a while. Am I supposed to find you something else now?'

She made a few last snips then said he was done. He stood up and looked at himself in the reflection of the drinks cabinet. There were lines on his face he didn't recognise. But the fading scar on his forehead apart, he felt he looked much as before, in the Yard. Except for the clothes. They were, now he thought about it, a shocking mess.

'I don't suppose you have a number for the chief constable?'

'Cyril?' Back in the chair, cognac in hand, she waved at him and said, 'You seem to forget I was the belle of the London stage for a while. I've no end of ancient admirers. No end of suitors since Maurice died. Could have got married ten times over if I wanted. The chief constable? Private line at work and his home number, too. Anyone else? The Archbishop of Canterbury? The leader of the Labour Party? The Lord Chief Justice? If it's the Aga Khan, I'll have to ring round any number of racecourses and–'

'Just the chief constable will do, thank you very much.'

Her eyes narrowed.

'You're up to something. I recognise that look. Fools may think you an ingenuous puppy. I don't.'

'I have absolutely no idea what you mean.'

'What's up your sleeve, nephew?'

'Joining the dots. The iron now, please.'

She raised her glass.

'It's in the scullery with an ironing board. While you're at it you'll find several tins of Cherry Blossom. Little tip. It's always a good idea to match the colour of the polish to the shoe. I don't know which of your sorry pairs you plan to wear tomorrow, but they could all do with a lick and a spit and some brush-work.'

'The chief constable...'

'I'll call Cyril Simpson first. He'd put the telephone down on you in an instant. Who'd blame him?'

Renard topped up his glass a shot and listened. The actress in her was never distant. Veronica Sallis was transformed when Simpson answered, once again the starry, coquettish character she'd portrayed on the stage. He could understand why so many men of a certain age remained starry-eyed about her.

'Speak to my nephew now, Cyril,' she said after a prolonged session of sweet talk. 'I don't give a flying fig what lesser men may have said about him; take it from me he's a damned good fellow. One you can trust. Louis?'

Then she left the room.

The Chief Constable of Kent sounded flattered by Veronica's attention then puzzled and more than a little alarmed by what Renard had to say.

'You're sure of this?' he asked eventually.

'As sure as I can be. Tomorrow, sir...'

A long pause then Simpson said, 'Tomorrow I'll do as you ask, Renard. On your sorry head be it if you're wrong.'

The line went dead. Veronica was waiting outside the door.

She'd fetched the iron, the board and a box of brushes and shoe polish herself. Perhaps so she could eavesdrop.

'Slippery customer, our Cyril. You don't get to hold a job like that if you aren't.' She handed him the polish. 'I hope you know what you're doing.'

He smiled, kissed her cheek, said he hoped so too.

Then he went upstairs and remembered how to wield an iron and a shoe brush.

After that he got the gun.

PART FIVE

CHAPTER 99

Maurice's suit was double-breasted and black, a decent fit. Renard's shoes were shiny, his socks matched for once, and his shirt was freshly pressed. Veronica looked him up and down after breakfast, tightened the tie with a few admonitory words, then, when she felt the bulk of the holster beneath his jacket, asked if a firearm was really necessary.

Yes, he said. It was.

She kissed him on the cheek and said, 'You're all I've left, you know.'

He held her shoulders, smiled and told her the same.

Then, leaning on the pillars of the portico of The Pantheon, she watched him head off to the Hillman Minx, newly polished Church's Oxfords crunching on the gravel.

He'd called the Castle the night before and established when Lieutenant Tobias Mortimer was due to arrive at his office. Nine thirty, it seemed. Not a man for early starts. It was a short drive to the coast. The green Morgan sports car was there in the drive, behind the barred gate and the sign that said "Crecy".

The Mortimers were a military family with a history, he reminded himself, parking the Minx on the verge.

The leather holster felt uncomfortable and very obvious beneath the suit jacket, which was, for some inexplicable reason, somewhat tighter than he remembered the last time he'd worn it, two months before when Veronica was trying him out for her late husband's wardrobe.

There was a brass door knocker in the shape of a rampant horse, the symbol, Renard recalled, of Kent. He rapped three times then Mortimer was there, still in what looked like a silk dressing gown with a Paisley pattern, a mug of tea in his hand, sleep in his eyes, skin pale. The smell of booze hung around him along with the hangover.

'May we speak, Lieutenant?'

'About what?'

Renard looked behind him. Hunting trophies on the corridor wall, a stag, a pheasant in a glass case, a golf bag and a polished shotgun in an open case further along. A hat stand with a uniform jacket on it and a leather holster with a gun just like his.

'It would be easier if I came in,' Renard said. 'I'm afraid I have to make a confession.'

Mortimer grunted.

'Half an hour. Then I need to bathe and get dressed. Another bloody day in the Castle dealing with the fallout from you fools in the police. Be grateful it's me, not you.'

———

The kitchen was untidy. Unwashed mugs, dirty plates in the sink, a bottle of Scotch half-empty on the sideboard. There was the smell of fried food and what looked like unfinished devilled kidneys on a plate.

'A confession?'

Renard opened the jacket and showed him the holster.

'You have a weapon, Inspector. How impressive. I didn't

realise they were so numerous we were handing them out to everyday rozzers.'

'I am an everyday rozzer no longer,' he replied with a quick smile. 'It seems my face doesn't fit in Dover, whatever your father's ambitions. Yesterday I was suspended.'

'Oh dear,' Mortimer said without a flicker of sympathy. The news was, it seemed, both tedious and a surprise.

'Since I no longer serve, it seemed only proper I returned this weapon to its true owner.'

Mortimer screwed up his unshaven face.

'Huh?'

'The stash of weapons we found at Frank Lee's cottage...'

'Bloody tea-leaf. Stealing our guns in times of war. The man ought to be put up against a wall.'

Renard took the revolver out of its holster.

'In that case you'd feel the same about me. I helped myself to one before you arrived.'

'You went for a Webley? Not an Enfield? Idiot.'

'You have a preference?'

'I can pick and choose, Renard. I keep one of these old things out in the hall. You can kill a man with one so long as you're close up. It's the difference between fine wine and plonk. A man like you probably wouldn't notice.'

'True,' Renard said. 'I apologise. Weapons aren't my speciality.'

'You stole from my armoury?'

'There seemed so many guns at Lee's place. I believed I might be in danger of meeting German agents. It seemed wise to be armed.'

'I thought my father gave you one.'

'My aunt snatched that and if you know her, you'll understand there's no snatching it back. For her personal protection, she said. This one looked rather newer. Shocking of me, I agree. I don't know what I was thinking.'

Mortimer gave him a cold stare, held out his hand, snapped his fingers.

Renard hesitated for a moment then slid the weapon across the table.

It was in the lieutenant's fingers when he said, 'If you don't mind my asking... May Dobson. Was she a regular plaything of yours? Every couple of nights? Or just when you felt like it?'

The pallor vanished from Mortimer's cheeks, replaced by a sudden flush.

'What?'

'She was fifteen, Lieutenant. You knew that. You surely understood it was against the law. As well as quite improper.'

'Is that why you're here, Renard? A prurient interest in my love life?'

He shrugged.

'Sex life, you mean. I doubt there was much love in it. I merely wondered...'

Mortimer placed the gun on the table, by his mug.

'Who the hell are you to ask these questions? Stealing my weapons. You said yourself. You're not even a police officer anymore.'

He tried to reach over for the Webley, but Mortimer beat him to it.

'I'm merely curious. A man of your social standing. A fifteen-year-old child, the daughter of an unfortunate police officer. I was always led to believe *droit de seigneur* was a myth concocted by sensationalist historians.'

'The father was a traitor, I hear.'

'Oh, yes,' Renard said, looking right at him. 'That.'

Mortimer seemed slow and confused. Perhaps the booze had clouded his head.

'For what it's worth, Renard, not that it's any of your business, she didn't look fifteen. Not a bit of it. The girl was gorgeous. I thought I was going to teach her a few things. I thought wrong.

God knows what grubby secrets Anna Schmidt had passed on.' He laughed. 'Not that I'm complaining, mind.'

Renard smiled and said nothing.

'Why are you looking at me like that?'

'I was under the impression the name she worked under was Dawn Peacock. That no one outside Shearer's circle was aware she was anything but an English dancer with a sideline in prostitution.'

The flush in Mortimer's cheeks grew yet rosier.

'Of course I knew what was going on there.'

'I'm sure you did, sir. But not from Captain Shearer.'

'What are you really here for, Renard?'

'To return the gun I took. But if you want to talk–'

'I don't. You can leave now.'

He didn't move.

'What was it you said to May?'

Mortimer's eyes narrowed and he muttered, 'Come again?'

'Something that incriminated you, I believe. A stupid boast. One she mentioned to Anna Schmidt that rang alarm bells, that told her you weren't to be relied upon. Poor May had no idea she was really working for the Germans. As I said, she was a child. Did you make her a promise? For when the Nazis come? "I'll look after you. I'll make sure you stay safe and comfortable. I can see your family, your mother and father are protected too. When Hitler's here we'll all be fine. Just remember what I did. Be grateful. And open your legs when I, your lord and master, demand it of his teenage mistress".'

The man opposite laughed. There was egg yolk, Renard saw, dried on his dressing gown. Other stains too. The kitchen smelled of whisky, much as Joe Dobson's must have the night he died. Treachery, it seemed, took its toll.

'You really are a fool. You come here, no longer a policeman, on your own. You make these allegations...'

'You killed him. You attacked a vicar who came to call and disturbed you. They're not allegations. They're established facts. I talked to Maud Perkins last night. She knew you were May's secret visitor. That when you came to call, Anna Schmidt would always place a pillow over the microphone next to the bed. She was afraid what you'd say between the sheets I imagine. A rather better spy than you, it seems.'

Mortimer was toying with the gun again, his mind somewhere else.

'May was such a beautiful child. What happened was a great shame.'

'Perkins also saw your very individual car last Friday when you came round to meet your German comrade.' He leaned forward to make the point. 'That means you were the last person to see Dawn Peacock... Anna Schmidt... alive. I trust you're aware this has implications.'

Sometimes, there was a moment a guilty man glimpsed the shadow of the gallows in front of him. Renard had come to recognise it over the years. Come to have mixed feelings about it, too. He was not a fan of hanging men usually, and women never. Though there were times he was prepared to make exceptions.

Mortimer was staring at the table, the dirty plate, the booze bottle on the sideboard.

'I can't help but wonder, Lieutenant, if you'd have turned back from the cliffs that night had you known May and her mother were trapped down there in Shakespeare Halt. Would you have switched off your lamp for the Luftwaffe bombers who were about to blast them to pieces? Allowed that young girl to live? Perhaps even Harry Lee, too?'

No answer.

'I imagine not,' Renard went on. 'A soldier must always do his duty. Whether it's murdering a woman in a bunker on those same cliffs. Shooting dead an unfortunate youth in the faint hope you might pass the blame for a treasonous outrage to him. Or, when that fails, drugging a bereaved father then hanging the sorry man from his own skylight with a length of electric cable, while depositing a German radio in his chest of drawers.' Renard tapped the table. 'A *German* radio. Without a code book.' He looked around the kitchen. 'I wonder where you keep that here...'

Still Mortimer stared at him, a baleful expression on his long, drawn face.

'What I would most like to know is whether this has any effect on you. Is there no sense of guilt? Regret even? Do you never have doubts? Or can you cover them up with boundless whisky and the hope the Nazis will provide you with a new whore when they come?'

'You bloody fool,' Mortimer muttered.

The gun was up, pointed straight across the table.

'I would appreciate an answer before we hang you, sir.'

That got a laugh, at least.

'Men like me don't hang. Never have. Never will. Farewell, Inspector Renard. A poor and damaged fellow, so very much out of his depth. A fool who does not know his place.'

All the same, his hand shook as he held out the weapon.

'You're surely not going to shoot me as well, are you?'

'Why shouldn't I?'

'It seems excessive.' He looked around the room. 'And while your kitchen is a little messy...'

'Damn you,' Mortimer grunted and then he fired.

CHAPTER 100

Breakfast in the Raglan was simple due to rationing: one slice of bacon, one egg, a single triangle of fried white bread. She ate on her own at the table she'd shared with Shearer the night before, with a small pot of stewed tea brought by Eric who kept giving her the look.

Eventually she said it.

'I know. You don't allow visitors upstairs.'

The man seemed locked in permanent misery.

'Back before the war we'd have them here trying to set things up for divorces. Taking some fancy woman into a room like it was evidence of adultery or something. Half the time nothing happened, and I got dragged into making statements for the judge. Not my business, dealing with lawyers.'

She finished the bacon though it was fatty and undercooked.

'Perhaps you should take this up with Captain Shearer.'

'Don't like listening to people going at it, either. You made a lot of noise if you don't mind me saying. My room's right on the floor above.'

Jessica Marshall closed her eyes and wanted to laugh.

'Perhaps, Eric, you're in the wrong business. I can't imagine there are many hoteliers who never get to hear the sound of people making love.'

'Don't like it,' he said again. 'Not right. This came round for you this morning. Telegram.'

Calhoun moaning about something again, she thought. Canada had quite escaped her thoughts over the last few days. Shearer had put her work in touch with a wider world. With London and Sydney, Bombay and other outposts of empire. Places she'd dreamed of working one day. Anything except returning to the grey misery of Toronto and Yonge Street.

She stared at the landlord until he walked away then ripped open the envelope.

SUPERB PIECE THIS MORNING. VACANCY FOR WAR REPORTER. JOB YRS. TERMS V. GENEROUS. STORY MOVING ON FROM DOVER. SEE ME SOONEST. CHRISTIANSEN. DAILY EXPRESS. 120 FLEET ST.

The telegram from the most famous editor in England left her speechless, not quite able to believe it. She didn't even notice Eric had returned and taken hold of her half-finished plate.

'Good news?'

'Possibly,' she replied, tucking the telegram into her bag.

'Anything else you'd like, madame?'

'Poached haddock and an egg. A croissant. Pancakes with maple syrup. An interview with Churchill. Or Hitler. Either would suffice.'

'Very funny.'

'You did ask...'

Back in her room she looked at the typewriter, the camera, the notes she'd made. Thought of all the sweat and effort she'd put in over the years.

Yet it was a story David Shearer had dictated – invented, perhaps – that got her the break she'd longed for all along.

Jessica Marshall sat down in front of the Remington, wound a fresh page into the carriage.

Then she typed.

I would rather be ashes than dust.

CHAPTER 101

Dan Kelly burst through the back door with such force he nearly took it off the hinges.

Grey smoke drifted across the kitchen, with it the smell of gunpowder. Tobias Mortimer lay on the floor, writhing, screeching, clutching the bloody mess that was his right hand.

'Sir...'

Renard was leaning back on his chair, eyes closed, thinking of the meeting to come.

'What is it, Kelly?'

'Er... well...' He pointed at Mortimer whining on the tiles. 'You shot him?'

'Don't be ridiculous.' Renard got up and went over to take a look. The hand seemed bad. 'He tried to shoot me. Are the rest here?'

Kelly was gawping round the place.

'There were some cars turning up when I heard a bang. I guess so. I mean... who?'

'Good.' He bent down to look at Mortimer. The Webley, the gun Mortimer Senior had given him, was in two pieces, barrel separated from grip, scattered across the tiles. 'I don't know how you cuff a man with half his fingers blown off. Any suggestions?'

'Jesus Christ,' Mortimer bleated. 'I'm bleeding here. I need a doctor.'

'You'll live,' Renard told him. 'For now.'

There were noises outside. Then a tall, distinguished-looking man, bald as a coot with a neat salt and pepper moustache, smart in a grey pinstripe suit and black trilby, marched in.

'Chief Constable,' Renard said.

Dan Kelly watched, open-mouthed.

Cyril Simpson came and stood over the injured man on the floor.

'And what, Inspector, would you like me to do with him?'

He had it all clear in his head. His mind was working again now, quickly, the way it used to back at the Yard, before.

'Put him in a van. Get him to hospital. Canterbury, Maidstone. Anywhere but Dover. Your men?'

'They are my men, Renard. Maidstone. None local. As you asked.'

'Excellent.' He pointed a finger at Kelly. 'I want none of this to go near Dover. Not a word to the nick, the Castle, anyone. Not until I say so.'

'You're the boss,' Kelly said with a quick shrug.

'I am bleeding here!' Tobias Mortimer whined.

'Three counts of murder,' Renard said. 'Attempted murder since he tried to shoot me too. As to the treason...'

Simpson bent down and looked at the whimpering officer on the floor.

'We haven't hanged a soul in Maidstone for ten years, Lieutenant Mortimer. May have to send you up to Wandsworth for that. Not sure we're up to the job.'

'Get me a bloody doctor!'

Renard nodded at Kelly, who dragged the man out, shrieking still.

There were five police vans in the lane and a large Black Maria with barred windows.

'This is your call,' the chief constable said as they watched a complaining Mortimer Junior being hauled towards the custody truck.

'I want half an hour with him on my own. Oh and...'

He nearly forgot.

Renard walked back into the bungalow and found Mortimer's holster and gun.

'And this,' he said as he left.

CHAPTER 102

Shearer began the morning meeting the way he always did, by going through the day's papers and the wire coverage abroad with Ian Henderson and Fred Lumsden.

'You look happy,' Henderson noted as he came in.

'I'm always happy when things go well.'

Lumsden had seen the *Express* already. He didn't seem cheerful at all when he turned up.

'Out with it,' Shearer said.

'First things first.' Lumsden took a seat and got his little dog to park himself by the desk. 'No one in Dover's going to be fooled by this Sergeant B nonsense. This town's never been good at keeping secrets. They all know Joe Dobson hung himself, supposedly.'

'No supposedly to it,' Shearer said.

'Well, they all know he ended up dead. Now this...' He brandished the story in the paper, a whole page, with a teaser on the front. There was a picture of Jessica Marshall looking right into the camera and next to it a silhouette of a police officer with a question mark for a face. 'Everyone's being told he was a traitor. Got his wife and kiddie killed. Murdered a woman here, Frank Lee's lad too.'

'But he did,' Henderson said. 'The police say so. Talk to Superintendent Chalmers. The case is closed.'

Lumsden shook his head.

'Is it indeed? Will there be an inquest on any of them? Something the public can listen to? I'd sit through that. I've done a fair few in my time. Amazing what comes out if you've got a good coroner in the chair.'

Shearer and Henderson exchanged glances.

'You know the answer to that, Fred,' the younger man said. 'We don't have a coroner right now. There won't be an inquest on those poor blokes who Dobson got killed down Shakespeare Halt either. In times like these–'

'In times like these it's more important than ever people hear the truth. It's to do with trust. If you don't have it, they'll think everything you say's a lie before long.'

'I don't care what they think,' Shearer said. 'Only what they do.'

Lumsden threw the paper back on the desk.

'What's the bloody point?'

Shearer let him stew for a moment then said, 'Haven't you noticed? Either of you?'

'Noticed what?' Henderson asked.

'How... quiet it's been. Relatively.'

Fred Lumsden nodded at the ceiling.

'Been planes coming and going up there day and night. What are you talking about?'

'How quiet it's been here. If you–'

His telephone rang. Shearer took the call, put his hand over the mouthpiece, looked at them.

'I need to take this in private. Henderson, go and tell Mrs Marshall to get here. Eleven, not midday like I suggested. We'll resume then.'

Lumsden glared at him.

'Do you really want me hanging round, Captain? I'm not your dogsbody.'

A shrug then Shearer pulled out a bottle of champagne from his desk drawer and told Henderson to find a bucket and some ice.

'Come, come, Mr Lumsden. I have an important announcement. An old newshound like you wouldn't want to miss it.'

CHAPTER 103

The day was bright but marked by an autumn chill. Sluggish warships cruised the Channel, like grey sharks waiting for their moment. St. Margaret's was a beautiful spot on the Kent coast, secluded, pampered, a hideout for the wealthy. Not far away along the cliffs artillery batteries were reloading, soldiers drilling, military vehicles roamed back and forth. Yet below, in the cluster of homes around the tiny bay, it almost seemed as if the war had never started. Hedges were trimmed, lawns mown, flower borders manicured. Here and there the Union flag fluttered from flagpoles, the largest, that on Agincourt Lodge, flapping from the tower.

It was a pleasant walk down the steep hill. When he got there Sir James Mortimer, the Lord Lieutenant of Kent, sat at the wrought-iron table in his philosophers' grove, surrounded by the statues that peeked out of a privet hedge. The little bower he'd made for himself was shady, perfumed by rose bushes now shedding their petals, a perfect refuge. He was bent over flowerpots and a tray of compost, whistling to himself.

'Geraniums, Renard,' Mortimer said, looking up. 'Every year I take some cuttings. Never had to buy a plant in ages. These...' He lifted a tiny sliver of green stem. 'They came from Antibes. We have a small house there. Lord knows when we'll see that again. Mediterranean species. They grow very well in St. Margaret's. We have the shelter and the climate, usually.'

He gestured towards a chair at the wrought-iron table and Renard sat down.

'I imagine you're here to talk about what happened at the police station. Quite shocking. Chalmers is a vindictive man. Most incompetents are. Don't worry. I'll see it's dealt with.'

Renard unbuttoned his jacket.

'Still carrying your gun, I see.'

'Indeed. Thank you for the gift.'

'Probably for the best. Who knows what's round the corner?'

Renard took the weapon out of the holster and placed it on the iron table.

'Do you garden?'

'No time or place for it in London.'

'You're in Kent now. A good hobby for a man. Calming. Perhaps Veronica will teach you. Such a wonderful woman. Half the gentry here would sweep her off her feet given the chance.' He smiled. 'Me included.'

Renard nodded then asked, 'Why did you want me in charge of Dover police station?'

Mortimer rolled his eyes.

'What a strange question. Isn't it obvious? You're a man of great experience. Chalmers is a time-serving fool. In times like these–'

'I was rejected by the Yard because they feared for my mental state after Dunkirk.'

The geranium cutting went into the pot.

'Ah, yes. That mystery. You never did clear it up for them, did you? Still. What's done is done. You're better now, aren't you?'

'Was it because you thought that, when your friends from Berlin arrived, I'd be the more biddable?'

Mortimer put down the knife he'd been using and frowned.

458

'Perhaps I was wrong there. What the hell are you talking about?'

Renard raised the gun, pointed it across the table.

'A young woman called Dawn Peacock died. The entire family of Joe Dobson. A deprived and miserable boy, Harry Lee. All because of you.'

'Put that thing down,' Mortimer ordered. 'Don't be so stupid.'

'All the talk about hating Mosley–'

'I despise the man!'

'You're doing his work.'

'You fool. You've no idea what you're talking about.'

'I should shoot you now. Save the expense of a trial.'

'Then do it!'

Renard edged the Webley inches to the left and fired.

The head of Aristotle exploded into shards that flew all round the little bower. Mortimer had his hands over his head and was shaking, whimpering.

'I apologise for the surprise, sir. This is not the gun you gave me. Your son just tried to kill me with that.'

'Tobias? What on earth did you want with Tobias?'

'To arrest him on three charges of murder.'

'This is insane!'

Another shift in aim, another bullet. This time it was Socrates and Mortimer shrieked as the flakes of marble rained all round him.

'First,' Renard said, 'I want to know why. Mosley…'

'I am no lover of Mosley! For God's sake…'

The third shot was wild, so close to the man's head he might have felt it passing.

'If you don't talk, I'll kill you here and now.'

Mortimer pointed a trembling hand down towards the tiny bay and the grey Channel.

'Think about this, Renard! We've lost. Can't you see it? Adolf will be on our doorstep any day now. When he arrives, there'll be the bloodiest battle this sorry country's ever seen.' He slammed his fist on the table. 'We've lost. All this nonsense of Winnie's about fighting on the beaches. In the streets. You don't believe it, do you?'

'It doesn't matter what I believe. The law...'

'To hell with the law. We're defeated. It's time to recognise the fact. I'm no fan of Mosley. Of Hitler, either. I've been a loyal member of the Conservative and Unionist Party all my life. Unlike that chancer Churchill, who'll cosy up to any damned outfit that'll take him. I'm a pragmatist.' He tapped his chest. 'A patriot. A true one. I wish to spare this country yet more pain. We must negotiate. An armistice. A compromise.' He looked around. 'I'm not the only one who thinks this way, Renard. Far from it.'

'I would like their names.'

'I'm sure you would. There you'll be disappointed. For God's sake, man, see sense. Before it's too late.'

'And what of the Jews?'

Mortimer's face screwed up with distaste.

'What of them? They get their arses kicked periodically. Whenever they climb too far out of their box. Then someone puts them back in their place and we start up afresh all again. You don't imagine Hitler wants to sweep every last Yid off the face of the earth, do you? He's an admirer of this country. He never wanted this war. If the fools hadn't ditched Chamberlain and brought that warmonger Churchill to power, we'd have peace now. It's still possible. We let Adolf carve out what he wants of France and those damned countries to the east the average Englishman couldn't find on a map. Then, together, as allies, we turn on the real enemy. Russia. Together. Stalin.' Another slam of the table. '*He's* the monster who threatens our way of life. Everything this country's ever stood for. Stalin. Not the fellow in Berlin.'

Renard said nothing.

'How long have you known?' Mortimer asked.

The dot. The line. The riddles that joined them.

'I knew the moment I realised you'd given me a gun that had been tampered with. Made to harm the firer, not the target. We did weapons training at the Yard. A metal sleeve inside the barrel to stop the shell. A crude and simple trick. Though from what it did to your son, an effective one.'

'How is Tobias?'

'Did he play the piano?'

'What? No.'

'Then I don't think he's going to learn. Even if he has the time before he hangs.'

Mortimer groaned.

'Be sensible, Renard. You're here on your own. You're out of the police, disgraced. We can find a way round this. I'll make sure you're safe when Jerry comes. You and your aunt. No repercussions. No vengeance. No Germans billeted on you. I guarantee it. The discussions have taken place.'

'Have they?'

He waved at the grey sea.

'You think we've no channels of communication across a slender stretch of water like that? There are advantages to working with these people. Treat them reasonably and they will render the same in return.'

Another shift of the gun and this time it was Plato reduced to shards that flew all over Mortimer, leaving him cowering across the table.

Renard was getting angry. That didn't happen often.

'I saw the dot, but I couldn't find the line. Because of that, innocent people died. The Lee boy. May Dobson–'

'It wasn't me who set up that whorehouse. I never would–'

'Your son was her keenest customer, didn't you know?'

No answer. Renard turned the gun straight on him.

'I want your code books. Your records. I want everything.'

'Will you listen to me? This is about saving lives, not losing them.'

Renard stopped. They were here. Men in uniform crowding into the garden. Cyril Simpson was among them, issuing orders. Kelly joined the uniform group headed into the house.

The chief constable strode over.

'Cyril...' Mortimer murmured, eyes down.

'Jimmy,' Simpson said cheerily.

'Permission to blow his bloody head off, sir,' Renard said.

'Granted, Inspector. I'm only sorry it'll be your pleasure not mine.'

He took aim, straight in the face, two feet from him, no more.

'There's a safe in the study,' Mortimer cried. 'In the tower. For pity's sake, Cyril, I did this for us. Hitler will be here any moment. Do you want this country to turn into the Somme? Or Passchendaele? We both know what that was like.'

'I want the combination,' Renard said.

The man's head went down, his voice a tone lower, a shade quieter.

'Twenty. Zero Four. Eighteen Eighty-Nine.'

'Sounds like someone's birthday. I wonder whose?'

'Adolf's,' Mortimer roared back. 'Who do you think?'

Renard extended the gun across the table and pulled the trigger. Mortimer screamed. There was a click, then nothing.

'Oh dear,' Renard said. 'It appears your son had just four shells loaded. What a shame.'

'You *are* insane,' the old man whimpered.

The Black Maria was manoeuvring in the drive. Simpson told two of his officers to handcuff Mortimer and put him in the back.

'If his son bleeds on him, so be it.'

They watched the man stumble off between two uniformed officers.

'The Lord Lieutenant of Kent,' Simpson said. 'Heaven knows they can turn up anywhere.'

'You had no idea, sir?'

'None.' Simpson looked at the gardening tools and the

flowerpots on the table. 'Nice geraniums. He really doesn't think he's a traitor, does he?'

'Bad people rarely believe they're doing something villainous, in my experience. Even murder. They can rationalise everything. Blame it on rage, or jealousy, others. Or a simple quirk of fate. Never on themselves.'

The chief constable seemed to approve of that idea.

'You sound more like a trick cyclist than a police inspector.'

'I'm not sure *what* I am anymore, sir.'

'You're a Kent police inspector. If you want to be.'

'You'll keep these two?'

'In Maidstone, as you said.'

'Outside the military?'

Cyril Simpson didn't look confident.

'As best I can. Murder is one thing...' They watched Mortimer being pushed into the van, hands cuffed behind his back. 'Treason, especially in a chap of his standing, well... I have calls to make. And you?'

'Just the one,' he said, then shouldered the gun.

'Er, Renard,' Simpson stopped him as he got up to leave, 'one more thing.'

'Which is?'

'The gun! Did you know there were no shells left in it when you pulled the trigger on him?'

'I was reasonably confident, sir,' Renard said.

'You might have killed the man!'

'True. Will you excuse me now?'

CHAPTER 104

There was an unexpected air of jollity in Shearer's office when Renard arrived. A bottle of champagne sat in a silver ice bucket on the desk. Jessica Marshall was there in a summery dress, the kind she might have worn for a garden party. Ian Henderson, Shearer's deputy, looked pleased with himself. Only Lumsden appeared less than happy.

'Am I interrupting something?' Renard asked as he took a seat, unbidden.

'Not at all.' Shearer grabbed the bottle, popped it, began to pour. 'I'm sorry I only have four glasses.'

'Duty,' Renard said.

'But I thought...' Shearer waved his hand. 'Never mind. Good news is good news. Find our visitor a glass, Ian. Let's share.'

The younger Ministry man vanished for a brief while, returned with the glass, placed it on the table, then said he had to go and deal with a report.

Renard watched him go, left the champagne flute where it was and said, 'I told you. Not for me. What news might that be?'

Shearer raised his glass and smiled.

'What I tell you here doesn't go out of this room. Not right now. It'll be common knowledge soon enough.' He let them wait for a second. 'We have intelligence. *Unternehmen Seelöwe*. Operation Sea Lion. Hitler's game-plan to invade England is on hold.'

They didn't touch their drink, didn't say a word until Jessica Marshall broke the silence.

'Is this for real?'

'Oh, yes. They're not the only ones with spies.'

The German army, Shearer said, had come to accept that an invasion across the Channel could not succeed until the Luftwaffe had mastery of the skies. The hard-fought summer war in the air, the Battle of Britain, much of it over Kent, was a victory for the RAF. As a result, the German army commanders had told Hitler a seaborne invasion was likely to fail.

'You can imagine the creature in Berlin is furious,' Shearer added. 'The Führer's turned on the Luftwaffe and Göring. So Göring has turned on his Luftwaffe squadrons.' He laughed. 'There's a rumour the fat man asked them what they needed to defeat our pilots. And one of them said... "Give us Spitfires".'

'How can you know that?' she asked.

He tapped the side of his nose, then winked.

'They can't launch an attack across the Channel now. Given the winter weather, they can't contemplate an invasion until next summer at the earliest. By then we'll have turned the tide. There will be no other opportunity. From this point on we take the war to Hitler.' He raised his glass in a toast. 'To the victory. However long it takes.'

Jessica Marshall took out her notebook and began to write.

'Not yet,' Shearer said with a sudden sharpness. 'I told you. Not a word outside this room. When there's a story, Jessica,' he winked, 'I'll let you know.'

'What does this mean for us, then?' Lumsden asked. 'For Dover?'

It was Renard who answered.

'It means the battle moves on. They bomb the hell out of London and the cities. Not so much this place. A long, slow war of bloody attrition.'

Shearer nodded.

'That would seem to be the case. How do you know?'

'I didn't, Captain. I guessed. I do that a lot. It's invaluable when no one tells you the truth.'

There would still be bombs in Dover, Shearer said. Shells from across the Channel. Aerial sorties, sea attacks. But once September was over, life in the town would change. It would not be a return to normality. The place would still be a frontier fortress and the Castle would only continue to grow in importance as the tunnels and the radar systems there expanded. But a degree of escape from the daily bombardment of the town would begin.

'It's happening already,' he added. 'Surely you've noticed. So...' He raised his glass again. 'Will no one join me in a toast?'

Jessica Marshall did the same. Then, reluctantly, Lumsden.

'Inspector?' Shearer said with a smile. 'If I may still use that title. Surely you'll drink to that?'

Renard reached into his pocket and pulled out a pair of handcuffs then threw them on the desk.

'Pleasant as your news is, sir, this is not a social visit. I'm here to arrest you as an accessory to murder. Do I need to use these? Or will you be reasonable and walk to the police station of your own volition?'

Shearer refilled his glass, then, a little nervously, he laughed.

Lumsden began to get out of his seat.

'No one need move,' Shearer said. 'We've barely started on the champers. Nor do I have time to indulge your fantasies, Renard.'

'Lieutenant Mortimer is about to be charged with the murder of Dawn Peacock. Anna Schmidt, as you first knew her. He's making a statement that says you asked him to pick her up from Effingham Terrace for interrogation after you'd read the message she left with Mrs Marshall here.'

'And why would I do that?'

'Because you'd come to learn she was a double agent. Treating with the Germans as much as you.' Renard read from his notes. '"The devil's favourite piece of furniture is the long bench". You realised this was a coded plea for help based on an old German saying. Schmidt was sending out an SOS to her controllers. *Not* to you.'

'Renard...'

'I haven't finished, Captain. Anna Schmidt's bordello was little more than a mile from here. Her theatre was just across the road. If she was in fear of her life from the Nazis, she would never have needed to resort to such subterfuge.'

Shearer sipped at his glass and stayed silent.

'Is this true?' Jessica Marshall asked. 'Is this why you really killed my story? David?'

A shrug, then he said, 'Mortimer was ordered to interrogate her as he saw fit. That was all. Not to kill her.'

'He tortured the woman,' Renard pointed out. 'He beat her up. He cut her with an army knife.'

'That was never meant to happen. I knew nothing of it, Renard. Believe me.'

Fred Lumsden muttered a curse and shook his head.

'Look,' Shearer went on. 'We'd suspected she was playing both sides of the game for a while. Mortimer offered to interview her–'

'I'm sure he did,' said Renard.

'The means, I left to him. He said she had some kind of seizure.'

'He strangled her, Captain. After cutting her. I saw the wounds. The bruises his fingers left around her throat.'

Shearer waved a dismissive hand in his direction.

'I know nothing of that. I gave the lieutenant no instructions except to interrogate the woman. How he went about his work was up to him.'

'She was never going to come out of that bunker alive.'

For the first time, the man looked rattled.

'What on earth are you are talking about?'

'Mortimer had to kill her. He was working for the Germans too. As was his father. They're both in police custody in Maidstone now.'

Shearer shook a little as he put the glass back on the table.

'This is impossible. Sir James Mortimer is the Lord Lieutenant of Kent–'

'Who's been in regular contact with Berlin for months. His son was a regular at your whorehouse. Taking May Dobson, a fifteen-year-old girl, to bed.'

'No...' Shearer waved the idea away.

'In return for sleeping with May, Mortimer promised she and her family would be safe when the Germans came. The girl told Dawn Peacock – Anna Schmidt – thinking this would find its way to you. Instead, Schmidt realised how very leaky her network had become and tried to send a plea for help to Berlin through Mrs Marshall here. You then placed the woman in the custody of a man who was bound to take her life. Because he knew that if you got your hands on Anna Schmidt, the chances were you'd discover the truth.'

'Bloody hellfire,' Fred Lumsden roared, livid as he got to his feet. 'Murdered women! Children in brothels. Is there nothing you won't do?'

Shearer lit a cigarette and said, 'Sit down.'

'Enough's enough. Do you have no scruples?'

'Do scruples win wars?' the man snapped back. 'Would you thank me for my so-called morals if they were the reason you found yourself living under the Nazi jackboot? The woman was a traitor. Here to do us harm.'

'You dispatched Anna Schmidt to a cruel and violent death,' Renard said.

'If what you say is true.'

'Lieutenant Mortimer boasted of it this morning before he

tried to kill me. He's also going to be charged with the murder of Harry Lee. And of Sergeant Joe Dobson, a bereaved serving police officer, an innocent man he hoped to frame. There's a team from headquarters searching his home and that of his father at the moment. I'm sure we'll find evidence that they've both been feeding the Germans information for months. That Mortimer Junior was waving that lamp above Shakespeare Halt. And you, Captain, knew nothing?'

'No,' Shearer said, going red in the face. 'I did not.'

Lumsden struggled to his feet again.

'You damned monster. To hell with your bloody tricks and ruses, Shearer. I am done with you!'

He cursed again, stormed out, dragging the dog behind him.

Jessica Marshall sat there, silent, in shock.

Shearer helped himself to more champagne then leaned back in his chair, took a swig, closed his eyes and went on.

'If what you say is true, Renard, *if*... then Mortimer should be in our custody, not yours. Treason is not a matter for the local police.'

'Murder is.'

'Treason, I believe, takes precedent. I can get a man in the War Office to explain this to you if you like.' He smiled across the desk. 'Yes. I believe that would be a good idea. Jessica, the Inspector and I need words in private.'

CHAPTER 105

Fred Lumsden was a hunched figure on a bench seat by the harbour. Benny lay at his feet looking miserable out of sympathy. The bay was busy as always: repairs, small launches, gangs of sailors and workmen tackling the vessels there beneath a renewed canopy of barrage balloons. She took the seat next to him and waited. It was a while before Lumsden spoke and then all he said was, 'I've been a bloody fool.'

'Why?'

He turned and stared hard, right at her.

'Are you kidding me?'

'No, Fred. Why? He's right, up to a point, isn't he? This is about survival. About beating Hitler. We've started.'

He pointed at the sky.

'Those brave boys up there did that. You heard him. Hitler daren't attack us because he can't control the Channel. Putting a girl in a brothel, murdering a woman, even one of theirs... that's hardly the same.'

There were a couple of fighters in the sky. Spitfires or Hurricanes, she always struggled to tell the difference from afar. Patrolling through the clouds. Waiting on the next onslaught which, if Shearer was right, would probably head north, skirting Dover, seeking London.

'You helped him,' he said. 'You were a party to this.'

'We both were.'

He turned round, clutched the dog's lead tight to him.

'Did you know that story was made up? Sergeant B my arse. That poor man Joe Dobson lost everything: his family, his life. Now he's going to go down as a traitor too. All because David Shearer says so. Did you know?'

She gazed at the busy grey horizon and said, 'David dictated most of it himself in my room at the Raglan. It was a rewrite job mostly, on my part.'

'Ah. Like that is it?' There was a bitterness in his voice she'd never noticed before. 'I see.'

'Do you?'

'I thought you were a reporter. A real one. Or wanted to be. I thought–'

'Dammit! Don't lecture me! You worked for him too.'

'Dogsbody, Jessica. I never spread his lies.'

'Really? You didn't seem to have a problem when they were about a dead fisherman who happened to like the Fascists. Or is it just wrong to lie about the good people?'

That hurt him. She could see the sudden flash of pain on his face.

'Fred. When this is over... whenever... I can come back to Sergeant Dobson. Tell that story properly. I will.'

The pain was gone, contempt in its place.

'The first rule of reporting, Mrs Marshall. There's nothing worse than naivety. You seem to have it in spades.'

'Oh, do I?'

'Yes. When this is over the only stories you'll be telling are the ones folk want to hear. Heroes and villains. Black and white. Winners and losers. And...' he jabbed a stubby finger in her direction, 'you'll be feeding them that day in and day out.

Sometimes I think this bloody country's only happy when we're either fighting someone or telling ourselves we're better than the rest. Joe Dobson was a decent family man, an intelligent fellow from what I heard. Look what it did for him.'

'I know, Fred,' she whispered, her voice low, fading. 'I know.'

'He deserved better.'

'Lots of people do.'

Lumsden struggled to his feet the way old men sometimes did, then told the dog they were off.

She stood up as well, getting mad with him, with herself.

'What exactly do you expect me to do?'

'Whatever you want. We're all just puppets here, aren't we? Pathetic little marionettes with the likes of David Shearer pulling our strings.'

She thought of telling him about the job in London. How she was going to leave Dover. The story had moved on. A plum post in Fleet Street beckoned. A war reporter for real. The break with a big newspaper she'd been praying for year after year.

He was about to shuffle off, past the engineers working on the shattered wreck of the *Codrington*. Then something struck him. Fred Lumsden turned and stared right at her.

'Know why I came to this sorry little town almost forty years ago? Not long after old Queen Victoria died?'

She waited. There was nothing to say.

'I grew up in a pit village. My dad was a miner. My brother died down below. A fire. He was just sixteen. I was having none of that. I got as far away from all that muck and grime and squalor as I could manage.' He waved at the harbour. 'Every morning I'd walk past that stretch of water on the way to work. I'd say to myself, "Look where you are, Fred. Not staring at filthy miners coming off a shift. This is where the world starts. And one day I'll get on one of them big liners, head off out to see it".'

He took a step nearer.

'Never happened, Jessica. Not like it did for you.'

'I'm sorry.'

'I wasn't asking for your apology. The point is, I fooled myself all these years thinking this is where the world starts. But you know what? For half the idiots round here, those White Cliffs are where it ends. They're not interested in what's out there. Only in us. John Bull with his top hat and his cane and his stupid flag for a waistcoat round a belly so fat he can't see his feet. When this nightmare's over and we win – and we will – that's the story the likes of you will be writing. Here's another cliché you'll be chucking at them. "We'll never forget". Right. Truth is they'll never damn well remember, not properly, because you won't tell them the truth to begin with. What they should be thinking about. No. You'll just feed them all the myths that'll one day take us right back here again. Staring at that grey stretch of water, hating and fearing everyone who's on the other side. You...' the dog began to whimper as if it had never seen him so mad, '...make me sick.' He looked as if he might weep. 'But nothing like as sick as I make myself. Good day, Mrs Marshall. I hope you have a good war. Whatever that means.'

She watched him amble off and felt regret they'd never meet again. Then, shaken, she walked back into the office of what was once, in a time of peace, the Mountbatten Hotel.

Henderson was downstairs at the desk.

'I want to see him.'

The young officer didn't even look up from the page he was reading.

'Not now. Bad time.'

'It's important.'

The way he stared at her then was much the same as Lumsden had outside. Contempt bordering on distaste. Maybe you only needed to sup with the devil once and that was it.

'Ian. I said–'

'Did you hear me? He's busy with that lunatic copper and he will be for a while. I can deal with it. Your next story. What's it going to be? The night in the tunnels? He told me about that.' He laughed. 'You were there with that barmpot, weren't you? Right odd one, he is. Thinking he can march in here and throw his weight around.'

He put the papers he was reading on the desk by the miserable woman who ran things there.

'I feel the next piece needs to be lighter in tone. More human. Good for morale. The story about Joe Dobson was what we needed at the time. But you can't keep piling the misery on people. I want something brighter. Cheerier. A bit of fun.' He winked at her. 'You know what fun is, don't you?'

She thought of slapping him, but perhaps he'd have liked it.

'If you want, I can come round and we could try and run up a little something in your room later. I've got ideas too.'

The woman on the desk was listening. Jessica Marshall walked over, bent down to her and said, 'Could you give Captain Shearer a message for me?'

'Such as what?'

'Such as... goodbye.'

CHAPTER 106

When Renard got back to Temple Ewell, Veronica was wandering the kitchen, once more complaining about how rationing so diminished the choice of menu. He left her to it, took the fly rod out of its case and went down to the sleepy river. He wondered if he'd ever master the flight of Danvers' supposedly magical *brown bugger* across the bending stretch of water beneath the willows where trout swam lazily in the current, oblivious to his efforts.

Four times he made a clumsy effort to pitch the line in their direction, once almost catching the trees themselves. Then he heard the crackle of gravel in the drive and put the rod away. Poppy Webber, out of her hospital gown for once, emerged into the garden clutching an envelope.

Before they could speak his aunt dashed from the house, ushering them to the picnic table by the river and the seats there, a tray in her hands with two glasses of wine and a plate of water biscuits and cheese.

'Have you noticed anything?' she said, standing there quite resolute.

Poppy Webber looked mildly embarrassed.

'His hair!' Veronica cried. 'I cut it. Also, his clothes. Much smarter. Or rather less dishevelled.' She cocked her head and pointed at his feet. 'The colour coordination of the socks leaves much to be desired. But then he is just a man.'

'I have changed from business clothes to casual. There's nothing wrong with my socks.'

One was brown. The other navy.

Veronica growled and left them.

The stern, somewhat fierce doctor he'd met at the Institution seemed to be in abeyance.

'I came to apologise, Louis.'

'For what?'

'For shouting at you at the hospital yesterday. I was stressed. Work. Some bad news from home. What's more, you were really quite persistent, which was the last thing I needed.'

'I was pursuing a murder case.'

'I was dealing with a stream of injured men and women.'

He grimaced.

'I get carried away sometimes. It was thoughtless. The living and the dead. It's obvious who should come first.'

'Indeed,' she agreed. 'It is. All the same... Here.'

She handed him the envelope. The crest of the Institution was on the reverse.

'I found time to run some tests on your sergeant. There was a substance in his blood. I haven't had the chance to get to the bottom of it yet, but this may be enough to convince a coroner to investigate further.'

Renard took the envelope but didn't open it.

'Thank you,' he said. 'I imagine it was a sedative. Something that made him drowsy. Probably knocked him out.'

She sighed then laughed, just briefly.

'I keep coming here to offer you revelations, only to discover you're aware of them already.'

'True,' he said with a smile. 'Am I right?'

'I imagine so. The man had been drinking too. There were splinters in the back of his legs. I'm no criminal pathologist but as an amateur, I'd guess he'd been dragged across a wooden floor. I can't imagine how someone could inflict those wounds on himself. You knew?'

He had guessed. There was little else he could do in Dover.

'It was kind of you to come.' He placed the envelope, still unopened, on the table anyway. 'The case is closed.'

She looked younger now she was in normal clothes, not the white jacket of the hospital, a stethoscope round her neck. Her blouse was pale with blue pinstripes, a silver chain with a cross hung round her neck. Much like one Delia once wore.

'By closed, you mean... what exactly?'

They sat at the table and sipped the wine. It was a while before he answered.

'I mean I understand what happened. There will be consequences.'

'A man in court? How exciting.'

He said no more.

'Oh, I get it. Police work. Confidential.' She pointed to the rod on the lawn and said, 'You're fishing?'

'Just like you.'

When she smiled, the years rolled off her. The war too, he imagined. It occurred to him that it was so long since he'd had a conversation like this – warm, casual, meandering, with anyone except his aunt. The illness – she was right, it *was* an illness – had placed a barrier between him and the world. Now, a murder case successfully resolved, a place back in the police earned, it was vanishing.

Poppy Webber got up, clapped her hands and picked up the rod.

'Let me show you how.'

Before they could begin there was the roar of a motorbike engine down the drive. Dan Kelly propped up his BSA Gold Star near the ha-ha and ran over.

'Sir!' He saw she was there and for some reason, blushed. 'Miss. I mean, Doctor...'

'Hello, Constable Kelly,' she said, and he blushed even more.

'I just got a call from Maidstone. I'm to take a few days off and turn up at Canterbury for duty on Monday.'

'Jolly good,' said Renard.

Kelly didn't seem to think so.

'Is it? I don't know anybody in Canterbury. Not a soul. They're all posh up there.' He was pleading, it was plain. '*I don't know anybody.*'

'You'll know me.'

Kelly beamed and cocked his head from side to side.

'I was hoping you'd say that. They're sending you there too?'

'The chief constable's decision. There are... ructions in Dover, it seems.'

'I don't mind ructions. Quite enjoy them actually.'

Poppy Webber covered her mouth, laughing.

'Don't snigger. I mean ructions are part of the job, aren't they? You don't become a copper if you're not up for the odd punch-up. When you're in Canterbury and me too, does that mean we're like... a team?'

'We will be working together, yes.'

'A team!'

'How nice for you both,' she remarked.

'Not nice for any villains,' Kelly said and brandished a fist. 'If we can take down the lord lieutenant, I don't give a rat's arse for the chances of any common criminals out there.' Another blush. 'If you'll pardon my French.'

'Kelly...' Renard's eyes drifted towards Poppy with a little nod. 'I do have company.'

He grinned at that.

'I noticed.'

'My aunt will be here any second.'

'Right.' The leer vanished in a second. 'Well then, I'd best be off.'

CHAPTER 107

The train to London was late. Of course. Jessica Marshall had sat on the hard platform bench for an hour. Desperate to flee Dover, she'd grabbed her case and the battered Remington the moment she saw the engine wreathed with grey and black smoke finally chugging towards the station. Then the platform manager dashed out and yelled at the few people waiting, ordering them not to board until he said so. The Folkestone line was still closed at Shakespeare Halt and they had to take a circuitous route through Canterbury into Victoria.

'Goddamn it,' she yelled out loud, much to his shock, then walked to the bench at the far end of the platform, away from the gaggle of soldiers playing cards and smoking by the ticket barrier.

A couple of minutes on she looked up to see Shearer marching towards her, smiling as if nothing untoward had happened in the world. In his hands was a small bouquet of wilting roses, five or six stems.

'Trouble on the tracks as usual,' he said, holding out the flowers. 'Lucky me.'

'Where did you steal them from? The municipal flowerbeds?'

He placed the blooms on her lap and sat down next to her on the bench.

'There's a cynical side to you at times. I imagine you feel it comes with the job.'

'You're a romantic at heart, aren't you?'

He seemed to take that literally.

'I am, in fact. As you'll come to learn. I should warn you Christiansen may come across as something of a tyrant. He's an excellent man all the same. Old-fashioned, but he'll pay you well and I'm sure the assignments will be just what you fancy.'

'Jesus Christ...' She closed her eyes, laughing, crying, a little of both. Of course, he would have known about the telegram. Perhaps he'd even organised the offer of a job. 'Who are you, Shearer?'

The question seemed to surprise him.

'I told you when we first met. Don't you remember? I'm the man who'll make your career.' He leaned in and whispered in her ear, 'Do you doubt it now?'

She had to ask.

'Is it true? Everything that Louis Renard described about the Mortimers?'

'The pair will be in military custody by the morning. It's not something for the civilian police.'

'And you never knew? You *never* suspected?'

It was his turn to laugh.

'Good lord, Jessica. The old man's the Lord Lieutenant of Kent. His son... They're as near as royalty here.'

'Royalty can still turn treacherous.'

He looked down the platform. No one was near enough to hear them.

'We should have known. Not me. That wasn't part of my remit. I won't catch the blame.'

'I'm sure you won't.'

'Of course not. Still, one learns more from one's mistakes than the successes.'

He left it there. That wasn't enough.

'I want to know,' she said. 'I want you to tell me exactly what happened.'

'Why?'

'Because I'll never speak to you again if you don't.'

He wasn't pleased about that.

'Very well. I know it'll go no further. Mortimer was in the office when I became convinced Anna Schmidt had turned. He offered to use his military interrogation expertise on her. I decided to take the risk and let him.'

'But you–'

'I'm not one for interrogation. It isn't a skill I own.'

She was surprised by that at first, but not when she thought about it. Shearer was in some ways a shy man. One happiest in the shadows. Confrontations were for others. He simply wished to work behind the scenes, pulling strings as Fred Lumsden had said, arranging his puppets.

'Did you really believe Dobson was a traitor?'

He frowned.

'To be honest, I wasn't sure. We'd heard he'd been making odd comments in the police station. About how he'd work for the Germans when they arrived.'

'Hardly a crime.'

He picked at the flowers, thinking.

'The point is that, even if it was someone else, by placing the blame on Dobson once he was dead, I might have gained some advantage. Having your enemy believe you're an incompetent idiot is no bad thing. They drop their guard. And then you pounce.'

She was speechless for a moment.

'Have I offended your sensibilities, Jessica?'

'I'm not sure I have any left. It's just a game of chess for you, isn't it?'

He shook his head.

'No. Much more than that. A game of life and death.'

'The poor man was innocent! You'd have known that if you'd listened to Louis Renard.'

He nodded and said nothing.

'Why didn't you?'

'Because Renard came here as damaged goods. The man vanished to Dunkirk and still no one knows why. He returned wounded, ranting and raving, or so I was told. It was only because his beloved aunt talked the chief constable into taking him on that he was there at all. They nearly put the fellow in an asylum, for pity's sake. So naturally I assumed he was unreliable, confused, to be tolerated and indulged to keep Dame Veronica Sallis sweet. Obviously, I was mistaken. The chap appears to have a gentle exterior and steel within.' He smirked. 'The very opposite of me.'

She understood a little of what he meant. There was something fragile, damaged about Renard. Not that she could put her finger on it exactly. The unbending interior was there too, well hidden.

'He's a good man. A decent man. I understood that the first time I met him. You didn't.'

'True,' he agreed. 'A fellow with morals. Unlike me, you mean. But as you said, you always fall for bastards.'

She told him to take the roses and shove them up his rear. He affected not to notice.

'The *Express* will provide you with many opportunities in London. And beyond. Make sure you always steal the very best.'

'I will. The trial of a lord lieutenant of the land for treason, for a start.'

He gazed at her, open-mouthed then said, 'Are you serious?'

'Damned right I am. Sir James Mortimer, arraigned for treason and God knows what else. His son could hang for three murders I can think of. If they don't shoot him as a traitor. There's quite a tale. It's the first thing I'll demand of this man Christiansen – the right to cover it.'

'Oh Jessica, Jessica...' He wound his arm through hers and she didn't move. 'Poor mite. There's still so much I have to teach you.'

CHAPTER 108

'The Lord Lieutenant?' Poppy Webber asked, an inquisitive smile on her face, 'of Kent?'

Kelly had slunk off to his motorbike and vanished up the road.

'About the fishing...'

'You've nicked – is it all right if I say "nicked"? – Yes, it is, you've *nicked* the Lord Lieutenant of Kent?'

'And his son. They were collaborating.'

She gasped.

'With the Germans?'

'No. With the Welsh. Of course it was the Germans. The son killed Dawn Peacock. Harry Lee. Sergeant Dobson. He was the one who waved in the planes to Shakespeare Halt.'

She punched his arm.

'Blimey, Inspector Renard. That's two fine feathers in your cap.'

'It's not public yet. I'd be grateful if you could be discreet.'

That offended her.

'I'm a doctor. I'm always discreet. Will you have to appear in court as a witness?'

'I don't know.'

'Will they hang them? I hope not. I don't approve of hanging and kindly don't tell me I'm wrong. They should just be locked up for good.'

No, Renard told her, he didn't approve of hanging either.

Something about the way he said that seemed to stir her interest.

'You must have sent a few men to the gallows.'

'Don't ask.'

'Do you ever wonder if it was the wrong one?'

Renard closed his eyes.

'Do you ever stop asking perceptive questions?'

She grimaced, then smiled, said sorry and passed him the rod.

'Show me how you do it, Louis.'

He walked to the river and made an attempt at a cast. As usual the fly went where it felt like – on this occasion, to a stretch of weedy water the fish rarely visited.

'You're making a beginner's mistake,' she announced, joining him at the edge of the river.

'Which is?'

'You think you're casting the fly. When really you should be casting the line.'

Dots on the horizon. Something to join them. He'd had Sir James Mortimer in his sights since the evening he'd examined the crippled Webley in his room. If only he'd taken his eye off that distant fly and worked harder to define the line that led to him. Dobson and his family, Harry Lee too, might still be alive.

'Also,' she added, 'you're trying too hard. It's important to relax. This is a leisure pursuit, not athletics. Give it here.'

Naturally, he obeyed.

Poppy Webber stood on the bank, legs slightly apart, eyeing the still water.

'Keep back. I don't want to catch you.'

'Oh,' he said. 'I am disappointed.'

For a moment she turned and grinned. Then, with a few slow, balletic movements she made the cast perform lazy semicircles across the water. Three times she did this and never let the fly reach the surface once.

Finally, she brought the line in and handed the rod to him.

'Your turn. Let me help.'

Behind him, one hand on his waist, the other on his rod arm, she guided his movements with a gentle firmness, back and forth.

'There.' She stood back. 'You're getting the hang of it. I want you to drop the little fellow right under the willows over there. Mind the branches. I saw something rise. Who knows? Perhaps this is your lucky day.'

It took four goes but finally the brown bugger landed squat on the water in the shadows. A second or two later Renard felt as if he'd received a sudden electric shock. The tip of the rod bent with such force he had to hold on hard to keep it spilling from his hands.

'Got him!' she cried. 'Tight line but don't pull too much. Not the reel, leave that alone. Pull him in with the line and the rod, let the spare fall down at your feet. Steady, steady. I'll get the net.'

It felt as if he'd caught a shark. But by the time he'd got the fish to the bank and Poppy Webber had caught it in her net, he saw it was small, a brown trout barely nine inches long. She picked the fish out of the mesh and, with the care of a doctor, released the hook from its mouth then handed it over.

'Congratulations. You seem to be good at catching things today.'

The gleaming trout barely struggled in his fingers. It lay there, gasping, its bright eyes seemingly both terrified and resigned.

'Supper for one,' she said. 'Do you want me to show you how to gut it?'

Renard bent down to the water and let the river flow over the gently moving trout. The creature wriggled in his fingers as if grateful, glad to be alive, back where it belonged. Then he released it and watched as the fish swam through the limpid water, back to the shade of the willows where a mist of evening midges had gathered above the surface.

'Well,' she said, arms folded. 'At least you know how to catch another.'

He put the rod on the table.

'I only ever wanted to catch one. To know what it was like. Take the rod if you want. If your father could use it...'

Something he'd said had saddened her and he'd no idea what.

'That was the other thing I came to tell you. He's not well. Dad. I'm moving to Edinburgh. There's a job for me in one of the hospitals. I can look after him. Your friendly amateur pathologist at the Institution is packing her bags.'

There was a silence between them, one neither seemed to wish to break.

'I'm sorry to hear that,' he said finally. 'About your father. I hope...' He didn't want to say the rest. That was all too late now. 'When do you go?'

'When I want. I finished at the Institution today. Couple of days to pack. Sort things out.' She inched closer. 'I haven't gone yet.'

There was a cough nearby. Poppy mouthed 'oops' and stepped back. Veronica was there.

'I'm sorry to interrupt. Dreadfully rude of me. I never realised you were... well.'

Renard stifled a laugh. He'd never seen his aunt embarrassed before.

'I wondered if you'd care to stay for supper? It's just chopped pork and salad I'm afraid. If I'd known we had a guest...'

Poppy Webber beamed.

'I'd love to.'

'Oh, and Louis. Danvers noticed someone had dropped a letter in the box this afternoon. No stamp. They must have been passing.'

She handed him the envelope. He took one look at the handwriting and the warmth of the moment, her presence, the bright spark of life she brought with her, vanished in a second.

'You must excuse me,' Renard said and strode off to the house.

CHAPTER 109

'Think about this for a moment.' Shearer wriggled along the bench until they touched then his hand slunk round her waist. That, she promptly removed with a slap.

'Don't ever call me "mite" again.'

'How would it look if we were to see an aristocrat of Mortimer Senior's standing in court accused of treason?'

'I believe it would look like what is popularly known as "justice".'

Her words seemed to go right over his head.

'You see, it couldn't possibly be in public because then the man would be given a pulpit to demand we strike a peace with Hitler. Even *in camera*, word would get out.'

There was not the least indication the train for London was likely to leave soon, or that she could board to get away from him.

'Wait... wait... You mean he's going to get away with–'

'There's a secluded mansion in the wilds of Scotland. We keep people like Jimmy Mortimer in cold storage there. Safely out of the way where they can do no harm.'

Jessica Marshall was getting madder.

'In the manner to which they're accustomed, I imagine.'

He squeezed her arm.

'Comfortable though not pampered. They're aristocrats, love. Etonians and Wykehamists, the cream of society, or so they'd like to think. This is England, not Russia. We can't just bump them off.'

'He's a traitor.'

'He is indeed. Though the man's put in years of public service.'

'Good God. What about the son?'

Shearer winced.

'Oh yes. Him...'

Silence.

'Don't tell me, David. Don't you dare tell me...'

He unwound his arm.

'Lord, that man has caused me problems. I went out of my way to distance him from the catastrophe with the Schmidt woman. Look where that got me.'

'Look where it got *her!* And that boy. Sergeant Dobson and his family. Dead and buried.'

He barely seemed to hear.

'If Anna Schmidt was still alive, I might have turned her. It's the first thing you do with a captured agent. Scare the living daylights out of them, then see if they'll switch sides in return for staying alive. Most are self-serving nobodies at heart. Not zealots anxious to die for the cause. That fool deprived me of the opportunity, quite deliberately, it seems. Anna Schmidt might have been invaluable.'

She could scarcely believe what she was hearing.

'He's a murderer.'

'And a traitor. Who might help us win the war if he continues to supply information to the Nazis which we have invented for him. Jessica, I *use* people. Have you not noticed yet? That's what I do. I'll place Lieutenant Mortimer back in a meaningless bureaucratic role in the Castle, where I can watch him like a hawk.

From there he can send spurious messages back to Berlin. In return I may allow him to continue to breathe.'

'But they'll know about his father!'

He folded his arms and looked decidedly disappointed with her.

'Sir James Mortimer has renounced his role as lord lieutenant due to ill health and is reposing in a sanatorium in Scotland for the duration. There'll be an announcement in the Court Pages of *The Times* tomorrow. Should his son disappoint me once more, I'll put a bullet through his skull myself and dump him in the briny. As he knows full well.'

'Have you told Louis Renard all this?'

There, for a moment, he looked guilty.

'Please. I'm not entirely heartless. It was difficult enough for the fellow getting roasted by a mandarin from the War Office for thinking he could arrest me. The fate of the Mortimers, I'll leave for another day. One wouldn't want to affect the chap's mental condition if indeed it is still a touch delicate. All in good time.'

'I feel sorry for you,' she whispered. 'Truly.'

He took her hands, looked directly into her eyes.

'Don't. This is the stage we play on, the theatre of our war. Until a day or two ago, its limits ran no further than poky little Dover. Now it's so much larger. The world.' He came closer. 'My world. Yours too. Ours to roam and shape.'

The station manager came out of his office and yelled at the squaddies waiting at the end of the platform to get on the train.

'I hate you,' she said.

'A natural reaction I suppose. I'll be spending a lot more time in London in future. My remit is increasing. Let's celebrate for both of us with supper at the Savoy next week. I'll be staying at my club but it's men only. So, afterwards, it would be your hotel of course–'

'No. Absolutely not. God, you're insufferable.'

She grabbed her case and the Remington and hurried to the

first-class compartment. Shearer followed, hands in pockets, the paltry bouquet beneath his arm, whistling all the time.

'I really, really hate you,' she cried through the open window as finally the train began to move.

'Understandable,' he called back, running alongside as it picked up speed. 'We can work on it. I'll call. Farewell, Mrs Marshall!'

Then the bouquet of stolen roses flew through the window and landed on her seat.

Chapter 110

Greetings, my dear inspector,

I trust this letter finds you well, for the time being at least. The sight of you coming out of Dunkirk was a pitiful one, I must confess. You should learn to duck and dive. It is one of life's great talents.

Still, here we are, waiting on Adolf. A time of challenges and opportunities for us both. I am pleased you have found some modest role in the police service once more. Though the Kent Constabulary is hardly Scotland Yard, is it? If only you'd been quicker, wiser, more stony-hearted, our paths might have crossed before now.

Perhaps they have.

In any case, rest assured they will again one day.

You need not fret about Dame Veronica. I have no professional interest in your aunt. In truth, I admired some of her performances once, before I moved on to more suitable entertainment. Attractive and elegant as she is, I find the lady too old and a touch scrawny for my taste. I prefer the soft, warm touch of younger flesh. But that you know.

Now, who will take delicious Delia's place? There's a

question. Someone, surely. I can't believe a man like you has lost his spark, Louis.

Do you really think it died in France?

Think only this of her: that there's some corner of a foreign field that is forever England.

There will be others. For both of us.

A most cordial au revoir from your admiring friend and colleague in crime.

Morven Graves, Esq.

———

Renard was in the hall, the letter in his shaking hands, when they found him.

His aunt took his arm.

'Louis. What on earth is wrong?'

All he could do was stare at the page. Then at Poppy Webber.

'I'm sorry, but you'll have to stay here tonight. Tomorrow, pack your things. I'll drive you to Edinburgh.'

She shook her head.

'Tomorrow?'

'It's not safe anymore.' Renard showed her the letter. 'He's here. Graves. The man's looking for someone. Someone close to me, I think.'

There was a shocked silence then Veronica announced, 'I'll go and prepare the guest room.'

Poppy Webber touched his arm and reached for the letter.

'May I, Louis?'

He handed it over. Her intense dark eyes slowly scanned the page, an expression on her face that was as professional as it was personal. A plane passed, low and noisy, overhead. The vixen was outside somewhere shrieking again, a sound so human it made him shiver.

'This man is sick,' she said. 'Evil. He's boasting, isn't he?

Boasting of... I'm so sorry. He wants to taunt you with... with what he's done.' A pause. 'With Delia.'

Renard took back the letter, folded it carefully and stuffed the thing in his pocket.

'He may wish that. He's failed. I've known Delia's dead ever since I came back from Dunkirk.'

Perhaps the man was intelligent enough to realise that, too. And this was all a part of some strange and deadly challenge.

She took his hand.

'Grief's a ghost, Louis, not a shadow that vanishes with the light. It's a spectre that appears whenever it wishes and vanishes that way too. You'll carry her with you a long time, I think. Forever, even.'

'A ghost may be exorcised.'

She squeezed his fingers then let go.

'Is that what we really want? They're part of us. It may be easier to make your ghost a friend than fear it as a foe.'

She was, he thought, a remarkable woman. One he could talk to for hours.

'You sound like a psychiatrist.'

That amused her.

'Funnily enough, I studied that a little. Freud and Jung. Sex and dreams. The Nazis are rather enamoured of Carl, or so they claim. Freud was a Jew, of course, so he had to flee. He died here in London. He was a great fan of Shakespeare, you know. A man with more than a passing regard for the English, possibly because you offered so many avenues for his research.' She hesitated. 'There. I got a smile, Louis. We all have to smile from time to time. Most of all when it's the last thing we feel like.'

'Scotland Yard has little interest in what they call trick cyclists, I'm afraid.'

She tapped his jacket.

'Then they're Luddites. It's interesting. Enlightening. Modern.

We're more than flesh and blood and bone. This Morven Graves. Have you kept all his letters?'

They were upstairs in his bedroom, every one of them.

'If you'd allow me to read them... There's something compulsive, fanatical here. It seems it's aimed very directly at you. Do you have any idea why?'

A good question. One he wished he could answer.

'I chased the man in London for more than a year and I still can't picture him in my head.'

She thought for a second then said, 'He wouldn't like that idea. He wants you to acknowledge him. That seems important. He can't have seen us together, Louis. Can he? At the hospital? On the cliff?'

Renard had been racking his head about that ever since he read the letter. Morven Graves seemed invisible, a man who could go anywhere he liked and never be found.

'He found this place. I've no idea. You'll be safe here. He only attacks women on their own. I can drive you straight to Scotland. We'll leave at dawn. I still have a weapon. I'll check outside first.'

She nudged his elbow.

'Louis. I can drive myself.'

'Then...' Graves was right about one thing. The spark, the need for love and company, was undiminished. 'Then I'll accompany you if I may. I can take the wheel when you don't feel like it. Two days, it'll take us. We can stop off somewhere. York. Northumberland.'

'Three days,' she whispered. 'There's a charming inn I know in Stamford.'

'Three then.'

She put a finger to her lips.

'Or thinking about it... perhaps four. Do you know Berwick? Lovely town. On the border between England and Scotland. There's a small hotel in Sandgate.' She peered at him very directly. 'I went there for a naughty weekend with a boyfriend from medical school. He was a total wastrel sadly, but the sea air and that lilting accent of theirs. Kippers, Arbroath smokies and whisky... as many nights as you want.'

Renard was feeling rather warm.

'And after...?' he asked.

Just a word. One that hadn't entered his head for months.

After...

That was one of the many things war stole without your noticing. The chance to plan, to dream, to hope.

'I can't think about after, Louis. Only now.'

He couldn't take his eyes off her.

'If now is all we have, best we make the most of it.'

CHAPTER 111

The train chugged through Canterbury, the cathedral majestic in the distance, the town low, sprawling, dull in comparison. As dusk descended, she sat by the window and watched as it rolled on past picturesque villages, lush farmland, flocks of cattle and sheep, the trellises of hop fields where a few people still worked gathering the crop for beers to come. Her mood varied between the furious, the outraged and the deeply amused. Of course, she'd see David Shearer again. It seemed there was no avoiding him. Even if she wanted to.

An hour or so in, the carriage door opened and a man entered lugging a large and battered leather suitcase. He doffed his hat, said a pleasant hello, heaved the valise onto the rack then took a seat by the door.

'Please excuse the intrusion.' He had a calm and cultured voice, an apologetic tone too. 'I hate to disturb you. Our brave soldiers appear to be taking control of the rest of the carriages. Much as I welcome their courage in the field, their behaviour when it comes to drink and tobacco and language is not to my liking.'

'Letting off steam,' she said, thinking she might be glad of polite and personable company after the strains of Dover.

The fellow nodded in agreement.

'I imagine you could call it that. Please don't think me a snob. I simply appreciate peace and quiet on a train journey. That is why one books first class, after all. Not that our military friends take much notice of such distinctions.'

'Perhaps,' she said, 'they feel they've earned it. Or are about to.'

He looked forty or so with the amiably forgettable face of a minor civil servant. His suit, once doubtless smart, was creased and had seen better days. With a cheery nod he sat down and began to read a newspaper. The *Daily Express*.

Jessica Marshall saw her picture byline on the story about her night in the theatre with Louis Renard. It was a strange feeling. Immediately, she returned to gazing out of the window. Deer grazed in the meadows of what looked like a country estate where the grass was pockmarked by a rash of molehills. The landscape was rising in the distance, a line of undulating downs getting closer. London, she assumed, lay on the other side.

'Excuse me.' The man waved the paper in her direction. 'I do hope I'm not being presumptuous. Unless I'm mistaken, this is you, isn't it?'

The article. The picture a dead police sergeant had taken of her by the harbour. Not a bad one, either.

'Afraid so.'

He kept looking at her very intently.

'I saw you in Dover, didn't I?'

'I was there, sure...'

'No, no. I mean the other night. That dreadful show. The Hippodrome. You were in a box with your husband. I foolishly bought a ticket for the stalls. Sheer boredom on my part. I recall looking up and thinking... what on earth is a smart-looking couple like that doing in a dive like this?' He waved the paper again. 'Now I know.'

It was odd being recognised. The hills she'd seen before were so much closer. The train appeared to be headed right for them.

The man had noticed too. He got up and closed the windows then the door.

'I'm a regular on this line. We're coming up to the Sevenoaks Tunnel. Two miles. The longest in the region. It's always wise to close the window. Otherwise, we'll be choking on filthy smoke and dust for a good ten minutes. Trust me, it's the last thing you want on that lovely dress of yours.'

Now they were on a gently curving bend. The tunnel mouth emerged ahead, a black hole cut into a vast hill so high the summit was out of sight even at a distance.

'Did you know...' he pointed to the approaching rise, 'that somewhere close by above us, right up there, is Biggin Hill? Spitfires and Hurricanes. Brave men. Sacrificing their lives to save ours.'

For some reason the idea of all that rock, thousands of tons of it, soon pressing down over her head felt strangely disturbing.

'No. I didn't.'

He leaned forward.

'The chap you went to the theatre with... your husband...'

'He wasn't my husband.'

'A friend then?'

'Yes.' Leave it there, she thought. 'A friend.'

'A good friend?' he wondered.

'Not really.'

It was crazy. All the time in Dover, shells falling, armed men everywhere, and only once had she felt afraid. That grim moment she'd bumped into the corpse of Joe Dobson hanging from his skylight. Yet now, for some reason, her skin prickled with the same quick, bright chill of fear.

'You were with him in a box in the theatre, Jessica,' he said with a quick and knowing grin. 'Please. An attractive woman like you. A tall and handsome man. Forgive one assuming...'

She glanced at the door. There was a guard on the train, surely. The squaddies too, but they might be anywhere.

'Who are you?'

'Me?' He laughed. 'Just a fellow who travels.'

'Doing what?'

'Selling things, mostly. Rare goods, for the ladies. Always the ladies. Luxuries that are scarce because of that fellow in Berlin. If there's anything you'd like?'

He was staring at her legs quite openly.

'Stockings. I have an excellent line in stockings.'

The wan evening sky vanished. She was about to get up and find another carriage when the train shook so hard she had to grab the arm of her seat and fall back, swamped by the sudden darkness. The carriage lamps came on slowly, dim in their glass shades, casting the kind of faint ochre light she associated with gas. Then they failed altogether as the carriage rattled once more from side to side and the smell of smoke and burning coal leaked in through the windows. By the time the dim illumination returned, they were deep in the tunnel, sooty bricks rushing past, the carriage filled with the deafening boom of iron wheels on rough Victorian track.

He'd moved to the seat opposite and she'd never even heard him. Now he sat there smirking under the faint waxy lights. The suitcase was next to him, the lid open. His hands were pale, the fingers long and dextrous, those of a pianist or a surgeon. He reached inside the case and retrieved a pair of stockings, flesh-coloured, long, sinuous, and wrapped them tightly around his hands.

'Silk. A miracle spewed out of the mouth of a little worm. Nothing fake or man-made. I would never countenance that.'

There was an emergency cord on the other side. His side.

'Please...'

He shuffled closer.

'So soft,' he said and flexed the stockings into a tight and narrow band. 'Strong, too. And sensuous.'

She reached across to grab the cord. He pushed her straight back onto the seat, hard, with a force that took her breath away.

'Do you like the feel of silk, Jessica?' He smiled, the very picture of a wolf as he came closer. 'I do. In fact, I'd say I love it.'

ABOUT THE AUTHOR

David Hewson's three decades as a leading European crime, mystery and thriller writer have encompassed the Nic Costa series in Rome, the Arnold Clover books in Venice, The Killing adaptations in Copenhagen and the Pieter Vos books in Amsterdam, currently optioned for Dutch TV. His work in the audio field won him an Audie for best original audiobook with Romeo and Juliet, narrated by Richard Armitage. A former journalist with the *Times, Independent* and *Sunday Times* he lives in Kent.

A NOTE FROM THE PUBLISHER

Thank you for reading this book. If you enjoyed it please do consider leaving a review on Amazon to help others find it too.

We hate typos. All of our books have been rigorously edited and proofread, but sometimes mistakes do slip through. If you have spotted a typo, please do let us know and we can get it amended within hours.

info@bloodhoundbooks.com

Printed in Great Britain
by Amazon

52727222R00290